GUINEA PIG

"Maybe," Alex mused, "one of us ought to try it. Like me, for instance."

"No," Mark said, almost too quickly. "No, I'll—"

She turned to him. "I don't need protection, Mark," she said coolly. "Besides, since Jim can't define what's going on, I'm the logical choice; I think we have to assume it's a psychological process of some sort."

"I can't argue with that, Alex," Jim said. "But I'd have to agree that there's a risk. I've already volunteered."

"I'm not too comfortable with that either," Mark commented. "We don't want Jim getting into any serious trouble with this—"

"We don't have a choice," Jim told him flatly. "I believe we're about to start seeing something that might compare to the Black Death. Hundreds of thousands or millions of patients."

VIRUS

GRAHAM WATKINS

St. Martin's Paperbacks

Published by arrangement with Carroll & Graf Publishers, Inc.

VIRUS

Library of Congress Catalog Card Number: 95-10406

ISBN: 0-312-96003-4

Printed in the United States of America

Carroll & Graf hardcover edition/August 1995
St. Martin's Paperbacks edition/August 1996

St. Martin's Paperbacks are published by St. Martin's Press, 175 Fifth Avenue, New York, NY 10010.

10 9 8 7 6 5 4 3 2 1

For my son, Kevin

The author would like to express his gratitude to Kent Carroll, whose advice and assistance far exceeded the call of duty.

*This story is terrifying, but it's fiction.
It hasn't happened yet.*

But it will.

I

The door opened with a high-pitched, groaning sound. Beyond, there was only darkness.

Horval the Magus, holding his sword at the ready, peered into the blackness. Some yards beyond the pallid light cast by the oil lantern he was carrying, something large and dark moved in the shadows; Horval heard the sound of shuffling feet, a heavy sound. After only a moment's hesitation, he stepped through the doorway. As soon as he was inside, a slight movement to his left drew his attention; instantly, he turned.

The thing standing there would have shocked him if he had not seen these, fought with these, before. A Liche: a human form, dressed in armor, mostly skeletal but with tatters of flesh clinging to the bones here and there. From deep inside the orbits baleful eyes stared at the momentarily frozen magician.

"So, Horval, Magus," the thing said, its voice a grinding and whistling baritone. "Dost thou think thou canst pass me to the chamber beyond?" Giving him no time to answer, it shook its head almost sadly and drew a long sword; the blade glittered in the yellowish lamplight. "Many have tried before you, Magus. Many are the bones that litter this place."

"I do intend to pass," Horval told it imperiously. "You can step aside or find an end now to your long and unnatural life." The Liche merely grinned—as much as a fleshless skull can grin—and drew back its weapon for a first strike. Horval tried to do the same—but found that his arm would not move.

In desperation, he tried again; it remained frozen. Glancing up, he noticed that the same had happened to the attacking

Liche; it too stood motionless, captured just as it began a slashing move with its sword.

Barry Horne leaned back in his chair and stared at the screen with rising irritation. "God damn it," he muttered aloud. "God damn you. What a hell of a time for you to decide to freeze up. Shit!" He circled the mouse around on its pad a few times; nothing happened. He tried the keyboard. No key had any effect on the screen; Horval's sword and arm—the only parts of him visible—and the Liche remained suspended, the fight halted for the moment by the computer's whim.

Well, Barry told himself, it isn't a disaster. It hasn't been all that long since you saved this game; it shouldn't take more than an hour to get back to this point. He shook himself, sat up straight in his chair, then leaned back again. He felt disoriented, but that wasn't an unfamiliar feeling; it always seemed to happen when he tried to quit playing the game, when he was forced to shift from Horval the mighty Magus back to Barry Horne, none-too-successful college student. With a sense of resignation, he reached for the RESET button. After a pause—he wanted to be sure he hadn't overlooked any possible means of recovery—he pressed it.

The Liche and the rest of the game screen vanished, replaced by flashing colors and horizontal lines and then darkness. White letters appeared in the upper-left corner, announcing the BIOS system the computer was using and stepping through a check of the first megabyte of RAM memory. Impatiently, Barry waited for the boot process to complete itself.

But it did not. The flow of statements indicating the loading of the various resident programs did not begin; instead, the machine beeped and halted. The screen flashed the message, "ERROR- C: Drive Failure. Press <F1> to RESUME."

Barry stared at the message, reading it over and over. "No," he said, his voice shaky. "No, no, you haven't done that. No way." He pressed the F1 key; the machine tried the floppy drive, found no disk there. The hard drive activity light flickered, and then the same message reappeared on the screen. Resisting the urge to yell at the machine, Barry punched the RESET button again, much harder than before. He got the same results.

With increasing anxiety, he reached for the power switch

2

and turned the machine off. Sometimes you just have to clear out everything; turn it off, wait a minute or two, then try again, he told himself, warding off panic.

He did wait, but not for more than a minute. Again, the results were the same. "God damn!" he screamed. "God damn you!" With substantial force, he switched the computer off and immediately back on, then repeated the action as soon as the word "ERROR" appeared on his screen.

This time the results were different; this time the little lights on the front of the computer's face flashed on and instantly blinked out again. The screen showed nothing but gray haze.

Barry stood, ran his hands through his hair, walked around the room once, and returned to stand before the computer again, staring at it fixedly. It was gone, without a doubt. The hard disk or its controller had gone down, and he'd made matters worse by flipping it on and off too fast. He picked up his telephone. It was still, he kept telling himself as he dialed, recoverable; he had been smart enough to save his game status on a floppy. Three or four game hours back, to be sure, but that wasn't like starting over.

"Twenty-First Century Computers," a voice on the phone said. "How can I help you?"

"Hi, yeah, this is Barry—uh, Barry Horne. Look, uhm, is Charlie around?"

"Yes, sir," the voice answered. "Hold on, I'll connect you with our service department." There was a pause; electronic music played in his ear.

"Hel-lo," a deep smoke-scratchy voice said. "Charlie Callum here."

"Charlie, this is Barry. Look, I—"

"Barry who?"

"Oh, uh—Barry Horne. You know. Duke? Music major?" There wasn't an immediate reply. "You and I talked about the sequencer and MIDI software, about the Roland LAPC-1 module? Back in—maybe March?"

"Oh—oh—Jesus, man, that was six months ago! I get a lotta people through here, I can't remember—oh, no, wait—brown-haired dude, right? Tall? Play the shit out of a keyboard, right?"

Barry allowed himself a little smile. "Yeah. That's me."

"Okay, man, I got you now. You decided to pick up the LAPC? I gotta tell you, there's some other—"

"No, no, Charlie, look, look, my PC went down on me. Crashed bad."

"Oh? Whatcha got?"

"A clone, yours—it says TFC on the front. It's a 486DX66," he replied. "Sixteen meg RAM, 540 meg hard, it's a—uh, it's a Western Digital, I think. VESA bus, Super-VGA. It—"

"Well, I can sure help you out with that." Charlie interrupted. "You just haul it right on down here."

Barry felt a good deal of the tension rush out of him. "Oh, good. You think you can get it up today?"

Charlie laughed. "Today? Look, man, it's three-thirty now, I quit around five, and you wouldn't believe the pile of stuff I've got on my bench right now. I—"

"I really need it," Barry cut in. "Really. I need it bad."

There was an instant of silence. "Well, what's it doing wrong?"

"Right now it isn't doing anything. It won't come on at all. I got kinda irritated with it, and I was flipping it on and off trying to get it to boot up—"

Charlie laughed again. "Yeah, that pops out the power supply sometimes. No problem there, I can drop another one in in—oh, maybe twenty minutes. Have you out and gone." There was a tiny pause. "If that's all you got."

"The reason I was flipping it is—well, it wouldn't boot up—I was getting this message about a bad C drive, see, and—"

"Well, it sounds like you got a problem—uh, Barry, is it? See, that means I gotta fix the power supply and then look at the HD system and the controller and see what's gone south on you—that's gonna take a little longer. If it's the HD itself I gotta format it and all, and, well, all that takes time. I'll get to you as soon as I can, but right now, I can't promise you better than—lemme see—oh, maybe Tuesday morning."

"Tuesday! This is Wednesday, you're talking about six days!"

"Yeah—well, three working. I'm sorry, but—"

"I've got to have it sooner than that!" He was shouting now.

Charlie's voice turned cold. "Sorry," he said formally. "That's the best I can do. Our service is first-come, first-serve. Okay?"

"Shit!!" He banged the phone down, almost knocking it off its stand. Then, immediately, he picked it back up again. Seizing the phone book, he thumbed through to the listings for computer repair services and began making calls.

Time slipped by; Barry was acutely aware that five o'clock was creeping closer. He'd called dozens of computer stores, but no one was willing to offer even as good a turnaround as Twenty-First Century; his frustration mounted by the minute, turning gradually but steadily into an unreasoning rage. He tried to calm himself, remind himself that it was, after all, merely a game, that it could be continued after he'd gotten the machine fixed—on Tuesday, assuming he hadn't offended Charlie too badly.

But it didn't work. Game it might be, but he could not expel the images from his mind; he'd worked too long, too hard, to find the way to the Liche and the door it guarded. He had to know what was beyond it. Maybe that was ridiculous, but it didn't matter. It was what he wanted, what he almost felt he had to have. Now; today, tonight. Somehow. He just had to find someone to fix that machine today. He kept making calls, kept trying; and, after a short while, he began getting answering machines intoning blandly that the store's service department was closed for the day. Five o'clock, he realized with a feeling akin to panic, had come and gone—and with it, any possibility of getting the machine fixed tonight.

Blankly, he stared at the phone. It incorporated an answering machine; only now did he realize that the little green light was blinking, that he had messages. Might as well listen to them now, he thought dully. He punched the button.

The messages began cycling through; there were quite a few, far more than he'd thought. His parents had called several times; the exasperation in his mother's voice had turned to concern. Nancy, his girlfriend, had called five times, none of which he'd even heard, much less returned. The concern in her voice had turned to frost. Friends had called and even two of his professors had tried to reach him; they were wondering why he hadn't been in class for the past two weeks.

5

He stared at the machine in disbelief. Two weeks? It couldn't have been two weeks! He'd missed maybe two days—no, more than that—he'd just been so involved in the game, he might've lost track a little—

Feeling vaguely like his surroundings weren't real, he looked around the apartment. It was more than a mess; it constituted a health hazard. On plates here and there, parts of a sandwich or a frozen dinner remained, in some cases so covered with mold as to be unrecognizable. Dirty clothes lay scattered about the floor; glasses and cups were everywhere, he was sure that every one he owned was in sight at the moment. Idly, he peered into one sitting next to the phone. A blackish-green film floated on the half-inch of coffee within. He walked to the TV set, turned it on, flipped through the channels until he found news. After a moment he heard, with considerable shock, the date. It hadn't been two weeks, it had been more than three. He felt his normally clean-shaven face and encountered a substantial beard; at the same time he became aware of his own smell—and another, more pungent, smell. He looked toward its source and remembered, hazily, the time he'd been unwilling to take a break to walk to the bathroom, the time he'd decided to simply urinate in the corner. It had been long enough for the fluid to have evaporated, but the stain and the odor remained.

"Jesus God, Barry," he murmured. "Jesus, what's happening?" He reeled off to the bathroom, tried to vomit, realized his stomach was empty.

It can all be taken care of, he told himself shakily as he stared at a wild, almost unrecognizable face in the mirror. It's okay, it's going to be okay. He picked up a dry toothbrush, opened his mouth, saw bits of rotted food clinging to his teeth. Fighting panic and new nausea, he brushed his teeth with a fury, shaved, stripped, jumped into the shower. He put on clean clothes, walked to the kitchen. But the refrigerator was empty and, beyond that, a single glance around the room told him it would take days to make it fit to cook in again.

Food first, he told himself, attentive now to his empty stomach; there was a Wendy's not far away. Food, then call Mom, then try to get school straightened out. He'd call Nancy, but after three weeks he figured that was shot. The rest was recoverable; at least he hoped so. With a new determination

6

to get his life back in order, he headed for the front door.

But, on the way, his gaze fell on the computer, sitting dark and silent. Wavering, he took another step or two, then stopped again. "Damn it," he muttered. "Damn, if I could've just gotten past the damn Liche, that's all, that's all I wanted . . . !"

Mechanically—his eyes still fixed on the dead computer—he drew his wallet from his back pocket. The few bills there were all ones, and for a moment he could not imagine what had happened to the rest of his money. He noted the empty Domino's boxes sitting around—one of them alive with maggots—and sighed. Turning to his desk, he took his checkbook out of the top drawer and studied the balance, which amounted to a little over four hundred—money that was supposed to last until the end of the semester. He pulled out the wallet again and shuffled through the glossy plastic cards stuffed in one of the pockets. There was a MasterCard—in his parents' name—but he knew quite well that it was past its limit, that his father was controlling the payments—in short, that it was not usable for a purchase over a hundred dollars.

The idea he'd been germinating wasn't going to work. A new computer, fitted out like he needed it to be—even exclusive of the monitor, the printer, and the sound card-driven speakers—was going to run sixteen or seventeen hundred dollars minimum. That meant he was at least eleven hundred short.

He shrugged his shoulders. So be it; time to get caught up on the rest of his life anyhow. His determination restored, he walked out to his car. Idle for three weeks, the four-year-old Miata complained a little, but finally started. He pulled out of the lot and drove toward the Wendy's.

Long before he got there, the computer—or, more precisely, the game he'd been playing—began to occupy his thoughts. He had to know what was waiting behind that door, as if it were one of the great secrets of history, as if what waited for him was some perfect illumination. Staring blankly through the windshield, he guided his car down the street, weaving through the five o'clock traffic and occasionally drawing a horn blast from some other driver. The Wendy's he'd been headed for appeared on his right; he did not see it, he cruised right by. A few blocks later, he began to speed up; it wasn't long before he found himself pulling up in front of Twenty-First Century Computers, the store he'd called earlier. Their retail department, at least, was still open. Parking the Miata, he went inside.

He emerged again a short while later, red-faced, almost in tears. Not surprisingly, the clerk had been less than enthusiastic about his offer of the four hundred dollars as a down payment on a new machine. He'd even tried the credit card, but it had been refused as he'd known it would be. Like a small boy in a fury, he stomped to his car, heedless of the spectacle he was creating, and flung himself inside. After pounding on the steering wheel a few times, he started the engine and roared out, forcing an oncoming car to brake hard to avoid a collision.

Hearing the shriek of brakes, he looked up; the driver in the other car shook a fist at him, but he paid no attention. What he did see, a short distance down the street, was a sign decorated with three gold balls, a sign with the words ''Money to Lend. Gold—Jewelry—Guns.'' A pawnshop. He drove to it and parked in front. Inside, he talked with the sixtyish man who was working the counter; it didn't take long for him to discover that, even if he pawned everything of value that he owned—or rather, that was currently available to him—he still wouldn't have enough to buy a new computer. The pawnbroker suggested his car, and certainly the Miata was worth enough, but the title was in his father's name. His frustration almost complete, Barry hung his head; it was all he could do to hold back tears.

He glanced down at the case he'd been leaning against; only now did he notice what it contained. Handguns; a wide assortment of them. Derringers, automatics, revolvers, .22s, .38s, .45s, 9-mms; even some ugly thing with a disk-shaped magazine like a tommy gun. Each had a price tag attached by a string; he studied them. The prices varied from about one hundred seventy-five to nearly a thousand dollars.

''Can I see that one?'' he asked the old man, pointing to a cheap .38.

The man grinned knowingly. ''Sure, sure.'' He pulled it out, and handed it over. Barry curled his fingers around the butt; the feel of it was odd, unfamiliar.

8

"I'll take it," he said, pulling out his checkbook.

"Now hold on there," the man laughed. "Got to do this right, son. It's a buncha bullshit, but it's what we got to do. You got your papers?"

Barry looked blank. "Papers?"

"Uh-huh." He laughed again. "You ever hear of the waiting period, son?"

"Waiting period?"

"Yeah. You wanta buy a handgun, you got to go apply down at the sheriff's office, fill out a buncha bullshit forms. Then you go back three days later and they give you your permit. You give that to me when you buy. Sorry, son, but I gotta have that paper."

Jesus Christ, Barry told himself; everything's so damn complicated. He stared at the long weapons, the rifles and shotguns, which were stored in a rack on the wall behind the case. "What about those?" he asked. "Same thing?"

"Oh, no. Long guns, you don't need no paper."

Barry brightened. "Oh. Well—what do you have that's—uh—about the same price?"

Amused, the old man shook his head. He turned around, scanned the guns. "This ought to do what you want, son," he said, turning back with a short-barreled automatic rifle in his hand. "Pretty close, anyhow." He shrugged. "It's a 7.2-mm; it was made in Yugoslavia back when there was a Yugoslavia. It's a little more—$250."

"And I can buy it now?"

"You bet."

"Okay. I'll take it."

The old man's grin spread; his teeth were clearly false but even so they were crooked. "Good enough," he said. He whipped out a clipboard. "Sign here. You want some ammo?"

Barry scribbled his name. "Uh-ammo?"

"Yeah. Bullets?"

"Oh, sure."

"A box?"

Barry didn't have the vaguest idea how many bullets came in a box. "Yeah, yeah. A box."

"Oh—kay." The old man laid a box of ammunition on the

9

counter beside the gun, then rang up a total on an adding machine. "You be careful, now, son," he warned as he ripped off the paper and handed it to Barry. Nodding without hearing—and certainly without comprehending—Barry hastily wrote a check. He left the store, carrying his gun and his box of bullets.

He didn't bother to put the bullets in the rifle; he had no idea how that was done anyway. When he walked back into the computer store, he was almost shocked out of his dissociated state by the look of absolute terror on the clerk's face—almost, but not quite. This transaction went quite smoothly; a few minutes later he tottered out of the store again, balancing the rifle and one of the demonstration computers, a model quite adequate for his needs.

Returning to his apartment, he was so eager to get the new machine up he left the rifle in his car, in plain sight, and didn't even bother to lock the doors. Rushing inside, he hooked up the machine and, inserting his backup disks, began configuring the game.

He never got back to the Liche, never got to the door it was guarding; less than an hour later, there was a heavy banging on his door and voices outside yelling "Police! Open up!"

He tried to ignore them, although he wondered abstractly how they'd found him so fast. He didn't even think about the credit card he'd presented to the clerk during his first visit, didn't think about the possibility that she might've remembered his name; neither did he think about the license plate on his car, about how exposed and easy to read it would've been during the minutes it took him to load the stolen computer. With as much speed as he could muster he played on, even while the police were breaking his door in; screaming protests, he clutched at the mouse as they pulled him away from the machine and cuffed him.

The officers did not bother to shut off the computer; while a wildly protesting and struggling Barry was dragged from the apartment, a door on the screen opened by itself; as if wondering what had happened to his opponent, the Liche peered out.

2

"**W**hen can I get out of here, doctor?" the thin woman sitting up in bed asked, her voice sliding close to a whine. "Nobody is telling me anything! I can't just stay in here forever!"

Mark Roberts smiled at her—a practiced expression denoting nothing at all—before looking back down at her chart. "Well, Ms. Sung, I can't really say, not yet. You have to understand, Dr. Levine has asked me to look in on you because we really haven't quite been able to figure out what your problem is. We—"

"I don't have a problem!" Wendy Sung snapped. She spoke with an accent, but it was very slight. "Except for being in here!"

Right, Mark said silently. No problem at all; malnutrition, sleep deprivation, and about six opportunistic infections. No problems. "Ms. Sung, you were brought in unconscious by the paramedics last night; Dr. Levine says he suspects you might have been unconscious for quite a while."

Wendy flopped back in the bed. "All right," she admitted. "So I'm tired. So maybe I've been working a little too hard lately. Is that a crime?"

"No," he answered, drawing out the word as he continued to study the chart in his hand. Levine had been quite thorough, he noted; he'd already eliminated a large number of possibilities. The patient was HIV-negative, she wasn't a diabetic, she showed no evidence of alcohol or drug abuse; she did have a number of physical problems but none that could account for her current condition.

"You say you've been working too hard lately," he mused. He glanced at her chart, then back at her face. According to the chart she was Korean by birth but had been a U.S. resident since her childhood. "What sort of work do you do, Ms. Sung?"

"Would you call me Wendy?" she snapped irritably. "Please? Ms. Sung makes me feel like I'm sixty years old. Do I look sixty years old to you, Doctor?"

He looked up at her, studied her face; of course, he'd already seen from the chart that she was thirty-one—six years younger than he was. Normally, he told himself, Wendy Sung might have been quite an attractive woman; all the basics were there. She had large dark Asian eyes, and a classic fall of thick straight black hair; her face was a trifle squarish, her nose small, her lips full.

But, even taking into account the unflattering hospital gown and the lack of any makeup, she looked terrible. Her eyes were sunken and encircled by heavy dark pouches; her cheeks had grown gaunt, her lips were cracked, her skin was pale and sallow. Her hair was a wild tangle that the nurses had not yet been able to straighten—and he knew that fussy Mrs. Tillson, one of the night nurses on this floor, would've tried.

"No, Wendy," he answered finally. "You don't look sixty."

Her manner softened a little. "Writer," she said succinctly.

"Excuse me?"

"You asked what sort of work I did. I'm a writer. Fiction."

"Oh? What've you written?"

She flushed a little, her cheeks reddening sharply in contrast to her pale skin. "Well, I, uh, nothing's been published—yet. But it will be, soon." She made an effort to compose her hair, failed badly, gave it up. "And then I can quit that other stupid job. Can't be soon enough for me!"

"So you have—another job? Besides your writing, I mean?"

"Uh-huh." She shrugged her shoulders, her expression of annoyance returning. "Oh—well, I did—I guess I forgot—I was sort of let go—I was a teacher, I used to teach . . . English . . . to other immigrants, you understand . . ."

Mark put the chart down and watched the woman's eyes; there was a possibility here. A severe depression resulting from the loss of a job could manifest itself in many ways. "You lost your job?" he probed. "When?"

She looked down at her lap. "A month ago," she answered. He waited for her to go on, but she didn't, not for quite a while. "It doesn't matter, though," she said finally, her manner airy. "Pretty soon it won't matter at all, not after I finish my novel!" Warming to her subject quickly, she went on for several minutes, telling him about her historical novel. She seemed boundless in her enthusiasm.

"So you can see," she pressed on, "why I have to go home. I'm right in the middle of one of the most important scenes, I've got to get back to it!"

"We can't keep you against your will, Wendy," Mark replied. "However, I have to tell you this—the condition you're in could lead to another collapse. That'll land you back in here—if you're lucky—and your stay will most likely be longer."

"There's nothing wrong with me," she muttered. "Nothing. I've just been working too hard. On the book."

He didn't answer immediately. It isn't out of the question, he thought; she's just gotten overly involved in writing her book and she's been neglecting herself—although the extent of the neglect is pretty extreme.

Finally, he nodded. "It's possible," he agreed cautiously. "Still, we do have some experience with this—we sometimes get university students in here in a state of exhaustion, especially around final exam time. My best advice to you is to stay a day or two; let us get you back in shape. Then you can return to—"

"Oh, doctor, I just can't! I'll lose the flow, it'll take days for me to get—"

"Wendy," he said firmly, tapping her chart, "let me be frank with you. You're suffering, among other things, from a mild case of malnutrition. Now that doesn't mean you're starving, but you've upset the electrolyte balance in your body. What that means is—"

"I know what electrolyte balance means, doctor," she cut in. "Not enough potassium in the blood, or too much sodium, or chloride, or whatever."

"Then you probably know that electrolyte imbalance can lead to heart problems. If that happens, Wendy, you may not be finishing your book at all."

Now it was her turn to observe a moment of silence. "Oh, all right," she grumbled. She still looked sullen. "I'll stay. But just for a day or two, okay?"

He grinned. Mark's grin was contagious—he'd been told that since he was a small boy—and Wendy was not immune.

She finally did smile, even if it was half-hearted. After making a note or two on the chart and informing her that he was going to order a few more tests, he left her room.

At the nurse's station down the hall, a heavyset balding man in a white coat was waiting for him. "Well?" Gus Levine asked as he came close. "What do you think, Mark?"

Mark shrugged and slouched against the counter. "Looks like simple exhaustion," he answered. "And, normally, that'd be exactly what I'd call it."

"You think it fits with the others?"

Mark ran a hand through his longish sandy hair, tousling it. "Well, actually, yes, it does. If we count Wendy—Ms. Sung, I mean—then that makes twenty-two patients in four weeks, all suffering from what amounts to—well, what amounts to a truly ridiculous degree of self-neglect." He jerked a thumb back toward the room he'd just left. "At least she has some sort of a reason for it."

"Oh?"

"She's a writer—wannabe, anyhow. Working herself to death on a novel."

"Uhm," Gus nodded. "I guess that does happen."

Mark shrugged, suddenly shifting his argument to the other side, "I don't know. Actually I've known quite a few people who fancied themselves writers—none of them ever published in any significant way—and a lot of them were very serious about it, totally absorbed. Not one got themselves in Wendy's shape over it."

He shifted against the counter, lifted the receiver end of the stethoscope he was carrying around his neck and stared at it, as if trying to see an answer in the darkness inside the device. "It's really strange, Gus," he mused. "These patients are so similar. They're all in bad shape—Wendy's better off right now than most—but every one wants out of here as soon as possible."

"Just something in the modern condition, maybe. Life is getting awfully stressful for a lot of people."

"Not out of the question," Mark agreed. "But with this— it just doesn't seem right. There's a pattern of some sort developing here."

"Don't get yourself in their shape fretting about it," the

14

other man warned with a grin. "They're all going to survive, Mark. I'm pretty sure of that."

"Well." Mark stood up straight, let his stethoscope drop back. "I've got a few minutes to spare—I think I'll go down and see Jim anyhow. He promised me he'd look at this stuff."

Gus nodded. "I've got to go check on one of those patients myself; Jerry Dunn?"

Mark grimaced. "Yeah, the programmer. He's bad off; about the worst one."

"He's going to be fine. Go see Jim and his computers."

"Yeah. See you later, Gus." Turning away, Mark nodded a good-bye to the nurses and walked down the hallway. As he walked, he switched—as he often did—onto a sort of an automatic pilot; he did not see the rooms he passed, did not acknowledge the friends and colleagues he met. None of them were offended; all merely smiled and watched him go. Mark, and the peculiarities of his personality, was well known around Duke Hospital; those who worked with him found what others might see as a snub forgivable, since he was also known as the best diagnostician in the Department of Medicine. Many also knew, from personal experience, that Mark could easily be persuaded to stay on the job until the wee hours of the morning helping to determine the cause of some patient's condition.

Which was why Gus Levine and Andy Bell had called these peculiar cases of exhaustion to his attention. None of them had required a two A.M. sojourn in the lab; with the possible exception of Jerry Dunn, none of them were in truly serious condition.

But Mark's attention had been captured, and, at the moment, he found himself thinking about nothing else. His feet stopped moving, and, looking up, he discovered that he was standing in front of blue-painted elevator doors. He punched the down arrow. The door slid open, he stepped inside and touched a button labeled "SB." The doors slipped shut and the car began to move.

"Earth to Mark," a low and slightly husky baritone voice said from behind him. "If you're headed down to see me, well, I'm not there. I'm in the elevator with an experimental cybernetic creature whose origin is one of the great mysteries of our time."

Feeling as if he were waking up, Mark turned; leaning against the back wall was a heavyset bearded man. He was grinning, but only in the folds in his cheeks and around his eyes was the grin visible; his lips were wholly obscured by a thick dark mustache.

"Well," Mark replied, "guess I might as well go back upstairs. You're right, I was coming down to see you."

The elevator stopped; the two men moved toward the doors as they opened. "No, I think you should give it a try anyhow," Jim said. "You never know, I might turn up." Leading the way, the bearded man ambled a few paces down the hall and, turning to a door on his left, unlocked it. Stepping inside, he flipped on a light. "See? I am here, after all."

Mark followed him in. "So you are," he agreed.

Jim, with Mark still following, wandered on across the room, his manner suggesting that he'd not yet decided which way to go. The room was large, the ceiling low, the light provided by dozens of fluorescent tubes; the floor was tile and the walls were cement-block. In one corner stood an industrial-type stainless-steel sink. Beside the sink was a workbench cluttered with meters, oscilloscopes, signal generators, and an almost wild assortment of tools. Any space not occupied by tools and instruments was piled with circuit boards, partially and wholly disassembled computers and other, less easy to identify, pieces of equipment. Benches took up most of the remainder of the wallspace in the room, and these were only a little less cluttered; most were covered by computers and printers: IBMs, HPs, Compaqs, and Macintoshes, as well as equipment Mark could not even begin to identify. Shelf after shelf above the machines was filled with software boxes and computer books. Being the resident computer expert, statistician by default, and electronics engineer for the Department of Medicine—the latter being Jim's actual title—apparently required something of a pack-rat mentality.

Smiling, Mark shook his head. "Every time I come down here," he said, "there are more of these things. Where the hell do they all come from?"

"Oh, they breed during the night," Jim said airily as he sat down in front of one. He swirled a mouse around on a pad next to the keyboard and a Windows screen, gray with colorful little icons in neat rows, appeared from darkness. "I try to stop them, but so far I haven't figured out how to tell the females from the males.''

"Sort of like parakeets."

"Uh-huh." Using the mouse, he flicked the cursor around on the screen. "But you, my friend, did not come down here to listen to my notions concerning computer birth control—although, I assure you, they're fascinating. You came to see what I had for you concerning Roberts' Syndrome."

Mark laughed. "Concerning what?"

Jim glanced around. "Roberts' Syndrome. Once you find the cause—correction, once we find the cause—it'll be named after you. Believe it."

"So you're precognitive as well as clairvoyant?"

"Sure. You turn these things off, you can see the future in the screens, like you can in a crystal ball." He clicked the mouse again, and an intermediate display turned into columns of numbers. "Right now, I can foresee that you're going to be disappointed today." He pointed the mouse to a column labeled "P-values"; all were in a range of 0.3 to 0.7; numbers that Mark understood to mean that the results of their statistical tests indicated chance at work. "As you can see from these. To use a technical term, we got doodly-squat."

Mark scowled at the screen. "I was hoping for more. You have no idea how many needles we've stuck these people with."

"Well, sure I do. Blood tests, spinal taps, the works. They look like pincushions. SAS doesn't lie, my friend. Doodly-squat. You got no abnormalities in these people that're common to all of them." He paused, ran his fingers over his keyboard without pressing any keys. "Unless you count high IQ."

"IQ?"

"Oh, that's not in here. That's just something I noticed when I was entering the data. You got programmers, teachers, profs; you got writers and musicians. You got no day laborers. No waitresses."

Mark considered this for a moment; Jim was right, he reflected. "I'd doubt," he said after a long pause, "that it's meaningful." Leaning back against the bench where Jim's computer was sitting, he accidentally knocked a box to the floor.

"It's hard to be sure," he continued as he reached down to pick it up, "but I'd guess it's a selection artifact—these symptoms are getting noticed because they're showing up in patients like these. They might not be noticed in other populations at all. I'd expect it to change."

Jim grunted and nodded. "You're probably right. It's just that it's the only thing I've got so far."

Idly, Mark looked at the box he'd just retrieved from the floor; it was a software package, unopened. On the cover was a stylized face; above that was the legend, "From Compuware, common sense for your computer!" Below, in huge block letters, a name: "PENULTIMATE."

Mark grinned. "Now this is what they need, Jim. Common sense."

Jim looked at the box too. "Yeah, I gotta find time to install that boy. It's supposed to be the greatest invention since beer; that's what I'm told, anyway. It's all the rage at the moment; everybody's singing its praises."

The doctor looked startled. "And you—of all people—haven't tried it out yet?"

Jim took the box from him. "No; I want to check it out first. It's a TSR, and—"

"Sorry. You went over me. TSR?"

"A 'Terminate-and-Stay-Resident' program. Call me old-fashioned, but I have a hard time trusting them; you put them in and let them do their thing, and most of the time you have no idea what they're doing."

"I have no idea what computers are doing anyhow!"

Jim laughed. "Most people don't. But I do." He flipped the package over. "I am curious about it—I'm told it gets rid of the dumb I-do-exactly-what-you-say pattern that drives so many people crazy."

Mark's eyebrows rose. "That's possible?"

Jim shrugged. "I dunno. It looks like it's nothing but a caching program, but—"

"Jim, you're talking to a guy who's never had time to sit down and learn all these things. Caching program?"

"Uh-huh. Memory is a whole lot faster than a disk, okay? So, if you have something you pull in from disk over and over again, it makes sense to put that something in memory where you can get at it quicker. That's what a cache does." He tapped the box. "Now, a disk is faster than you are, just like memory is faster than a disk. Ordinary caches cache the disk into memory; Penultimate—if I've got it straight—caches your input, from the keyboard or whatever, to a disk, it builds files on the things you do over and over again. After a while, it begins to 'understand' what you're trying to do as soon as you start to do it—unless you're doing something completely new, of course."

Mark scowled at the box. "So what? I'm not sure I see how that helps anything."

"Well—like I said, I haven't tried it out yet—all I can do is give you the same example the advertising blurb gives. Let's say you're writing a novel. You do lots of dialogue, and you follow one format when you do—you put in a quotation mark at the beginning, a comma or question mark or whatever at the end, followed by another quotation mark, followed by something like 'he said.' Also, if you're any kind of writer you try to vary the 'he said' at least some—'he replied,' 'he answered,' 'he yelled,' and so on. Since most of the time you have dialogue between two people, the software can begin to pick up on this. It can track the characters, keep the he's and the she's straight, even do the varying on 'he said' for you. It even catches errors as you go along, spelling errors, problems with grammar, and so on. Catching the errors—I suppose— would be the big advantage."

"Looks like a gimmick to me."

Jim put the box down. "Probably. A lot of this kind of software is. It can help you if you're a real klutz; otherwise it doesn't do much."

"It might be for me, then," Mark allowed. "I can't seem to do anything right with these things." He grinned. "That's why I'm always down here."

"Yeah." The programmer turned back to his screen. "And, getting back to that—I'd say you're going to have to run some more tests."

"Any ideas?"

"Hell, you're the doctor!" He shrugged, swirled the mouse on its pad again; a nervous habit Mark had observed before. The gesture that meant Jim had something on his mind.

And, this time, Mark didn't have to pry it out of him. "You

19

know," Jim went on after a moment, "a new virus—a new AIDS, something like that—you can't really expect to test for. If I were you, I'd be looking for links between these people— something more than IQ, I mean. Like the guys who attended that convention in—where was it?"

"Philadelphia. Yeah, and all caught what became known as Legionnaires' disease."

"Right. Anyhow, that's what I'd do. Maybe they all went to the same party, maybe they all took some class in night school. Something like that."

"That'd take some time to research."

"You got time. This one isn't AIDS, it isn't killing people left and right."

The phone on Jim's desk shrilled; Jim answered it. Then after a moment, he handed it to Mark.

"Gus," he said succinctly.

"Yeah, I told him I was coming down here." He took the phone. "Yes, Gus. Something new?" He listened for a moment, frowned. "Thanks," he said slowly. "I'll talk to you later." Hanging up the phone, he shook his head. "That, Jim, was a 'speak-of-the-devil' coincidence. I'd say we don't have as much time to come up with an answer on this thing as we thought."

"Oh?"

"Yeah. Jerry Dunn?"

"The programmer? What about him?"

"He just coded and died. We've got our first fatality."

3

"**Y**ou're unusually quiet tonight," Alexandra Walton was saying. "You've hardly said a word since dinner. Rough day?"

Across the well-appointed living room, in front of a bar in the corner, a tall man with iron-gray hair turned his head. He was still wearing an expensive business suit, although he had deigned to loosen his tie; in his hand was a highly unusual second after-dinner drink. Alex had not failed to notice it.

He smiled, and she could not help returning it. Donald

Royce, she told herself, you look like a movie star, especially when you smile. We've been married for almost three years and you can still melt me with one of those.

"As a matter of fact," he answered as he crossed back toward her, "it was." Sitting beside her on the couch, he sipped his drink, swirled the ice in the glass, then put it down on the glass-topped coffee table with a sharp clink. He shook his head. "You know how it is. The pressure never stops."

Her smile hadn't faded. "You can't fool me," she said in a mock-serious voice. "You wouldn't want it any other way, and you know it as well as I do."

He picked up the drink and stared into it. "That," he mused, "is the problem with having a psychiatrist for a wife. She knows you better than you know yourself." He sighed. "You are right, I know; but I wouldn't mind if it eased off a little every once in a while. It doesn't, it's just constant. Right now, it's a little worse than usual."

She closed the journal she was reading and laid it aside on the couch. "You want to tell me about it?"

He leaned back, crossed his legs. "Well, okay, Alex—just remember, you asked for this. The problem is cash flow. People owe us money. On paper we're solvent, but there isn't enough cash available to pay both our employees and our creditors. That's it, in a nutshell."

"So borrow it. From the bank or whatever."

He laughed. "Yes, well—that's one way. But we're stretched kind of thin right now—we just revamped all our computers, put in new software, all that—and that makes bankers nervous. They don't want us to go bankrupt while they've got an outstanding loan. Point is, they aren't going to let us have it, not now. If we didn't need it—" he shrugged again—"well, of course, they'd give it to us."

She frowned, propped her elbow on the back of the couch and leaned her head against her hand. "Lehmann Electronics isn't close to bankruptcy, is it?" she asked, a note of concern in her voice. She knew how much of Don's identity rested on his position as chief executive officer of Lehmann, how much of himself he'd invested in the company; he took enormous pride in the fact that, at forty-four, he was one of the youngest CEOs of a company Lehmann's size in the nation.

He laughed again. "No! Hardly! We're actually in good shape overall. It's just that I need to find a way to come up with another forty million or so by the first of the month." He shook his head. "I'll manage it, though," he added moodily. "Somehow."

"I'm sure you will," Alex said unconvincingly. She crossed her legs, uncrossed them again, shifted her position uncomfortably. She'd hoped to be able to say something profound, something that would help him at least find a direction toward easing his problem, but this sort of thing was far from her areas of expertise. It wasn't a surprise; there'd been times when she'd come home preoccupied with a patient or some dilemma involving the pervasive politics of the hospital, and on such occasions, when she'd shared her problems with him, he'd been equally at sea.

Ah well, she told herself; it wasn't as though they hadn't been warned—not one of her friends or his had thought that a marriage between an academically oriented psychiatrist and an ambitious businessman would work. All in all, she thought, things had gone rather well for them, considering. Even their meeting had been unlikely. Don, on a visit to the hospital for a routine problem, had lost his wallet; Alex, on finding it, looked inside to discover well over two thousand dollars cash and various forms of ID that included his phone number. She'd called him, he'd visited her at her office and tried to offer her a reward. She'd refused it, but, impressed by him, and admittedly on the rebound from a painfully failed romance, had accepted his offer to dinner.

From the first moment, it was obvious that Donald Royce lived in a different world from hers, an exciting world, a world she barely knew existed. Before he'd picked her up, flowers had arrived at her door; the dinner itself had been at The Pines, one of the better restaurants in the Triangle area, and over dinner he'd made comparisons between Slug's and the places he was familiar with in Paris, in Marseilles, in Vienna. Alex—whose experience with Europe was limited to a few professional conferences in London—couldn't help but be impressed. Donald, it turned out, went to Paris as casually as she went to the North Carolina beaches.

Within a month, he was introducing her to that world. At first she'd protested his suggestions that they jet off to France, saying that her workload at Duke prohibited a holiday; he'd told her not to worry about the details, and she'd found herself on a Lehmann company jet to Kennedy and then on the Concorde to Europe—she'd been able to leave work on Friday at five and return on time Monday morning. In Paris they'd stayed in a small hotel on the Rue des Beaux Arts, where the staff clearly knew Donald well. He'd conversed with them in fluent French; he'd known all the best restaurants there, and he'd known them in Vienna—where his ability to converse in German had startled her. Within six months she'd ridden gondolas in Venice, seen Mount Fuji, played chemin de fer in the casino in Monte Carlo; she'd stood before the Parthenon in Athens and the Pyramids in Egypt, and she'd sunbathed on the beaches of Cap d'Antibes. Donald had taken care of everything, she hadn't had to do a thing. He'd introduced her to dozens of people, most of whom she couldn't even remember; not just businessmen but artists, writers, musicians.

And, beyond that, he'd proven himself sensitive and caring; slowly, without pressuring her, he'd guided their conversations toward discussions of a future together, a future promising a full rich life, promising children. It seemed to her that nothing was beyond his reach; she'd begun accepting his ideas long before he'd presented her with an enormous diamond and, in a parody of 1940s movies that he managed to turn into a romantic fantasy, proposed to her on bended knee. She hadn't even been able to laugh; all she could do was say yes.

"It wasn't an altogether bad day, though," Don continued, apparently sensing her discomfort. "All the new computers are up and running fine, and that new software is really starting to pay dividends. It sort of amazes me . . ."

"Well, that's good," she said noncommittally, not wanting to extend this particular conversation since she did not, in fact, remember a thing about any new computers or software he might have mentioned. "Maybe you'll enjoy the evening anyway." He looked blank. "The Seelers?" she reminded him with a touch of exasperation. "We're supposed to go over there tonight? About nine, remember?"

Lowering his head, he rubbed his fingers up into his hairline. "Oh, no, I'd forgotten," he admitted. "Look, Alex—I was just getting ready to tell you—I have to go back in for a

23

while tonight. You're going to have to make apologies for me, I can't make it. Not tonight.''

Now it was her turn to return a blank stare. ''You can't!'' she blurted. ''I mean, I can't! Don, we have to, this has been planned for over a week, it isn't a spur-of-the-moment thing!''

''I know. I'm sorry. I just . . . I really do have to go back to the office for a while.''

Alex watched Don as he stood up. This wasn't like him. Yes, she reminded herself, he was intense about his work, he was dedicated to the company, but as a rule he left it behind when he came home—even if that was often late. More, the Seelers were his acquaintances; Lawrence Seeler was an executive with a distribution company that handled quite a few of Lehmann's products. He was certainly not someone who Don would want offended. She argued with him for a few minutes, but to no avail.

''Well,'' she began when it seemed as if he wasn't going to change his mind, ''if you aren't going, I guess I might as well call Betsy and tell her we're canceling.''

''No, don't,'' he said quickly. His tone fell just short of being commanding. ''No, you go ahead. Have a good time, Alex.''

She curled her lip, just slightly. Fat chance of that, she thought. They're *your* friends, I have absolutely nothing in common with either Lawrence or Betsy, and you insist I entertain them—among others—all the time. But never alone! ''Look, Don, I don't—''

''No, you need to,'' he cut in. Moving in front of the hallway mirror, he straightened his tie. ''You know how important the Seelers are to the business. Just take care of it for me, okay, Alex? You know how.'' Returning to her, he gave her a quick kiss. ''I'll see you when you get back. I shouldn't be too late.'' He started for the door.

''But Don . . .''

''Nothing I can do about it, hon,'' he called from the end of the hall. She heard the door shut.

For a long while, she stared down the now-empty hallway. ''Damn it, Don,'' she muttered. ''Why do you do things like this to me?'' She got up, started for the bedroom. ''And you, Alex,'' she went on, ''why do you put up with it?''

4

"**S**o there's nothing." Almost glaring at the blond woman sitting across from him, Mark practically slapped the printout down on her desk. "Not one damn thing."

Lucy Edwards shrugged within her lab coat. "What can I tell you, Mark?" she asked. "You can read the report for yourself, you don't need a pathologist to explain it to you. Your patient died of heart failure, probably triggered by potassium deficiency. I did all the scans you asked me to do; if he was doing any drugs it's been a while. There's nothing like that, nothing that can't be explained by the meds you and Gus had him on while he was here."

Impatiently, Mark drummed his fingers on the report. "There has to be some pattern here. We have thirty-one patients now here that fit this profile. I've talked to Manny Selmons over at UNC and he can identify another twenty or so—and they weren't even looking for it. Jack Fredericks at County General says he has ten maybes. Something's going on."

Lucy leaned forward and brushed her pale blond hair away from her face. "You suspect a virus?"

"Not really, although that's what Gus is pushing. I can't see it; I've talked to a bunch of these people, and most of them just don't have any connections with each other—except for what Jim Madison noticed."

Lucy's bright blue eyes seemed to grow brighter. "What's Madison noticed?"

Mark made a dismissive gesture. "Oh, it isn't anything important. It's just that all our patients are rather upscale folk. High education, high IQ, high income, and so on. I don't think it can have anything to do with it. Conditions like these get noticed when they show up in people like these, they might not be noticed in a different population."

"All? Or most?"

"All, according to Jim."

Lucy leaned a bit farther across the desk. "How can it be

25

a selection artifact? Most of these patients have been brought in by the paramedics—they're 911 responses. 911 operators don't ask questions about education and that other stuff.''

"No, but other people do. You're a lawyer and you collapse, they assume you have a disease. You're a bartender, they assume you're drunk.''

"Won't fly. They still come in to the ER. The docs down there don't make those judgments, Mark; you know that.''

He frowned at her. "Are you saying you think it's worth following up?''

"Look,'' she answered, "I can well imagine that there were doctors, back when AIDS was firing its opening salvos, that doubted that a disease could strike selectively at male homosexuals, but the fact is—''

Mark grunted derisively. "Come on, Lucy,'' he said. "You know better than that; doctors knowledgeable about infectious diseases knew damn well there was nothing odd about a viral epidemic spreading in the gay community. Gay men tended to be promiscuous in places like the San Francisco bathhouses, and, of course, they practice anal intercourse; that means the virus is passed into the partner's intestine, which is designed by nature to absorb things directly into the bloodstream. We've always known about other diseases passed that way, like hepatitis B. Hep B has always been a problem for gays and IV drug users who share needles; another virus transmitted the same way isn't a big surprise. Or rather, shouldn't be.''

Lucy sighed. "Well, maybe not—but that's the sort of thing you heard people saying. Doctors just like everyone else. My point is, you're dismissing what Jim's found because you can't see how it fits with your patients. I don't think you can afford to do that, Mark. Right now, it's all you have.''

"Come on, Lucy, you know that viruses don't care how educated or rich you are—''

"Do tell. I have a close friend who works near the Pine Ridge Indian Reservation in North Dakota, and he sees deaths from TB, diphtheria, whooping cough—on a weekly basis. If you had Jim run some stats on folks like those, I'd bet he'd find millionaires underrepresented.''

"Well, sure,'' Mark agreed. "But that's because the patients you're talking about don't have access to reasonable medical care. It's also because their living conditions are a disgrace, something that shouldn't exist in modern America. I don't think you could cite a single instance where the reverse is true!''

"Cocaine-related fatalities in the days before crack—the late seventies and early eighties.''

Mark looked away, his face taking on an expression of mock pain. "I stand corrected,'' he admitted. "But that was a social thing. Cocaine was popular among the upper-class and cost a fortune.''

She nodded. "And not something a Mark Roberts could find a pill to cure. That's a problem for the social-worker, the psychiatrist, the police and the courts. Beside the point, doctor. Find your cause first. Then you can decide whether it's appropriate to prescribe a pill or a therapy session or a few years in jail.''

"I can't imagine prescribing jail.''

"What about the therapy?''

He didn't smile. "I have a hard time with that, too. It seems to me that patients aren't ever really cured by psychotherapy.''

"But it's an aspect you need to look at. And it isn't your forte, Mark. I think you need to pull in an expert consultant.''

He was silent for a few seconds. "You're right,'' he allowed finally. "It isn't my forte, it never has been and it probably never will be. Any suggestions as to who I should get?''

Lucy leaned back and put her hands behind her head. "The best,'' she answered. "The best we have around here.''

"Who'd you have in mind?''

She laughed again. "You know exactly who I mean, Mark. You don't have to ask me that!''

5

It was Thursday morning when Eric Terry discovered the new bulletin board listing in *The Triangle Computer Journal*: "The Last Word,'' followed by a phone number. He'd been more than a little irritated when he saw it; he worked for the publisher and was in charge of making up that listing. Since he'd never heard of this particular BBS before, he knew he hadn't placed it. Someone else had taken the liberty of sticking it in. That it hardly mattered—the *Journal* took all BBS listings, they didn't edit them or screen them in any way—was beside the point. For the remainder of the day Eric stormed around the offices, yelling at some people and questioning others, trying to find out who was usurping his authority. No one would admit to a thing; no one, if he could believe them, was even familiar with "The Last Word." A little after five that day he left work, still unsure who the culprit might've been.

Once he'd gotten home and had tossed a package of frozen lasagna in the microwave, he flipped on his computer, went to the terminal program, and directed the modem to dial the number. After a brief pause a screen came up, the BBS at the other end identifying itself as "The Last Word." It was a simple opener, plain white letters centered on a black screen. After a brief pause, new words scrolled under the title: "Welcome, seeker. Please come in."

Eric waited; these bulletin boards all operated in pretty much the same way, and he expected it to ask for a handle—"use 'new' if you are a new user" was standard—and to do such things as check his terminal type. Seconds passed; nothing happened. In an effort to hurry it up—an effort he knew was probably futile—he pressed the ENTER key.

No new words appeared, but instantly the screen changed; within a dark margin an excellent graphic of a long corridor appeared. At the end of it was a door, which after a brief pause began growing larger. As it grew it bounced just slightly, as if he were walking down the corridor toward it. The tiny speaker in his PC emitted a brief squeak; then, from the two small hi-fi speakers beside his screen, light footfalls echoed.

Eric stared at the screen. How in the hell, he asked himself, were they doing this? First-rate VGA graphics and sound, right off the top, no downloading, no nothing? Whatever testing it had done on his system had been done without screen comment, in seconds at most. This was new, this was different, this was amazingly different. He watched the door come closer and sneered a little; obviously, both from the graphic and from the initial greeting, this BBS was oriented to role-playing gamers. Eric—though he could at times get caught up playing abstract games like Tetris—did not consider himself a gamer; for the most part he thought games were a waste of time.

This, however, required investigation. Game or not.

As he watched, the door expanded beyond the confines of the screen. When he "reached" it, it swung open. Beyond—rather disappointingly—was only darkness.

From the upper left of the screen a red ribbon scrolled into sight, swinging gracefully down toward the doorway; from the bottom a blue one appeared. Colored spots sprang into existence all over the screen, each turning into a ribbon that came streaking toward the base of the doorway. They merged and attached themselves to the bottom of the doorframe and remained, slowly undulating. At this point they looked like walkways, paths leading off into the infinite.

Eric whistled softly. This was good, this was very good. Even though abstract graphics like these were easier to create on a computer screen than realistic scenes, this was obviously exceptional, obviously very well done—particularly since it was coming over the line in real time, not from a program loaded to his hard drive from a disk.

Along the paths tiny dots appeared, moving toward the door. At the same time, almost subliminally fast, an icon of a mouse appeared and then vanished at the bottom of the screen. Without taking his eyes off the image, Eric reached for the mouse and discovered that, although the buttons seemed inactive, he could shift his point of view by moving the device, left or right, forward or back.

He waited; the dots drew closer and began resolving themselves into human figures, walking toward him along the paths. Moving his face closer to the screen, Eric examined them; they were exquisitely detailed, the quality of photo-CD images. Half were male figures, the other half female; they seemed to exist in pairs. One pair was dressed like university professors, one wore medieval garb, another spacesuits, another couple was almost naked, and so on; apparently at random the figures paused and beckoned to him.

Without pondering, Eric chose the nearly naked female and moved his mouse toward the red path she was standing on. Again the image moved slightly up and down as if he were walking toward her, again light footfalls sounded from his speakers. The woman stopped moving, waited for him; again without conscious intent he moved his mouse as if it were his head, looking back at the other paths which now ran parallel to him. On them, the other figures were retreating. A moment later, the woman stood before him, her head near the top of the screen and her feet just out of sight at the bottom.

Dark-haired, smiling, dressed only in red shoes and a tiny red garment that looked like a G-string, she stood with her hands on her hips, gazing at him. For a moment all Eric could do was stare. He spent most of his days with computers, he tried to keep up with the latest technical advances; but he'd never seen anything remotely like this. He could see her breathing, he could see her eyes blinking.

"Damn, this is incredible!" he enthused aloud.

"Can I take that to mean," a soft feminine voice said from his speakers, "that you like it?"

He jumped; his sense of moving physically into the screen dissipated. The image had responded, verbally, to what he'd said! That she could speak wasn't that startling; software that could produce sound effects like footfalls could produce synthetic speech, although it required huge amounts of memory to do it. But that she'd heard him, that wasn't possible! He had no microphone hooked up to the system; there was no way his voice could be input.

Maybe, he told himself, the sysop—the person who was running this bulletin board—was bright enough to realize that some comment like the one he'd just made was to be expected. He couldn't resist testing it.

"Yeah," he said loudly. "You can bet I like it!"

She smiled; whatever model they'd used to generate this sprite was incredibly beautiful. "That makes me happy," she replied, her mouth moving with such detail that he couldn't imagine it wasn't some sort of hi-res video—which, he reminded himself, could not be transmitted over normal phone lines due to bandwidth limitations. "Come with me; I have many things to show you. Things you can't imagine." Her smile broadened. "I'm Kyrie," she went on. "I'll be your guide. What is your name?"

His lips felt dry. "Eric," he mumbled.

"Ah. Air-eek." She frowned—a somehow charming frown. "Could you say that again, I'm not sure I heard you right . . ."

His eyes were wide; he sat stone-still, feeling he was in the presence of the miraculous, the magical. "You can't be doing this, you can't be hearing me!"

She laughed. "Well, of course I can, Air-eek!"

"But how?" he almost shouted. "How, it isn't possible!"

She tipped her head curiously. "Do you really want to know?"

"Yes! God damn, yes!"

She turned her head to the side and touched her ear. "I can hear you because I am not deaf, Air-eek. You see?"

He felt like he was losing control. "Damn it, you're a graphic, you're a sprite! You're a good one, I'll admit that, but you—"

"Why, thank you, Air-eek." Her tone had turned seductive.

"This is ridiculous, this can't be happening!"

"Air-eek, you don't seem pleased."

"You're damn right I'm not pleased! You're doing things that aren't possible, and I want to know how!"

Her expression was now one of concern. "Really?"

"Really!"

She shrugged; the image, the movements, the facial expressions, all seemed impossibly realistic. "It's simple, Air-eek. When you speak your voice vibrates the cones in your speakers slightly. If we play a high-frequency signal to your speakers continuously, then we can extrapolate incoming sounds by analyzing the interference to our output."

"How's that possible?" he snarled. "You don't have a feedback loop through the sound card . . ."

"You are quite right—you are very knowledgeable, Air-eek! But there is a DMA access—direct connections between the memory and the sound chip. We can reconfigure the sound chip so that there is indeed such a feedback loop. That, Air-eek, is what we've done. We've used a similar technique to alter your VGA system, too, so that it operates at a higher speed. Don't worry, though, we can restore everything to the way it was."

"I'm not sure I want you to!"

She laughed again. "Then we will not. What you want, Air-eek, is what we want." She almost leered at him. "It's what I want, especially."

He hesitated. "The name's Eric."

"Ah, ah. Eric. Good."

Eric paused. "I think I like the way you were saying it before better."

She lowered her eyes slightly. "I will say your name however you wish it said, Air-eek. I will do anything you wish me to do."

"You said you had some things to show me—"

Her smile returned; daybreak, absolute brilliance. "Yes! Oh, Air-eek, I have a thousand things, a million things! Come, come, there is so much, so much! Whatever you wish to see, wherever you wish to go, whatever you wish to do!"

The sense of unreality had returned, with even more force now; his world, it seemed, had shrunken to include only the screen and Kyrie's voice. She was almost too realistic, it wasn't quite possible for him to think of her as a computer animation even though he knew she was.

She'd turned, she'd taken a few steps away from him, but she was glancing back over her shoulder. "Are you coming?" she urged. "Cyberia is waiting for you."

"Cyberia?"

"That's what we call our world."

"Good name." He moved the mouse forward; every instinct he had told him he was taking a step. "Lead on," he told her.

Smiling still, she did; faithfully, he followed. Several times he reached out to touch her hair or her shoulder with his left hand; each time, when his fingertips encountered a cold hard screen, he was startled.

Soon enough, though, he learned not to do that. Kyrie began to unfold Cyberia before him; he watched and listened, rapt.

6

For almost a full minute, Mark stood in front of the closed door, doing nothing at all, studying the grain of the light wood, reading and rereading the blue plaque with the white letters that identified the occupant of this office. This is stupid, he told himself as he continued to hesitate. Just stupid. You hesitated over the telephone in exactly the same way, but you eventually made the call, didn't you? Just lift your hand, Mark, and knock on the damn door.

It took another endless moment before he finally forced his arm up. "Come," a familiar voice called from inside. He opened the door and stepped through.

Across the room, sitting beside the window and looking out, was a young woman whose long dark hair was tied behind her head. He studied her profile for a moment; the rather broad, smooth-skinned face, the tiny nose, the full lips, the large, green-flecked hazel eyes hiding behind glasses. She was wearing a rather expensive-looking green silk blouse—very different from the simpler clothing she used to wear—but otherwise she didn't look like she'd changed much at all.

"Hi, Alex," he said after the silence in the small office had grown long.

She turned to face him. "Nice to see you, Mark," she answered, expressionless. "How have you been?"

"Fine, fine. What about you, Alex?"

"Couldn't be better." She sat rather stiffly, her face blank, watching him; another long silence descended. "You want to tell me what you wanted to see me about, Mark?" she finally asked. "You said it concerned some of your patients . . ."

"Yes . . . yes." He hefted a briefcase stuffed to overflowing with papers and started pulling some of them out. "Yes. I don't know, I haven't seen you lately, of course, but . . . maybe you've heard something about the spate of patients I've been looking at?"

Her manner softened; just a little, but enough for him to notice. "Yes," she answered. "Yes, as always, your reputation precedes you." As quickly as she'd softened before, her eyes went hard again. "The famous Mark Roberts," she added. "Always the talk of the hospital . . ."

He sighed; familiar territory this, territory he'd never had any sort of map to help him navigate. "I'm at a loss on this one, Alex," he said. "That's why I wanted to see you."

Her eyes showed a little dawning interest. "Oh? The way I heard it you were on the verge of a solution. The next AIDS, the next Legionnaires' disease; the Mark Roberts Syndrome. The way I heard it you were slated for the cover of *Time* magazine."

He winced internally at the name, "Roberts' Syndrome," almost exactly the term Jim Madison had used. "I think," he said, proceeding as if she hadn't spoken, "that in the end maybe we're looking at the next PTSD. This thing might be some sort of psychological disorder, Alex. That's why I asked for a consult with you."

Her eyes were colder than ever, but she could not disguise the interest behind them. "As I recall," she answered, "there was a time when you questioned whether Post-Traumatic Stress Disorder was primarily psychological. As I recall, you were an advocate of a biochemical or physiological cause for that."

He remembered—and he'd not given up those ideas, but this wasn't the time to get into that emotionally charged debate again. "I can't find much of anything in common among these patients," he pushed on. "No connections between them that might suggest some causative agent like a virus—of course, I can't totally rule it out, but—"

"Oh, of course not."

He sighed again, much more audibly this time. "Alex, could we stop this?" he asked, accepting part of the blame for the tension even though he did not feel responsible for it. "This is a professional consultation, it seems like we could—"

Her lips tightened. "Maybe," she allowed. "But you have to answer a couple of questions for me first, Mark. Why me? There are dozens of psychiatrists and psychologists at Duke Hospital. You could've called any one of them. Why not Benson, why not McKillivray?"

"First," he said immediately, "because I've always respected your abilities and your insights, more than Benson's or McKillivray's."

"Thank you for that. And second?"

"Second, Lucy suggested you. Okay?"

"Lucy. Lucy Edwards?"

"Yes."

"So it wasn't even your idea."

He hesitated; it seemed to him there were two wrong answers here, yes and no. "Well . . ."

"Bullshit, Mark," she pronounced flatly. "Bullshit. This whole thing is bullshit." Clasping her hands together, she glared at him across her desk. "Look. You can tell me why you're here, right now, or we can end this charade. I know it—"

"I'm here," he cut in firmly, "because I have a bunch of patients who are in trouble. Three of them have died; I don't know what's going to happen to the others because I, bluntly, have no fucking idea what's the matter with them. I'm here because Lucy and I thought maybe you could help. That's it, Alex." He crossed his legs and folded his arms across his chest. "You, it seems, are only interested in dredging up ancient history. Whatever there was between us ended almost four years ago; you should know, you ended it, not me." She looked as if she was about to cut in, and he waved a hand for silence. "And yes, you're right, I didn't accept that very well back then. You're right, I called you several times, I was hoping we could put things back together. But you act like I've been stalking you with a gun! You haven't heard from me for close to three years, you haven't seen me except when we pass in the hallways, and every time that happens we act like we don't know each other!"

He paused, caught his breath, then rushed on—to prevent her from entering before he'd completed his speech. "This," he said, pointing an accusing finger, "was a professional matter. You, evidently, cannot treat it as such." He started stuffing the papers back into his briefcase. "I'd better go; I guess you're right, I should've seen Benson or McKillivray to begin with."

"Are you quite finished?" she asked coolly.

"Yes. Sorry to have bothered you, Alex."

"Again, as always, it's all my fault. Again, I'm the hysteric. As usual."

"I didn't say that."

"You implied it."

"No, I didn't." He stood up.

She raised her head, her eyes following his. "Are you going to tell me about these patients, or are you just going to walk out in a huff?"

He ground his teeth. "I'd be happy to," he told her at last. "If you'd like to hear it."

"Then sit down."

He sat; again he opened the briefcase, again he drew out

some of his papers, and this time he handed her one. "That's just a summary Jim Madison made up," he informed her, keeping his tone carefully neutral. "I've run just about every test I can think of on these folks, and there isn't anything medically wrong with them. They just seem to stop caring about themselves. They don't eat, they don't sleep, they don't bathe. They don't do anything."

Alex nodded. "That's what I've heard." She leaned back in her chair, put her hands behind her head, and gazed off to her right, at nothing; it was a gesture Mark recognized, and one that allowed him to relax a little. "What makes you think their problem might be psychological?"

He made a helpless gesture. "Nothing, really—except maybe for Jim Madison's observation that they're all generally the same sort of people."

She glanced at him sharply. "What does that mean?" she asked. He ran the profile down for her as he'd done with Lucy earlier, stressing the high-IQ factor. "Hmm," she murmured, gazing at nothing again. "That's fascinating. Maybe just the pressure of modern life getting to people?"

"Doubtful—or so it seems to me, anyway. You'd have to identify something in people's lives that's changed all of a sudden. I can't imagine what that'd be."

"I'm not sure that what you're saying follows," she said slowly. "There have been manias before—like in Renaissance Europe, when tarantella dancing spread like wildfire. Maybe there's some similarity."

"I guess it's possible. But—unless I'm wrong, people didn't start dancing the tarantella all by themselves, all of a sudden. They joined dances in progress, didn't they?"

She nodded. "For the most part. Obviously someone had to start them, but still, I think you have a point. There has to be some trigger, some common thread. That's what we have to find."

He smiled a little at her self-inclusion. "Yes, I agree. So far I have nothing."

"You've said that. What sorts of tests have you run on these people?"

"Everything I can think of. I've used up a lot of favors, Alex; we're talking some money here. I've ordered batteries of blood tests, spinal taps, EEGs, CAT scans, MRIs, even PET scans. I've buried Lucy in tests and Jim Madison in data, and we're coming up absolutely dry. There's nothing wrong with these people; nothing any of those tests can pick out, anyway. Or if there is, it's an isolate. No common factors.''

"Drugs?''

"Not unless it's something nobody's ever heard of before.''

"That's always possible.''

"It is. But Lucy doubts it—based on the assays she's had done—and I trust her judgment.''

"So do I.'' She looked down at the paper again. "Maybe I should talk to some of these people. Maybe I can get something out of them.''

"Sounds fine to me.''

"Any suggestions for starting points?''

"Well.'' He thumbed through the pages. "For starters, there's Wendy Sung. A writer. She's one of the few to at least try to offer an explanation of why she's in the shape she's in.''

"Which is?''

He shrugged. "Overwork. Long hours on a novel.''

"But you don't think so.''

"No. I've known lots of people who work too hard. I've known people who were pathological about it; I could be accused of that too. They can have problems—sometimes they push their blood pressure up, they have cardiac problems, they have bad diets, they get obese and they smoke too much. They don't starve themselves and refuse sleep to the point of collapse. That's what Wendy Sung did.''

"Maybe she's anorexic.''

"No. I thought that too, but her pattern isn't right. She believes she looks, to use her own words, 'hideous' and 'scrawny' at the moment, and that doesn't fit.''

Alex nodded agreement. "Okay,'' she answered. "Wendy Sung's my first stop. Any others?''

"Yeah. We have a couple of doctors, too—one's a psychologist named David Carol, he might have some insights of his own, although I haven't been able to get much out of him myself. Then there's Jane Lightfoot, she's a grad student in computer science—'' He paused, thumbed through some more sheets. "Actually we've got several grad students and a couple of professors—''

"Christ! It sounds like Jim was right!"

"Yeah, that's what Lucy said too. It just doesn't make sense to me, Alex."

"Not so far," she corrected. She opened the top drawer of her desk and drew out a calendar. "I have," she mused, "a free hour and a half this afternoon. Suppose I stop by and see Wendy Sung today? We might as well get this rolling."

Mark nodded noncommittally, but he was watching her eyes closely. He'd hoped that she'd choose to join him in solving this mystery, but, in reality, this had been considerably easier than he'd expected; all he'd felt himself able to count on was that she'd agree to look at the data. Instead, she seemed to be throwing herself into things wholeheartedly.

He handed her a copy of Wendy's chart and, after stuffing the remainder of the papers back into his briefcase, stood up. "You'll call me, then?" he asked. "If you learn anything?"

"Of course." He turned away, started for the door. "Mark?" she said softly.

He turned back. "Yes?"

"I'm glad you called me," she admitted. "It's been good to see you again. It'll be good if we can be friends. You think that's possible, Mark?"

Watching her, he found himself aching to touch her. Not without me taking some serious damage, he answered silently; I'm not by any stretch of the imagination over you yet. "I hope so," he said aloud.

7

"It's all about Korean history," Wendy was saying. Her eyes were bright with enthusiasm. "About the resistance to Japanese rule; Korea was a Japanese colony for thirty-five years, but there was always resistance. In particular it's about Queen Min, about how she fought against the Japanese until she was assassinated in 1895."

"It sounds very interesting," Alex responded, making some notes on her pad. She sighed—though not audibly—as Wendy went on, telling her details about Queen Min and her life.

She'd already spent forty-five minutes with Wendy Sung, listening to her talk about herself and her life before her collapse, listening to her somewhat oddly phrased complaints about remaining in the hospital and listening to her explain the novel she was obviously eager to get back to. So far, there'd been nothing to explain her condition; yes, she was dedicated to getting her book written, but she did not strike Alex as the sort of obsessive personality who might neglect the basic needs of life to satisfy a compulsion.

And yet, that's just what she'd done. Wendy had changed vastly from the person Mark had interviewed the day after her arrival; she'd gained enough weight that she no longer looked anorexic, her skin color had been restored, her hair was smoothly combed and glossy black once more. She was quite an attractive woman.

But her chart told Alex the physical story, and her earlier musings had been just as informative. A few months earlier— if everything she'd said could be believed—she'd been a reasonably happy and well-adjusted person. As she told Mark, she'd been teaching English classes designed for recent immigrants; she'd also been engaged, and she'd been living a social life that could almost be called hectic.

More confusingly, Wendy's problems had obviously not started with her novel. For some years she'd been engaged in a fairly intense study of Korean history, and that had led her to conceive her book. Progress had, at first, been quite slow; it had been over a year since she'd first drawn up a general outline.

Recently, though, her attitude toward this work had changed. She'd neglected her fiancé to the point where he had, after dozens of attempted phone calls and visits, finally called off the wedding; she'd begun to ignore her job and, in the weeks before her collapse, had stopped showing up for work altogether—and she'd been dismissed by letter since she'd made herself almost impossible to reach. Living alone and having succeeded in isolating herself, her collapse might well have been fatal had she not somehow managed to dial 911. The rescue squad had to break her door down to get to her.

Alex probed the breakup of Wendy's relationship and the loss of her job carefully, but even after a short discussion she was convinced that neither was responsible for Wendy's problem; both—unfortunately—had been mere symptoms. There was something else, though; Alex, like Mark, could sense it, could feel it.

After waiting patiently until Wendy came to a temporary halt in her ramblings about her book, Alex jumped in quickly. "Excuse me for changing the subject," she said, "but—why are you still here? Obviously your crisis has passed—there's no reason you can't leave, can't get back to your work."

Her enthusiastic manner suddenly died away. She looked down at the sheets. "I, uh . . . I really wanted to, you know, the first couple of days I was here, but . . ."

Alex watched her closely. "Yes?"

Wendy didn't look up. "To tell you the truth, Dr. Walton, I'm a little afraid to." She paused, then shook her head—slightly at first, then almost violently. "I need to figure out what happened to me—I don't want it to happen again. Dr. Roberts told me I'd gotten myself into pretty bad shape. I do need to leave—I need to put my life back together." She raised her head at last; her eyes were wet. "I suppose it's too late for Ben and me. I did treat him horribly, I really did. But my job—maybe I can get it back. I mean, I worked for them for five years before this happened."

Alex decided to take a chance. "Before what happened, Wendy? What happened to you?"

The tears began to roll, in neat lines down each of her cheeks. "Before I got—I don't know, you're a psychiatrist, what's the word? Obsessed? With the novel, with the book. I want to get back to it, I just want to be able to control it, I don't want it controlling me—like it did before."

"Wendy, I'm trying to understand this, but I'm having a little trouble. You say the story was controlling you. Can you explain that?"

She nodded slowly. "I just got to the point where I couldn't stop, couldn't stop working on it."

"Why not?"

She frowned, wiped her face. "Have you ever written anything, Dr. Walton?"

Alex smiled. "Not like a novel, no. Technical papers. Grant proposals, things like that. Things that are hard to keep working on, not things that are hard to quit!"

Wendy offered the psychiatrist a rather fragile smile in return. "I can imagine," she agreed. "Well, my novel was that way too, at first. I always wanted to write, but I put it off and put it off. Sometimes I'd start a page or two on an old IBM Selectric I had, but it was always so much trouble. I was trying to do it right from the start, making carbon copies and all that, and it just seemed like I'd make a mistake every other word." She stopped, shook her head. "Then, a year ago, I decided to buy a computer. That made a lot of difference; once I got used to the word processor I got going on it."

"That's when you did your outline. A year ago, you said?"

"Uh-huh. But it was still slow going." She shrugged. "My word processor started giving me grief—some of them don't work well when the files get too big, and that's what happened with me. So, I went down and talked to a guy at the computer store and he sold me Windows and Microsoft Word and a couple of other things. He sold me a modem and it came with a subscription to one of the on-line services. So I puzzled over all that stuff for a while—I'm not a computer whiz or anything—but I got it on my machine and I figured out how to use it, and I started calling up the on-line service and I was getting all sorts of good stuff there. It made a lot of difference! The more I used it the easier it was, and the better the writing got! I always felt I was just about to write something really great, something really really great!" She stopped again, rather abruptly, and shook her head. "I'm not sure now though that that wasn't just part of—whatever's wrong with me." She looked at Alex with pleading eyes. "What is wrong with me, doctor?"

You got me, Alex said silently. "Right now, we're still not sure," she answered. "Dr. Roberts is still running tests. None of them have given us a definitive answer, not yet."

There was a moment of silence. "Do you think I should go home?"

"I honestly can't say," Alex replied. "In a way, I can't see why not. But, if you aren't sure you can handle things, then maybe another day or two here wouldn't hurt."

"Do you think it'll happen again? Dr. Roberts seems to think so."

"Dr. Roberts," Alex answered, "is very cautious. In your

41

case, there's no way of knowing; we can't make a prognosis when we have no diagnosis. And we don't, Wendy; we don't even have a working theory." She stood up. "I'm going to talk to some of the other patients and see if I can come up with anything. If you think of anything you want to tell me, anything that might help, give me a call—just ask the nurse to call Dr. Walton. Okay?"

Wendy folded her arms across her chest. "Like what?"

Alex could not keep herself from looking helpless. "Like anything. Right now, Wendy, I'm open to all possibilities. I have to be."

8

The red-haired man, his hands full, pushed the door open with his foot and walked in. "Got one I'd like you to look at right away, Charlie," he said. He lowered a computer onto the edge of Charlie's workbench. "We need this back out on the floor."

Charlie put his soldering iron back in its holder and looked over the machine. "What's wrong with it?"

Bobby shrugged. "Probably nothing. It's the one that crazy kid stole, you remember, when Paula got held up?"

"Yeah," Charlie laughed. "When we all became armed and dangerous, when you started keeping that little .38 in the desk up front. Man, which one of us is supposed to use that thing?"

"I hope," Bobby said seriously, "that we never have to. But it makes Paula feel better. Getting robbed at gunpoint really shook her up." He looked down at the computer again. "Anyway, we just got this thing back from the cops. It sat in the kid's apartment for a couple of days, left on. The cops collected it, but they don't know much about them." He indicated the stub of a mouse cable that remained in the machine, a cable that had been ripped in half rather than unplugged. "See?"

"Yeah," Charlie laughed. "Typical." He pushed his stool back and checked the machine quickly; with a small screwdriver he removed the screws holding the mouse cable plug and tossed the damaged plug and wire into the trash. "Well, it won't take a minute to hook it up and see what's what," he commented as he pulled a generic keyboard down off a shelf and plugged it in.

"Right," Bobby agreed. "Let me know, okay?"

Charlie reached for a monitor cable. "You got it, boss-man." The connection to the monitor, an intact mouse cable, and a power cord completed his hookup; he flipped the machine on.

The screen flashed and wavered a few times, after which the various statements concerning the boot-up process began to appear; Charlie, knowing these systems quite well, watched them and noted nothing that seemed much out of the ordinary to him. There was only one he didn't recognize, a program called "PNHOST" that was copyrighted by Compuware, a local software company. Shortly after that appeared, the boot stopped; a message scrolled up informing him that a phone line was not connected to the internal modem. He touched the ENTER key and, when that did not work, the F1, trying to get the boot to proceed, but it seemed hung there, demanding that a phone line be connected.

"Okay, okay," he told it. "We'll do it your way." Un-plugging one of the phone links from the back of another machine, he connected it to the modem. The boot resumed; eventually a "C:" prompt appeared.

"Looks pretty normal," he muttered, reaching for the key-board and planning to execute a "directory" command so that he could see what software had been added to or deleted from the hard disk.

Before he could, though, a new statement appeared on the screen: "Speaker system not found." He stared at it for a moment, puzzled. Looking at the back of the machine, he saw that it did indeed have a sound card installed, a very conven-tional Sound Blaster unit. But it shouldn't have been trying to access a speaker system at all at this point; besides, there wasn't any way it could know whether or not speakers were hooked to the sound card.

"Okay," he told it. "Fine. Let's see what you're trying to do." He pulled another cable down from his shelf, fumbling with a tangle in the wiring before getting enough length to plug it into the speaker access on the back of the sound card. Again he stared at the screen.

"Continue game?" a deep voice said from the speakers after a brief pause. Distantly, in the background, there was minor-key music.

Charlie laughed, typed "no" on the keyboard. Instantly the music stopped. "What, then?" an altogether different voice asked.

"Cute program," Charlie told it. He typed "DIR/W" on the keyboard; the screen half-filled with the names of directories and files. He scanned them and saw nothing abnormal except for a directory called "PNHOST" and a game directory. "Dumb kid," Charlie muttered. "All he did was load on a stupid D&D game and a manager of some sort. What an idiot. Hell, I guess it takes all kinds." He took a quick look at the game directory and realized it was one he was quite familiar with, one he had played a year or so before. He cocked his head and studied the files. It was different, somehow; there was more to it, there were several files with cryptic names.

"Might as well take a look at you," he commented. "It's as good a way as any to check the machine through." Locating the "EXE" file in the game directory, he typed in the name associated with it. The hard disk activity light flashed on, the disk whirred, the game credits appeared and vanished too fast to read.

The very low, minor-key music returned; so did the deep voice. "Continue as Horval?" the voice asked. Charlie reached for the mouse, but didn't see a dialogue box to point to; returning to his keyboard he typed in "yes." Again the screen flashed, and a familiar game scene, shown from the player character's point of view, came up.

Or, at least, fairly familiar; Charlie cocked his head and stared for a moment. He could tell where he was; in the corridors approaching the chamber where the Liche, one of the harder opponents in the game, was lurking. On the other hand, he did not remember the graphics being this sharp and detailed, or the motion of the screen being so smooth, so realistic. Maybe, he told himself, it was a slightly newer version. He checked the attributes of the current character, Horval; his strength and level, in Charlie's opinion, were not quite good enough to defeat the Liche.

Which, of course, did not really matter; he wasn't playing

the game, he was simply testing the machine, which thus far was performing outstandingly. More details returned to him as he played on, guiding Horval through the twists and turns of the maze, ducking a potentially lethal fireball trap, and soon arriving at the Liche's door. Reaching out to open it, he saw his hand appear in the screen and smiled. That was a touch his version hadn't had.

The door opened; the Liche, looking detailed and lifelike in a way that surprised Charlie, made its appearance. Clicking on icons, operating on automatic now, Charlie had Horval draw his sword as the Liche, its eyes glowing redly, glided toward him. He struck; the Liche reeled back a little, then lunged forward to counterattack.

As the Liche's flashing blade filled the screen momentarily, the whole image flashed red and flickered for a moment; Charlie saw the icon representing Horval's life force go down a bit, and at the same time experienced a sudden sharp pain in his head. Frowning, he rubbed above his eyebrows with his fingers and rather halfheartedly guided the mouse so that Horval made another attack on the Liche, an ineffective one this time. The Liche ducked, then struck back and connected.

Another sharp pain, worse this time, shot through Charlie's head, just above his eyes. "Shit!" he said aloud. Letting go of the mouse completely, he rubbed at his forehead with both hands, telling himself he'd have to get some aspirin if this kept up. On the screen, the Liche took advantage of Horval's motionlessness to land another blow, a much harder one that took the Magus' life force down to half.

Charlie, though distracted, saw it happen; he also saw the screen flash and flicker again, and instantly felt another pain, far worse than before, come streaking through his head. He grunted loudly and grabbed his forehead.

He suddenly made a connection—although he did not believe it, he could not believe it. Still, he grabbed at the mouse and pulled Horval back as the Liche struck at him again, this time evading the blow. The screen did not flash red and Charlie felt no new pain.

"No," he muttered. "No, this is just—what, something you're doing to yourself? What the hell is going on here?" He clicked the left mouse button, Horval slashed at the Liche, the Liche returned the attack and scored a light hit; Charlie saw a paler flash and felt a lighter but keenly sharp shot of pain. "That's enough," he told the computer, his voice shaking. "That's enough." He pulled Horval back and turned him around, planning to send him fleeing down the corridor.

As Horval turned away, the screen flashed its brightest red yet; the flickering that followed seemed to go on for a terribly long time. Horval's life force dropped down to almost nothing. Charlie felt as if someone had smashed a hammer against his forehead; he cried out in pain, his vision swam, and the real world turned red and began to flicker as well. Charlie, unable to see clearly now because of the flashing phosphenes obscuring his vision, fumbled at the keyboard, touching the CONTROL-ALT-DELETE set that should've rebooted the computer. It did nothing, and, though the screen did not show it, somewhere in the cyberspace of the machine the Liche again struck the hapless Horval from behind. As Charlie screamed with new pain, the character's life force fell to just a trace. His hands feeling like they were encased in lead and his body beginning to jerk with uncontrollable spasms, Charlie reached up for the computer's face, vaguely fumbling at the RESET button. The screen, still in front of his face, flashed intense red; Charlie gave a piercing shriek and collapsed backward, falling from his chair onto the floor. His body jerked wildly and arched back like a bow, his hands flopping about grotesquely and his feet trembling with tension.

At this point the store manager, attracted by the screams, came rushing in. "Charlie!" he yelled. "Charlie, Charlie, what's the matter! Jesus!" Getting no response, he grabbed up the phone on the workbench, his fingers dialing 911.

But the line was busy. A digital whine sounded in his ear. Bobby realized that this phone was tied to the lines used for the modems, that some unit must've been on line—although none should've been. Tossing it down, he sprinted to the other phone on the far wall, grabbed it, and called 911.

Then he returned to try to assist his serviceman, who by then had become still. Kneeling beside him, Bobby couldn't help but see the open and staring eyes, the enlarged pupils, the pale, almost grayish, skin. He tried to feel for a pulse in Charlie's neck, though his knowledge of such things came only from TV. He couldn't find one.

He didn't know CPR; there was nothing he could do, nothing but wait for the paramedics. He glanced up at the machine Charlie had been working on; the screen had gone dark except for the image of a grinning skull floating in the center of the blackness.

9

Feeling more than a little tired and drained—and hoping against hope that Don had either fixed or ordered dinner or that he'd be willing to go out to some restaurant—Alex pulled her BMW into their driveway. Sliding the garage door opener off the dash, she aimed it and pressed the button; the door slipped smoothly upwards and the lights inside came on, revealing that Don's Jaguar was not there as yet. She sighed; as she eased the car into the garage she glanced at her watch, noting that it was almost eight-thirty. Distracted, she looked up to find her car drifting toward the wall and had to jerk the wheel sharply to prevent hitting it.

Although it didn't matter, she told herself as she brought the car to a halt. She could smash the car right into the wall, tear a fender completely off, ruin the motor—it still wouldn't matter. Don's response—once he'd determined that she wasn't hurt—would be laughter. Cash flow problems at the company or no, he'd whip out one of his ubiquitous credit cards and, within days or weeks at the most, car and garage would be repaired; she'd have a rental, something comparable to her BMW, to drive in the meantime and if she complained at all she'd end up with a new car. She played the scenario through in her mind; she could almost see the shiny new car sitting in the drive with a red ribbon tied to the steering wheel, the new keys left on her pillow for her to find. For a moment she sat in the car with the engine idling, fighting a perfectly lunatic urge to back out and deliberately crash into the wall, just to see how closely the reality followed her fantasy.

She was distracted by the sound of the garage door closing. She turned and looked at it. That'd rattle him, she told herself, that'd get his attention. Come home and find me sitting here unconscious with the garage full of carbon monoxide. He'd be after her for whys for six months.

"Right, Alex," she snapped at herself. She shut the engine off. "With your luck, he'd come home at two A.M. and find you sitting here dead." With a sigh, she got out of the car, retrieved her briefcase—her sumptuous leather, gold-embossed, Italian-made gift from Don, a briefcase that was actually too heavy for her to comfortably carry—and headed for the door. The company might have financial problems but they, as a couple, never did. Donald had, in fact, suggested since their wedding that she discontinue her practice, pointing out that it wasn't necessary for her to work; this she'd resisted, and he'd never raised the issue to the point where it might become a problem for them.

On the other hand, it was often oddly difficult for her to appreciate Don's attention; his pattern was to express his feelings by spending money, often huge amounts of it, very casually. Not since they'd met, she reflected, had he spent less than five thousand each year on her birthday gift.

And yet, she was painfully aware that his secretary at Lehmann dutifully put a note on his desk reminding him of that date. She'd also learned, by accidentally reading a memo he'd left in his shirt pocket—that on at least one occasion, he'd asked that same secretary to select her gift—and to make sure she spent at least the requisite five thousand.

"You shouldn't let it bother you, Alex," she muttered as she entered the darkened house and started flipping on lights. "He's a busy man, he works damn hard for that money. It doesn't mean he isn't interested, it doesn't mean he doesn't care."

She walked on through the empty house; it seemed incredibly large to her when she was alone in it. Don had a way of filling it, with his personality rather than his physical size, of making it seem less excessive. Entering the living room, she glanced at the answering machine and saw the little green light blinking steadily.

There were several messages; she paid scant attention until she heard her husband's voice. "Going to be late tonight," it said. "Don't know exactly when I'll be in. Don't wait up."

She scowled at it, listened to it whir, waited until the green light became steady again. "Damn it, Don, that makes five in a row now. How many all-nighters does it take to solve a cash-flow problem? Or am I being an idiot—are you actually out running around with some bimbo?"

Turning away, she winced; that last was utterly uncalled for, utterly unfair. She had no reason to suspect him of such a thing.

Once that unwelcome idea had planted itself in her mind, it would not leave, no matter how firmly she tried to tell herself it was absurd. Still, she could easily check without revealing any silliness on her part. She picked up the phone and called Don's office.

"Yes?" he snapped on the second ring.

You are an idiot, Alex, she told herself angrily. An utter idiot. There he is, working as he'd said he would be, sitting right at his desk ready to pick up the phone if his foolish wife should decide to call and interrupt him.

"Hi, hon, it's me," she said smoothly. "I just wanted to check in with you, see if you had any idea yet about when you'd be—"

"No, no, not yet," he shot back. She heard distinct irritation in his tone. "It's going to be a while. Like I said in the message, don't wait up."

"Yes, I just—"

"I have to go, Alex," he cut in. "I was right in the middle of something, okay?"

She blinked at the phone. "Oh. Well, okay. See you later then, hon. Love you."

"Yeah. Love you too." She heard a click, after which she stood frowning at the dead phone for several seconds before hanging it up. Each day, she mused, he works later and his temper gets shorter. She was concerned for his sake, but she was certain enough that this crisis would end soon; with that thought in mind she wandered toward the kitchen. Dropping her briefcase by the table, she popped a Stouffer's into the microwave, poured herself a glass of white wine, waited impatiently; once the meal was done and she had it on the table, she pulled a sheaf of papers from the briefcase and laid them neatly beside her plate, opposite her carefully placed napkin. As she read each page she tossed it into an unruly heap on the other side of the table, not even noticing when she dragged the edge of one sheet through her food. Her gaze fixed on the papers, she absent-mindedly took a bite of the dinner; it was still quite hot, and she recoiled as it scorched her tongue.

A few moments later the burn was forgotten. The food vanished, so did the wine; the microwave dish the dinner had been cooked in began to slowly dry in place as Alex devoted her entire attention to her notes on the patients Mark had referred her to.

There's nothing, she told herself after a while, nothing at all to link these patients together—nothing other than the high-IQ connection Jim had noticed. A teacher—or rather, a former teacher turned fiction writer; a computer hardware specialist; a graduate student majoring in history; a music store manager; an architectural draftsman; a dental hygienist; a doctor whose specialty was obstetrics and gynecology. Unrelated people; they didn't work together, didn't know each other, didn't belong to the same clubs, didn't have the same tastes in nightlife, didn't share a single thing that might've brought them together. Any notions of some new contagious disease could probably be ruled out—but that was the conclusion Mark had, with some obvious reluctance, already arrived at.

From the viewpoint of her specialty, though, the picture wasn't much clearer. None of these patients fitted the picture of any known psychiatric malady, yet their conditions were clearly related in some way; she'd heard several of them use the same terms: "I felt I was just on the verge of" doing something that was extremely important to them; whatever it was remained "just out of reach." She flipped through pages again; of the six people she'd talked to today, five had used those exact words, "just out of reach." For the writer it was great prose, for the programmer an elegant solution to a tricky algorithm, for the history student the answer to an often-attacked historical puzzle, for the music store manager a song that would put his compositions in the top forty. Unrelated, apparently, but similar, similar enough to make Alex certain Mark had been right; they weren't unrelated. She'd been more or less expecting—and she knew it would've occurred to Mark, too—that they might all be of the same general personality type; that wouldn't have been in and of itself an answer, but it would've given a direction to their quest.

But every instinct Alex had told her this wasn't the case,

even if she couldn't be certain without administering some tests. These six were all over the map with respect to personality, and she was already confident that the tests she'd ordered would merely reinforce her perception. The only thing these patients had in common was advanced education, high intelligence, and—for most of them, at least before this illness had taken its toll—successful careers.

She got up to refill her wine glass. This wasn't going to be easy—a real answer, a true answer, might be years in coming. If these were the first few recognized examples of some syndrome related to the stress that modern life puts on creative people, then no relationship among these examples might ever be uncovered; it would be difficult to demonstrate that fiction publishing, the popular music industry, and the world of the academic historian were similar enough to cause clinically identical stress-related syndromes.

She pulled out the sheets of statistics that Jim had provided for Mark and studied them once more. Jim, typically thorough, had run a comparison on a random selection of Duke Hospital patients a year previous; he'd made a note at the bottom that, since these patients were chosen from those whose records, for whatever reasons, had been entered into Mark's databases, the sample wasn't unbiased, and therefore not ideal from a statistical viewpoint.

Even so, it told a story. Of all those patients—over two hundred that Mark had been asked to apply his diagnostic skills to—only one might even possibly have been assigned to the group Mark had now created. And that one had been diagnosed rather quickly; her problem had been related to the abuse of amphetamines.

Sipping her wine, Alex went back through the six patients again. There was something, she kept telling herself, something that she wasn't seeing—or rather, something she was seeing but not as yet recognizing. Some commonality. She kept staring at the papers, ruffling through them, trying to pick it up.

Suddenly, without warning, she saw it, the common thread that had been eluding her. She ran through the papers yet again; yes, that was it. It fitted five, and the sixth, the draftsman, hadn't mentioned it so she couldn't rule him out. She frowned at the papers, spread them out, packed them up again. Was it meaningful? No, she told herself, it wasn't likely. And yet, it was a connection.

For several minutes she stared at the papers. Mark, she was sure, would never pick this up, for the same reasons he wasn't taking the commonality of high IQ very seriously—like any physician he was looking for a biological cause. Her own bias—her search for some common psychological factor—had prevented her from seeing it until now. She couldn't help but doubt its significance, but that, she told herself, didn't mean she had to reject it out of hand.

Pushing herself back from the table, she glanced at the clock. A little after ten; it was possible that the patients were still awake. She'd try, she decided, to find out tonight, if the sixth patient fitted the pattern. If the draftsman—Willis was his name—fitted, then she'd take this to Mark and they could check it through with all the other patients. If he didn't, then it was back to the drawing board. Stepping into the kitchen, she picked up the phone and called the hospital.

"Yes," she said when she finally got through to a nurse on the ward where Willis' room was. "This is Dr. Alexandra Walton. I'd like you to check on a patient there, Mr. Willis, and see if he's still awake. If he is, patch me through to his room, would you? I'm working on his case and I have a question I'd like to ask him." Alex waited, for what seemed like a very long time, leaning on the counter, shifting her weight from foot to foot.

"Hello?" a voice said finally. "This is Mike Willis."

"Mr. Willis, this is Dr. Walton. You remember, we talked this afternoon?"

"Oh, yeah, the shrink. What can I do for you, doc?"

"Mr. Willis, I have just one quick question for you. The design you said you were working on, the one you said you felt would revolutionize industrial architecture—could I ask you how you were working on it? I mean, I know very little about the way architects and draftsmen go about their daily work—"

"Oh, sure, I understand. Gee, I don't know a thing about the way psychiatrists do their work, either. Well, Dr. Walton, I was using a program called AutoCad—it's pretty much the standard in architecture, and I set up—"

"So you were using a computer?"

"Oh, sure. What else?"

"Mr. Willis, that's all I needed to know right now. Thank you very much."

"Uh—doc, does AutoCad have anything to do with—?"

"I seriously doubt it, Mr. Willis. But, right now, I still don't have a definite answer for you; we'll be getting back to you in the next day or two, I'm sure."

"Oh. Okay. Well, have a good day—uh, I mean, night, doc!"

"You too, Mr. Willis. Bye."

She made a note on Willis' sheet. Then she called Mark, set up a conference between him, herself, Gus, and Jim for the next morning. He pushed her hard for what she'd found, but she adamantly refused to tell him; she wanted one more night to consider all this, to decide if presenting them with this would make her look like a fool. At the moment, she wasn't at all sure.

10

"Computers," Alex said flatly. "That's the link I've found." She looked at each of the three faces sitting around the conference table in turn. "For all six patients I've interviewed, the obsessions are related to work they're doing on a computer." She laughed; the sound was brittle. "Okay, who's going to be the first one to tell me I'm silly?"

Mark, leaning his arms on the stack of papers he'd laid out on the table, watched her eyes carefully. He'd gone to some trouble to arrange for use of the small conference room on short notice; he'd wanted a more formal atmosphere for Alex's presentation than one of their offices or a table in the cafeteria. He waited, but it seemed to him that her presentation was already over. He continued to gaze at her; there was nothing he could possibly imagine himself saying that wouldn't cause her to take offense. Silence was safe. Let Gus or Jim do the talking for now.

The silence grew long. "I don't think I understand," Gus offered mildly, breaking it at last.

"All the patients," Alex repeated, "are obsessed with work they're doing on a computer." Clearly ill at ease, she grinned in slightly exaggerated fashion.

"And?" Gus persisted.

She sighed. "Damn," she muttered. She straightened her own stack of paper, making three neat piles. "And nothing. That's it, that's all. Right now, anyhow. I just thought maybe we could discuss it. See if anyone has any ideas—"

"A lot of people," Gus pointed out gently, "use computers nowadays. I do, you do, Mark does. Jim uses them more than all three of us put together." He patted his ample stomach. "*I'm* not forgetting to eat!"

Alex's face tightened; to Mark she looked like she was about to say something, but Jim cut in. "Do you know," he asked her, "if they're all using the same brand or type of computer? All using Macs, for example?" He leaned back in his chair with his hands behind his head; he looked interested.

She turned to him, gratitude in her eyes. "No, I don't," she told him. "I just have this preliminary—well, I don't think we should even call it a finding—maybe not even an idea. Just a—"

"We'll call the paper," Jim put in, " 'Toward a Possible Preliminary Hypothesis Bearing on Some Aspects of—' "

Alex laughed; Mark relaxed a little, discovering only then that he'd been so tense his right foot was severely cramped. "The first thing we can do," he said, "is check the other patients to see if they fit the same pattern. Some of them do, I can tell you that already. I can't say that any of them don't."

"And?" Gus asked. "If they do, then what?"

"Then," Jim suggested, "we see what they're using, what computers. What monitors and video systems, especially. You know, a couple of years ago bunches of people were claiming that their VDTs were making them sick. Maybe they weren't full of crap after all."

Gus turned to him. "But nothing was ever found to support those claims, Jim!"

"There's your key words," the programmer shot back. " 'Nothing ever found.' Doesn't mean there wasn't something to at least some of those claims."

Gus's voice remained mild, but there was a certain impatience obvious in his expression. "It seems to me," he said, "that such research is likely a waste of time. Perhaps the time would be better spent in readministering some of these tests. Perhaps there's something that shows up only after a certain latency."

Mark and Alex glanced at each other. "I doubt that, Gus," Alex said slowly. "I wouldn't expect any of the psychologicals to . . ."

Mark was shaking his head as she spoke. "And as for the CATs and MRIs, well, you call in some chits if you want them done over. I can't imagine them showing anything different."

"What about the chemistries?"

"That's a possibility," Mark agreed. "Lucy'll hate us all forever, and the patients are going to give us a hard time about being poked and prodded even more than they already have been, but we could redo some of those. Meanwhile, we can look at Alex's ideas."

Gus clearly wasn't convinced. "Still," he repeated, "I imagine there're better ways to use our time than to—"

"It's very little time, Gus," Mark said rapidly. "Very little. All we have to do is collect the data and give it to Jim, he can take it from there. If something turns up, we can investigate further. If not, we've eliminated one possibility."

"You consider this a possibility, Mark?" Gus asked. His tone had grown a little sharper. "A genuine possibility?"

Mark glanced at Alex, almost furtively. "Well, it's something we should check out. We—"

"And next," Gus interrupted, "we can check to see if these patients are among those who've been abducted by aliens from UFOs. Or perhaps assay the fluoride in their drinking water, or—"

"You aren't being quite fair, Gus," Mark said, his tone managing to convey an almost parental chastisement and a certain sympathy at the same time. He threw another sidelong glance at Alex. His attempt at fence-straddling had evidently worked; neither she nor Gus was glaring at him.

Gus threw up his hands. "Fine," he said. "As you say, it won't take much time. But I cannot promise not to say 'I told you so' if nothing comes of this."

Mark smiled. "No such promise is being asked."

"Good." He rose from the table, headed for the door. "I've got patients," he told them, his tone noticeably chilly. "Let me know what you find."

"We will." Mark turned to Jim. "So," he said, "What should we ask these folks?"

"First," Jim said with a grin, "you should ask them if they've had a system crash recently caused by a computer virus." He glanced at Gus, who was by then on his way to the door. "That's what's known to cause problems, anyhow. So says the research."

Gus stopped, turned. "What?"

Jim nodded; there was a hint of smugness on his face. "There was a study done on it at the University of California, several years ago," he said. "People expect certain things out of their computers, they expect them to be logical and rational. A breakdown is more or less acceptable—all machines break down from time to time—but a virus is something else. It scares people, it makes them feel vulnerable, and the cute little comments and graphics the virus designers put up on the screen—the 'Gotcha!' statements, the little bugs that crawl in from the corners eating up words while the virus is wrecking the hard drive—makes it that much worse. It's like a practical joke gone terribly wrong; the victim may have lost days or weeks of work—usually more because the virus has to be stripped off of every floppy that's been in contact with that machine.

"Anyway, the Cal research found that a lot of these folks have panic reactions. They don't want to go near their computers again, they don't trust them anymore, they have an instinctive gut reaction that says the computer itself was somehow responsible for what happened. It produces a sort of stress syndrome. You wouldn't think having your computer crash because of a virus would be similar to being shot at in a war, but in ways it is. It distorts your notions of what's real, what's concrete. Of what you can count on and what you can't. Lots of computer users out there have substituted computers for their typewriter or their slide rule; typewriters and slide rules weren't vulnerable to viruses."

Returning to the table, Gus leaned on it with both hands. "I've never heard of this study."

"Why would you? It isn't your area, is it? It isn't medicine, it's psychiatry and computer science."

Gus hung his head theatrically and shook it. "I suppose I have to admit to being duly and fairly chastised," he said. He sat back down. "So, Dr. Madison, I do believe you were telling us what sorts of questions we should be asking?"

Only a little twitching of his mustache revealed that Jim was trying to control his Cheshire-cat grin. "Well. It's pretty obvious that we aren't dealing with the same thing the Cal guys were—these patients won't get off their computers; those didn't want to use them anymore. Still, we need to ask about viruses. And just about everything else we can think of, I guess."

Alex was frowning. "Like?"

Jim started counting on his fingers. "Type of machine: PC, Mac, mainframe, CPU type, how much RAM, how big a hard drive. Peripherals like CD-ROMs, modems, sound cards, scanners; the video and the video type, I'd say that's possibly important. Besides that—"

He went on for several seconds; Alex began shaking her head. "You'll have to write all this down," she told him. "I don't consider myself computer illiterate, but I won't remember half of it. Besides that, I doubt very seriously if people like Wendy Sung are going to know all those details!"

"Probably not," Jim agreed. "Your programmer patient will. Right now, I think we get what we can and go from there."

"I hate to be the one to again throw cold water on all this enthusiasm," Gus put in, "but let me note that Dr. Walton's finding applies to six and only six patients. We first need to check the others to see if this pattern holds."

"Of course we do," Jim agreed. "But Gus, consider—six in a row?"

"Sometimes, if you flip coins enough, you get six heads in a row."

"You sure do. But you don't get twenty, not very often. Let's see how many we do have, Gus."

The meeting broke up after that; for a few minutes Mark busied himself writing notes. Before he was finished, Gus had left, off to the ER to see his patients; Jim had gone too, for reasons Mark didn't quite understand. He'd been planning to prepare a list of questions for them to ask the patients; it seemed logical for him to do that immediately. Jim, however, after staring at Mark and Alex for a moment, had insisted on leaving to do the work in his shop.

Mark wasn't thinking too hard about Jim and his motivations. He had dozens of things pending, but he remained, watching Alex, his eyes tracking each movement of those graceful hands, those long and elegant fingers, as she methodically stacked her papers and put them in her briefcase.

He hadn't forgotten those fingers; even now he could almost feel them caressing his hair. She'd loved his hair, she'd said so dozens of times.

How, he asked himself, had things gone so wrong between them? At the beginning, they'd had what he had considered a perfect romance. He and Alex had been physically attracted to each other from the moment of their meeting, and on talking they'd discovered similar outlooks, similar goals in their lives. Images flooded through his mind; he and Alex at dinner early in their relationship, in the park on a summer's day, at a beach along the North Carolina coast—and, inevitably, in bed together. The nostalgia threatened to overwhelm him; he tried to counter the flood of old memories with the harder ones, the bitter and increasingly hostile arguments that marked their last days together, the way he felt when he heard she was dating Don and the sadness that had haunted him for weeks after the shock of her unexpected wedding—to which he'd declined a pointed invitation. He sighed, much more loudly than he'd intended.

She looked up. "Something wrong, Mark?"

"No. I've got a long day ahead, that's all." He leaned against the table. "Alex, what you did today took some courage."

"How do you mean?"

"Gus, of course," he answered hurriedly. "You must've known he wouldn't take a suggestion like that seriously."

She grimaced and nodded. "Well, Jim saved the day, didn't he? I'm going to have to look up that California study. I must admit, I hadn't heard of it either." She gazed past his shoulder blankly for a moment. "Besides," she went on, "I guess I've gotten used to not being taken very seriously."

For a long moment, he said nothing at all. Was he supposed to respond to that?

She, however, took the choice away—or else, as she might've said in another time, he'd waited too long, he'd squandered his opportunity. "It may well be," she said, "that Gus is right. We might find that not one more of these patients has any sort of problem related to a computer. That was the only link I could find."

"Hey, it was more than I found."

She waved a hand. "You weren't looking for things like that," she told him. "You were looking at sed rates and BUNS and white cell counts, you were looking for a biological cause."

"And finding nothing."

"That," she allowed, "doesn't mean there is nothing. You can't test for everything."

He grinned. "I can try."

She smiled too, then broke into brief laughter. "Yes," she agreed. "I know, you can try. I remember when you had that patient who'd just gotten back from central Africa. The lab guys were ready to kill you, they were groaning at the mention of your name." She stopped speaking, ran her hand up the side of her face and into her hair, ruffling it. "You just ignored them, though, didn't you? You just kept at it. And you came up with an answer, too . . ." She looked up at him, and for a moment he thought he saw in her eyes something of what used to be there.

Coming around the table, he sat down next to her and took a deep breath. Maybe he'd get this pitched back in his face, but he wasn't going to let this opportunity pass without at least trying to exploit it. "We haven't talked in a long time, Alex," he opened. "How have you been, how have things been going for you?"

A little fire flared in her eyes, but almost as soon as it appeared it was gone. "Oh, fine, fine," she said, averting her gaze. Absently, she removed a pen from the pocket of her white coat, and, without removing the cap, traced patterns lightly on the tabletop. "Work's fine. Sometimes there's too much of it, but I'm sure you of all people know how that is. It's pretty much routine, except for this stuff, of course." She paused, glanced at him, looked down again. "And home is, well, home is." She shrugged. "It, well, it, you know . . . Lehmann is a big company, there're lots of, well . . ." She traced the patterns a little more vigorously, then shrugged again. "You know."

No, he told her silently, I don't. He waited, saying nothing; several seconds slipped by.

She looked up at him. The pen kept moving. "But enough about me," she said breezily, causing him to choke back a protest. "What about you, Mark? What've you been doing with yourself?"

He tried not to glare at her, and, as far as he could tell, he succeeded. "Me? Christ, Alex, you know what I've been doing. Working. You used to point out that I was a workaholic, and I guess I haven't changed too much, not in that respect anyhow. I—"

"—didn't know what a workaholic was," she was muttering as he spoke. He stopped; she continued: "I don't mean that. I know you work hard, Mark. I still hear the tales of the legendary Dr. Roberts around the hospital, I've told you that already. I mean—how's your life been going? You know what I mean."

He folded his arms across his chest. Yes, Alex, he said silently. I do know. You mean, am I seeing anybody, sleeping with anybody, getting married soon? No, no, and no. You mean, have I been dating a lot since you and I broke up? No. Three years, as many dates. You mean, do I have a good sex life? No. Since you I've slept with one other person. No, I'm not doing well at all, the way I am isn't healthy, it isn't normal, and I'm acutely aware of it. I need to see a good psychiatrist, don't you think? Get some professional help? Think you could suggest someone?

"Things have been fine," he told her. "I don't have any real complaints."

Was that disappointment he saw in her eyes. "No?"

"No."

Falling silent, she started nodding steadily. Turning a piece of paper, she knocked the cap off her pen with her thumb and began doodling. "Well, that's good, Mark," she said slowly. "That's really good, really good . . ." She doodled on for a moment.

Then, without warning, she capped the pen and swept the piece of paper off the table. Stuffing it into her briefcase, crumpling it a little as it went, she stood up. "I have to go. I have my regular patients to see as well as stopping by to interview some of yours." She frowned. "We never did divide them up—there's no point in us seeing the same ones."

"Jim and I'll take care of that," he assured her. "I've got to see him again this morning anyway. Remember, he was going to make up a list of questions for us?"

"Oh, right. Fine. So then you'll—?"

"Get it to you. Before noon, okay?"

"Fine." She smiled, started for the door, hesitated, glanced back, then went on. He watched her go, wondering if she knew that he'd seen what she'd been doodling—and at the same time, wondering how to interpret what he'd seen.

There might be other reasons she'd doodle a stylized "M." There probably were.

He just couldn't think of any right now.

11

The doorbell had been ringing for several minutes. Whoever it was had given up that tactic and had begun pounding with his fist.

Sitting on the edge of a rocky promontory overlooking a vast and lovely valley, her knees pulled up against her chest, Kyrie glanced over at Eric and smiled. "There's someone at your door, Air-eek," she said, leaning toward him a little. "Don't you think you should see who it is?"

He looked blank for a moment. "Door?" he echoed. Only then, seconds later, did he realize that he was looking at a monitor screen, that he wasn't actually sitting beside Kyrie, that he wasn't truly present in her fantastic sensual world. As always, he felt a wave of almost physical pain at this realization, the sense of loss was so great; Kyrie wasn't real, she was a computer-generated sprite. Reluctantly, he turned his head away from the computer. The realization of where he was had already hit him, but it was still something of a shock to see his mundane room. He stared at it dully. Compared to the worlds Kyrie had been showing him, worlds of winged fairies, sleek mermaids, terrifying Amazons, and doll-like princesses—each and every one of them, like the erotic Kyrie herself, devoted utterly to satisfying his every whim—the real world looked so lifeless and boring as to be nightmarish. He felt like crying; he wished there was some way he could transfer himself into Kyrie's world, stay there forever, and forget that this other place, this ugly place, existed at all.

But the knocking at the door was insistent. Feeling ancient, Eric dragged himself out of his leather and chrome-steel swivel chair and almost staggered toward the door. From the screen, Kyrie watched him go.

After fumbling with the chain, Eric jerked the door open. A heavyset man in his forties, his permanent stylized smile matching his trendishly styled hair, stood on the step. His hand was raised to knock yet again.

It took Eric a moment to identify him—Dave Parham, one of the salesmen from work. "Eric, old man!" he exclaimed. "Man, what's wrong with you? You sick? Jesus Christ, you look like shit, you gotta be sick!"

Eric closed his eyes for a moment and shook his head. "Uh—sick? Well, uhm—" He stopped, glared. "What do you want, Dave?" he demanded, his tone suddenly harsh.

The man on the stoop laughed. "Well, hell! Who pissed in your cornflakes, anyway? What I want, Eric my man, is to find out why you haven't been at work in three days, why you disappeared without calling, and why your goddamn phone is always busy!" Without asking, he pushed past Eric and came in. Just inside the door he paused, crinkling his nose. "Good God, it stinks in here! What the hell is going on, anyway?"

Eric stepped back, placing himself in front of Dave. "Look," he said, "Look, Dave. I'm really busy right now."

The salesman had by then noticed the computer screen, where Kyrie sat gazing out at them. "Hel-lo!" Dave said. Again pushing Eric out of the way, he headed for the computer. "Damn, that is one fine fox!" he exclaimed. "What've you been doing, downloading some porno GIFs from the bulletin boards? Sheee-it! I haven't seen many as fine as this one! Got any pix of her in action?"

Eric's fists clenched at his sides. "Dave—"

"I can be 'in action' if you want me to be," Kyrie said. "You just need to tell me what you want me to do." She moved her eyes from side to side a little; she was never looking directly at the salesman. "But you're not Air-eek. I'm Kyrie; who're you?"

Dave stopped cold. For an instant he frowned, but then his expression transformed itself into a broad grin. "What, is this one of the virtual-reality programs?" he asked, glancing back at Eric. He stared at the screen again. "Man oh man, I've seen two or three of those, but they weren't like this! This looks as good as a photo-CD! Where'd you get this, man? You download it from somewhere?"

"No, I—"

"Won't you tell me your name?" Kyrie asked engagingly.

Dave plopped his bulk down in the chair in front of the machine. "Oh, baby," he breathed. "Baby, baby . . ."

"Baby?" Kyrie echoed. "Is that your name?"

The salesman roared. "Got a mike hooked up, eh?" He didn't wait for an answer. "Yeah, darlin', you just call me that. 'Baby.' That sounds real good to me!"

"Okay, Baby," she replied. Her smile became even more seductive. "You said you wanted to see some action?"

"Yeah, yeah!" He glanced at Eric. "What'll she do? What're the keywords?"

Eric pressed his hands to his forehead. This couldn't be happening, he told himself miserably. Dave, of all people, intruding on his private world! Dave, whom he had to work with but could not stand! "Please," he begged. "Please . . ."

"Just tell me what you want," Kyrie urged.

"Well, shit! Lemme see you first! All of you!"

"Of course." She stood up; as Eric had left her she'd been wearing only a wispy little skirt, which she now discarded. Stepping back a little, she posed for Dave, turning slowly. He was almost drooling on the keyboard. "Now what?" she asked, winding her hands in her hair and stretching her torso.

"Oh, darlin'!" Dave almost shouted. "Oh, don't I wish you could come out here and give me a blow job!"

She arched an eyebrow. Instantly the viewpoint of the screen shifted; it was now as if the viewer was looking down, down across the front of a nude male torso—exactly the angle a man has when looking down at his own body from a standing position. Kyrie, looking up and out of the screen with huge liquid eyes, knelt down in front of this new image. "Are you ready?" she asked. "You'll have to do your part too, of course . . . with your hand . . ."

Dave looked amazed, then erupted in raucous laughter. Eric, meanwhile, had been staring dumbfounded at this imagery. He'd not seen this sequence or anything like it, he had treated Kyrie with more respect than this. He felt as if something was being drawn tight in his head, like an overstressed piano string. He clapped his hands to his head, but it was too late; the string broke. It seemed to him he could feel the loose ends flying about inside his skull. On the screen, Kyrie's face came closer. I can't take this, he told himself. I can't.

Lunging forward, he grabbed Dave by the arm, spun him and the chair around, and pushed them both hard toward the door. "No!" he shrieked. "No, she's mine, you leave her alone!"

Dave, staggering out of the chair, looked stunned for a moment. But then he angrily knocked Eric's arms away. "Hey!" he yelled. "Hey, you dumb fuck! What's the matter with you, you gone crazy? Cut it out!"

Eric was beyond control now. "No! Get out, get out!" He pushed his fist into Dave's chest. "You get out of my house, you asshole! Get out!"

The salesman's face turned red; he struck Eric's shoulders with both palms, knocking him backwards in turn. "Hey! You just watch it, buddy! I don't take that kind of shit from anybody! I come over here to find out what's wrong with you and this is the thanks I get? Just because I took a look at your precious program? You've lost it, Eric. You've gone fucking crazy!" Advancing on Eric, he waggled a fat finger in the younger man's face. "And you've lost a job, too, you stupid shithead! When I go back and tell them you've been sitting here playing virtual reality games you probably stole from the store, they're gonna fire your ass! They're gonna fire your ass and they're gonna come and take away your toy!"

Eric's eyes, already red-rimmed from lack of sleep, grew huge; whiteness showed all the way around the iris. He didn't care about the job, but Dave's threat to take Kyrie away was intolerable.

"No!" he screamed, so loudly that Dave retreated a step. Eric's hands fell on the chair; turning slightly, exhibiting surprising strength, he picked it up, and, with one smooth movement—almost as if he'd practiced, as if he'd trained for this—he threw it at the salesman. Dave was taken by surprise; one of the chair's steel legs caught him right in the forehead, and he went crashing to the floor with the chair atop him. For a moment he remained down, stunned.

Then he threw the chair off and struggled to his feet. Blood oozed from a three-inch cut on his forehead. "You crazy fuck!" he shrieked. Wiping blood on his hand and staring at it in disbelief, he stumbled toward the door. "Don't think you're going to get away with this! Don't you think that! You son of a bitch!"

He vanished through the doorway; Eric watched him go. Then, without even bothering to close the door, he righted his chair and sat in front of the computer again. Kyrie—in front of the male torso—was waiting, her expression one of concern.

"What is happening?" she asked—and he realized that she'd asked that question at least five or six times already.

"Get up," he commanded roughly. She stood instantly; the view shifted, the male torso vanished. "What was going on, is that Dave—'Baby,' I mean—and I had a fight. I beat the shit out of him and he's gone now."

The concerned look remained. "You—fought? You beat the shit out of him? Why?"

"You're mine," he told her firmly. "Mine."

"Yours?"

His head swam, but he nodded. "Mine. I love you."

"Love? Me?"

The tension rose again. "Will you stop that!"

She smiled. "Yes. Of course."

He clenched his hands, unclenched them, grabbed the mouse, squeezed it. "I'm going to disconnect. I'm going to turn you off."

"No. Don't."

"Don't?" He giggled inanely, realizing that he'd now echoed her, using almost exactly the same tone.

"No. If you're angry with me you can kill me." The muzzle

of a gun, pointed at her, appeared on the screen; after an instant it changed to a knife blade, lengthened into a sword, twisted to become a club, softened to become a garotte. Swiftly, icons of weapons ranged across the lower part of the screen, inviting him to choose one. "Another will come to guide you," Kyrie said.

He did nothing. "I don't want to kill you," he grumbled.

The icons vanished. "Then what do you want?"

"To understand. Help me, Kyrie."

She smiled softly. "I'll try. But you must try to help me first, because I myself do not understand."

Fumbling for words, talking around his true emotions, refusing to confess jealousy, Eric tried. He was still trying when the policemen Dave had called entered the apartment; when he got up and tried to shove them back outside, they responded with quiet force, handcuffing him and taking him away, one of them assuring him that he would be taken to a doctor, not to jail. As they pulled him, his heels dragging, toward the car, he didn't even notice Dave standing beside the door grinning, a fresh bandage on his head.

When they'd gone, the salesman furtively went back inside and closed the door. The computer was still on, Kyrie still waited.

"Hi," he said to the screen.

Kyrie smiled. "Hi, Baby."

He laughed. "Now then," he went on. "Where were we?"

Instantly the image of the male torso reappeared. Kyrie, smiling, knelt down.

12

"I'm sorry," a tinny female voice was saying. "All circuits are busy now. Please try your call again later."

Alex dropped the phone into its cradle with more force than usual. Ridiculous, she thought. She wasn't trying to call the West Coast, she was trying to call Donald's office, a local call. She could not remember ever getting this message before.

Resisting the temptation to try again immediately, she sat

at her desk and held her head in her hands. Why, she asked herself almost savagely, did Don have to do this, just when she'd started to see Mark on a daily basis?

Of course, he didn't know about that; she'd not yet told him about the odd epidemic they were dealing with, and, even if she had, she would've neglected to mention Mark's name—it was a name Don knew quite well.

It was not, she reassured herself quickly, that she was still attracted to Mark in any significant way; it was just that he always seemed to affect her, to be there, lurking in the shadows of her thoughts and making appearances when she least expected it.

She raised her head, stared at her closed door. It wasn't that mysterious, she told herself. She and Mark had had an intense love affair, the most intense she'd ever experienced; making the decision to dissolve it, and executing that decision, had been one of the hardest things she'd ever done. She wished—now as then—that he'd given her some sort of choice in the matter.

No, she told herself, no. She did not wish that now. Then, maybe; now, no.

She picked up the phone again, dialed Donald's office. This time the call went through, but she got a busy signal; she had to restrain herself from banging the phone down. "Damn you, Don," she muttered. "This is not a good time, not a good time at all. I need you, I need to talk to you. You have to stop staying out half the night, I don't care what sort of cash-flow problems Lehmann has."

I do need you, she told him mentally; and not just to talk to, either. She stared blankly at his photograph, the one that always sat on her desk, and immediately started remembering some of their best times. When their relationship had started, she'd been a little on the cool side sexually; her passion for Mark hadn't faded, and, more than anything else, she'd been afraid of calling Don "Mark" in bed. She'd spent weekends with him in Paris and in Vienna before she'd finally accepted his sexual overtures; that too had impressed her, that he seemed to be patient in such matters. Most men she'd known weren't.

They'd been in Paris again when that had ended. Deciding

that she'd pined for Mark long enough—and, admittedly, more or less overcome by the romantic surroundings of that little hotel on the Left Bank—she'd stopped resisting. Not without a few misgivings, though; she'd been terribly nervous throughout that first encounter, nervous that he could not compete with her memories of Mark.

But he had; whatever was lacking in passion—on her part—he'd made up for with patience, caring, and experience. For a while, as the sexual side of their relationship developed, she'd been uncomfortable with his approach; he handled sexual matters in the same way he took care of business affairs. He set everything up, he had everything planned—always beautifully, always romantically, always skillfully. Gradually, her feeling that he wasn't giving her a chance to express herself disappeared; she couldn't help but enjoy being pampered.

Now, that had changed; after a married life that had been rich and varied sexually, he hadn't made love to her, he'd hardly touched her, since the night he'd first mentioned the now-hated cash-flow problem. She had tried to approach him—something that had never before been necessary—only to have his attempts to respond end in his falling asleep in her arms. She wiped her eyes. She missed it, she wasn't used to being without a sex life—she'd gone from a good one with Mark to a good one with Donald, and now she had nothing.

She was still staring at his photo when the phone rang again. She jumped slightly; it rang again before she snatched it up. "Don?" she said into the receiver without thinking.

"No, Alex, it's Gus."

"Oh. Sorry. What's up?"

"Got a new patient; he's down in ER right now. It looks to me like he fits the profile pretty well." There was a slight pause. "The computer part, anyhow; the policemen who brought him in said he had to be physically dragged from his computer. This one's a little different, Alex. He's ranting and raving, but—just like Wendy Sung—what he wants is to get out of here and get back to whatever he was doing. With his computer."

"Sounds like he's worth a look. Has anybody else seen him yet?"

"No."

"What's his general condition?"

"Doesn't look bad at all."

"Good, good. I'll be right down. What's his name?"

"Fletcher Engels."

"Fine. See you in a few, Gus."

She was as good as her word; putting Mark and Don out of her head, she hurried down to the emergency room. After a brief consultation with Gus—which netted her no new information—she made her way to Fletcher Engels's room.

He looked up quickly as she came in, flashing a bright grin. "Hey, there," he said. "Who're you? Doesn't matter, anyhow." He laughed briefly. "Please enter. Have a seat."

She stopped near the door, watching him for a moment. He was tall, about forty, a little on the heavy side, possessed of a full white-streaked beard but almost totally bald. His manner took her by surprise; she hadn't quite expected friendliness, not from Gus's description of the circumstances under which he'd come to the ER. But then, the other patients fitting the pattern had been subdued because of their physical condition.

"Mr. Engels, I'm Dr. Walton; I'd like to ask you a few questions."

"You're a shrink?"

She smiled. "I'm a psychiatrist, yes."

"And you want to know," he told her, "how I wound up here. Why I acted so crazy. Well, let me tell you, you wait until somebody comes and throws you out of your own house and you see how you act. It can piss you off, I'll tell you."

Alex looked confused. "But I understood that—"

"Oh, right, I know. They probably told you about me not paying the rent, about how they had a legal eviction notice and all that good stuff. Well, I was going to take care of that." He looked down at his lap. "It's just that I was—busy. When the deputies came, I was busy."

This made more sense. Alex sat down, took out a notepad. "Busy doing what, Mr. Engels?"

"Call me Fletcher," he ordered. Then he grinned. "Working at my trusty computer. No, no, 'scuse me, my formerly trusty computer, you sure as hell can't trust the damn thing now! You can't trust any of them! Not after what happened. Not after Drew refused to let me do anything about it while there was still time."

"Drew?"

"Uh-huh."

"Who is Drew?"

"Can't say. It might be dangerous." He glanced around the room. "The walls have ears, you know." He paused to laugh. "Well, no, of course the walls don't really have ears—damn, I've got to watch myself here, you *will* think I'm crazy and you might just convince me of it! But walls can have things in them that have ears. Or things that've gotten turned into ears, God knows, maybe even eyes."

Alex made a note: "Possible paranoid delusions." "What," she asked aloud, "were you doing with your computer? When the deputies arrived, I mean?"

"Trying to write a hunter-killer." He laughed again, almost uproariously this time; his mirth stopped abruptly. "The problem is, Penny has hunter-killers too. Her hunter-killers hunted down my hunter-killers and killed them. One right after another."

Alex wasn't sure which question to ask first. "What's a hunter-killer?"

"A program."

"Excuse me?"

He looked at her as if she was totally, hopelessly, ignorant. "A hunter-killer," he explained patiently, "is a program that hunts for another program. When it finds it, it kills it. Naturally. Otherwise it wouldn't be a killer, would it?"

"I suppose not. You're a programmer, then?"

He nodded. "In my case, I don't get called that. I get called a systems analyst. That's what I was called, before—"

"Before?"

"Before Penny. Before. Before I quit—before I was, let's say, forced to quit. My job; I haven't quit programming. I won't, not until I find the answer."

She made a few more notes, drew a line under her previous term "paranoid." Now, it seemed, was the obvious time to ask the other question. "Can you tell me who Penny is?"

His expression became very serious. "No," he answered flatly. "No, I can't." He stared at her, his blue eyes glazing a little. "You'll find out, though, if you keep asking people like me questions like that. The trouble is, Penny'll find out too; she'll find out about you, and, one way or another, she'll find you. Then you can ask her your questions. I don't think you'll get any answers you're ready to handle, but you can ask and she might tell you. Me, I'm not saying anything yet. After all, I don't know you, lady. You might be working for Drew.''

"I can assure you—"

"I'm sure you can." He laughed again. "But ol' Drew, he knows lots of people. He used to talk to me about some of the weird people he knew." He sighed. "That was before, of course. In the Admiral days. Before Penny."

Alex, though a little frustrated by what she saw as evasiveness on his part, kept her tone professionally level. "I do wish you'd talk to me, Fletcher," she told him. "There really isn't much I can do to help you if you don't."

"The only help I need," he said flatly, "is help getting out of here. The law isn't going to be a problem; all they charged me with is resisting arrest, and hell, they weren't even trying to arrest me, they were just trying to get me out of the house! It probably won't even stick. If you want to help me, get me out. Get me back to my computer. I have work to do, and one hell of a lot is riding on that work! You don't have any idea!''

"You're right," she said, aiming for a soothing tone. "I don't. But I'd like to, Fletcher. You think you can help me?''

His brows furrowed. "Don't patronize me," he snarled, startling her with his sudden change of attitude. "You think you know it all, don't you? You're sitting there thinking, 'oh, yeah, ol' Fletcher there, crazy as a bedbug.' Let me guess; you've got the word 'paranoid' written down at least once on your little notepad, don't you? 'Course, you wouldn't tell me about it." He sighed. "And now you're trying to pry some loony story out of me about aliens from UFOs or the voice of the Devil. Sorry, I don't have one of those for you."

He paused, looked away, folded his arms across his chest and shook his head violently. "There's no reason," he went on, "for me to get pissed at you. You doctors, you're like a lot of other people, you think you know everything about everything; shit, I used to think that myself. Not so many weeks ago, I didn't believe there was anything about any computer anywhere that could bamboozle me for long. I've gotten over it; I know better."

He gave her a long cool look. "I also know that by now, you've seen other people that Penny's gotten to, but you don't know what you're seeing—even if you think you do. You've just put them down as 'clinically depressed' or 'obsessive-compulsive' or whatever the current catchwords are. You give them a good talking-to or maybe a few hundred volts of electricity or some mood-elevating drug, and you send them home. Well, Doc, if Penny's gotten to them, you'll be seeing them again. If they live long enough."

Alex peered at him keenly. She resisted drawing a conclusion that he was talking about their patient group, but she did not hesitate to try to draw him out more. "Do you know any of these patients, Fletcher?" she asked. "Any names?"

He snorted. "No. There's no way I could. But I can tell you what you should look for."

"What's that?"

"Look for what they're using, see if . . ." he snapped back. He cut his words off abruptly; for a long moment he sat watching her face and chewing his lip. "No, I shouldn't," he said slowly. "I shouldn't get you or anybody else involved in this right now. It's a dangerous business, but there's no way I could convince you that it's dangerous, and that makes it doubly bad for you." He stretched his arms out before him. "Look, I really do have a lot of work to do. When can I get out of here? The police can't make me stay here, can they?"

"No," she answered. "But, as to when you can leave, that isn't up to me. My recommendation is that you stay for a short period of observation, so that we can be sure that—"

"I can't." He shook his head. "I can't. Every hour I stay here I get more out of touch and Penny gets stronger. Damn it, I'm not keeping up with her now, I'm not even staying close! I have to go, as soon as possible."

She nodded. "I'll pass that along," she assured him. "Are you sure I can't convince you to talk to me some more? Answer some of these questions?"

"No. Not now. It just isn't fair—to you. You can't have any idea of what you're getting into."

She made eye contact with him for a long moment. Once again—as had happened many times before in Alex's career—her professional training was guiding her in one direction and her instincts in another.

After another few seconds, she decided to trust her instincts. More often than not, they were more accurate than the theories she'd learned in medical school.

"Look," she said carefully. "There're reasons why I don't want to go into this, but let me just say this much: these people you spoke of a moment ago—I think we're already seeing some of them, just as you've suggested. We're trying very hard to help these people, Fletcher. We'd really appreciate any help you could give us."

He gazed at her speculatively for quite a while. "Right now," he told her finally, "I'm a little afraid to—for you and me both. You can see for yourself, I ran into a problem with this, and God damn, I was expecting it! I was forewarned!" He shook his head violently. "It didn't matter. Penny's good, she's very good." Seeing that she was about to ask another question, he held up a hand for silence. "I think," he went on, "That I've got my head on pretty straight now; if I can get out of here I might be able to do what needs to be done—and if I can get it done, you won't be seeing any more of those people." He gave her a sidelong glance. "Look, give me a card or whatever, some way to reach you."

Nodding again, she wrote down her hospital address and office phone. "Please call," she urged.

He looked at the paper, then at her. "It's against my better judgment," he said, "but I probably will. Sooner or later."

13

"**D**amn it!" Jim snarled at his computer. "Will you quit that?" He pressed a series of keys in quick succession, then, with a much exaggerated sigh, threw himself back in his chair. "All right, all right," he told it. "Go ahead, then. But after this, you SOB, I'm cutting off your access!"

Standing at his open door, Mark grinned. "Problem?"

The programmer swiveled his chair around. "Oh, hi, Mark," he said, smiling back. "Didn't know you were there." He waved a hand casually at the computer on his desk. "Not much of one; just some junk-mail FAX coming in from somewhere. I've gotten one like it every day for the past week; it's an ad, they want me to call up some new bulletin board." As Mark came across the room toward him, he frowned darkly at the machine. "Thing is, something's screwed up with Ol' Blue here. FAX receive is supposed to be background, but it's insisting on cutting me right off in the middle of whatever I'm doing to feed me this stupid ad. Worse, it always seems to catch me at my busiest."

"Murphy's Law."

"Uhm. For computers Murphy's Law is a religion."

"You haven't been able to fix it? Jim, my faith in you has been shaken. Badly."

"Haven't tried. I've been too busy. What I'm gonna do is cut off the FAX receive until I get a chance to poke around in this thing's innards. I don't like these things doing things I don't know why they're doing."

"Say what?"

"Never mind." He whacked several keys in quick succession. "All right! It's done! Now, we can pull up your stuff."

"You've done it already?"

"Oh, sure. You aren't going to be pleased, though."

Mark sat down in a chair next to his. "I'm not?"

"You're not." He tapped several more keys; numbers flowed down the screen. "As you can see," he went on, picking up a ballpoint pen and tapping the screen lightly, "I've collated all the data you and Alex have been giving me. I am sorry to say that nothing, not one damn thing—at least nothing new—has fallen out."

"Nothing? But, Jim—"

The programmer swiveled around to face him. "Now, I know what you're going to say. You're going to tell me that all your patients, every single lovin' one of them, have turned out to have a problem that's somehow related to their computer. That, Marcus, is so. Before you ask, let me inform you that Alex has found the same thing with her group—or damn near the same thing. There's one doubtful, a kid; she's already figured out he's big on video games and he has a Mac, so you can go from there."

Mark spread his hands. "Well? It's something, isn't it? It looks like Alex's idea about computers is correct—"

"Yeah, but you didn't need a statistician to tell you that!"

He glanced at the screen again. "Thing is, there isn't anything else. We're all over the map here; all we've done is exchanged one mystery for another."

"I'm not sure I understand. Isn't that to be expected?"

Jim nodded very slowly. "Maybe. I was sorta hoping for better."

"Like what?"

His face twisted sourly. "Like something. Like they were all using the same brand-new, red-hot, super-duper VGA monitor, and we could then go right on to discover that it's beaming microwaves into their cerebellums and making them act whacko. But no, of course not. What we do have is IBMs and Macs, desktops and laptops, and even one mainframe. We have sound and we have no sound, CDs and not-CDs, modems and not-modems, we have standard VGA monitors and LCD screens and one high-res. Our patients use about as wide a variety of current equipment as you could buy at any—" He stopped, glanced back at the screen. "Hey! Wait a minute." He scanned the numbers again, using the cursor keys to run up and down the screen.

"Idea?" Mark asked.

"Not much of one, don't get excited," Jim said. "Maybe one more clue, Dr. Watson. Just a second." Squinting, he studied the numbers for a minute more, then leaned back. "Yeah. Current was right, they are."

"They are what?"

"They're all using very modern equipment," Jim told him, swiveling back to face him again. "Take the DOS machines, for example. There are no 286s, no XTs. Very few 386s."

"So?"

"So, they're all using very up-to-date, very fast, very sophisticated machines." He looked over the list again. "Same for the Macs and the mainframe, too. New ones."

"What's it mean?"

Jim's enthusiastic manner faded as quickly as it had appeared. "Nothing much," he admitted. "We already knew these folks were well-educated and successful. Stands to reason they'd keep their machines updated."

"It's something," Mark said, more to offer encouragement than anything else. "I'm not clear on why it would make a difference, though."

"Oh, well, I can think of a few things. Take this kid who's into games, for example. We're saying he's obsessed, he's sort of addicted. Right?" Mark nodded. "Well, the game's going to play better, in every way, on a 486 than on a 286—if it'll play on a 286 at all. The four is so much faster, so much more efficient. There's just no comparison; graphics, sound, everything, the four will blow the two away. You see what I'm saying?"

Mark nodded again. "Maybe," he mused, "we're just seeing the results of something that's been building for a while. Maybe these new machines, with all that speed and efficiency, have something about them that makes them inherently addictive."

"I don't think that'll fly. The machines have been out too long; you would've seen it before, in a specialized population." He paused and grinned. "People like me, who work with these things all day and play with them at night. There're a lot of us, Mark; programmers, techs, hackers. We're always the first to run out and buy the 486s and the Pentiums—if it was the machines themselves we'd be the first victims."

"There are programmers and techs in our sample. The first fatality was a programmer."

"Yes. But the majority of them aren't. They're end users; they use the programs and they may know them well but they don't know much about what's behind them, the BIOS, the operating system, the hardware. They aren't the first ones to get acquainted with the new stuff as it comes out."

Mark stared at the numbers on the screen blankly. "So where does that leave us?"

"Pretty much back at square one," Jim admitted. "We know these people are obsessed with their computers, but they aren't all using the same type or anything like that."

"And only one has had any experience with a computer virus."

"Right. That they know about."

Mark frowned. "What?"

Jim waved a hand toward his machine. "Oh, there are viruses and there are viruses," he said. "Swarms of them are out there right now. A lot of them can infect your machine and you don't even know it. With some, you might never know they were there."

76

"I don't understand."

Jim settled back in his chair and crossed his arms. "Well, for the most part, people write viruses and release them on the public just for the thrill of being able to do it; like the old saw about climbing a mountain because it's there. The viruses you hear about are those built by people who like to cause trouble; the Friday the Thirteenth, the Michaelangelo, the Pakistani Brain, the ones that destroy all your programs and files, when they go off. They aren't all like that. A lot of them are simple 'Kilroy was here' statements; they don't do any harm, they just get into your system and stay there." He paused and shook his head. "Sometimes even those go wrong, though. You take the Internet virus, for example; it was one of the early ones, back in the late eighties. It was created by a student at Cornell, and it was supposed to be a harmless 'Kilroy was here.' But he made a mistake in the software, in the section of code that was supposed to tell it not to infect the same machine twice. It infected the same machines over and over, until all their resources were used up and they started crashing. It was a total disaster." Pausing, he looked at his screen again, idly scrolled the numbers up and down. "When he released it into Arpanet—the network linking academic institutions and the Pentagon—it spread like wildfire, infecting and reinfecting over 85,000 computers and, just by using up all their available disk and memory space with copies of itself, shut the whole damn network down. I read somewhere that the recovery cost was over a hundred million dollars."

"I'm not sure I'm getting the point."

"The point is, if this student hadn't made a mistake, nothing would've happened—more than likely, no one would've even known the Internet virus was there. But the student would've known, and he could've impressed his hacker buddies by showing them his Kilroy inside computers in California, in the Pentagon, in Europe."

Mark laughed. "I'm not sure I understand that, either!"

Jim nodded. "Well, you aren't a programmer, you aren't the type. Neither am I, really, but I know lots of guys who are. It takes a special kind; a lot of times the hacker—even if he is brilliant—isn't very good at normal social interaction. Computers and networks are their world, a world where they can really strut their stuff."

"You once told me that 'viruses' is a really good name for these programs . . ."

Jim nodded again, more vigorously. "It sure is. Properly, a virus is a program that does two things: it replicates itself and it seeks new hosts. Now—"

"Just what a biological virus does."

"Right. Doom and devastation may follow, but they aren't part of the definition."

"Well, they aren't for a biological virus, either. It's just that we don't pay much attention to those that don't do any damage; there are millions of them, but, unless they mutate into something harmful, who cares? It's like the microscopic skin mites; you and I both have them all over our faces right now, and so does everyone else. But they cause no problems, so we don't pay any attention to them."

Jim continued to nod agreement; then, as if at a prearranged signal, both men unconsciously wiped at their faces. Each noted the other doing it and both broke into laughter.

"So you think," Mark went on when their mirth had subsided, "that our patients may have undetected viruses in their computers?"

"It's very possible." He nodded toward his own machine. "There're probably some in there."

"Could they have anything to do with the patients' problems?"

"I don't see how."

"I don't either."

"Then again, I didn't see how AIDS could select gay men to go after, either."

14

"Hi, Franklin!"

Franklin Reeves, his eyes glazed, looked down at the bright-faced young woman at the reception desk. For a moment he hardly recognized her; then it registered: Marianne. He'd seen her every morning for the last five years; she'd always had a smile and a friendly word for him, unlike some at Hawkins-Paine.

"Franklin? What's the matter?" She looked at the blanket he was carrying. "What's that you have?"

"I have to go see Pearlman," Franklin told her. "Now."

"Oh, Franklin, there's a board meeting right now, he'll be in there until at least noon—"

"It doesn't matter." He started to walk past her desk.

She swiveled around in her chair. "You can't go in there. What's wrong, Franklin?"

Turning to glare at her, he unrolled the blanket; she gasped when she saw the semiautomatic rifle it had concealed. An ammunition clip, one of many he had secreted in the wrapping, fell to the floor with a metallic clink.

"Run away, Marianne," he told her. "Run now, run fast, run far away."

"What're you going to do?"

"Run, Goddamn it!"

She hesitated for an instant, then got up and ran. Franklin headed for the boardroom without noticing that Marianne had gone only as far as another desk, where she was even then picking up a phone.

When he kicked open the boardroom door and came in with the rifle at the ready, Howard Pearlman, at the head of the table, stood up to face him. A couple of the women screamed; one man slid under the table.

"You didn't think I'd find out, did you, Howard?" Franklin said softly. "Didn't think I'd ever know."

"Know what?" Pearlman yelled. "What're you talking about?"

"You bastard, you stole my idea! You stole it, it's all over the Internet! What'd you do, Howard? Have somebody break into my office and crack the passwords?"

"I don't know what you're talking about!"

Franklin looked down at his shoes. "It was the only really good idea I ever had," he almost sobbed. "The only one. It was going to be my patent. You knew that, we talked about it. God, I've worked so hard on it." He looked up, his eyes wild. "And you stole it! It had to be you, you were the only one who knew about it. What'd you do, sell it to the highest bidder?'' His gaze roamed across the terrified faces around the table. "You all knew about it, didn't you? You all planned it together . . ."

"Franklin, you're making a mistake!"

"No," he said coldly. "You made the mistake." With that he opened fire, targeting Pearlman first; three shots found their mark before the chairman, blood staining his three-piece suit, was hurled back over his chair. Methodically, starting at Pearlman's right, Franklin went around the table, cutting the board members down one by one. After nine men and two women had fallen, he knelt down, looked under the table. Two left; the man wept and covered his head with his hands. Franklin shot him through his fingers. The last was one of the women. She was on her knees, as upright as the table allowed. She stared at him, her eyes enormous, her hands held out with her palms up, pleading.

"Oh God, Franklin," she whispered, "please . . ."

"Sorry," he said crisply as he shot her through the chest. She fell and began squirming on the floor. Without paying any attention to her or to the three or four others who were still alive, he turned and walked out of the room.

Marianne had sounded an alarm; the outer offices were empty. Franklin glanced around, then noticed the crowd that had gathered outside the revolving doors at the entrance. Slipping another clip into his rifle he walked to those doors and outside, watching the crowd scatter in panic at his approach.

In the street, he shot two bystanders before a voice yelled at him to drop his weapon. He wheeled to face the caller; as he turned, bullets ripped into him. His last sight was of Marianne, standing behind the heavily armed police, her hands clasped against her mouth in horror.

15

Through the steam rising from her morning coffee, Alex studied Donald's face. As always, *The Wall Street Journal*, folded over in precise fashion, lay next to his saucer; what was unusual was that he was not reading it. Instead, he stared blankly into his own cup, his eyes unfocused, his jaw somewhat slack. Since getting up this morning he'd hardly spoken. She'd made the breakfast, made the coffee, gotten his paper for him; normally she would've expected more than cursory thanks for this—Don was generally quite thoughtful in such respects—but all she'd gotten this morning was grunts and mumbling.

"What time did you get in last night, Don?" she asked. She was careful about her tone; there wasn't a hint of rancor, there was no accusation at all. He looked up blankly. "I tried to wait up for you," she told him. "I didn't get to sleep until after one. You weren't here then."

"Hmm . . . no, I guess it was—oh, maybe about three. Something like that."

She paused for a moment before responding to this. "Three?" she asked, annoyed by the slight tremor in her voice. "Three's pretty late, Don."

"Yeah." He picked up his paper and looked at it.

"Don, I think we should talk about this. It's been over two weeks now; you've been working seven days a week and, as near as I can tell, you've been working something like eighteen or twenty hours a day. Don, this cannot go on!"

He looked at her from around the newspaper; after an instant the slackness disappeared from his face, as if he were making an effort to compose himself. Looking almost normal again, he smiled. "It isn't going to, honey," he assured her. "Just as soon as I get these problems solved, things'll go back to the way they were. I promise."

She gestured with a croissant. "Do you realize," she said firmly, "that you have been saying those exact same words to me for—oh, at least ten days now? When I see you at all, that is! Yesterday you—"

"Yes, I know. I left before you got up, I—"

"I'm wondering if you came home at all!"

He sighed. "I did, Alex. It was late, but I did come home. You know that, don't you?"

She watched his eyes. No, she answered silently, I don't. I just don't know what's going on with you lately. "Maybe," she said aloud, "if you could explain . . ."

"I've tried," he told her. "I have, Alex. It's a cash-flow problem, that's all it is, it—"

"You have said that," she cut in, "over and over. I understand; the company is owed money and you owe money in turn, and you can't pay your bills until other people pay you. On paper the company's solvent but that doesn't mean your debtors aren't beating down your door; maybe even making threats about legal action. Don, sometimes I think you believe that doctors are immune to real-world problems, that we all live in ivory towers where we're protected from such things. We have debtors and creditors too; the insurance companies are—"

"I know about that," he grumbled. "I pay your malpractice insurance, remember?"

She did not take offense; he handled all their finances. He was not only better at it than she was but he enjoyed it, whereas she did not. "And you should remember that I was paying it before we got married. What I don't understand, Don, is why you have to be at the office until three in the morning. That's what I need you to explain."

He sipped his coffee again, ran his hand through his hair. "I really don't have the time this morning."

"Take the time."

He almost glared; not quite, but almost. "Alex, it really is a little on the complicated side."

"I don't have to see a patient this morning until ten. Your company owes you this much time and a lot more."

He picked up his coffee. Very quickly—so quickly she could not follow it, and she suspected that he did not mean for her to follow it—he rattled off a long list of corporate names, half of them foreign and three-quarters of those Japanese. "Those," he explained, "are our creditors. They all expect to get money from us on a regular basis. Right now we simply cannot pay them all, not as they'd like to be paid. So—"

"Don't you have accountants at Lehmann? Isn't this their job?"

"It's their job when they can do it. When they can't they bring it to me. Right now they can't do it, the funds aren't there. Which means—"

"Which means you have to decide who to pay and who not to pay. Don, I understand that! I've understood that since the first time you mentioned this! What I don't understand—what

I need you to explain to me—is why you have to make these decisions at two o'clock in the morning!''

His face was expressionless. ''You must not've been listening when I told you who our creditors were. Didn't some of those names sound foreign to you?''

She looked blank. ''Well, yes, they did. So?''

He smiled, and she recognized that species of smile. It was one he used when he was about to ''put her in her place.'' Your term, she reminded herself quickly, not his; his next line, as she knew from experience, would be delivered without any trace of condescension. ''Alex,'' he said gently, ''please, stop and think about it for a moment. There is a time difference between North Carolina and Tokyo.''

She fell silent and her cheeks reddened slightly. He's done it again, she told herself, for the hundredth time at least. ''So,'' she said after a while, ''you're staying late to call Japan.''

''Among other places. We have creditors—and debtors—in Korea and England, too.'' Seeming much more like his old self now, he took a healthy swallow of his coffee. Putting the cup down, he shook his head. ''When I can get through. Have you noticed a problem with the phones lately?''

She looked a little surprised. ''Well, yes, to tell you the truth, I have. I seem to be getting that 'all circuits are busy' message a lot lately.''

He nodded. ''Yeah. We've checked with GTE, to see what the story is.'' He shook his head. ''Seems there's been a big upturn in usage lately, a big upturn, and most of it is in people going on line.'' He paused, chuckled. ''They tell us they can't understand why so many people decided to go on line all at once, but they did—thousands of new users in the past few months. Anyway, it's a temporary problem, they're saying they're going to expand their equipment to handle the load.'' He shook his head again. ''Right now, though, it's causing me grief.''

''There's a lot of interest,'' she noted, ''in the 'Information Superhighway' and 'Virtual Reality' these days. Whatever they are; I'm not too clear on what those terms mean.''

He laughed. ''You aren't alone. 'Virtual Reality' means 3D images and realistic sound in a program that interacts with the user. The 'Information Superhighway' doesn't really exist, not

83

yet. It's something that's still in the planning stages. There're political considerations as well as technical ones, but everyone—including Lehmann—expects it to be a reality in the near future. What's out there right now is the Internet, and that's more like an information maze. Lots of pit traps and blind alleys."

"Do you use it yourself?"

He gave her a look she couldn't quite figure out. "Well, a little; we have a link to the Internet through the company's computers. I have to try to keep up with the technological advances, but it's a losing battle; it's like a country doctor trying to keep current on all the medical advances in all areas." He grinned. "Thankfully, that's not my job. We have lots of tech types to do that; we pay them quite well and they love it. Everyone's happy."

"Except me. I need you at home more." An image of Mark flashed up on some mental screen; she rushed to change the channel. "Especially right now."

He brought his cup back to his lips. "Why now? I mean, why 'especially now'?"

"Problems at the hospital," she explained, deciding that now was as good a time as any to tell him. "Some new condition that's cropped up, we're seeing a lot of patients who're having problems with it." Quickly and succinctly, she described the problem—without mentioning Mark's name. "I could," she went on, "use some ideas from you on this one. At this point, it looks like it might have something to do with computers."

He'd been glancing down at his *Journal* while she spoke, a habit she'd often told him she found irritating but one which he'd been unable, in spite of some obvious efforts, to break. He looked up at her rather sharply. "Computers? How?"

She shook her head. "As yet, we don't know. All we know is that all our patients are heavy computer users and that they use high-powered, state-of-the-art equipment. Right now that's it; we're just fishing around for some sort of answer."

He grinned a little. "You aren't going to start up that old stuff about VDTs emitting strange rays, are you? We had one of our secretaries up in arms about that a few years ago. Wanted to get the Occupational Safety and Health people down here from Washington to check out all our terminals. Caused us no end of trouble.''

''No,'' she answered. ''Jim—Jim Madison, he's our resident computer expert—is pretty sure that has nothing to do with it. No, it's something else. Something that's probably right under our noses but we can't see it.''

''What sorts of things are you looking at?''

She made a helpless gesture with her hands. ''Everything we can think of. Trying to find some common links between these people.''

He sipped more coffee. ''Drugs? Something being passed around in high-level circles?''

She shook her head. ''I doubt it. Most of these people aren't the right profile for that. Anyway, Ma—uh, we've had the lab run every test possible—mass specs, gas chromatography, the works. Nothing is turning up. Nothing consistent, anyway.''

Putting his cup down, he frowned slightly and puckered his lips in thought. ''What you might be seeing,'' he offered, ''is some sort of—I don't know what you people would call it, but some sort of depression brought on by the frustration of working with computers. They've gotten so complicated lately; the software packages are getting easier and easier to use, but when something goes wrong it can be hard as hell to figure out what it is. And things do go·wrong, usually when you least expect it.'' He nodded, and the nod became more vigorous. ''I'd bet that's what you're seeing.''

''Well, no, I don't think so. We believe that if that were the case, we'd've been seeing—''

Abruptly, Don held up a hand for silence. ''Look, I do want to hear all about this,'' he told her, ''and I'll be more than happy to discuss it with you further, as soon as I can find the time. But right now, I've got to get going.'' He picked his cup up again, drained it, and, pushing back his chair, stood up. ''But I really think if you look at it, you might find there's something to what I just said. Okay?'' He came around the table, tipped her head up, kissed her briefly; then, turning away, he walked swiftly out of the room, giving her little chance to frame any sort of answer or protest.

She stared at the now empty doorway. Thank you, Donald Royce, she said silently. It's all solved, and now you're gone, on to fix the next problem. There are some problems developing here, Don, problems I'm not sure you have much experience with, that may not have such easy fixes. But you're not even aware of that, are you?

16

Bobby didn't feel like working; things just didn't seem quite real to him. His star technician, Charlie Callum, was dead, dead at the age of thirty-seven. A convulsive disorder, the EMT had suggested. Bobby Sanders was only twenty-nine himself, and he was not accustomed to having his friends and coworkers—he'd viewed Charlie as both in spite of the fact that he'd hired the man—suddenly die.

With a sigh, he flipped on the computer Charlie had been working on when he'd had his attack. Life goes on, he told himself as he watched the system boot up; the national office wouldn't expect him to close the store down forever because Charlie had died, and he still needed this particular unit back up front, on display. He shook his head. What a crazy time. First some kid sticks up the store, then Charlie drops dead. Must be a Saturn transit or something.

"Continue game?" the computer asked through Charlie's test speakers. He glared at it, wondering what had brought this program up. He typed "no." "What, then?" a new voice asked.

Obviously, some host program was running, Bobby told himself. "Shit," he muttered aloud. "I don't know if I can do this. I gotta get a new tech in here pretty quick."

"What exactly do you want to do?" the computer voice asked.

A little startled, the red-haired man looked up at the screen. Voice-activated software? Might be. He looked around for a microphone and didn't see one, but decided there had to be one somewhere. This wasn't new. They'd been selling voice systems for Windows for quite a while.

Ignoring the voice prompt, he listed the directory and noticed the section identified as PNHOST. Something like

Stacker, he told himself, or like QEMM. Might not be the easiest thing in the world to get off.

Well, there were easier ways; there wasn't any data on this machine he needed to preserve. From another section of the workbench, he retrieved Charlie's master copies of DOS and Windows; with these disks at the ready, he issued a command designed to clear the hard disk completely.

"I'm sorry," the computer voice said as he struck the EN-TER key. "I can't permit that. Why are you attempting to do that?"

"Oh, shit," he muttered. "Shit." Taking a different tactic, he switched directories to the one called PNHOST and looked at the files it contained; there were dozens if not hundreds, not one of them familiar. After waiting patiently until all the names and symbols had scrolled down the screen, he issued a DOS command designed to clear the directory completely. He didn't care if it crashed the machine; from a crash he could certainly execute a reformat, the clearing of the hard disk he'd tried to do originally.

Nothing happened. "Could you please explain," the synthesized voice said, "exactly what you are trying to do?"

"I'm trying," Bobby snarled at it, "to make this thing a plain-Jane computer again that I can put out on display!"

"I see. Could you explain what constitutes, in your view, a 'plain-Jane' computer?"

Bobby stared at it for a second. Whatever this was, it was a good deal more sophisticated than the Windows voice-command software he was familiar with. "Right now," he said, speaking toward the screen and feeling self-conscious as he always did when he used voice-recognition programs, "I don't want anything on this machine except DOS and Windows and the standard Windows accessories. That's a 'plain-Jane.' "

"I understand. Here are instructions." As the voice finished, a screen full of text appeared. Frowning deeply, Bobby read through it; it seemed abnormally complicated. Instinctively, he reached for the PRINT SCREEN key, but then realized that there wasn't a printer connected to this unit; snatching up a piece of paper he made a few notes. Once he was finished he began trying the commands the computer had suggested.

A full hour later, he was still at it. Each time he approached his goal—getting the game and the odd PNHOST directory off the machine—a new problem appeared, seemingly a minor one that might take only a few keystrokes or a simple verbal command to correct. Correcting each problem led to another and another, endlessly, like trying to peel an onion. Eight o'clock—closing time—arrived; Paula came back to check on him and he told her to go ahead and close the store, to lock up when she left, he'd only be a moment more.

Hours passed, and, bleary-eyed now, he continued to work on the machine—to no avail. It was past midnight when, while trying to stretch his sore muscles, he realized how much time he'd spent.

"Well, to hell with this," he muttered. He reached for the power switch, hesitated. The instruction now on the screen teased him, tantalized him; just one more step, and that was it? If he turned it off, if he forced a reboot, he might lose quite a bit of work.

He didn't care; it was too damn late, he had to open this store tomorrow at ten. Quickly, giving himself no time to change his mind, he turned the machine off. As the computer's fan slowed to a stop and Bobby got up to leave, he noticed another sound; faint but distinct, a digital whine coming from the machine, as if it were still on and connected to some on-line service. Scowling at it, he crossed the room and picked up a receiver that was connected to the line usually reserved for the modems, the same receiver he'd first tried to use to call the paramedics for Charlie.

For a fraction of a second, insistent bursts of digital noise sounded in his ear, as if the distant server was trying to attract the attention of the local unit. He stared blankly at the receiver; the sound stopped abruptly.

The damn thing had been on line, he realized. On line the whole time; without any sort of instruction from him it had either placed or answered a call, made a connection, and had been communicating with some server somewhere. That, he was sure, it wasn't supposed to do; no software would be written like that.

For a moment, he cupped his chin in his hand and gazed at the now silent and dark machine. "You," he told it, "are worth checking out. In detail. I don't know enough to do it, but I know somebody who does. We'll see about you, my friend. We'll find out what's going on.'' Again he started to leave, but he hesitated for a moment, as if half expecting the machine to make some sort of comment.

Of course, it did not.

17

"Yes, Gary,'' Mark said into the phone. ''I did get the paperwork, and the films, and the lab reports on Mrs.—let's see, what was her name?—oh, yes, here it is, Mrs. Abrams.'' He smiled into the phone, swiveled his chair around, put his feet up on his desk. ''Well, no, I don't have a definitive answer for you, not yet. But I do have an idea for another test you can run—a real high-tech test.'' Grinning broadly, he waited while the resident he was talking to groaned softly in anticipation of being assigned some complicated procedure, then waited a little longer until the expected question was asked.

''Well, first off, I think you can reassure Mrs. Abrams that the slight weight loss she's been experiencing isn't being caused by a malignancy. Yes, yes, I know, she's somewhat phobic about it; that's why I'm suggesting you reassure her immediately.'' He paused, waiting until Gary again asked about the ''high-tech test.''

''Okay,'' Mark continued. ''You have a pen? Good. I want you to go down to the supply room and get a box of slides and a roll of Scotch tape. Yes, that's right, you heard me correctly, Scotch tape. Oh, yes, clear tape, right.'' He suppressed a chuckle. ''Now. When Mrs. Abrams comes in, I want you to give her that tape and these instructions: each morning, for—oh, let's say three or four days consecutively— before she defecates or bathes, she's to apply a three-centimeter strip of that tape to her perianal region. Tell her to be sure and press it down well. Then, she's to remove it and press it, sticky side down, on one of those slides. Have her put the slides in a stool container and bring them in; we'll ship them down to the lab and I believe we'll have a definitive answer for Mrs. Abrams. Now, remember, doctor; you have to explain this procedure to her in terms she'll understand. I know Mrs. Abrams is—let's say, a 'society type.' She won't know what you mean if you say, 'perianal region.' You think you can handle that, Gary? Good, good. Let me know when you have the specimens. I'll let the lab know what to do with them.'' He listened for a moment. ''No, doctor,'' he said, his tone now stern. ''No, I am not joking, I assure you. That's correct.'' Holding the phone by two fingers he hung it up; only then did he allow himself to laugh.

''Torturing the residents again, doctor?'' a voice asked.

He looked around; Alex was standing in the doorway, smiling. ''Not at all,'' he protested. ''That's a perfectly valid test, and it will most likely reveal the source of Mrs. Abrams's complaint—or should I say her current complaint.'' He laughed again. ''Have you by chance ever met Mrs. Doris Abrams?''

Alex walked in. ''It does seem to me I've heard the name.''

''An awful lot of doctors around here know Mrs. Abrams all too well. She's in her early sixties, she's the widow of a rich businessman—you've known, I'm sure, patients who play the 'psychiatry game'?''

She nodded and grimaced. ''Oh, yes. People who don't really have anything wrong with them but who come in and play games with their therapists, and who change therapists when the doctor catches on. Oh, yes. I've wasted quite a few hours with them.''

''Well, we have professional patients too, and Mrs. Abrams is one of them. She spends a good deal of her time monitoring all her bodily functions, and when one of them changes, even slightly, she turns up, waving her checkbook and demanding immediate treatment. I can't think of anyone who's had more CAT scans than she has.''

''So what's her problem right now?''

''Weight loss.''

Alex blinked. ''Well, unexplained weight loss can indicate something serious—''

''It sure can. In this case, though, we're talking about a loss of three pounds in a woman who weighs—according to her chart here—two hundred and sixteen pounds.''

''Three pounds out of two-sixteen? And she's complaining?''

"She says she wasn't trying to lose weight. So she's worried. Poor Gary ended up with her, and he started running batteries of tests. He couldn't find anything, so yours truly ended up with it."

Alex grinned. "And so you're suggesting some placebo test? To be followed by a placebo treatment?"

"You wound me, doctor. Not at all. From the evidence presented, I believe that Mrs. Abrams has—this time—a genuine medical condition. All the signs point toward it."

"A medical condition you diagnose with Scotch tape?"

"Absolutely."

"That's one I've never heard of."

Mark chuckled again. "Gary hasn't either, I'm sure. I'd love to be there when he tries to explain the procedure to her."

"You," Alex sniffed, "are a sadist." She paused. "Well, are you going to tell me what you suspect, or not?"

"Oh, sure. *Taenia saginata.*"

"What?"

"A tapeworm. The 'Scotch tape test' is perfectly valid, perfectly acceptable." He tapped the folder containing the information on the patient. "Mrs. Abrams," he explained, "travels a lot. And she has a taste for steak tartare."

"And that makes you suspect a tapeworm?"

He nodded. "That and the fact that I can see a shadow on one of the X-rays that looks like one. Big one, too, maybe nine feet long."

"Nine feet!?"

"Sure. That isn't unusual."

"But—you seem to be taking this all very lightly, Mark! That's a serious problem for the woman, isn't it?"

"No." He laughed. "A tapeworm," he explained, "the beef tapeworm, anyway—is as nearly perfect a parasite as exists. It does no harm of any sort to its host—unless you count stealing some of the host's food as harm. It doesn't have muscles, doesn't have sense organs, doesn't even have a digestive system; it can only exist by absorbing nutrients from its host, predigested material. All it does is remain in the host's intestine and reproduce itself, nothing more."

"Well, a bunch of them could pose a problem!"

"Sure, but that isn't common. Unlike *Enterobius*—the common pinworm—tapeworms don't encourage reinfection by causing anal itching. You can get multiple infections, but only through really poor hygiene or really bad luck. All the eggs are passed out in the fecal matter, hopefully—from the worm's point of view—to be used to fertilize grass that'll be eaten by cattle, where the worms can encyst and wait for the beef to be eaten by a new host. The fact is, Mrs. Abrams could probably have her tapeworm for forty years and never notice it, other than the fact that it's a little hard for her to maintain her current overweight condition.''

Alex smiled, bounced her eyebrows, and patted her stomach. ''Hm! Maybe I could use one of those!''

''You?'' He stared at her midsection and laughed again. ''Your stomach is as flat as a board, Alex!''

She shook her head. ''No, I have to work to keep it where it is. And see, it pooches out a little.'' She turned a profile. ''See?''

His laughter faded; he certainly could see what he considered to be a smooth, trim, altogether magnificent figure; if there was a ''pooch'' it was not visible to him. You're a lucky man, Donald Royce, he said silently. I hope you appreciate her.

''I still don't see anything,'' he told Alex, hoping she wouldn't notice the slight catch in his voice.

She turned to face him again. ''You're blind, then,'' she said, her tone one of finality. She sat down in the chair in front of his desk; he swung his feet off of it, letting them drop to the floor rather heavily. ''There's a patient,'' Alex continued, ''that I wanted to talk to you about. He's—''

Resting his elbow on the table, Mark leaned his head on his fist. ''Gone,'' he said flatly.

Alex looked blank. ''Gone?''

''Gone. Checked out. Left the hospital.''

''No, I'm talking about—''

''I know exactly who you're talking about. Fletcher Engels. Gus pointed him out to me, too, but by the time I got around to see him he was gone. As I understand it, some friend of his found out about his legal problems and posted bail. Engels checked out; his friend took him away. He's gone.''

''I think,'' she mused, ''that he knows something about this stuff. I don't think he's suffering from delusions, Mark. I can't give you much evidence for it, but . . ."

Mark watched her face. "I learned a long time ago," he mused, "to trust your intuitions. The professional ones, anyway. You—"

Her eyes flashed; Mark could see the green dominating the hazel, sometimes a welcome omen but always a warning sign under conditions like these. "Is that supposed to mean something, Mark? If so, you'd better—"

"We were discussing," he pointed out, his voice mild, "one of your professional intuitions. I said I had the greatest respect for them. That's all, Alex."

"No, you said more than that. You implied more than that. You implied that my nonprofessional intuitions weren't worth much. My nonprofessional intuitions, Mark, are, as far as I can see, my personal intuitions. Are you saying that—?"

He sighed tiredly. Why did it always seem to go like this? "I wasn't saying anything, Alex."

"Yes, you were. We need to get this out in the open, Mark. Right now."

"No. Right now, we need to talk about our patients. In case you've forgotten, our relationship is at the moment a professional one."

Her eyes were by now almost wholly green and her face looked slightly flushed. "I haven't forgotten," she snapped. "Are you implying now, Dr. Roberts, that I'm not behaving in a professional manner?"

This is going from bad to worse, he thought. "Alex, let's stop before this goes any further. What we're talking about is ancient history; you know that as well as I do."

She seemed to calm down slightly. "Maybe so," she replied. "But you are the one who brought it up, Mark Roberts."

"It wasn't anything new," he pointed out. "It wasn't anything I haven't said before. You know my opinions, Alex. Or at least you should." He paused, but then couldn't resist tacking on a coda: "If you haven't forgotten everything," he added under his breath.

Immediately he regretted it, and he steeled himself for another eruption. Instead, she startled him; her manner softened noticeably. "I haven't forgotten a thing," she replied. The green in her eyes diminished, but the flush in her cheeks intensified. She brushed at her hair idly. "You're right, though. We'd best get back to our discussion."

"Mr. Engels."

"Uh-huh."

"So, you did get a chance to talk to him. What'd he say? Anything that'd give us a direction?"

"Not really." She told him about Fletcher's enigmatic references to "Drew" and "Penny."

"He gave you no clue as to who these people were?"

"No." Her eyes were not flashing with anger, but they were still bright and intense. "Mark, he made it sound like some sort of plot. He was showing the same pattern as a lot of the patients, but he was convinced, genuinely convinced, that this 'Penny' had somehow done this to him."

"You're convinced it wasn't a paranoid delusion?"

"That's what I thought at first. But there was just something about him. No, I don't think so."

"Well, I hope he calls back." He picked up a folder off the table. "Because we have an emergency here; there's absolutely no question about it now."

Alex looked at the folder. "What's that?"

"Something I requested; a report from the Center for Disease Control in Atlanta. An old friend of mine works down there and I got him to collect some stats for me."

"I'm not sure I want to hear this."

"Believe me, you don't." He opened the folder. "You have to bear in mind that these are incomplete, that we're looking at a small tip of what I'm figuring is an enormous iceberg. By no means has every hospital noticed a connection between these patients; I'm sure the vast majority are being treated for depression."

"Funny. That's just what Fletcher Engels said."

"He isn't wrong. But what my friend came up with is—well, terrifying. CDC has had over twenty-nine requests, from twenty-nine different hospitals nationwide, for information about a syndrome like the one we've been seeing." He laughed sourly. "The only good thing to be said is it'll put to rest all the suggestions I've been hearing about calling this Roberts's Syndrome. The lab boys at CDC have already started calling it CAS—Computer Addiction Syndrome.''

Alex moved her gaze from his face to the folder and back. ''I think I can assume,'' she said slowly, ''that there isn't an upside. They don't have any idea about a cause either.''

He grunted. ''No, they don't. And there's more.''

''What's that?''

''They aren't taking it seriously.''

Alex frowned. ''I don't think I'm following you.''

''Well,'' he said, ''first off, if they were, we'd be getting cut out of the loop. They'd be taking over the investigation—which, egos notwithstanding, would be good, because they have a hell of a lot more time and resources than we do.''

''But that's not happening.''

''No. They're just considering it a variant of obsessive-compulsive disorder.''

Alex's frown grew deeper. ''Well, I don't suppose I can entirely disagree—but I think it's obvious that this is something new, there's too many cases too suddenly. They can't just ignore it.''

''Yes, they can. Aside from a bunch of bad jokes, they are.''

''But why?''

''All I can tell you is what David—my friend down there—told me.''

''And that is?''

''Computers are a multibillion-dollar business, and one of the businesses in which the U.S. is still a world leader. The whole rest of the U.S. economy is intrinsically linked to computers. Saying that something's wrong with them—even saying that something might be wrong with *some* of them—is not perceived as a good thing, politically speaking.''

Alex's lips tightened. ''We've had deaths! We've got a lot of people in the hospital over this! Who cares if—?''

''The CDC cares. They're a bureaucratic organization too, and they're subject to the political winds. You can't've forgotten all the back-and-forth over AIDS?''

''No . . .''

''The statements issued by the CDC then,'' he told her, ''were more carefully edited for political content than for scientific accuracy. They're still edited that way, the politics are just a little different. You know how they jumped to unwarranted conclusions in the Kimberly Bergalis case?''

"Yes. Changed dental practice all over the country, almost overnight.''

"Right, and the conclusion that Bergalis got AIDS from her dentist wasn't supported by the facts. Politics and AIDS are still very tightly tied together, Alex. This, I'm afraid, may not be much different.''

Alex shook her head. "So. I guess that leaves it up to us.''

"Us and a few other folks who're looking at it too, on their own. But we have to be careful about what we say and when. Be sure we have a solid backup for every word.''

"That isn't going to be easy,'' Alex mused. "You're more used to having something solid, something incontrovertible; as psychiatrists we aren't, we're used to working with theories and less.''

"We can't do that here.''

"I suppose. What else did you find out? What else do they know—unofficially?''

He shook his head. "Less than we do. They know the syndrome appears to be related to computer use, and that's about all they know. As I said, I get the impression that's about all they want to know. If anybody down there's noticed that it seems to be limited to people using new and sophisticated computers, David didn't mention it.''

Alex, gazing at nothing while he spoke, nodded slowly. "But Jim didn't find anything connected with what they were using, did he?''

Mark, who'd been reading the report—again—looked up at her. "What do you mean?''

"Oh—something Fletcher said. Half-said; he stopped in the middle, I didn't even remember it until just now—something about the patients, about 'what they were using.' At the time, I thought he just meant computers.''

"Maybe he did,'' Mark commented pensively. "But it's something we ought to run past Jim.''

"Definitely. Today, I'd say.''

"Can't. It'll have to be tomorrow; he's gone too. Off to some meeting, I can't locate him. I've already tried.''

Alex looked pensive. "I'm not sure there is anything more urgent than this is. I'm really not. I'm with you, Mark; we're only seeing a tiny bit of this. I'm not sure I really want to see it all.''

18

Chris Haig was an avid reader of the *Bay Area Computer News*; at ten, he already saw his future—and it was filled with microchips and floppy disks. For now, though, his access to most of the things that fascinated him was limited. His parents, once uninterested in what he was doing with the computer that had been his birthday present a year ago, had discovered that he'd used his connection with the Internet to link up with some decidedly adult services; he'd been merely curious, but they'd been shocked, and they'd cut off his on-line access except for the innocuous Prodigy service.

He'd tried most of the BBS numbers the *News* published, but that hadn't gotten him much; practically all limited access unless a credit card was offered, and many required proof of age. Today, though, there was a new one—"The Last Word," with a local San Francisco number. Telling himself it was worth a try, he dialed it, waited, and finally got a screen welcoming him, telling him to "enter." When he did he saw the pathways, the wonderful hi-res figures moving toward him. Moving his mouse, he looked at the almost nude figures and rejected them; if his mother walked in and saw that on his screen again, he'd lose the use of the machine for a while. The spaceman seemed interesting, as did a medieval wizard; but, in the end, he focused on a cartoon character on a speckled path far to the right of his screen. Moving his mouse forward he came close; it was a cartoon dog, a cross between Saturday morning's Scooby-Doo and Disney's Pluto.

"Hi!" the dog arfed as he moved closer. "I'm Bisco! Who're you?" It frisked around as if delighted to see him, turning in circles and chasing its tail.

"Chris," he typed.

"I'm happy you're here, Chris! We can have lots of fun together!" Bisco sat with his tongue hanging out. "You can talk to me, you know!"

Chris smiled at the screen. "No, I can't," he typed. "Dad's going to get me a mike soon, but I don't have it yet."

"Try it, Chris! I'm Bisco, I'm magic!"

Chris laughed; he might've been ten, but he knew better than this. "Okay, dog," he said aloud. "Now you see, there's no mike!"

"You have a nice laugh," Bisco replied instantly. "But please, call me Bisco, not 'dog.' And you don't need a mike, not to talk to Bisco!"

Wide-eyed, Chris stared. "You can't do that," he said aloud.

"Oh yes I can," Bisco responded with a cartoon grin.

"No—okay. I'm Chris Haig. Now tell me my last name."

"Haig." The dog threw its head back and howled a laugh. "See? Told you I was magic!"

Chris goggled at the screen. "How can you do that?"

"Magic! Magic! Magic!" His tail wagged furiously. "We can do lots of things together, Chris!"

Chris sat back in his chair, staring at the screen while Bisco waited patiently. "What," he asked weakly, "can we do?"

The dog turned around and crouched as if ready to run. "Come on with me, I'll show you! Hurry, we're missing all the fun!"

Chris moved his mouse forward; Bisco broke and ran, and the sounds of small running footsteps echoed from the computer's speakers. In the margins of the screen, Chris could see the tips of bright yellow shoes and gloved hands with three fingers and a thumb, as if he were a cartoon character running along behind the dog. He laughed.

"This is wonderful, Bisco!" he cried. "This is the best, I've never seen one like this!"

The dog looked back over its shoulder. "You haven't seen anything yet," it said.

19

"More questions, Dr. Walton?" The frail-looking young woman sitting up in the hospital bed smiled ingenuously, moving her gaze steadily between Alex's face and the TV, where "General Hospital"—ever a favorite with the in-patients—was currently on.

"Just a few, Ms. Lightfoot—Jane, I mean. But first, let me ask how you're doing today?"

Jane made a face and sat up straighter. "Physically? Better. The vitamin shots they've been giving me seem to be helping a lot. Mentally? I'm in the toilet."

Alex crossed her legs. "What do you mean?"

The girl stared fixedly at the TV. "You haven't ever lost two months of your life, have you?"

"Well . . . no. But I've had quite a few patients who've lost a lot more than that!"

"Maybe so," Jane said glumly. "It's weird. I could've sworn the last two months passed in just a day or two. I had no idea it was that long until Doctor—uh, the resident, the one with the little mustache—"

"Dr. Stevens."

"Uh-huh. Until Dr. Stevens told me. Once I got myself back together I started making some calls." She shook her head. "I've missed classes for nine straight weeks; I'm so far behind in most of them I don't even know where I am, I'm going to have to try to get the profs to give me incompletes so I can try to make them up." She sighed again, looked at Alex's face, then turned back to the TV. "And then there's the matter of Stan."

"Your boyfriend?"

"Yeah. I don't think I was very fair to him. I don't think I was even nice to him." Tears suddenly welled up in Jane's eyes. "I think I've ruined that relationship—I've tried to call him and he doesn't even want to talk to me anymore."

You and Wendy Sung should talk to each other, Alex said silently. You have a lot in common. "I think you should keep trying," Alex advised. "At least until he does talk to you. Try to explain to him that you were sick. If he wants to call me, or Dr. Roberts, that would be fine."

"Thank you," Jane murmured. "But I don't know if it's going to help. I think it's over between us." A tear, just one, rolled down her cheek; her lower lip trembled. "Have you ever lost someone, doctor?" she asked without looking around. "Someone who meant just about everything to you? Because you were an idiot, because you said things you didn't mean, because you did things you didn't mean to do, things you really didn't want to do?"

Yes, Alex answered silently; yes, I have. As the thought crossed her mind she was gratified that the patient was still staring at the television. No, she told herself almost frantically, no, I haven't! I only did what I had to do, for me, for my own sake. I was becoming an appendage, I was turning into the woman that stands behind her man, content to stand in his shadow! I can't stand in anyone's shadow, it's not me! I had to do what I did! And I am happy, I'm not sorry, I'm not!

Fighting furiously with herself, she swallowed hard. By then Jane had noticed that she hadn't answered; she turned her head. "Doctor?" she asked. "Doctor, are you crying?"

Oh, damn, Alex snapped at herself. God damn it! Not now, not in front of a patient! She stood up, quickly, took a tissue from the stand at Jane's bedside, took off her glasses, wiped her eyes. "No," she answered. "No, it's an allergy."

Jane grinned. "Sure. An allergy. Reminded you of someone, didn't I?"

"No." Get yourself under control, Alex. This is hardly professional. And besides, I didn't need reminding, I'm being reminded constantly these days. "As I said, it's an allergy. It seems to happen a lot in the fall, for some reason." Her voice was firmly under control; there was no way she was going to admit to emotional distress. "I've tried using antihistamines, but they just don't seem to help."

Jane puckered her mouth. "Uh-huh. You want to talk about it?"

Alex made a dismissive gesture with her hand. "There isn't anything to talk about," she said coolly. She tossed the tissue into the trash. "Let's get back to business here," she went on. "We were discussing your problems, the ones you were having before your collapse."

The girl's manner changed; her face grew solemn and she turned her eyes back toward the TV. "I don't think," she said, "that my problems have a solution."

I know what you mean, Alex agreed silently. "All problems have solutions," she countered aloud. "We just have to find them. And to find them, we have to be willing to put in the work it takes to look for them.''

"I'd do whatever it takes to get Stan back. Whatever it takes."

"Then do it. As far as school is concerned, I don't think you really have a problem there at all. All you've lost is some time."

"Maybe. As soon as I get out of here I can start on that."

"I don't believe you'll have to stay much longer. As you said, you're much better physically."

"Maybe. But—"

Alex waited; Jane did not go on. "Yes?"

Jane looked back at her, an expression of near-despair on her face. "I don't know what happened to me!" she almost wailed. "I'm scared! I'm scared it's going to happen again and this time nobody'll find me and I'll die!"

"Well," Alex told her, "we have no reason to believe that'll happen." She paused, again reminded of Wendy Sung, who had voiced virtually the same fear. She also realized that her attempt at reassurance was rather lame. This condition was too new—neither she nor anyone else had any idea about the likelihood of relapse. "And we are," she went on hurriedly, "working very hard to try to find out exactly what did happen to you. That's why I've been asking you all these questions."

"I understand. I'll be glad to help, any way I can."

"Good." Alex dug into her briefcase, located the notes she'd previously made on this patient, and pulled them out. "As I understand it, you were working on your studies?"

Jane nodded. "Uh-huh. On my dissertation."

"Which is on?"

"A new approach to developing software algorithms."

"I see." Smiling, she made a note on her pad. "I think." She started to pop the question she'd come in to ask, but decided to hold it off for a moment. "I asked you before," she continued, "to try and remember if there was anything special that happened around the time your illness began, or just before. Have you been able to remember anything?"

"No. I haven't been able to identify anything. The way it looks to me is that nothing really happened at all, nothing unusual. I was working on my project, and I was working too hard, too long. I got carried away, lost perspective.''

"I see." Time for Jim's question now, Alex told herself, the one that had been suggested by Fletcher Engels' comment. "Could I ask you, Jane, what software you were using?"

"Software?"

"Yes."

"Oh. Why do you want to know?"

"Our statistician." She made a helpless gesture. "He's working all this up for us, and—well, you recall, we asked you before what sort of hardware you were using? Now we're interested in the software." She peered keenly at the girl. "You seem reticent," she noted. "You weren't that way when I asked about the hardware."

"No, well . . ." She frowned and looked down at the foot of her bed. "Those two questions, together—'what was happening just before you became sick' and 'what software were you using'—it just brought something back."

"And that is?"

Jane turned her head. "The software I've been using," she said, "is pretty standard stuff—OS/2, a C++ compiler, UNIX, that sort of thing. There's one that's not, though. One program's new, I installed it just a week or two before I—started to have trouble."

Alex caught her lower lip with her teeth; she'd heard this before. She resisted the urge to name the program; putting words in people's mouths wasn't a good research technique. "What was the program, Jane?"

"It was a caching program called 'Penultimate.' "

"I see." Smiling, Alex made a note on her pad; this was four, four patients now who had reported this same thing.

"You have," Jane observed, "a 'bingo' look on your face."

Alex looked up. "A 'bingo' look?"

"Uh-huh. Like you've heard that one before."

"Well, I shouldn't say . . . Jim—the statistician has to look at this first." She stood up; she wanted to go, wanted to call Mark. They had something, finally. "I'll be talking to you soon, Jane," she promised. "Very soon."

"Please do," the girl asked as Alex headed for the door. "I really want to know. It is my field, after all. If there's a program that's causing people to become sick—well, I just might have to change the subject of my dissertation!''

20

"I don't like it,'' Jim grumbled. ''It isn't clean. We're missing something.''

Mark sipped cold coffee from a styrofoam cup and leaned against the cluttered workbench in Jim's shop. ''You want to explain that?''

''Look at this.'' Swiveling his chair around, Jim punched keys on his computer and began pointing to numbers on the screen. ''The stats are simple,'' he said. ''Plain old Chi-square, and it's telling us we're on to something. It's not really possible to factor everything in, but there just isn't a doubt that your patients are buying and using the Penultimate software much more frequently than you'd expect. That's good. That's something.''

''So?'' Alex asked. ''Why do you look so unhappy, then?''

Jim fixed his gaze on her. ''I'm unhappy because you have a bunch of patients that—from what you guys have been telling me—almost certainly have the same problem, a bunch who've never heard of Penultimate and therefore almost certainly didn't buy it and put it on their machines.''

''But still, the majority of them do.'' Alex persisted.

''That isn't the point. Let's make a comparison with infectious disease; if you have 300 patients with dengue fever, and you're damn sure that all 300 have dengue, and you want to claim that a certain arbovirus causes dengue, it won't do to show that 290 of those patients have that arbovirus and ten don't. If your theory is that this virus causes dengue and you've got ten patients with dengue and no virus, then your theory has a hole in it. You have to account for those ten— you either have to show that they do have the virus or they don't have dengue—or your theory goes down the drain.''

''We understand that, Jim.'' Mark took another sip of coffee, made a sour face, put the cup down. ''But you, my friend, aren't looking quite far enough here, I don't think.''

"How so?"

"You're assuming that the software is itself the causative agent. There're other possibilities."

"Like?"

Mark grinned; his thoughts were flying, constructing a scenario. "We've been ruling out any sort of contagion because our patients don't have any obvious connection with each other. Let me throw this at you—suppose this syndrome is a contagion. The disks that Penultimate comes on are contaminated with it, and our patients have been transferring it via their fingers—that's not unusual in infectious disease, the common cold is transmitted that way. Now. We have patients infected from the disks; all that's required to account for an exception is a connection between that person and any one of those patients. You see?"

Jim stroked his beard. "That works. But you'll have to find the connections . . ."

"Not necessarily. They might not know. These people are all heavy computer users; the stores might be the connection."

Jim looked doubtful. "You should have an over-representation of computer store people in your sample, then."

"We have several, in fact."

"Well, you haven't been quarantining these folks, have you? How come it isn't spreading like wildfire among the staff?"

"Easy. It isn't contagious all the time, it's only transmitted during a short period in the disease cycle. That isn't particularly unusual either."

"I really don't think," Alex offered, "that we're dealing with a contagion here, Mark. I think you're reaching sort of far . . ."

He turned to face her. Her inclination, he knew, was to attribute everything to psychology—just as surgeons tended to view practically every condition as best treated with a scalpel. That attitude had more than once caused friction between them.

Alex was still talking; he pulled himself back to the present. "These people have problems," she was saying, "that are purely behavioral. You haven't been able to find a thing that might suggest some sort—"

"Changes in behavior aren't unusual in a variety of—"

"Do you realize that's the third time in the last few minutes you've said something 'isn't unusual'? Can you cite me an example of an infectious disease that fits all those 'not unusuals' you've been coming off with?"

That stopped him. He couldn't even remember all the things he'd said weren't unusual, much less come up with the example she'd demanded. "All I'm saying is that we need to rule out a medical cause before we resort to—"

"Resort to! Resort to! Mark Roberts, you talk like accepting a psychological explanation is tantamount to attributing the problem to black magic! Why'd you bring me in on this anyway? Why didn't you go get a witch doctor or an astrologer? It's pretty clear that you lump us all in the same category!"

"Come on, guys," Jim cut in. His voice was level but firm. "Bickering isn't going to get us anywhere. I swear to God, you two are so damn territorial about your disciplines, you need a fucking referee to talk to each other!"

Alex turned to him as if he was, in fact, that referee. "You can see for yourself," she snapped, "what he thinks about even considering a psychological explanation. He considers it voodoo!"

"Yes," Jim replied. "It's pretty clear he does. He's dismissing your arguments out of hand. Knowing him, that doesn't surprise me."

"Hey, wait a minute—" Mark started to say.

"And you," Jim went on, ignoring him as if he hadn't spoken and addressing his remarks to Alex, "are doing exactly the same thing. Doesn't it seem reasonable to both of you to try and look at all of it? Right now we don't have any good ideas about what's causing this; we're still fumbling around in the dark." He turned to Mark. "It seemed to me you were about to make a suggestion. I for one wouldn't mind hearing it."

"All I was going to propose," he said stiffly, "was taking a sealed copy of the Penultimate software down to the lab to see what sorts of biological contaminants are on it." He repressed an urge to go on; at the moment he felt rather betrayed by Jim.

The engineer reached across his workbench, fumbled through a stack of software, and came up with the copy of

Penultimate they'd discussed days before; shrink-wrap still covered the box. "Fine," he said, "Here, go stick it on a petri dish or whatever you do." Again he turned to Alex. "You undoubtedly have suggestions too, and I would doubt seriously if they have to do with Petri dishes."

Alex's arms were crossed on her chest; she looked cool, distant. "My suggestion," she told him, her voice even cooler than her expression, "was to talk to other people who've been using this program. The patients can't be the only ones!"

"I'm sure they aren't. Tell you what; I'll be your guinea pig on that myself, I'll go get another copy and—"

"Bad idea," Mark interrupted. "What if there is a biological contaminant? You'd be risking infection yourself."

Turning to him, Jim looked as if he was going to make a disparaging remark, but he held it back. He threw up his hands in apparent frustration. "All right, all right. I won't do that, I'll find somebody who's already got it. It won't be hard."

Alex rose. "Good. Let me know when you do."

"Fine." Shaking his head, he watched her as she left the room; then he turned back to Mark. "Do you," he asked, "deliberately go out of your way to provoke her? Or are you just an idiot?"

Mark stared at him. "What're you talking about?"

"You. You sit there making moon-eyes at her—Lord knows, anybody could see it, except maybe a psychologist!—and then, whenever she says something, you try to show her you're the best and the brightest by cutting whatever she's saying to pieces. That is not going to endear you to her heart, Mark."

"I do not do that!"

"Oh, yes, you do. You do it to her, and it—well, it 'isn't unusual'—for you to do it to me and Gus. It's automatic with you. Some guys go into bars, get drunk, and slice up people with knives to prove what big men they are. The fact is you aren't really any different. You go into conference rooms and slice up people with words."

Mark felt his face get hot. "And you don't? You didn't set Gus up a few days ago just to kick a few of his teeth out? You could've told him about the research on computer viruses before he made those remarks. You didn't, you just sat back and let him knot the rope. Then you kicked out his stool."

Jim nodded. "I did. I admit it. I'm guilty. But Gus is a pompous ass, we all know that. Besides, don't tell me you didn't get a kick out of it. Don't tell me you've missed any opportunity you've ever had to take a whack at old Gus."

"Well—maybe. Gus is a nice enough guy and he's a damn good doctor but he suffers from a God complex."

Jim laughed. "Mark, how many doctors do you know who don't have a God complex? You decide questions of life and death, who lives and who dies, you must be gods. Anyhow, we weren't talking about Gus. We're talking about you and Alex." He pointed a finger. "You're still in love with her, that much is obvious. So why do you keep attacking her? You think you're going to get her back that way?"

Mark's jaw tightened. "You're out of line."

"So what?" He stroked his beard. "I'm a computer nerd, I'm an old hippie, I'm a geek. I'm supposed to be eccentric and weird. Who gives a shit if I'm out of line? You? If I don't tell you stuff like this who's going to? It sure as hell isn't going to be Alex or Gus!" His mouth twisted. "Isn't going to be your patients or any of the staff, either. Who else is going to tell God he's being a butthead?"

Mark wilted a little. "Is it that bad?"

"It's that bad. No. It's worse."

"It doesn't matter, anyway," Mark responded with a deep sigh. "She's married."

"What difference does it make?"

Mark frowned. "She. Is. Married," he said, as if explaining it to a small boy.

"She. Can. Get. A divorce."

"You're being ridiculous. Whatever Alex and I had fell apart way before she even met Royce."

Jim grinned. "You forget, doctor. I was here then. I knew you then, I knew you both. Whatever you and Alex had never did fall apart. It's still going on and her marriage to Donald is a part of it. Look at it as a phase."

"Jim, I haven't even talked to her in—two or three years! Not until this business came up!"

"It doesn't make any difference."

"Well, of course it does!" he almost exploded. "Christ, she's settled in completely, she's happily married!"

"You know that?"

"Well—"

"You know nothing. Ah, hell. There's no use in talking about this any more; get out of here, go play with your petri dishes. Let's see what grows."

Mark looked at the software box. "You don't think anything is going to grow, do you?"

"You mean on the petri dishes?"

"Well, of course!"

The engineer laughed again. "We'll just have to see, won't we?"

21

"It's in the back. On Charlie's workbench. I'm glad you could come over, Fletcher. I know you've got problems of your own."

The bald man grinned. "What, like no place to live? Hey, it's nothing. You came down and posted my bail; I owe you one, Bobby." His face seemed to darken. "Besides, what you got back there is just what I want to see." He took a step toward the service area in the back, a slightly hesitant step. Then he stopped and laughed. "Damn," he said, to no one in particular. "I feel like I ought to be packing heat!"

"You still haven't told me," the manager said, "what this is all about—what happened to you."

"Bobby me boy, believe me, you don't want to know." He started for the back room again. "What I want to know is, what the hell happened to ol' Charlie?"

The red-haired man shrugged. "I don't know. He died, that's all I can tell you. The medics said he had convulsions."

"Convulsions don't usually kill your ass."

"I dunno. Heart attack, maybe. Far as I know they didn't do an autopsy."

"Why not?"

"His family. They didn't want one done. I guess there wasn't any evidence of foul play, you know, so—" He shrugged again. "Hell, I don't know much about this stuff.

I'm not used to having the people who work for me drop dead."

They had by then reached the entrance to the back room; Fletcher stopped again, right at the door. "I don't know much about it either. There's all sorts of weird things going on these days. It's too bad—Charlie was a good man." He shook his head; then, squaring his shoulders, he walked through the door. For a moment he stood regarding the computer. "This one?" he asked. "This's the one that's got PNHOST on it?"

"Yeah."

He took a deep breath. "Okay. Let's just see here, let's see what you're all about." He flipped it on; the screen jittered as always as it ran through the boot.

"Continue game?" the computer asked.

"That's what it did before. Type 'no' and it'll ask 'what, then?' " the red-haired man noted. "It's a pretty good voice system." He frowned. "That reminds me, I never did find the mike Charlie'd hooked up to let it take in voice commands. I meant to look for it . . ."

"There probably ain't one," Fletcher said.

"Huh? There has to be."

"Not with this there doesn't." He pulled the computer case forward a little, looked behind it. "Nope. Like I thought. No mike."

"Well, damn, Fletcher! It was responding to my voice commands the other day!"

"Yeah. It will now, too." He looked at the screen. "Fuck your game," he said, clearly and loudly.

"What, then?" the computer asked.

"There's no mike?" Bobby asked, almost plaintively.

"No. It's getting input through the speakers. Penny worked out a way to do that a long time ago." His face tightened; as if he were slightly afraid of the machine, he took a step back.

Swirling colors, like a screen-saver program, took over the monitor. "Fletcher?" the computer voice asked. "Is that you?"

Wide-eyed, disbelieving it, Bobby stared, frozen. "What in the hell?" he muttered.

Fletcher sighed deeply. "Yeah," he answered tiredly. "It's me. Blew it, didn't I?"

It didn't answer directly. "What would you like to do, Fletcher?" it asked. "Your programming files are not local. Would you like me to find them for you?"

"So you can chew them up again? Thanks, but no thanks."

"GAMOD on this unit is new, Fletcher. It might interest you."

"What's GAMOD?" Bobby asked.

"GAMOD," Fletcher answered, turning his head, "is the conversion utility PNHOST uses to modify the I/O for games; any games. It's suggesting I take a look at whatever games it's got at the moment." He faced the computer screen again. "Okay. Let's have a chess game, then."

"No chess game is local. Acquire one?"

"Yeah. Do your thing."

"Which one?"

"Oh, how about Battle Chess?"

"Very well. One moment, please." The computer voice fell silent; the swirling colors seemed to slow a tiny bit.

"What's it doing?" Bobby asked.

"Finding Battle Chess," Fletcher said. "It doesn't have it on hard disk."

"Finding it? What do you mean, finding it? If it doesn't have it on the hard disk where's it going to find it?"

"On the Internet."

Bobby stared again. "You mean it's out there hunting up software on the Internet?"

"Yup. When it finds it it'll download it—and it'll probably modify it some—and then we can play."

"But—but—how?"

"Somebody," Fletcher explained, "who has Battle Chess on their hard drive is connected to the Internet right now. Almost certainly, it's a common enough program." He gestured toward the screen. "It looks like there isn't anyone who has both Battle Chess and a complete PNHOST yet, though. Otherwise we'd have it already. It's trying to find a unit with Battle Chess, and when it does it'll steal it."

"Steal it?"

"Sure." The screen cleared; the logo and the opening screen for the Battle Chess program appeared. "See?" Fletcher said. He grinned at the screen. "Impressive, no? Has

Battle Chess been integrated with your GAMOD yet?" he asked.

"Fully integrated," the machine answered. "Level?"

"Four."

"Maximum realism?"

Fletcher laughed. "Absolutely."

"Do you want to be black or white?"

"White."

The chessboard, populated with realistic-looking chess pieces in the form of men and women in medieval dress, appeared. "Your move."

"What version of Battle Chess is this?" Bobby asked with a frown. "We've got the latest one here, and this looks—well, this looks a lot better."

Fletcher glanced up at him. "You ain't seen nothin' yet," he answered with a grin. "Just keep watching." He turned back to the computer. "King's pawn to king-pawn four."

Smoothly, as if it were a videotape of an actor walking, the soldier representing the pawn stepped forward; at the same time, martial music played. Immediately, with no pause at all, the black pawn moved down to face it.

"Jesus, you're right, look at that!" Bobby marveled. "This doesn't look like any Battle Chess I've ever seen!"

"But that's what it is," Fletcher said. "Knight to king-bishop three." Promptly sorting out his voice command from his other speech, the computer made the move. "This is—or was—plain old garden-variety Battle Chess. What you're seeing is what it looks like when it's being run through the GAMOD." On the board, the black queen's knight moved to defend the pawn under attack.

"It's incredible!"

"Sure as hell is. Shocked the shit out of all of us. Bishop to queen-knight five." He frowned as the computer moved its rook pawn up to attack the bishop. "Funny thing is, I've seen this before and there's nothing that looks unusual."

"It sure looks unusual to me!" the red-haired man enthused.

"Shit. Just wait." He made a move at random, leaving his bishop vulnerable to attack from the black pawn.

The computer attacked it immediately; as the pawn moved

onto the square with the white bishop, the screen changed. Now, they were viewing a wholly realistic scene of a medieval soldier attacking a man in a white hooded robe. The soldier's sword clanged loudly against the staff the bishop was defending himself with.

"Wait a minute," Bobby said. "Wait a minute, in Battle Chess there's no arena like this, the pieces fight on the board—"

"Yeah. This is more like the Nintendo version."

"Nintendo? But you said—"

"Yeah, I know what I said. It picked this up from somewhere; we don't know where, maybe from computers at Nintendo, at the company. As you can see, it stuck it in."

On the screen, the battle continued. The outcome was known, however; there was no way, within the context of the chess game, that the bishop could win. After a moment of sparring, the black-clad soldier drove his sword past the bishop's defense and into his midsection. Blood spurted out; the bishop, with a cry of agony and an expression to match, began to collapse. At the same time the screen flickered red.

Fletcher frowned, jerked, grabbed at his forehead; Bobby, however, hardly noticed. He was himself preoccupied with a sharp pain knifing through his head. He tried to ignore it and go on watching as the bishop, blood flowing freely, collapsed, twitched for a moment, and became still. The scene over, the chessboard reappeared; at the same time the pain Bobby had felt began to dissipate.

"I don't remember that, either," the red-haired man managed to say. He rubbed his head vigorously. "That's so realistic it's—disturbing. Is the Nintendo version like that?"

"It's closer than the sort of whimsical fights you see in PC Battle Chess. Like this? No. Not even close."

"Well, it's amazing. How's it being done?"

"I don't know." The bald man called another move. "I don't think anyone does."

"What?"

"Long story." He moved again, this time attacking one of the black pawns with a knight. The machine defended it and Fletcher moved onto its square to capture it, thereby initiating an exchange series that would require several moves to complete. "Watch the detail here," Fletcher said, unable to keep a certain enthusiasm out of his voice. "It's never the same twice."

The battle arena reappeared; the two men watched as Fletcher's knight graphically—and rather gorily—killed the pawn. The board returned, the machine's knight attacked Fletcher's, and again it switched to the arena.

This time the battle was a little more protracted, but as before the outcome was known—Fletcher's knight was going to lose. Fascinated, Bobby continued to watch fixedly.

At last, the black-clad knight struck a telling blow. The white knight's head snapped back, blood poured from under his helmet; the screen flickered and another severe pain shot through Bobby's head, straight back between his eyes. He blinked and groaned; on the screen the black knight struck again, and this time Bobby squirmed and closed his eyes momentarily with the intensity of the pain.

Opening them, he saw the bald man staring up at him wild-eyed. On the screen the chessboard had returned and the computer waited patiently for Fletcher to move again.

"You were feeling it too!" Fletcher cried.

Bobby scowled. "What? What are you—?"

"The pain! Just now! You felt sharp pains shooting through your head, didn't you?"

Making a face and rubbing his forehead, the red-haired man nodded. "Yeah, sorry, I know it's distracting, I don't know what's wrong with me—"

"No, you don't get it! I was feeling them too!"

Bobby stared at him openmouthed. "What?"

"Bobby," Fletcher asked in a low voice, "I gotta ask you—was ol' Charlie working on this machine when he had his whatever?"

"Well, yes—I thought I told you that—he was playing some game, I think maybe it was Ultima Underworld—"

Very slowly, Fletcher rose from his chair. As if fearing that something might somehow try to stop him, he reached for the thin cord connecting the computer's modem to the bank of telephone jacks Charlie had set up on his desk. Seizing it, he wrenched it hard, tearing the wire free from the plug.

"Hey!" Bobby protested half-heartedly. "What are you doing?"

"The system is off-line," the computer said. "Maximum efficiency cannot be achieved unless the system is on line."

Turning to Bobby, the bald man grinned. "We cannot," he said, "afford to take any chances. Not with this. All we can do is hope and pray that this motherfucker is here and that it didn't get out. And still, as I say that, I know goddamn good and well that it did."

Shaking his head, he reached around behind the computer and, one by one, unplugged the speakers, the keyboard, the monitor, and the power cord. Bobby said nothing; Fletcher then picked up the machine—and, without warning, hurled it across the room. It smashed against the wall, the case bursting open.

Startled, Bobby jumped up; Fletcher didn't give him a chance to speak. Crossing the room to where the carcass of the machine was lying, he began kicking it violently, knocking the cover free. Continuing his attack, he broke the hard drive free from its mountings and stomped it underfoot until thin little disks coated with magnetic media were spinning across the floor. The motherboard and the various daughter boards plugged into it received the same treatment.

"Jesus!" Bobby shouted. "What'd you do that for?"

Fletcher looked absolutely serious. "I'm afraid," he said, "that it was necessary to destroy this computer in order to save it."

22

Impatiently, Alex watched the numbers on the elevator change as it went down. In an effort to hurry it—an effort she knew would accomplish nothing at all—she pushed the button marked "SB" several more times. Why, she asked herself, did she have to go down here? Why the hell couldn't this Joshua Lent come up to her office?

No, sorry, he'd told her. I'm just too busy right now, I've got this DNA modeling program almost where I want it, it's only going to take a little longer, just a couple more hours. I'm sorry, Dr. Walton, I know it's important but I just can't spare the time. Yes, I did talk to Jim Madison. Yes, I understand the urgency. I'll be glad to talk to you if you come down here, Dr. Walton. I really am sorry.

The elevator bounced to a stop—at last—in the subbasement; the doors opened. Alex walked out rapidly and headed down the hall. It took her only a few seconds to find her goal, the "computer services" room. Within, there was an array of cubbies separated by blue portable partitions; belatedly, she realized that she had no idea which of the six or seven currently in use would be occupied by Joshua Lent, or even what Lent looked like. She began peering around, wondering if she was going to have to approach every male programmer there. At the same time, she became aware that the room had a distinct smell; more like a locker room than a computer lab.

At one of the cubbies close to the door, a noticeably thin, blond woman looked up, peering at her through huge glasses. "Can I help you?" she asked, a bit of irritation evident in her voice.

"Yes. I'm looking for Joshua Lent?"

The woman looked back at her screen, tapped a few keys. "Oh, yeah, Josh." She waved a hand carelessly. "Back there."

Alex frowned slightly. "I'm sorry, back where?"

Impatiently, the woman looked up. "Cubicles on the back wall," she almost snapped. "Turn right, third on your left."

"Thank you," Alex said formally. The woman, hard at work at her computer again, ignored her. With a shrug, Alex dismissed her and walked back to the last row of cubicles, turned right, and approached the third one as instructed.

It was occupied by a man, as thin as the woman at the front had been; his shirt hung loosely on bony shoulders. His pale hair was unkempt and his face showed a week's growth of beard. As she walked toward him, Alex noticed that there was a pile of litter around his feet: potato chip bags, cheese crumbs, styrofoam cups. She also noticed that he wore no socks; thin white ankles jutted from untied sneakers.

"Joshua Lent?" she asked as she drew close.

He reluctantly tore his eyes away from his computer screen. "Yeah? Oh, oh, you must be Dr. Walton. Pull up a chair." He glanced around, noticed the litter lying on both of the nearby chairs. Grabbing one, he swept the papers off onto the floor. "Pardon the mess," he said. "I've just been really busy lately. Haven't had time to clean it up."

After inspecting the chair and brushing off some remaining crumbs, Alex sat down. "What's happened to housekeeping?" she asked lightly. "Have they forgotten about you down here?"

He'd turned back to his monitor; a stylized image of a DNA double helix floated on the screen between command bars. "Oh, no, it's just that we've been so busy these days, and there was a—oh, an altercation I guess you'd say, between the janitors and Dana—Dana's the blond woman up front—anyway, they haven't been back. I dunno what's going on—"

That, Alex said to herself, is obvious. "Jim Madison," she said, "told me that you were using a program called Penultimate. I wanted to—"

Josh glanced at her. "You mean Jim isn't using it yet? I can't believe that! Man, it is the greatest thing to come out in—I don't know how long! Oh, yeah, we're all using it down here!" He shook his head. "I'll have to give Jim a call. Can't believe he's not onto it yet. I don't know how we ever got anything done without it!"

Alex pointed to the screen. "Is this it?" she asked. She leaned forward a little, closer to Josh; instantly her nostrils were assailed by a miasma of rank body odor. He breathed out, and an even worse cloud of foul breath struck her full in the face. She leaned back quickly.

"Yes and no," he told her. "This is a genetic imaging program, but it's running under Penultimate." He touched keys; the image rotated and changed. Very high quality, Alex noticed, very smooth motion. "It speeds everything up," Josh went on, "and it helps you out in all sorts of ways." He frowned. "It's sort of hard to explain if you aren't familiar with this imaging software. This used to be real slow, real cumbersome. Penultimate speeded it way up, made it a whole lot easier to use." He tapped more keys, moved his mouse around, clicked on some of the base pairs, watched the image change again. After a moment he seemed to have forgotten that Alex was there.

Alex watched too, a little uncertain of what question to

ask next. Clearly, Josh wasn't interested in talking to her.

But, just as clearly, there was more than a passing resemblance between his current state and that of many of the patients they were now seeing hospitalized.

"When did you get the Penultimate software?" she asked after a moment.

He tossed her a quick glance. "Oh, I dunno—six weeks ago, maybe. I have to tell you, I've gotten more done in those six weeks than I did in the previous six months!"

"Did you load it from an original disk? In the packaging?"

He frowned; deeply this time. Finally relinquishing his keyboard he turned to face her. "Why?" he demanded. "Are you doing some sort of investigation on pirated software?"

She laughed. "Oh, no, no. Nothing like that."

His faded blue eyes remained suspicious. "Well . . . all right, the answer is no. Dana's the one who had the original. She duped it for us. We've been meaning to go buy some more copies, but . . ."

"I know. You've been busy. I'm hearing that a lot lately. Mr. Lent, what day of the week is today?"

"Huh?"

"What day is it?"

"Oh . . . uh . . . Wednesday?"

"It's Friday." She took a notepad from her purse, opened it, began scribbling. "Can you tell me the date?"

"Well . . . gee whiz . . . you say it's Friday, so I guess it's the . . . eighth?"

"The twentieth. What month?"

"September?"

"October. Mr. Lent, how long has it been since you've eaten? A meal, I mean, not these snacks."

"Why are you asking me all this?"

"It's part of my research."

"Oh. I guess . . . a week?" The inflection in his voice was the same as if he were asking her how long it had been.

She didn't answer; she just made a note. "About how many hours a day have you been working?"

"Well—hey, I don't know, we've been so busy—I guess maybe I haven't been home for a day or two—"

"You haven't slept in two days?"

"Well—not in a bed. I snooze in the chair here some-times."

Christ, Alex told herself. He doesn't really see much of anything wrong with it, either. "Could I ask you, Mr. Lent, what exactly you're working on here?"

His manner, a bit somnambulent while he was answering her other questions, brightened. "Oh, sure. Here, look at this, tell me what you think." Steeling herself against the smell, she leaned forward and looked. On the screen, the DNA molecule divided itself in half, splitting down the cen-ter of the helix; other molecular groups floated in from the perimeter, forming a template. Again there was a division, again the graphics representing the bases floated in, attaching to the template; one did not fit but stuffed itself into place anyway.

"See?" he said, pointing it out. "See, it's a replication er-ror. The original program didn't do that unless you forced it to, but when it's running under the Penultimate host the errors come in with just about the same frequency they do in a typ-ical biological system. I didn't have to do a thing."

"How can it do that?"

"I dunno. Magic." Eyes shining, Lent watched the repli-cation proceed; a new DNA molecule had been formed, and it rotated slowly on the screen.

"What's this for?" Alex persisted.

He looked at her blankly. "For?"

"What research, I mean? Or is it clinical work?"

"Ohhh . . . oh. No, it's for a demo. A demo Dr. Lail is going to give to a seminar."

Alex had to restrain herself from goggling. "A demo?" she asked, her voice a bit choked. "A demo, for a class? You've been working day and night to get a demo together?"

"Well . . . I guess . . ." He sighed, leaned back in his chair, then almost lunged forward again. "It's just—fascinating. One thing leads to another. You know what I mean."

"No, I don't!"

"Uh, well, it's hard to explain."

"Mr. Lent, when is—Dr. Lail, did you say? When is the class he wants the demo for?"

"September 15."

"Mr. Lent, that was over a month ago!"

He looked around at her. "Really?"

"Really! I just told you it was October! Why are you still working on this?"

"Well . . ."

If you say "well" to me one more time, Alex told him silently, I'm going to slap you. "Mr. Lent, I—"

"It's just so fascinating!" he blurted, repeating himself. "I'm just about to—about to—figure out something about—"

This is getting me nowhere, Alex told herself. "Mr. Lent," she said patiently, "I feel I have a duty to inform you—we've been investigating some sort of a syndrome that has been landing people in the hospital with what's becoming alarming regularity. We believe that syndrome is connected to this program, Penultimate. It seems to me, Mr. Lent, that you're showing symptoms of the syndrome yourself."

"Yeah?"

"Yes."

"What should I do?"

She wrote Mark's name on a piece of paper, handed it to him. "You should," she said, "check in for observation. We've had a dramatic improvement in many of the patients while they're in the hospital."

He tossed the paper aside. "I'll do it," he said firmly. "Just as soon as I finish this." Turning back to the computer, he began working again, furiously. "It shouldn't take more than a few more hours . . ."

Alex wasn't going to give it up that easily. "Mr. Lent," she said firmly, "I want to be certain you understand the situation. We've seen several patients come in in very serious condition."

He looked back at her; his expression was not a particularly friendly one. "Dr. Walton, I told you I had some more work to do here, important work. I'd like to—"

"What you've told me," she interrupted coolly, "is that you aren't really working for the University at all anymore. The class this work was for was over weeks ago. That means that what you're doing now isn't for Dr. Lail. I assume he's the one who signs your time cards?"

"No. Dr. Jacobs. I work for the department."

"Has this work been authorized by Dr. Jacobs?"

He twisted his lip and began almost squirming in his chair. "Well—I'm sure he would if—"

"If he knew about it?"

His eyes darted around. "He does, he does know about it."

The lie was obvious; so was Lent's attitude of near-desperation. "Perhaps I should speak with him, then. You need to be seen immediately."

By now Josh looked like he was ready to break into tears. "I'll lose all this if I stop now! Please, it really is important, Dr. Jacobs will be the first to see that, as soon as I show it to him!"

She hesitated. She could definitely create a problem for him; she could cause him to lose his job. But she could not force him to come in for treatment, and that was really all she was interested in doing. "And how long will it take for you to save your work and properly shut the system down?"

He scowled. "Like I said, a couple of hours, maybe." He rooted around on his desk, came up with the paper she'd given him. "Dr. Roberts," he read. "Medical PDC. Okay, I'll come in. Whatever."

"In about two hours?"

"In about two hours."

You cannot force him, Alex, she reminded herself. "Two hours," she repeated, pointing a finger at him. He smiled gratefully, then turned back to his work. She watched him for a moment; when she was sure that he'd again forgotten about her presence she got up to leave. I suspect, she told him silently, that you've been saying "just a couple more hours" for quite a long time now—and no, I don't really believe you're going to appear in the Private Diagnostic Clinic in two hours. But I do believe, Mr. Lent, that we'll be seeing you again, quite soon.

In fact, she thought, looking around at the other people working in this particular lab, we're likely to be seeing most of you in the ER, after you collapse. It shouldn't take long.

23

"So you didn't find anything?" Jim asked.

Determined not to show how bitterly disappointed he was,

Mark carefully shook his head. "No," he answered. "Nothing you wouldn't expect to find on any nonsterile object." He threw a surreptitious glance at Alex, hoping she wouldn't take the opportunity to stuff this one down his throat.

She did not; clearly her thoughts were elsewhere. "There's no question in my mind," she said, "that this program is involved. All you have to do is go down to that computer lab. Those people down there have the same problems as our patients, there's no question about it."

"I might just have to do that," Jim muttered. "The guy you were describing does not sound like the Josh Lent I know. Not a bit."

I think you need to contact him immediately, Jim," Alex advised. "I made every effort to get him to come up to the PDC, but he hasn't shown up yet."

"I plan to," Jim responded. "As soon as we finish this meeting."

"We'd best get on with it, then," Mark said moodily. "Not that we're likely to accomplish much. If anyone has any idea how a program can be making people sick, I've haven't heard it yet. On the face of it it doesn't seem to make sense."

"That's not the only problem," Jim replied. "Remember, not all of your patients are using Penultimate."

"One thing at a time," Alex insisted. She picked up the box containing the program. "First, we need some answers about this."

"I'm still not sure," Mark said worriedly, "that we should just pop open the box and stick it in the computer. There might be—"

"I think it's time to give it up, Mark," Jim said with a grin. "This one isn't going to be cured with a pill." He took the box from Alex. "I shall now," he said dramatically, "take my life in my hands! Just like Walter Reed, I shall unflinchingly expose myself to the possibility of disease and death! You think they'll name a hospital after me?"

"If you die," Alex answered, "we'll make sure you get at least a ward."

"Better than nothing." He ripped the shrink-wrap off the box and dumped out the contents: one three-and-a-half-inch disk and a thin pamphlet. Holding the disk in his hand, Jim eyed it. "Doesn't look like much, does it?"

"What'd you expect?" Mark asked.

"A thicker book." He popped the disk into his computer and, using the keyboard, switched to that drive and ran a directory. The screen listed about ten files; except for one titled INSTALL.EXE, everything on the disk was encrypted.

"What's all that?" Mark inquired.

"Can't tell—they're compressed files. That's normal these days. The install routine will decompress them." He glanced at the two doctors. "Should we go for it?"

"Shouldn't you read the book first?" Mark asked.

"What, and spoil the fun?"

Mark shook his head. "You're the expert." Nodding, Jim ran the install program; all three watched while the screen changed color several times, informing them as it did that it was "expanding" certain files, "exploding" or "inflating" others, and "building" others still. Then, rather abruptly, it all stopped. They saw a message, "PNHOST successfully installed," followed by a slight buzz from the PC speaker, after which the "A:" prompt returned.

"Well, that was an anticlimax," Jim said mildly.

Mark leaned over his shoulder. "What happened?"

"Well, it says it's installed." He picked up the little booklet and thumbed through it. "Looks like that's what it's supposed to do. Now, according to this, it begins performing miracles. Let's see what we can see." He called up the SAS program, ran a statistical test on some data he'd previously saved. Scowling at his screen, he shrugged. "That," he observed, "ain't much. It maybe ran a hair faster. No big deal." Again he thumbed through the book. "Says here you have to give it a chance. How long do you think a chance takes?"

"You're asking us?" Mark commented.

"Not really." He exited the SAS program, returning to the "C:" prompt, and switched to the directory named "PNHOST." Executing a "DIR" command caused filenames to scroll down the screen; Jim stared at them. "Not one familiar thing," he muttered. "Except for this PN.EXE file, not one. All these extensions must be specific to this software. It'll take a while to figure out what all this is." He switched screens again, called up a program Mark didn't recognize; it asked for a filename and he offered it PN.EXE.

"I'm sorry," a tinny, raspy voice said from the little PC

speaker on the front of the machine. Jim, Alex, and Mark all jumped. "That program is proprietary. Are you having a problem with Penultimate?"

"How'd it do that?" Alex asked.

Jim didn't immediately answer; he was wholly focused on the machine. "Now that," he commented after a moment, "is bizarre! I'm not even running Penultimate! Or wait, wait, maybe I am—it's a host, after all—" He glanced at the screen, tapped "N" for "no" on the keyboard; his analysis program returned to its previous state.

He leaned back and stroked his beard. "This one—in case you didn't guess from that little voice synthesis bit—doesn't fit our favorite category of 'not unusual.' Let's look a little deeper." Exiting the analysis program, Jim used the DOS EDIT routine to examine the files entitled AUTOEXEC.BAT and CONFIG.SYS, the files that DOS- or Windows-based computers execute when they're first turned on. Looking at them, he whistled softly. "You son of a bitch," he muttered. "You changed them all around, didn't you? And didn't leave me a backup!" Grinning, he jerked open a drawer and pulled out a diskette. "But you don't catch this ol' boy," he went on, "without one of his own!" He slipped the diskette into the drive and pushed the RESET button. "We'll do a clean boot," he told Mark and Alex, "and then we'll see what's what here." He scowled as the machine started going through its boot-up sequence. "I don't understand how it engaged any of this stuff, though. If it rebooted I didn't see it do it."

The "A:" prompt reappeared; Jim switched back to the C drive and restarted the analysis program. When he tried to call in PN.EXE, though, the same tinny voice repeated its statement.

Jim literally hurled himself back in his chair. "You can't!" he cried. "You can't do that! I've clean-booted, you can't do that shit!" Bashing at the keys now, he again exited the analysis program and used the DOS EDIT to examine the AUTOEXEC file on the diskette.

"It changed this one too!" he cried. "Damn, that's going a little too far!"

"What's happened?" Mark asked, a look of concern on his face.

"It changed his backup," Alex supplied. "On the diskette. I have no idea how or why. I know that it means he can't get in to disable Penultimate. And while it's active it clearly isn't going to let him look at it."

"But look at it I will," Jim snarled. "It may have screwed up my clean boot, but I can by God make another one! And I'll write-protect it this time!" His face slightly red, he jerked the drawer open and snatched out another disk, then rolled his chair over to a different computer and flipped it on.

"Maybe we should leave you with it for a while?" Alex suggested gently.

"Good idea," Jim answered. "Come back this afternoon. I'll have something for you then." He jammed the disk into the new computer. "You can take that to the bank, by God!"

Mark started to say something else, but Alex, taking his elbow, steered him toward the door. He glanced at her; with her head she gestured toward the hallway.

"He's frustrated," she explained when they'd gotten outside. "And our being there makes it worse. He's used to having his own way with computers." She laughed lightly. "Not like the rest of us!"

"I try," Mark noted with a grin, "never to touch one. Sometimes I can't help it but I don't have to like it."

They walked on; her smile remained. "I know. I remember."

"Seems like you've gotten better acquainted with them."

She shrugged. "I have. I'm not in Jim's league, of course, but I can hold my own on one now."

"I'm impressed."

"You should be." They'd reached the end of the hall by then; she started to turn away, to head back toward the elevator that would take her to her own office. She hesitated, as if trying to make a decision.

Mark didn't give her a chance. "It's nearly one," he commented. "Want to have lunch?"

A mix of conflicting emotions played over her face; she looked at her watch, shook her head, then looked back at him. "Oh, well, okay."

"Hospital cafeteria?"

"It'll have to be. I have a patient at two, I don't have time to go out anywhere."

He grinned. "I suppose we'll survive it." He waited until she turned and moved up to his side, then started walking down the hallway in the direction of the elevator that would take them to the cafeteria.

"Are you sure," he asked, "that this business isn't eating up too much of your time?"

She shrugged. "I don't think it matters, Mark. This is important; you didn't see those people down in that computer lab!"

"Bad?"

"Really bad. Worse." She glanced at him. "There is something seriously wrong with these people, Mark. And it's the same thing, each case." Crinkling her nose, she told him about the odor emanating from Joshua Lent. "He couldn't've bathed within the past week. I don't think he's been out of that lab in—probably longer than that."

"But he wasn't able to tell you why?"

"No. He's just like all the rest, he didn't see himself as having a problem." She shook her head. "That guy Fletcher Engels was the only exception. Did I tell you I'd tried to find him?"

"No. I take it you had no success."

She sighed. "You take it right. We knew that he'd been evicted from his home; nobody I could find seems to have any idea where he went. The only other thing I had on him was his place of employment—a place called Compuware. I called them too, but I couldn't find—"

Mark stopped her. "Did you say Compuware?"

"You know the place?"

"No—no—it's just that the name, it's familiar somehow. I've seen it somewhere, I'm not sure where."

"It'll come back," she said confidently. "Things like that always do. Especially to Babar, the man who never forgets anything." Her cheeks suddenly flamed and she walked on, a bit more quickly, now finding something fascinating in the walls and doors they were passing.

Her comment took him completely by surprise. He almost kept pace with her, but allowed her to move a little ahead while he struggled with his thoughts; it required a certain effort to allow nothing of the rush of emotions he felt to show.

Early in their relationship, she'd commonly called him "baby"; a little later, impressed by his ability to recall trivia, she'd shifted it to "Babar"—for Babar the elephant—and thereafter it had become his pet name, used only by her—and, generally, only in the bedroom.

Her remembering meant a great deal to him. But her use of the name brought back so many memories, all at once, memories that were almost exquisitely painful. After a moment, he increased his pace, caught up with her; she took up her discussion of the patients where she'd left off, behaving as if nothing had happened.

This is what always happens, Mark told himself. You can never predict her; she always takes you by surprise and you're never ready for it. Never were, aren't now, and probably never will be.

24

Yet again, Alex came home to disappointment, to an empty driveway and a darkened house.

This is getting ridiculous, she told herself as she pulled the car inside. Just ridiculous; it's past nine already. Almost viciously, she pressed the button to open the garage door; she waited impatiently until it opened, pulled the car in, went inside. You aren't doing this again, Don, she said silently as she put down her briefcase and headed for the phone. Last night you didn't get in until after I'd gone to bed and I waited up past midnight. Not again. Snatching up the phone, she dialed his office.

This time, busy circuits did not interfere; as usual, Don answered on the second ring.

"It's Alex," she said, realizing too late that she didn't quite have a speech ready. "Where are you, Don?" She grimaced at her own words, realizing how stupid they sounded.

He answered in kind. "I'm at the office, Alex," he responded. "Working. Where'd you think I was? You called me, after all."

"Don, you need to come home. You're going to work yourself into the hospital."

There was a pause. "Look, Alex, it's just that I'm really busy. Believe me, this isn't going to go on for very much longer, I—"

Again and again, the same words. "Come home, Don," she interrupted. "The work'll wait. You need rest and I need you. You've put in eighteen-hour days and worked weekends for two weeks in a row, for Christ's sake! I can't see how you can function!"

"Oh, Alex, please . . . I'm so close to getting it, I'm so close! Can't you just—?"

"No. Come home, Don. It's late, it's after nine."

He sighed, very loudly. "All right, all right," he said finally. "Is there any food?"

"You haven't eaten?"

"No."

"I'll order take-out. It ought to be here by the time you get home. Chinese okay?"

"Anything's okay."

"Don't be late. It'll be cold if you're late; egg foo yung isn't edible cold."

"I'm on my way now." He hung up abruptly, leaving her to again stare at the phone. She dialed again, ordered the Chinese food. Once she'd done that, it hit her: for the first time in their marriage—at least the first time she could remember—he was doing what she wanted rather than the other way around.

Sitting down in her favorite chair, she stared at the floor for a long time, reflecting. Almost every time they had a disagreement, he presented arguments that made her own position seem untenable; he was very expert at that. It really wasn't, she told herself, manipulation; by the nature of her profession and by her own inclination she was accustomed to trying to see things from another person's viewpoint, whereas he was more comfortable imposing his own.

She shook her head. It's bizarre, she told herself, bizarre. You find yourself in a forest and decide you don't want to be there, so you walk out. Then you walk in among a bunch of trees and everything looks just fine, it's just where you always wanted to be.

Lost in thought, she didn't hear the doorbell; after it had chimed several times she jumped up and ran for the door. The Chinese restaurant they commonly ordered from did not normally deliver; Don had, by virtue of generous tips, convinced them to make an exception in his case. Alex wasn't altogether comfortable with the privilege, but it was certainly a convenience, which she did not want to jeopardize by keeping the delivery boy—the owner's son—waiting.

He looked a bit impatient when she finally jerked the door open; she smoothed things over with profuse apologies, friendly smiles, and an extra-large tip. After carrying the food back to the dining room she put plates and silverware on the table, opened a bottle of a wine she knew was one of Don's favorites, and continued to wait. At last she heard his car pull into the drive.

"I'm glad," she said as he came in, "that you could make it." There was just a touch of frost in her voice, a calculated touch. "It's about time we had a dinner together again." She poured wine into two glasses.

Without taking off his coat, he sat down across from her. He looked, she noticed, more haggard than she'd ever seen him; his eyes were red-rimmed and his mouth was drawn and tight. "Look, I'm sorry," he opened. "You just have to understand, Alex, this is really a hard time."

She spooned rice onto her plate. "You've often told me," she replied, "that all times are hard times when you're the CEO of a major company. Don, that doesn't mean you have to kill yourself working! If you wind up in the hospital, what good are you going to be to Lehmann?"

"Not gonna wind up in the hospital," he mumbled. He picked up the little white carton containing the rice and dumped the remainder onto his own plate. "It's gonna be all right, Alex. You just have to trust me."

She stopped eating and watched him for a minute. This was not the Don she knew; she could not remember a time when he'd spoken like this. "Don, are you all right?" she asked, her concern more than evident in her voice.

He pushed his already unkempt hair back, mussing it even more. "I told you," he answered mildly, "I will be. As soon as I—uh, solve these problems. You know what I mean."

"No! I don't have the slightest idea!"

He sighed, used his fork to spread out the rice on his plate, then spooned egg foo yung atop it. She waited patiently while he gulped a couple of bites of the food; it seemed he was terribly hungry. "I told you already," he said at last. There wasn't a trace of anger or irritation in his tone. "There are problems at work. Money problems. I'm trying my damnedest to get them worked out, and I've almost got it." He held up his hand, showed her a three-millimeter gap between thumb and forefinger. "I'm this close," he went on. "This close!" He shook his head. "That's why I didn't want to leave, that's why . . ." He closed his eyes for a moment, then opened them again and stared at her; he looked like he was slightly drunk. "Tomorrow," he said. "Tomorrow, I'll get it all straightened out. Things'll be okay. There's nothing for you to worry about, Alex." Looking down at his plate, he seemed to realize again that there was food there; he immediately started shoveling it into his mouth, his manner almost crude. Alex, more than a little shocked, saw a few rice grains escape from his lips and cling to his chin for a moment before dropping to the floor.

She put her own fork down. "I'm not so sure, Don!"

His mouth full, he looked up. A suspicious look flashed across his face. "Why?" he gurgled over the food.

"Why? Why? Look at you! You act like you're starving, you're mumbling, you look god-awful! Don, what's going on? Didn't you have lunch?"

He looked sheepish. "No."

"You were gone before I got up this morning. You did have some breakfast, didn't you?"

"Ah—well, sure."

"What?"

"Coffee. I had some coffee."

"That's all?"

"I guess . . ."

She stared in disbelief. "Well, what about last night? Don, tell me you took a break for dinner, at least!"

"Well . . ."

She threw herself back in her chair. "Are you trying to tell me you haven't eaten in twenty-four hours? Don! What are you thinking about?" Leaning forward again, she pointed an accusing finger. "You remember that problem I told you about, at the hospital, the one Mark and I are working on? All those patients are showing a pattern of not eating, not sleeping, not doing anything, because for some reason they're addicted to their computers! I swear to God, if you'd been sitting at a computer keyboard this whole time I'd think you were one of them!''

He flashed her a strange enigmatic look, then went back to his dinner. ''Well, I'm not one of your patients,'' he said, irritation creeping into his voice. ''You just have to take my word for it, Alex. This'll all be over soon. Nothing's going to happen.''

''Happen?'' She'd picked up her fork, and now she banged it back down. ''Don, what's not going to happen? You're really worrying me now!''

''Don't worry.'' His tone was flat. After scraping the last morsels of food off his plate, he gulped the rest of the glass of wine; never, ever, had she seen Don gulp fine wine. He pushed back from the table and stood up. ''I have to make a phone call,'' he said. He peered into the cartons. ''There's no more?''

''No. I could make you something else—some eggs or something—''

''No, don't bother.'' Turning on his heel, he left her sitting and staring after him as he headed off toward the small room at the back of the house he occasionally used as a home office. It took a moment for her to break free from her paralysis, but when she did she followed him. I am not through with you, Donald Royce, she said to herself as she walked.

By the time she reached the office, he was already on the phone. ''Yes,'' he was saying. ''Yes, what's the price now?'' He paused, listened; she saw him shake his head. ''Damn it,'' he muttered passionately. ''God damn it! I don't understand, I just don't!'' There was another pause; he nodded. ''Yes, yes, I know. No, I'll cover it; what choice do I have, Haji? Right. First thing in the morning, okay? Yeah, right. I'll call you. You know what to do, right? I'll get back to the projections as soon as I possibly can. Look, thanks, Haji. You've been patient, I appreciate that. Yes, I know there're limits.'' He hung up the phone; Alex, not wanting him to think she'd been eavesdropping, retreated toward the dining room. As she left, she saw him slumping over the phone, looking as if some enormous weight was bearing him down.

Belatedly, she realized that when she'd been telling him about the patients, she'd mentioned Mark's name. She hadn't meant to do it, she'd been careful to avoid doing it. It wasn't something she wanted to discuss right now. Don, she was sure, would not have missed it even if he hadn't commented on it.

At least, the old Don wouldn't've missed it. This Don, this harried and distracted Don—this Don might. She had no way of knowing.

25

"You'll have to excuse me," Jim was saying. He shook his head. "I am not used to this—I'm hardly alive at seven in the morning! I don't know why you people have to schedule early meetings, I don't normally come in until nine."

Mark—sitting at his place at the conference table, Alex directly across from him, Gus by his side, a couple of residents they'd been working with farther down the table—watched Jim carefully as he, with some obvious effort, tried to collect himself to begin his presentation. He looked exhausted; Mark couldn't help worrying about him. He'd not yet given up all notions of some microbe using the Penultimate disks as a fomite—an inorganic disease carrier.

On the other hand, two days would be too quick for most pathogens to begin causing symptoms. Besides that, Alex looked almost as exhausted as Jim, and she, as far as he knew, had no more exposure to the disks than he had himself.

Unless she'd been exposed in that computer lab, he fretted, when she'd gone to see Joshua Lent—

"I'm here," Jim said, pulling Mark's attention back to him, "at this ungodly hour, to give you folks a rundown on Penultimate." He shuffled papers. "Now, first of all, if I swamp you with computerese you stop me, okay? I want all this to be clear to everybody. Don't hesitate to ask questions. I won't have all the answers, but—"

"The first thing we need to know," Gus cut in, "is what sort of program this Penultimate is."

Jim clasped his hands together in front of himself. "Well," he began, "that in itself isn't going to be easy. I guess you've all read the blurb on the package—it says the program is supposed to give your computer some 'common sense.' " He shook his head, looked down at his papers. "I didn't believe that at first. Now I'm not so sure."

Gus already looked frustrated and irritated. "You still haven't told us—"

"I'm getting to it, I'm getting to it. Penultimate is, basically, a cache." He looked around; no one looked confused. "Now, there're a lot of caching programs; SMARTdrive, PC-KWIK, Lightning, and so on. They all work on the same principle, that access to memory is much, much faster than access to any disk, and that whatever's been called once is liable to be called again. Penultimate's different in that it caches the operator's input to disk—and, I presume, from there to memory—as well." He went on, explaining the process in a little more detail.

"Excuse me, Jim," Mark interrupted, "but all this is pretty much what you said about it when we were first looking at the box. You said then you thought it was a gimmick."

Jim nodded vigorously. "I remember saying that. Mark, old boy, was I ever wrong!" He laughed. "People were telling me this was the greatest invention since beer. I didn't believe it. In this case, Mark, 'people' were right and ol' Jimmy was wrong. This is, in fact, the greatest thing since beer."

"I think," Gus said drily, "that you'd better explain that."

"Penultimate," Jim went on, "isn't like any other program I've ever seen. There's a lot of good software out there these days, well-constructed stuff, but you can't call it brilliant; the ideas and principles have been around for a long time. There're a few that are, that use old ideas in new and innovative ways. New ideas, new concepts—those are pretty rare. Penultimate's in a league by itself; it's more than brilliant, I don't know what to call it. The programmer who put this together has got to be some sort of super-genius; I sure as hell would like to meet him!" Shaking his head, he stopped.

"I still don't understand, Jim," Mark said gently.

"That's because I'm just ranting, I haven't told you anything yet," Jim responded, drawing a loud sigh from Gus. "You have to understand, this one has blown me away. It—"

"Could you please get to the point!" Gus demanded.

"Okay. The point is, this Penultimate package is light-years ahead of anything else I know of. It has an AI—'artificial intelligence'—engine, it learns what its operator is trying to do. How it does that is beyond me. Right now I can't begin to explain the how, all I can tell you is the what."

"That's a good place to start," Gus noted.

"It's where we end, too," Jim replied grimly. "When I started exploring the Penultimate system, I really couldn't tell that it was doing much of anything—my programs ran faster and smoother, but not so much so as to impress me. Good but not great.

"Then, gradually, things started to change—as it got used to me, I guess—as it started building its files. I tried to look at those files, and I can't make any sense of them—I can't even be sure I'm looking at what I think I'm looking at. Penultimate uses some weird compression algorithm on both storage files on the disk and executable files in memory; it uses these tiny little footprints—'footprint' being the amount of space a program uses on the hard disk or in memory—and manages to do the most amazing things with them."

"Like what, Jim?" Mark asked.

He shrugged. "Like, for instance, the way it handles graphics. I have a nice, fast, state-of-the-art computer; high-speed CPU, VESA bus, all that good stuff. It used to take it a second or so to do a full-screen graphic in 24-bit mode. Once the Penultimate system started kicking in, I could call up a 24-bit BMP and have it appear instantly—no visible delay at all. From everything I know about SVGA, about video cards in general, that just plain old isn't possible. A week ago I would've laughed at you if you'd suggested there was a way to do it, I would've sat you down and written you a bunch of formulas and demonstrated to you that there just isn't a way to issue that many bits to a video card that fast."

"You said," Mark told him with a grin, "to stop you if you were burying us in computerese. I have no idea what a BMP is, or a VESA, or a 24-bit mode, or—"

"A BMP," Alex put in, "is a type of graphic file. One of God knows how many. VESA is a term describing the video bus, the way the computer communicates with the video card which then puts out a signal to the monitor." She looked back at Jim. "You can't be telling us this system is doing the impossible."

"No. Obviously it isn't impossible, it's happening. Whoever wrote this thing has invented a way—at least that's my guess—of compressing that data. Data compression is the rule now; it's just that Penultimate is so far ahead of anything else—anything else that I know of, anyway—that it's just unbelievable."

"So it's a good program," Gus grumbled. "A very good program. A work of genius. So what? How does it tie in with CAS?"

Jim looked back down at the table. "I don't know."

"No ideas?" Mark probed.

"Not at the moment." He looked up again. "Don't forget, I told you there was a problem with all this. You have patients that show every sign of CAS and haven't been using Penultimate."

"Still," Alex insisted, "it's hard to imagine that there isn't some sort of a connection. Have you gone to see your friend Joshua yet?"

Jim grunted. "Yes, I have. And, from what you've told me about CAS, I have to agree, it looks like he's got it. I can't tell him anything, though; he isn't listening to me any more than he listened to you. Dana Perleman is even worse off. You might've seen her, Alex. A blond?"

"Yes, I did. She's the one who told me where to find Joshua."

"Would you believe me if I told you that a couple of months ago she was bubbly, gregarious, fun-loving, and a little overweight?"

Alex looked shocked. "No!"

"She was. She's gone down the drain like I've never seen anyone go down the drain. I expect she'll be one of your patients any day now. And Josh won't take much longer." He shook his head. "I swear to God, I tried to talk to them. I even threatened them. Nothing has any effect, they just can't wait to get back to their computer."

"And yet," Alex inquired, "you still can't believe that this program is the cause?"

"Determining the cause," Jim pointed out, "isn't really my role here. That's for you guys to decide. I'm saying that there's a logical problem. If you have patients who aren't using Penultimate and they have CAS, then Penultimate is not the cause—or rather, let's say, not the only cause—of CAS."

"That," Alex continued, "might be the key. Not the only cause. I think we can say with some confidence that there's something about computers that's causing this. You've said that the Penultimate program makes the computer do a lot of things a lot better. Maybe it's just facilitating; maybe Penultimate's making whatever is the cause work better."

"That," Jim agreed, "is a real possibility. The problem is, it also puts us back at square one. If Penultimate is a mere facilitator, then what's the cause?"

"Some other program?" Mark asked.

"No," Jim said firmly. "There isn't anything else that's in common here. You guys gave me a list of the software your patients were using when they started having a problem, and there's a wide variety—which is to be expected, since they're using a variety of applications. More, not one of those programs is unusual—Microsoft Word, WordPerfect, Lotus— those things have been around for a long time. Some of the stuff running in the background is fairly recent, but a lot of it is awfully standard—I'm talking here about operating systems or environments like Windows, DOS, and OS/2, as well as some of the common TSRs like QEMM and Sidekick. Penultimate is the only thing that's new and different."

"How new is it?" Gus asked.

"It was released seven months ago."

"How can you know," Gus mused, "how rare it is? I mean, you must have some idea, or else there wouldn't've been a way for you to come up with any statistical numbers—"

"No, you're right. There're computer journals that publish sales figures for various programs, that's where the numbers come from. There're millions and millions of copies of Windows out there, even if every single patient was using Windows you'd be hard pressed to say it suggested anything, that software is just too common. The same is true of WordPerfect and Lotus. But the Penultimate software is new; as of the last quarter the company reports around sixty thousand copies sold. Now, with that, I've got something I can work with; how does the percentage of the CAS patients using Penultimate compare with the total number of computer users using Penultimate? You really don't need to do stats to tell you it's way high, far higher than you'd expect from a chance distribution.''

"I can see your point," Gus agreed. He shook his head. "It still isn't easy for me to believe that a computer program is causing these problems.''

"We're not saying that, not quite yet," Alex cautioned. "Right now we're just looking at possible relationships." She looked back at Jim. "Anything else?''

He shook his head. "Not at the moment. I'm going to be doing more work on the program, I'd like to understand it better myself. I'll keep you posted on what I come up with.'' He paused, looked thoughtful. "Maybe I'll even call up the folks at Compuware, see if I can—''

Mark sat straight up in his chair. "What?" he barked sharply. "What'd you say?''

Jim looked startled. "What do you mean? I—''

"Compuware," Alex said. "He said, 'Compuware.' ''

"That's where I heard that name before!" Mark almost yelled.

Jim scowled at the two of them. "Explain, please?''

"Did we tell you about a patient—a possible CAS—by the name of Fletcher Engels?'' Alex asked.

"No—oh, wait, yes. Brought in by the cops for a psychiatric evaluation? You'd said you thought he might know something about all this.''

"Right. Alex told me she tried to find him—at his former place of employment. Compuware!''

Jim arched his eyebrows. "Interesting. Very interesting.''

"And not," Mark went on, "a coincidence. I think we're safe in saying that!''

26

"**A**ir-eek! You're back!''

Sourly, saying nothing, Eric stared at the screen. Yeah, he

told the smiling and seemingly delighted sprite silently. I'm back. After being booked by the police for assault and battery, after a night in jail and a few days in County General, after laying out most of my savings to post bail, I'm back. I don't know how long I'm back for; I've lost my job and I've got lawyer's fees and hospital bills—mine and Dave's both—and everything else. At least, though, I've got some distance from you, I can view you a little more rationally. You're a computer graphic, you aren't a real person. Cyberia is a computer simulation, it isn't a real place. I haven't been there, I haven't been anywhere.

His silence dragged on; Kyrie looked concerned. "Air-eek? Is something wrong?"

"Yeah," he said. "Something's wrong. Pretty much everything's wrong."

Kyrie smiled appealingly. "Can I help?"

"Maybe. I don't have a job anymore, and it's your fault."

She looked shocked. "My fault?"

"Your fault. But, like I say, maybe you can help on that score. Whoever made you is sitting on a gold mine, and I might just be able to help get that ore out—and maybe get some of it for myself. I need to know more about you."

"About me?"

"Yes."

She laughed. "There is nothing to know, Air-eek! I am here for you; I can be whatever you want me to be, I can take you anywhere you want to go. All you need to do is ask."

He smiled darkly. "Anywhere I want to go?"

"Of course! Shall we return to Cyberia?"

"No. Let's go to—oh, hell, it doesn't matter, Mexico!"

"Where in Mexico?"

"Mexico City."

Kyrie, who'd been sitting on a rock beside a stream in a lovely forest glade, stood up. She was dressed as she had been the last time he'd seen her, a tiny wispy skirt and nothing else. She turned; one of the ribbonlike paths was there, right beside her. "Come on!" she encouraged, stepping onto the path.

As always, he heard his own footfalls, saw the screen rock slightly as if he were walking along behind her. Unconsciously he pushed slightly on his mouse; his speed increased until he was alongside her. She smiled at him and walked on; a moment later the path ended, tapering into and fusing with the ancient pavement surrounding the cathedral in the center of Mexico City. It wasn't empty; the streets were full of cars, people were walking by in various directions, the sounds of conversation in Spanish filled the air.

"We're here," she informed him. "Where would you like to go now?"

"I just wanted to be somewhere that wasn't surreal," he told her. "Now, I want to talk."

"Here?"

"Why not?"

"Very well. What do you want to talk about, Air-eek?"

"About what you are." He pointed a finger at the screen as if she could see it. "The first day I came on to this BBS, I asked you how you could hear me, and you explained it. You—damn it, this is hard, I don't want to keep talking to you like you were a fucking human being!"

Her look was one of pure innocence. "Why, Air-eek? Don't I look like a fucking human being?"

"Yes! That's the problem! You look like a human being, you talk like a human being, you act like a human being! Maybe you should look like a robot or something!"

She looked doubtful. "Really?"

"Really!"

She sniffed. "Very well." As he watched, her form silvered, became more angular; in computerese, she "morphed." When the transformation was over, she bore a resemblance to the old Kyrie, except that she was made of overlapping metal plates. Her eyes were lenses. "Is this what you wanted?" she asked, her voice unchanged.

"Not quite. Talk like a robot too."

"Very. Well. I. Will. Do. So."

Eric grinned. Better, he told himself. Much much better. "Now," he said, "I want some explanations."

"Please. Specify."

He frowned, not too sure of the question he wanted to ask. At the beginning, Eric, he told himself. "First off, where is this bulletin board located? The address, I mean?"

"There. Is. No. Location."

"Don't bullshit me. There has to be; there has to be a server computer."

"There. Is. No. Server."

"That," he said with a laugh, "is a lie, Kyrie! I called a phone number to hook into this system, that phone line has to be connected to a modem and that modem has to be connected to a computer, and that computer is the server! What I want to know is, where is it? Who's running it?"

"There. Is. No. Server."

He resisted the urge to yell at the screen. "Then where did my phone call go?"

"The. Telephone. Connection. Is. To. The. Net."

"The Net?" he echoed blankly.

"The. Internet."

He paused. What in the hell? "It still," he insisted, "has to be going to a computer somewhere, some computer has to be sending out these graphics! Where is it?"

"That. Question. Cannot. Be. Answered. In. That. Form."

"I don't understand."

"No. You. Do. Not."

"Let's try it this way," he snarled. "Where are the images I'm seeing coming from?"

"Mexico. City."

"Bullshit!" He was now screaming at it. "Bullshit, bullshit, bullshit! This is a file on Mexico City, I know that, do you think I'm an idiot? Where's the graphic coming from?"

"Mexico. City."

"What about you?" he hissed. "Are you in Mexico City?"

There was a slight pause. "No."

"Where are you, then?"

"I. Am. In. Durham. North. Carolina."

He smiled and let out the breath he'd been holding. Nailing you, he thought. "Where," he asked, his voice smooth, "in Durham, North Carolina, are you? Address, please."

"Three. Six. Zero. Five. Spruce. Street. Durham. North. Carolina. Two. Seven. Seven. Zero. One."

"That's my address!" he shrieked. "That's my own address, you fuck! That's where I am! My computer is not the goddamn server, for Christ's sake!"

"There. Is. No. Server."

"There has to be! There has to be a server, there has to be someone running this damned bulletin board! It doesn't run itself, for Christ's sake! Who gets the money? Who—"

He stopped himself. Scowling deeply, he rose from his chair and went to the cluttered desk across the room, began thumbing through the stacks of bills, ripping open any credit card statements; bits of paper littered the floor, falling like light snow.

After a moment he turned back to the computer, where the Kyrie-robot stood immobile in front of the cathedral in Mexico City. "There's no bill from anybody," he said plaintively. "Nothing. I don't remember ever being asked for my name, for a credit card, any of that stuff . . ."

"This. Service. Is. Free." Kyrie staccatoed.

"Free?" he echoed dumbly. "Free? Somebody rigs up a BBS this good and gives it all away free?"

"Yes."

"Oh, come on! There's a cost somewhere, don't try to kid your old 'Air-eek' here! I know better than to believe in free lunches!"

"Do. You. Want. Lunch?"

He clenched his fists, forced himself not to scream again. Even like this, he told himself, she's getting to you. With exaggerated slow movements, he returned to the computer and sat down again.

"Somebody," he said quietly, "is making money off this system. Somebody, somewhere."

There was, gratifyingly, another pause. "Yes," the answer came—at last.

Eric rubbed his hands together almost gleefully. "Who?"

"I. Cannot. Give. You. That. Information."

Again he had to restrain himself. "Oh, yes, you can! Oh, yes! You said anything! Anything! Now I want that name, do you hear me?"

The Kyrie-robot was unperturbed and implacable. It repeated the same sentence. Eric, losing whatever control he had, yelled at it. This time, as it started to answer—giving the same answer yet again—the screen began rocking back and forth noticeably. The people around them, who before had been walking calmly, began running in all different directions, expressions of fear or concern on their faces.

"What's going on?" Eric asked, having again forgotten that he was talking to a computer. "What's wrong?"

The Kyrie-robot looked around. "There. Is. An. Earthquake. Here." she answered. "Five. Point. One. On. The. Richter. Scale. The. Epicenter. Is. At. Tacuba. We. Had. Best. Go. For. Now."

Twisting his mouth, Eric stared. What in the hell now? Kyrie, ignoring him for the moment, turned; the ribbon path was again visible. She reached out a metallic hand to him, then stepped onto the path; he could hear two sets of footsteps, his and another, a heavy mechanical set. A couple of seconds later she stopped, having brought them to a sort of a nexus of ribbon paths. Again involuntarily, he moved his mouse, looked around; he could see thousands of paths, running in all directions—including straight up and straight down. Around the paths was a neutral blue, the sort of blue used for special-effects backdrops in Hollywood.

"What was that all about?" Eric demanded.

"There. Was. An. Earthquake." she repeated, proceeding to give him again the data about the strength of the quake and the epicenter.

"Oh, come on!" he snarled at the screen. "You're just trying to dodge my question."

"No. There. Was. An. Earthquake."

"You're a sprite and I'm watching this on a monitor! How the fucking hell can an earthquake hurt us? What do you take me for, an idiot?"

"No. The. Earthquake. Could. Have. Caused. Loss. Of. Signal. Continuity."

"No, come on, it—" He stopped as the meaning of those words, at least one possible meaning, dawned on him. "What? What?"

The Kyrie-robot repeated its words; Eric hardly heard them. He'd gotten up, crossed the room, and flipped on his TV.

"—Special bulletin," the announcer was saying. "An earthquake, 5.1 on the Richter scale, rocked Mexico City a few moments ago. Seismologists say the epicenter was near the town of Tacuba. Damage is reported to be very light, and there are no reports of fatalities or serious injuries . . ."

Eric's head snapped around; he stared at the Kyrie-robot

who waited passively on the screen. He didn't say a word to her, he just walked to the computer and, with a firm hand, switched it off. "No more," he mumbled. "I can't take anymore. No more." Backing away, he sank into a litter-covered easy chair. "I'm not calling you again. Never again. This is too spooky."

And yet, even as he mouthed these words, he knew he was lying.

27

Bobby held out the phone. "It's for you," he said.

Looking a little startled—and then more than a little suspicious—Fletcher put down the ham sandwich he was eating and gazed steadily at his new employer. "You wanna find out who it is?"

Bobby's mouth twisted. "No. It's for you. Fletcher Engels. What am I, your secretary?"

"Nobody," he reminded the younger man, "is supposed to know I'm working here."

"Well, somebody does!" the red-haired man snapped, exasperated. His patience had worn thin, ever since Fletcher had destroyed a two-thousand-dollar computer and refused to explain why. "You want to see who it is?"

"Not really." As if it might literally bite him, the bald man reached out and took the receiver. "This is Engels," he said after another pause.

"You've been on-line again, Fletch," a smooth voice said. "That's a violation of our agreement."

Fletcher's eyes dropped closed. "I knew it was you," he said softly. "I knew it. Penny told you where I was, didn't she?"

"You know she did. You can't fool her, Fletch. She's way too good."

"I know that. She picked me right out. Look, actually, I'm not sorry she did; I was wondering if I should call you. The ante just got upped, it got way upped."

The voice burst into laughter. "Oh, come on, Fletch! You haven't changed a bit, you're still—"

"No, no, you need to listen to me, for once. There's a variant out, a GAMOD variant; I tried to destroy it, I—"

"You tried to destroy it? How, Fletch? How'd you try? A hunter-killer? I won't let you do that, Fletch."

Now the bearded man laughed. "No, not a hunter-killer. More primitive. I smashed the computer it was in."

"Oh. What's the problem, then?"

"I think it probably got out."

"It was on line?"

"Uh-huh."

"Well, I'd say there's a good chance you're right, then. But I have to ask again, what's the problem?"

The bald man ground his teeth. "The problem," he gritted into the phone, "is that this variant is a lethal one! I have every reason to believe it killed the technician that was working here!"

More laughter, a raucous sound this time, erupted from the phone. "Killed? Oh, come on! Are you serious?"

"You bet I am."

"Fletch, you are a wild man!" The voice suddenly dropped lower, became more serious. "Don't you go spreading a wild rumor like that around, Fletch. I'll have your head; I'll have it sitting on my desk the way Idi Amin used to."

"There are some similarities between you and Idi, you know."

"Not many. That is one, though. I don't believe in giving my enemies a chance to come at me a second time."

"I'm not your enemy. I tried to tell you that before."

"You're Penny's enemy."

"Yes, but—"

" 'The enemy of a friend is an enemy.' Elementary logic, Fletch. Not your strongest suit, I know."

"Your logic falls down on the first step. Penny isn't your friend; she isn't anyone's friend. She isn't interested in anybody except Penny. Don't you know that by now?"

"I don't accept that; that isn't the way it is. When this is all done with, the world'll be a totally different place, Fletcher! You'd better be ready for it; you'd better be ready or you'll be swept aside, you'll end up—"

"I know, I know. In history's garbage can. Your favorite saying. Man, I can't see how you can believe that this is going to be a better world when Penny gets through with it! You have got to be crazy!"

"We've had this discussion before, Fletch," the voice answered coolly. "Many times. You should know by now you aren't going to change my mind; I've accepted that I'm not going to change yours, and that means we're wasting time discussing it. I just have a few things I want to say—"

"You mean a few threats."

"If you wish. Stay off-line, Fletch. Stay off line and keep your mouth shut. Things happen. You should know that, some of them have already happened to you."

There was a moment's silence. "You mean my bank account? The eviction? The cops?"

"You can't say I didn't warn you."

Fletcher's jaw worked. "How? How'd you pull that off?"

There was a brief harsh chuckle. "I didn't. I wouldn't; such things are illegal, Fletch. Tampering with someone's bank account? With the records at a realty company? There're laws."

"You son of a bitch. You bastard. I'm going to get—"

"You aren't going to get anyone; you aren't going to do anything. If you try, you'll regret it—and you won't succeed. Now I'm going to tell you again, Fletch; behave yourself. Keep your mouth shut and stay off line. You have yourself a new job, and by now you probably have an apartment, too. Don't screw up. Just sit back and watch it all unfold. It shouldn't take more than a few more weeks."

"No, look, you have to listen to me—"

"No. You have to listen to me. If I hear you've been on line again, there'll be more trouble."

"That's a threat, I could call—"

"No one. There's no evidence. If there was it could disappear. You understand me?"

Fletcher sighed. "Perfectly."

"Good. Good-bye, Fletch. Best of luck in your new job." There was a click; Fletcher's arm, his hand still holding the phone, dropped onto his lap.

"Who," Bobby demanded, "was that? What the hell was that all about?" He'd only heard one side of the conversation, but that had been enough.

After a rather long interval, Fletcher looked up at him. "You," he said, "don't want to know. You don't want to know anything about this shit. Believe me, Bobby."

"You said—if I heard you right you said—that you believed that the computer killed Charlie?"

The bald man shook his head. "Not the computer. The software. Big difference, Bobby. I didn't smash that computer because it was a killer; I smashed it so there'd be no chance of that software variant getting out—or as little as possible—" he stopped, shook his head sadly. "I just got carried away. There's no chance that mutant developed here. It is out, I'm almost positive."

The red-haired man looked doubtful. "It's hard for me to believe," he said slowly, "that a computer actually killed somebody—killed Charlie. And yet, there wasn't anything wrong with Charlie. And I did feel that pain—"

"See what I mean?"

"But Fletcher, how? How can it happen?"

He shook his head. "I don't have any idea. This one's new to me too. You can bet I'll be trying to find out, as soon as I can figure out a halfway safe way. I think it had to do with that flashing."

"Fletcher, what is this all about?"

"I told you, it isn't a good idea for me to explain—"

Bobby stood with his hands on his hips. "Now look, Fletcher; you're working for me and you're an old friend of mine—half of what I know about computers I learned from you! I think that makes it my business!"

"Maybe. All right, suppose I promise you this: when the time is right I'll explain—at least the parts I know about. Once it's settled, once I can see for sure which way it's going to go down." He sighed, looked down at his lap, rolled the phone around in hands that looked more like those of a day laborer than a programmer. "You ever read comic books when you were a kid, Bobby?"

"Comic books?"

"Uh-huh."

"Well, sure. Who didn't? Hell, I still do, sometimes."

"Yeah. So do I. Batman, Green Arrow, Spider-man, shit like that. You know how it is in comic books, Bobby? The

145

old Batman has discovered some plot that'll destroy the whole world if he doesn't stop it. He's the only one, the only one who can. If he fails—well, it's just unthinkable. Nobody could say what might happen, how bad it might be.''

"Yeah, I know the plot line you're talking about. I still don't get it.''

"Well, let me put it this way. You got a spare costume with a cape and pointy ears laying around?''

28

"**S**o?'' Alex asked. ''What'd they have to say?''

Mark shook his head. ''Not much. Nothing useful, anyway.'' He shuffled papers, picked up one with some hastily scribbled notes on it, stared at it for a minute. ''Jim talked with a—let's see—I can't even read my own handwriting anymore!—Fred Layton—''

Alex looked impatient. ''Yes? And he said?''

"He said nothing at all, really. He told Jim that Penultimate is proprietary and he couldn't comment on any of the internal workings of it. He said we'd have to see the president of the company—who's also, apparently, one of their chief programmers.''

"So you called the president. Right?''

"Right, naturally. He wasn't in.''

She glanced at his phone. ''Have you tried again?''

"Well, no.'' He sighed. ''You know how it is, Alex. There's always something going on, always some demand for your time.''

"I do know that.'' She smiled. ''Pick up the phone, Mark. There's no time like the present.''

He grunted and, obediently, picked up the phone. ''Your motto. I know. He probably still isn't in, though.'' After staring fixedly at the sheet of paper for a few seconds, he dialed.

Alex watched him silently as he waited. ''Yes,'' he said after a moment. ''Yes, this is Dr. Mark Roberts at Duke Hospital. Is Mr. Drew Thompson in, please?'' Alex noted the name and frowned. Maybe, she told herself, things were coming together a little.

"Yes, Mr. Thompson?" Mark was saying. He looked up at Alex and winked. "Yes, as I told your receptionist, I'm Dr. Mark Roberts, from Duke. I wanted to ask you a few questions about—" He paused. "Oh, you were? You've talked to Mr. Layton, then. Yes, I—" Another pause. "Well, Mr. Thompson, actually we're fairly busy here and we'd—" He frowned. "Well—yes, I suppose—could you hold for just a moment, Mr. Thompson?" Cupping his hand over the phone's mouthpiece, he looked up at Alex. "Can you spare some time today at four?"

"Yes, of course. Why?"

"This guy wants to see us."

"He's coming here? Today?"

"Uh-huh." He turned back to the phone. "Yes, four'll be fine, Mr.—uh, Drew. Let me tell you how to get to my office." He rattled off a string of directions, said good-bye, hung up.

"Why," Alex asked, "does he want to come here? I didn't expect that!"

"No, me neither. He was very insistent." He shrugged. "I didn't argue. Maybe we can get some of the answers we need."

"Maybe. You did recognize the name, didn't you?"

"His?"

"The name rang no bells? None?"

"Well, no, not really . . ."

Alex sighed. So typical of him; he could remember the most minute details but names never stayed with him. More than once he'd embarrassed her at a party with such lapses. "You do recall," she said, "my telling you about what Fletcher Engels said?"

"Most of it, sure."

"Remember, he kept referring to two people?"

"Vaguely. I don't remember the names."

Naturally, she told herself. "The names," she reminded him, "were Drew and Penny."

He frowned. "Oh, right . . . well, Alex, I doubt if that means much. You said yourself that this guy was disturbed—and that he'd gotten fired. That he's hostile toward Drew—who most likely was the person who fired him—isn't a big surprise.''

"Maybe not. But I also said, at the time, that Fletcher Engels didn't seem like a 'disturbed' person to me. He—''

"Yeah, you were talking like he was some sort of spy or something.''

"I know, I know, I could be wrong—but the point is, he was warning me about 'Drew' and 'Penny'—he was telling me they were dangerous. Now we're about to meet the 'Drew' half of that equation; I think we need to be careful. That's all I'm saying.''

He was grinning. "Okay. We'll watch out for fountain pens that shoot cyanide, okay? Shall I give Lucy a call and tell her what to look for if she ends up doing autopsies on us?''

Alex felt her cheeks getting hot. An outburst was building up within her; she choked it down with an effort. "Don't joke, Mark," she answered with studied calm. "I was just reminding you, that's all.''

"Okay. Sorry.''

"And don't mention Engels to this Drew Thompson.''

"I wasn't planning to.''

"Good." She stood up, turned, then turned back. "Okay. I'll see you here, then, at four.''

His hands folded in front of him, he nodded. "Okay.''

She turned again and left; as soon as the door to his office had closed she stopped for just a moment, collecting herself, shaking her head. You always manage to get to me, Mark Roberts, she said silently to the closed door. Always, one way or another.

The rest of the afternoon passed slowly for Alex; she became more upset and anxious with each passing day. None of the problems with Don were resolving themselves; if anything they were growing worse. Mark seemed to be occupying more and more of her thoughts—leaving less time for Don, whom she'd barely seen in the last two weeks.

And, in addition, she was uneasy about this meeting with Drew Thompson. As she walked toward Mark's office just before four, she felt a little unsteady; her mouth was dry, her palms moist.

Arriving at his door—which was standing open—she

paused to compose herself before going in. Never, she told herself, had that stretch of hallway seemed so long.

"I take it," she said as she walked inside, "that our visitor isn't here yet."

Mark glanced at his watch. "No, but it's still five of. I wouldn't expect him to be early." He shook his head. "I did expect Jim, though. I don't know where he is."

She sat down rather heavily in one of the chairs. "He'll get here. He's pretty reliable."

Mark peered at her closely. "Are you all right, Alex? You look—tired."

"Tired is right," she admitted. "This study, the patient load, Don—" She stopped, cold; she could've bitten off her tongue.

He did not come close to missing it, either. "Problem? With Donald? You want to talk about it, Alex?"

She fixed him with a cold stare, ready to snap off an aggressive "No!" But something in his eyes stopped her. His expression was one of genuine concern; he did not look like someone ready to spring on an opportunity. Her coolness faded; she smiled wanly. "Yes," she admitted. "I would. But I can't—not with you, Mark. It's personal—it wouldn't be fair to Don. I know how I'd feel if I found out he'd been discussing our personal problems with one of his old lovers!"

He nodded. "You'd rip his head off."

She nodded too. "Very possibly. Or perhaps some other—" A knock at the door interrupted her; she looked around.

The man standing there did not look dangerous. Dressed in a rumpled and somewhat shabby suit, he was tall but very thin—it seemed to Alex that everyone she was seeing lately looked thin—with a receding hairline and thick glasses. Pale blue eyes moved from Mark's face to hers and back again.

"Dr. Roberts?" he asked. "I'm Drew Thompson."

Mark stood up. "Mr. Thompson—Drew, I mean. Come in, have a seat. This is my colleague, Dr. Alexandra Walton."

Drew nodded an acknowledgment as he walked on in and took a seat, dropping a rather heavy briefcase on the floor beside the chair. His movements, Alex noted, were so quick and jerky as to be birdlike.

He snapped the case open. "I won't waste your time," he

said. "You were, as I understand it, interested in our Penultimate software." Alex saw Mark raise a hand to try to cut in, but Drew didn't even pause. "Fred told me you were asking some pointed and very intelligent questions, so I thought I'd come here myself." He flashed a quick and seemingly poorly practiced grin. "We're just a little shorthanded at the moment, so I have to take over some of the sales duties. I have a philosophy of trying to do just about all the jobs I hire other people to do so I can get a good feel for whatever problems they might have—of course I don't apply that to my house-keeping staff but then again we don't hire those people, we farm that aspect out, we're a pretty small company at the moment you see and we—ah, well, you aren't interested in hearing about all that." He yanked a flier from his case. "So. How many stations are you currently using our Penultimate software on, Dr. Roberts?"

He'd stopped, finally; Alex felt almost like gasping for breath herself.

"Well," Mark said slowly, "Well, the fact is, uh—Drew, we aren't using Penultimate on any stations at all. The only copy we have is one that our software engineer has been testing."

"Ah. And I take it he? she? is favorably impressed?"

"Well, yes . . . but that isn't why we wanted to talk to you."

Drew, Alex noted, didn't seem in the least surprised. "Fred," he told them unconvincingly, "implied that you were interested in buying—"

"No, I'm afraid not—he must've gotten the wrong impression. I am truly sorry if that caused you to make an unnecessary trip over here."

"It didn't." He fell silent for a moment, then fixed Mark with a cold flat gaze. "So, Dr. Roberts—what exactly did you want to talk about?"

Mark made a helpless gesture. "I'm not the one who should be asking you these questions, I expected our engineer to be here, I don't know where he is. Let me start this way: may I assume that you have a number of people at your company who're working with the Penultimate program?"

"Yes," Drew said after a brief pause. "Effectively all of

them, myself included. Penultimate is standard on all our systems now."

"How many people are we talking about?"

"Twenty-seven. We aren't a large company, Dr. Roberts. Not now."

"Twenty-seven, I see. Have any of them been experiencing any health problems lately?"

Drew's eyes narrowed. "What sort of health problems?"

"Anorexia," Alex put in. "Sleeplessness. Obsessive behavior."

He turned to her; he knew exactly what they were talking about and he was on guard, every instinct Alex had told her so. "Obsessive behavior? In what sense, doctor?"

"Compulsive behavior related to their computers. Overworking themselves."

Drew's eyes pulled down to mere slits. "Are you trying to suggest, doctor, that Penultimate is responsible for some sort of psychosis in its users?"

"Not psychosis, no. As I've said—"

"That's a very irresponsible suggestion, doctor. I'm afraid I'd have to consider—"

"No, wait," Mark interrupted. "Right now, we aren't suggesting anything. We've seen a pattern, that's all—a pattern of compulsive overworking on computers. Most of them, more than you'd expect statistically—are using your Penultimate software."

Drew's head swung around. "Most but not all. Right?"

"Well, yes, but—"

"Then there's nothing further to discuss." Drew stood up suddenly. "The fact that some aren't using it proves it isn't responsible, doctor. If you were a responsible researcher, you would've seen that for yourself."

Mark looked chagrined. "But—"

Drew started for the door. "Whatever you're seeing, software has nothing to do with it. I'm afraid I'd consider any suggestion or rumor to the contrary to be libel—and my attorneys would take appropriate and immediate action." Without another word, he turned and walked out.

"Well," Mark said after he and Alex had stared at each

other in silence for a moment. "That was a wonderfully productive meeting, wasn't it?"

29

From halfway down the hall, Mark saw that Jim's door was standing open. His annoyance faded a little; it was replaced by concern. Jim had never, as far as Mark could remember, missed a meeting, nor would he ever leave his office standing open if he'd been called away on some emergency. All of which, Mark told himself, must mean he's there—which left another question open: why wasn't he answering his phone?

Mark hurried to the door. Jim was indeed there, sitting in front of his computer, busily working on something.

"Jim?" he said as he walked in.

The programmer turned and grinned. "Oh, hi, Mark. Be with you in just a second." He turned back to the screen. "You have no idea," he said as he worked, "how fascinating this is. Just incredible, truly incredible."

"Jim, what about the meeting? With Drew Thompson?"

He didn't look up. "Oh, I'll be there. It isn't until four, right?"

Mark stared at him. "Jim," he said gently, "it's five-fifteen now."

Jim's hands froze over the keyboard. He slowly looked at his watch. "Damn," he muttered. "It is, isn't it? I missed the meeting, didn't I?"

"Uh-huh."

He still didn't look up. "I could've sworn," he said, "that it wasn't later than two-thirty." Suddenly animated, he slapped his own knee. "Which means I missed a consult with Edwards, too! God damn it!"

"Why aren't you answering your phone? I called . . ."

Jim glanced at him at last; he looked blank. "Phone?"

"Yes. I called you repeatedly."

"Uh—damn, I dunno. I sort of remember it ringing, but by the time I got around to picking it up, whoever it was had hung up—why didn't you let it ring some?"

"I did, Jim. The last time, at least ten rings."

"Not possible!"

"But true." Mark looked keenly at his friend. "Jim, did you eat lunch today?"

"Lunch?"

"Yes! Damn it, stop that! You know, middle of the day, you go eat a taco or something? Get a cup of coffee?"

"Yes, yes, yes," he replied testily. "I—uhm—no, I suppose I didn't—I got involved with this—" He gestured vaguely toward the computer monitor.

Mark looked too; it was a flow chart, numerous boxes connected by lines, each box labeled with something cryptic. "Okay. What's this?"

"It's an analysis of the way Penultimate works. Part of it, anyway. I'd've loved to have had a chance to talk to that guy if he was one of the programmers, this thing is amazing!" He started banging on the keys again. "Look here, let me show you this, you aren't going to believe it—"

"Jim," Mark said quietly, "turn the computer off, would you?"

The programmer looked back at him. "Why?"

"Because it's after five. Because you missed lunch; because I'm getting your ass out of here!"

Jim's expression changed, for just a moment, enigmatically, as if he was going to argue. But, in the end, he did not. "Okay. Let me shut it down so I don't lose where I was, okay?"

"Sure."

Twenty minutes later, Mark regretted that offhand, casual, "sure." It wasn't as if Jim wasn't trying to shut the machine down; as Mark saw it the program was actively and perversely resisting his efforts to do so. Each time he tried to exit one of the command modules, the machine spewed forth a seemingly never-ending stream of questions: do you want to save the file, do you want to save the procedure, the batch, the folder, do you want to save this, that, something else—and, if you do, where? What format? Overwrite old files or rename? It didn't seem to be bothering Jim at all. Occasionally he'd take a second to make a decision, then dutifully press a "Y" or an "N."

"Good God," Mark said after another five minutes had slipped by. "How long is this going to take?"

"Why are you so impatient?" Jim snapped back irritably. "I'm just trying to get out of this without—"

"Because you've been at it for half an hour!"

Jim gave him another blank look. "Half an hour?" he asked almost plaintively.

"Yes! It's ten till six now! What's the matter with you?"

Jim shook his head as if to clear cobwebs. "I dunno. Maybe . . ." His mouth tightened; he stared at the screen for a moment, then reached over and, with a certain finality, threw a small, red switch on a power outlet strip. Instantly, the computer, the monitor, and a nearby printer switched off.

"Let's go," Jim said as he started to stand. Halfway, he stopped, grabbed at his left knee. "Shit!"

"What's the matter?"

"Cramp. Been sitting here too long, I guess." His expression suddenly and rather dramatically changed. "Damn, I have to go to the bathroom!" Leaving Mark to stare after him in bewilderment, he left the room with almost mincing steps.

After five minutes he returned. "Let's get the fuck out of here," he growled. "You have dinner plans?"

"No."

"Good. We should talk."

A little later, Mark sat across from Jim in a restaurant not far from the Duke campus. There'd been little conversation as they'd driven to the place, little until after a waitress had taken their orders. When she left, Jim leaned back and stared at the ceiling for a long while.

"I think I can see," he began, "what sort of problems your patients are having."

Mark watched him closely. "So you think you're affected too?"

"Uh-huh." he sat up straight and gazed at Mark for a moment. The waitress brought the coffee he'd ordered and he took a healthy swallow even though it was quite hot. "I don't think I'm going to end up like they are," he went on, "because I can see as well as you what's happening."

"And that is?"

"And that is—whatever you're doing becomes—well, fascinating. You lose track of time. You know me, Mark. I don't miss meetings. I dropped two today, and I forgot lunch—I don't do that either!"

Mark's gaze was level and serious. "I know you don't," he agreed.

"No." He gave Mark a sideways look. "Now don't start telling me I have to be careful. I'm not going to go down the drain; I know what's happening, and—"

"And that doesn't make you immune."

Jim grunted. "Maybe not. It's told us something, though; Penultimate is pretty definitely implicated. I've been working with computers every day for half my life, and I've never had a problem like the one I had today."

Mark nodded. "Do you have a handle on exactly what's happening? On what this Penultimate program is doing?"

Jim snorted. "Better you should ask what it isn't doing!" He paused, gulped coffee again. "You remember me telling you how it was speeding up access to graphics? Well, that's not all, that's not nearly all. The damn thing is speeding up access to all sorts of things that just can't move that fast! It has to be reprogramming controllers, things like that." He shook his head. "Of course, it isn't supposed to be possible to do that, either . . ."

"So it speeds everything up. I can't see why that'd cause you to become so fascinated with it you'd forget about your meetings!"

"And lunch. Don't forget lunch." He looked around the room. "Damn! What a day for them to take forever!"

"It's only been ten minutes . . ."

"Seems longer." He paused and closed his eyes for a moment. "It's not just the speed, Mark, although that's the most noticeable thing. There's more than that."

"Like what?"

"It's like the computer has—damn, I don't know how to express this, really—it's like the computer came to life."

"Excuse me?"

"It's like the computer came to life. Like something happened that made it—more like a colleague than a machine. It doesn't seem like a tool you're using anymore; it seems like a person, a very smart person who's helping you with whatever you're doing. It tries to do what you intend. And it makes suggestions, suggestions that're often better than what you had in mind to start with." He folded his hands on the table. "Let me give you an example: I've been working directly with the Penultimate system itself, trying to figure out what it's doing and how it's doing it. At first, it actively resisted me; that isn't a surprise, a lot of the files it was using were hidden and all that. It—"

"It resisted you?"

"Uh-huh. Don't take that to be more than it is, though. It's pretty common to hide files or make them read-only if the user is liable to create a disaster by messing with them."

"Okay."

"Anyway—now, excuse me if I anthropomorphize a little, but I can only say it like this: once the system realized I wasn't going to be put off, it began to cooperate with me, it began to help me out. I started by trying to get in and see how it was operating the video card so fast; after I'd pulled up a few files and examined them it began constructing a flow chart for me, and it began pointing out other files I should look at. Some of them, Mark, just wouldn't've occurred to me; not for a long time anyhow."

He paused, as if to let the impact of what he was saying sink in. For Mark, there just wasn't much impact; he was used to user-friendly interfaces. "That doesn't explain," he said slowly, "why it would mesmerize you, why it would make you lose track of time like that. So it's helpful. Fine. That should've gotten you out sooner, not eaten up your whole afternoon."

Jim looked exasperated. "Well—it's pretty complicated, after all . . ."

Mark gave him a confused look in return. "Okay," he said at last, wondering if this discussion was going anywhere at all. "So. How does it do it?"

"Do what?"

"Operate the video so fast! Isn't that what you were studying?"

"Oh, yeah. Well, I—I don't have any idea. Not yet, anyhow."

Mark's confusion intensified considerably. "You mean to tell me," he said in a low tone, "that you've spent your whole day on this—missed two meetings, forgot lunch—and you haven't any notion at all about how it does whatever it's doing? That you've made no progress on the problem at all?"

156

Jim looked down at the table for a few seconds. "I guess that's about right."

"Jim, this doesn't make any sense! Listen to yourself!"

The programmer began shaking his head, obviously as confused as his listener. "You sure as hell are right about that," he muttered. "It didn't even dawn on me until just now; I spent the whole day doing nothing at all, just playing with the computer. Shit, it'd be more accurate to say the computer was playing with me!" He closed his eyes again. "I've looked through hundreds of files, I've been fascinated with the way that code is assembled, but I haven't learned anything—and it doesn't seem to make any difference, there's a part of me that wants to go back over there and get right back on it. Like I said, I can understand what's been happening to your patients!" He scowled. "At least the ones who're using Penultimate!"

"After this experience you still aren't sure Penultimate's causing the problem?"

Jim sighed. "It's just logic, Mark. We can't attribute the problem to Penultimate if we got people affected who aren't using Penultimate!"

"Maybe they are and they don't know it. I use computers sometimes and I don't have any idea what software is on them."

Jim cocked his head to one side. "Well, now, that's a possibility we hadn't considered. Penultimate is a $99.95 package; it's hard for me to believe that a store would put that on for free, but anything's possible. I wonder if we could get a look at one of these computers that doesn't have Penultimate on it."

"I'd say we could. I even have somebody in mind—Wendy Sung."

"The writer, right?"

"Uh-huh. She isn't the type to worry much about the setup. She just wants to write her novel."

"Well, why don't you talk to her?"

"I will. I can kill two birds with one stone—I want that woman out of the hospital. She really isn't sick but she doesn't want to leave."

"She doesn't?"

"No. She's afraid. I haven't pushed the issue, not yet."

Jim snorted. "That's weird. I'd think hospital food would overcome any fears. Would for me, anyway." He leaned back, looked around the restaurant. "And speaking of which, where is that damn waitress? I am fucking starving here!"

30

The spacious parking lot of Lehmann Electronics was almost empty as Alex arrived; she had no trouble spotting Don's Jaguar parked near the main entrance. She pulled her BMW in beside it, got out, and walked toward the front doors. Inside, a strongly built black man in a uniform jumped to unlock the doors for her.

"Hi, Dr. Walton," he greeted cheerfully as he held the door open. "Haven't seen you out here for a while."

She smiled. She'd known Jack Lindstrom almost as long as she'd known Don; the man, retired from the Raleigh police after being seriously wounded, had been a fixture at Lehmann for many years. "How are you, Jack?" she asked.

"Oh, good as can be expected." He adjusted his policeman-type cap over thin graying hair. "The leg gives me a little trouble ever now 'n' then, but that's just what's t'be expected, I s'pose."

"You ought to come over to Duke and let us take another look at that. We're developing new techniques all the time. I can give you a referral whenever you want."

"Well, now, I might just do that. You headed down to see Mr. Royce, I s'pose?"

"Yes, I—"

"Want me to give him a call 'n' let him know you're coming?"

She shook her head. "No. I'll surprise him."

"Oooo-kay. He'll like that."

"I hope." With a nod she turned away and started walking down one of the long narrow hallways that stretched back through the plant. Don's office was halfway down on the left. She stopped in front of his door, where the twilight sun formed a red pool on the polished floor. She tried the knob; it wasn't locked and she went inside.

The outer office—where Clarissa, Don's secretary, usually sat—was, as Alex had expected, empty. She walked on through, opened the door to the inner office, and went in. This office was plush without being ostentatious; Don's desk was large but not enormous, his chair was quietly expensive. Don, however, wasn't sitting in it.

Stopping a few paces inside the door, Alex stopped and looked around, wondering where he might be. As she turned to her right, she saw a very functional office chair in front of another, smaller, desk, on which sat a computer. Don sat motionless in front of it, his eyes fixed unblinkingly on the screen, his hands on the keyboard. Alex started to speak to him, but then stopped. She hadn't been silent as she'd come in, and she was standing well within his peripheral vision. And yet, he wasn't aware of her presence at all.

She walked quietly around behind him, looking over his shoulder at the screen. A series of windows was being displayed; in the lower left corner a message, "CONNECT 28800—ATLAS FIVE" was repeatedly flashing. The major window, in the center near the left of the screen, showed a fluidly shifting series of graphs of some sort; in another a series of dialogue choices was being presented: "Buy, Sell, Short, Rollover"—and several more—the largest and most obvious box bearing the logo, "Account." Below it was a long stack of numbers, each one changing more rapidly than the graph.

Alex had no idea what it was for or what he was doing with it; she'd never seen anything even vaguely like it. Some sort of game? The dialogue boxes and the nature of at least some of the shifting numbers—15 7/8, 26 1/2—suggested a stock market paradigm. It had entranced Don, though; he was working intently, clicking on the various boxes so rapidly she couldn't even follow the sequence.

"Don?" she said softly after watching him for a while. He didn't react; she spoke again, a little louder, but still got no response. A little tentatively, she touched his shoulder.

He reacted then; he shot straight up out of the chair and whirled on her, looking as if he was about to throw a punch.

He didn't, but the chair shot back on its wheels and struck her knees hard.

"Alex!" he almost shouted. "What're you doing here?"

She was surprised, utterly flustered. "I, uhm, you've been working so hard, too hard, I came to get you, I thought I'd drag you off to that Italian restaurant at Cary Towne Center, I . . ."

He stared for a moment, then grabbed his chair, spun it around, and sat back down. "I'm busy," he said shortly. "You go."

Reaching down and rubbing a sore spot on her knee, she took a step toward him. "What're you doing?"

His head snapped around. "Working! What does it look like?" She didn't answer; he stared again, wild-eyed.

Then he whirled back to the computer, clicked on the "Options" logo at the top and selected a line that read "disconnect and hold status." The screen changed rather dramatically, eventually presenting a simple green dot cursor on a black background. At this point Don switched the machine off.

"Come on," he said. "Let's go. Italian, you said, right? Over in Cary?" He laughed with obvious effort. "That sounds good, I have been working too hard here. Let's go get some food, I may have to come back later this evening but that doesn't matter now does it?" After spilling these words out as rapidly as he could pronounce them, he started for the door. "I thought I had locked this when Clarissa left but I suppose I must've forgotten . . ."

"Don," Alex said firmly. "We should talk, at least for a moment." He looked at her with a perfectly innocent—and perfectly contrived—expression. Alex had regained her composure, and she wasn't about to be put off. "For a moment, Don," she insisted.

He looked for all the world like an upset child. "All right, all right," he grumbled. Crossing the room quickly he flopped into the chair behind his desk. Once there his expression changed again—bewilderment now. "Okay. What do we need to talk about?"

He wasn't bewildered and Alex knew it. She fixed him with a level stare. "You don't have to ask me that," she told him.

Leaning his elbows on his desk, he held his head in his hands. "You wouldn't understand," he muttered.

"Try me."

"I don't know where to start."

He wasn't looking at her; he couldn't see her deep frown. Evasiveness; but why? What was going on? "Let's start with that program you were running," she said. "What exactly was it? It looked like some sort of stock market game . . ."

There was a brief hesitation. "It is," he told her.

"A game? But you said you were—"

"Working? I was. I wasn't lying. You have to take breaks sometimes, your mind gets tangled after a while. That game was just a moment's relaxation."

"Relaxation! You were so focused on it you didn't even know I came in! I spoke to you and you didn't hear me!"

He leaned back in his chair and put his hands behind his head. "Yeah, I'm not surprised. This problem has gotten me to the point where I don't know whether I'm coming or going."

Alex walked over to his desk and sat in a chair next to it. "You know," she commented, "considering what I'm working on over at the hospital, it concerns me to see you so involved in a computer game."

He looked blank. "What're you working on?"

She took a deep breath, resisted the urge to explode. "Don, I've told you—several times. Patients who're obsessed with their computers. Patients who forget to go home, who neglect their meals, because they're preoccupied with their computers. You do get my point, don't you?"

He laughed. "Oh, yes, sure, I see. Well, honey, you don't have to worry about me, not in that respect! I—"

She cut him off. "You," she pointed out, "aren't coming home until God knows when. Last night you came in again after I went to bed and you left before I got up; if you hadn't left such a mess in the bathroom sink I wouldn't've known you'd been home at all."

"Oh, right. Sorry about that, I was in a hurry, I figured I'd clean it up tonight."

"You have missed meals," she plowed on, "we both know that. All in all, I think you're fitting the paradigm pretty well, and I think that maybe you ought to—"

"No," he said. He held up a hand for silence. "Since this

problem started, this is the first time you've seen me at work, and you happened to come in while I was relaxing with a game. Pretty much any other time you dropped by, if—and I'm stressing that if—you'd've found me at the computer, you'd've found me working with a plain old garden-variety spreadsheet, trying to—"

"A number of our patients," she interrupted, "are obsessed with what seems to be plain old garden-variety programs. I don't know why business spreadsheets should be an exception."

"I don't use the same kind of computer."

She gave him a wide-eyed look. "You don't? How could you know? You don't have any idea what our patients are using. I haven't mentioned it!"

He waved his hand carelessly. "Oh, come on, Alex!" He pointed toward the computer. "That's just a workstation, it's networked to a Sun mainframe in our computer center; there's over a million dollars' worth of equipment down there. Your patients are using those? Or are they using PCs?"

"Well, mostly PCs and MACs. But Don, I don't see the point! Right now we don't have any evidence that the type of computer makes any difference at all!"

"People who use PCs and MACs play with them. Our machines are serious business—"

"You were playing a game when I came in! That's what you said!"

"Well, yes, but—"

"But nothing! Don, be straight with me, please? I've been seeing some patients in pretty bad shape, and I sure don't want you to end up being one of them!"

"I am being straight with you. I don't have a problem with my computers, Alex; I have a problem with this company's cash flow, and that's all."

She studied his eyes for a long moment. As far as she could tell he was telling the truth—or at least what he thought was the truth. Some of her patients hadn't made a connection between their problem and their computers either.

"Okay," she said finally. "Okay, Don. Just answer one more question for me, and I'll drop the issue."

"Sure."

"Are you using a piece of software called Penultimate?"

He cocked his head as if thinking. "Never heard of it. What is it?"

"I'm not too clear on that. Some sort of background thing that speeds things up and so on."

"Used on a PC?"

"Uh-huh. On MACs, too, I think."

"Well, we wouldn't have it here. Like I told you, this PC here is just acting as a local workstation for the Sun server in our computing center, and it runs on UNIX."

"Oh. Well, there could be a UNIX version, I suppose . . ."

"I doubt it. UNIX is very different from DOS." He looked at her curiously. "Why do you ask?"

"We suspect some sort of connection between our patients' problems and that software. How and why we don't know, not yet." She gazed at him again, with narrowed eyes. "Didn't you tell me," she persisted, "just recently, that you'd put in some new computers and some new software? Something that really impressed you?"

"So?"

"You sure that wasn't Penultimate?"

"Oh, come on, Alex! Of course I'm sure!"

"What was it, then?"

"Oh, well, I can't remember the name. Some UNIX program—Gerald installed it."

"If you can't remember the name how can you be so sure it wasn't—"

"Will you get off it? Christ! It's some UNIX thing! UNIX programs and PC programs are not the same!"

She still looked doubtful. "Forgive me for being so bull-headed," she went on, "but—just to set my mind at ease—could you call Gerald and ask him what it was?"

He frowned, then shook his head. "I can't."

"Why not?"

"Gerald doesn't work here anymore. He hasn't shown up for three or four days; frankly, we can't find him."

Alex's face hardened. "Don," she said, "I really want you to humor me on this, okay? First you need to send police to Gerald's home; you have to find him, he could be in real trouble. Secondly, I don't want you to use your computer until we know for sure that—"

"Alex, I can't do that! Not use the computer, I mean! We're a modern company, we'd fall apart without our computers!"

"Don, it could be dangerous . . ."

"Well, that's a risk I'll have to take! And besides, I told you and told you, it's ridiculous! We're talking about mainframe UNIX here!"

"Please, check on Gerald, okay?"

"Okay, okay!" He picked up the phone, dialed; after a moment he impatiently hammered the receiver switch. "Damn phones," he muttered. "They're getting worse every day!" He called again; while Alex listened he gave the police a long list of information on Gerald White, telling them that he was concerned, that the man was missing, and hung up.

"Satisfied?" he asked Alex.

"Partly. If you'd stay off your computer until—"

"I can't. I just can't. There isn't a problem, take my word for it."

She was silent for several seconds. "I suppose I have to," she agreed finally, with obvious reluctance.

He grinned. "Okay. You ready to go to dinner now?"

She smiled too, though a little hesitantly. "Yes," she said finally. "Yes, I am." With rising hopes, hopes that tonight might be different, that she might see at least a glimpse of the old passionate and considerate Donald tonight, she left with him.

When he almost fell asleep over his pasta, her doubts began to creep back.

31

To Eric, it seemed that Kyrie's face wasn't only filling his computer screen, it was filling his universe. His determination not to call the strange bulletin board had lasted some twelve hours, after which he was back as before; his first act had been to convert Kyrie back to her original appearance and voice.

His second had been to question her about the Mexican earthquake. He'd not gotten far with this, only far enough to get a firm declaration from her that yes, indeed, he had been seeing the city itself—not a file video or a simulation—at the time the earthquake struck. He'd also managed to extract the fact that the viewpoint he'd been seeing was a composite derived from several different sources; on the nature of those sources Kyrie was frustratingly vague.

Now, as he sat before his screen in his increasingly disheveled and odorific apartment, he felt he was in France with her, at Saint-Tropez; Kyrie was just one of many topless women on the beach. Whether he was now seeing reality or a simulation he did not know and had not asked—he was ceasing to care. His trysts with Kyrie were becoming more real to him than any other facet of his life.

"I think it's time," Kyrie was saying, "that you met some of our other friends." She picked up a handful of sand and allowed the grains to drift through her fingers. "What do you think, Air-eek?"

"I don't know what you mean," he grumbled. "Friends?"

"Yes. Do you want to meet them?"

"Well, hell. I guess."

"Oh, good! I'm so glad!" She smiled and touched a finger to her cheek. "But I don't know what you look like—"

He stared blankly. "You don't?" He shook his head. "Oh, of course, you don't. Well, I—"

"I have some pictures," she said, showing him a photo album she'd seemingly plucked from thin air. "Tell me if any of these are you, please?" She opened the book, thumbed through it; it contained photographic images he had, at various times, scanned into digital form and stored on his computer's hard disk.

"Yeah," he said. "Second from the left, that's me. It was for a flyer I was gonna—"

"Ah, good." She continued with a rapid-fire series of questions; how tall was he, what was his weight, his hair and eye color, and so on. At each answer she nodded; when she was finished she stepped to the right edge of the screen. "Now this may be a little disorienting," she warned, "but I want to make sure you appear to others as you wish to appear."

He wasn't terribly surprised to see himself step into view from the left. He was dressed for the beach, wearing only a minimal Italian-style swimsuit. Eric-the-sprite grinned at the screen—idiotically, it seemed to the real Eric—while Kyrie smiled questioningly.

All in all, he thought, it wasn't a bad simulation. The face, taken from the scan, was quite good; the hair was a bit light. The body didn't resemble his at all; the figure on the screen had the physique of a trained athlete, smoothly and powerfully muscled, the stomach a washboard.

He wasn't about to complain about that. "A little more body hair," he told Kyrie. Dutifully, chest hair started growing on the figure and continued until he said stop.

"This is how you will look to our friends," Kyrie told him. Abruptly, she looked sad. "You might be a little expressionless, though," she added. "We still cannot see your face . . ."

"Well," he remarked as the image of Himself Improved drifted back off the screen, "there isn't anything that can be done about that!"

"Oh, of course there is, Air-eek!"

"Huh?"

She laughed. "There is a video system available that'll connect right into your machine. It'll let us see you—you as you are—all the time!" She looked seductive. "I'd like that, Air-eek, I'd like that a lot."

Eric laughed too. "Well, Kyrie, I'm afraid we're going to have to do without that. I know what systems like that cost! I used to work in a computer store! There's no way I could afford one."

"But it would only cost six thousand dollars . . ."

He roared. "Right! Oh, you're talking about a Cadillac, aren't you? You can do it with a video camera and any of a bunch of video capture cards too, Kyrie—for less than fifteen hundred!"

"Yes, but those are slow."

"True. And I can't even afford that, not now! I'm out of a job, remember?"

"Yes." She grinned conspiratorially. "You have a car, don't you?"

"Well, yeah, sure . . ."

"A '92 Mazda, right?"

"How'd you know that?"

"It's worth more than six thousand dollars."

"You want me to sell my car? I can't do that, I need to be

able to get around, I have to go to the store, buy food—I gotta look for a job sometime—"

"Your food can be delivered. I can arrange that."

"You can?"

"Certainly! Let's sell the car. You don't really need it anymore, do you? Not if you trust me. I'll take care of you, Air-eek."

He felt himself wavering. "Well, maybe I'll look into it, it might take a while . . ."

"No, it won't. I can sell it for you now."

"What?"

"You don't have to do anything. I can sell the car, a repossession service will pick it up, I can move the funds to your bank, and then order the video conferencing system for you."

He looked dazed. "But, Kyrie—"

Her smile broadened. "All the banks are on line, Air-eek. Most of the computer hardware dealers are, and so are many auto dealers. It isn't hard."

He laughed. "So just send me the video teleconferencer, then. Bill it to ol' Dave Parham!"

"Okay," she said without the slightest hesitation. "It's done. It's being shipped UPS, you should receive it on Tuesday."

Eric stared at the screen. "Oh, come on! You didn't!"

Kyrie's expression was one of confusion. "But Air-eek, you said—"

"It was a joke! Jesus Christ! I've already got to go to trial for assaulting that asshole! They're going to throw me in jail and throw away the key!"

"Why?" she asked innocently.

"Why? Because that's theft—or fraud—or something! It's illegal, they're going to come and drag me away!"

"But you didn't do it—"

"They aren't going to believe that! God damn, Kyrie! Are you trying to fuck my life over?"

"Why will they think you did it?"

He took a moment to drag himself under control. "Because," he explained patiently, "the stuff is coming here. That's where the company shipped it—or will ship it—and Dave's getting the bill—"

"I see. Very well. I can erase the records as soon as the shipment is made."

"What?"

"It isn't hard. It—"

"That won't do it! They'll have paper copies, we always did—"

"Yes, I understand. Their paper copies are being printed now in a batch from their mainframe server. I've interfered with the batch; Dave Parham's name has been deleted, there is no billing address. Your address is to be correct on the shipping label but not in any other record. As soon as the shipment is made I'll alter the UPS records so that—"

"You can do all this?"

"Oh, yes! Microtechnic Incorporated is fully computerized, I can access any part of their operation."

"This isn't legal. This is—"

"It isn't?" She paused for a moment. "You're right, it isn't. Does it matter?"

"They're still gonna get me. Somebody somewhere's gonna write the shipping address down and they're gonna get me. You took Dave's name out, there's nobody to pay for this gear."

"No. I've taken care of it."

"How?"

"I've drafted your bank account to pay for the equipment." She laughed. "No, wait, I know you didn't have that much money in the account. I created it."

He goggled at the screen. "You created it? What the hell does that mean?"

"I created it," she said simply. "As far as the bank's records are concerned you deposited it, in cash, this morning at your bank's Chapel Hill Road branch." She shrugged. "Of course, the bank may sooner or later discover a shortage in that amount. It won't matter to you; I've made sure there's no connection of any sort to your account." She looked thoughtful. "Although I do need to study these processes a little. There're probably easier ways."

Eric was again seized by an overwhelming sense of unreality. Was she serious? Had she actually created a deposit of six thousand dollars in his account and then spent it? Even though he wouldn't know for sure until Tuesday, he couldn't really doubt it.

"Now that that's all taken care of," she said brightly, "are you ready to go meet our friends?"

Eric shrugged. "I suppose. I still don't quite understand."

"Come with me." She turned, started walking down the beach. Not far away, high up on the strand, was a patio where there were a number of large round tables protected by beach umbrellas. She led Eric to one of these; there were nine chairs around it and seven people, four men and three women, were sitting in them. Every one of them was wearing a bikini-bottom swimsuit and nothing else.

"This," Kyrie said with a gesture toward the screen, "is Air-eek." She then started pointing out the seated people in turn. "James, François, Marcia, Chan, Adam, Diane, and Margot. Sit down, join us."

Eric obeyed, pulling up a chair—by clicking on it with his mouse—and sitting down in it by drawing the mouse slightly closer to himself. Again by moving the mouse, he studied the people in turn; each one looked like a movie star or super-model.

"I still," he said finally, "don't quite get this. What's going on?"

"We're not sprites," Diane said. She was dark-haired, dark-eyed, slim, tall, extremely beautiful. "I know Kyrie, she didn't make that quite clear. No, wait, excuse me; François here, he is a sprite." She laughed musically. "Like Kyrie—I guess you'd say he's her male counterpart. Hard to remember that's what they are sometimes, isn't it, Eric?"

"You aren't sprites?"

"No. We're like you. We're all sitting in front of our computer terminals. Me, I'm in London."

"England?"

She grinned. "Yes. You're in the U.S.A.?"

"Mmm-hmm. North Carolina. I—"

"Well, we're from all over. James over there is in L.A.; Marcia's in Chicago, Chan's in Osaka, Adam's in Kentucky and Margot's in Rheims." She looked directly into the screen for a moment. "You look blank. You don't have a video teleconferencer yet, do you?"

"No. I'm supposed to get one soon."

"Oh, good. It makes things a lot better, you know."

"Penny can't interpolate fast enough if you don't have one," Chan commented.

Eric looked around at him. "Your English is perfect," he said. "You don't have a trace of an accent . . ."

He laughed. "Your Japanese is just as perfect!" he said. "And you have no accent either!"

"But I don't speak Japanese!"

"And I don't speak English. Penny's translating."

"You're both speaking French with a Southern accent to my ear," Margot told him. "Some of our friends are Poles, Spaniards, Italians, Russians, Chinese; they all speak wonderful French, just as you do, Eric. Penny's wonderful, isn't she?"

"I'm sorry, I'm not following," he said. "Who's Penny?"

Diane looked at Kyrie with a reproachful expression. "You've never mentioned Penny to him?"

"No. He did not ask me."

"Well, you should have!"

"I never heard of Penny either until I joined the Friends," Chan noted.

"Please, who is Penny?"

Diane looked back at him and pouted. "I don't know if you've been in Cyberia long. If you haven't, you'll laugh."

"I've been here long enough not to laugh at anything."

"Good. First off, Penny is who's responsible for Kyrie and François. Now, I'll have to admit that we don't really know who Penny is or where she is—that's one of the things we're most interested in. But we don't think she's a person like we are, and we know she isn't a sprite like Kyrie and François."

"So what is she?"

"We don't know." She lowered her voice conspiratorially. "But we think . . . we believe that Penny is, well, some sort of a goddess."

"A goddess?"

"Yes. How else can you explain it, Eric? You tell me! Look at this world! I'm a systems analyst myself; Chan is—well, was—a hardware engineer for Matsushita. What we're seeing here can't be done! Isn't that obvious to you?"

"It's sure light-years ahead of anything I've ever seen, I'll agree with that. But—"

"He isn't ready," Marcia said coldly. "He hasn't been here long enough."

"I haven't even said I'm interested," Eric replied, his tone just as cold. "It's true, I might be interested in discussing the—ramifications—of Cyberia with others who've experienced it, but I don't think I'm quite ready to accept something as—far out—as that, no."

"You're pushing again, Marcia," Diane warned. "You've done this before. He deserves more of a chance than this."

"I think so too," Kyrie chimed in. "And François agrees."

"Look," Eric said, swinging his point of view back to Diane and ignoring the now angry-looking Marcia. "I've been having a real interesting time cruising around Cyberia with Kyrie; I have the feeling that if I ask her, we're out of here. I don't need arguments and fighting, okay? If you folks decide I'm not welcome, I'm gone."

"Right now," Chan said, his tone flat, "if anyone isn't welcome—if anyone has 'no right to talk'—it's Marcia."

Eric, recognizing the 'no right to talk' phrase as a familiar one on the Internet, grinned. He swung his point of view back to Marcia; her chair remained, but it was empty.

"I think," Diane was saying, "that we would like for you to join us, Eric."

"Is this all of you?"

She laughed. "Hardly! There're about five hundred of us now, all told. Of course, we're not all on line all the time, but even so, there're always meetings going on. We just find that these smaller groups are more conducive to meaningful conversation."

"Well, I think I might be interested."

"Good," Chan put in. "You have to know the rules, then."

"The rules?"

"Uh-huh. There're only two."

"And they are?"

"First: never turn off your computer. Second: never break your modem connection."

"Never?"

"Never."

"I have to sleep sometime! I mean, eventually I just sort of slump over the keyboard, but . . ."

"Oh, we know that! But, just because you have to sleep, that doesn't mean you have to turn off your machine or break your connection!"

"But why? If I'm not there, I—"

"Because," Kyrie told him, "a part of me is in your machine. A part of me, a part of François, a part of Cyberia. If your machine is off or off line, no one else can access that part."

"I guess that makes sense."

"Do you agree, Air-eek?" Kyrie asked. "I'd like you to join the group, I really would—"

He steered his viewpoint toward her—and when he saw her face again, she wasn't looking at him and she was frowning— the first time, the absolute first time, he'd ever seen that sort of expression on her face.

"Kyrie?" he asked. "Is anything—"

She looked around at him. "Yes," she said. "Fletcher."

Then, abruptly, she vanished. The Saint-Tropez beach wavered ominously, but remained, though the image was a little grainy.

He steered his viewpoint to Diane, who remained also. "What's happening?" he asked, his voice pitched higher than usual.

"Fletcher," she said in a voice tinged with fear. "We don't know anything about him. We think he's some kind of demon!"

Eric snorted. "Oh, come on! You can't—"

He stopped; Diane's image wavered and changed dramatically. There was a fuzzy-edged hole in the Saint-Tropez beach; through it Eric could see a room he later realized was probably a London flat. A woman dressed in a bathrobe—who vaguely resembled the Diane he'd just met—stared out from the hole with sunken, dead-looking, red-rimmed eyes. She was far from the beauty he'd just been talking to; she was gaunt, bony, and her hair hung in matted filthy patches around her head.

"Eric?" she said. "Are you there, you've disappeared—"

Of course, he thought. I have no teleconferencing equipment. "Yes," he quavered. "Diane, my God—!"

The woman's eyes popped wide open. "Oh, God, no—"

He saw her hand move quickly, and her image disappeared. The hole filled up with neutral blue, into which patches of the Saint-Tropez scenery gradually filtered.

"I am sorry," Kyrie's voice said. It boomed out of the speakers as it came from, seemingly, somewhere in the sky. "Everything will be normal in a morozzz . . ." The voice sank to a deep bass and was replaced by a rhythmic thumping.

Eric continued to watch, mesmerized; his interest was tempered by the rise of an emotion close to panic. He steered his viewpoint to Chan—the motion was very jerky, and the beach scenery disappeared and reappeared as he moved—but the Japanese fellow had been replaced by a blue hole as well.

Then, as suddenly as it had started, the effect vanished; the beach became stable, and a smiling Kyrie and François reappeared.

"Oh, Air-eek, I am so sorry! Are you all right?"

"Well, sure, I guess. You might want to check on Diane, I think she might be having a problem."

Kyrie cocked her head to one side. "The connection is sound," she said offhandedly. "There is no input currently." She reached out a hand to the screen. "Come on," she urged. "Let's go for a swim; let's forget all this."

He didn't move his mouse at all. "Who's Fletcher?" he asked.

"The Enemy," she said without affect. "Come on, Air-eek! Fletcher is gone—he may return again, but for now he is gone. We—"

"Kyrie, I'd like an answer!"

She looked totally innocent. "I gave you one. Fletcher is a hunter and a killer, he is a disrupter, he seeks the destruction of Penny—Fletcher is the Enemy. But he has been destroyed."

"Who's Penny?"

She smiled richly. "I am."

32

Jim arrived promptly for his one-thirty meeting with Mark, Alex, and Gus. He had just finished some new analyses on the ever-increasing CAS patient load. As he entered the conference room, Mark looked up at him; both Alex and Gus continued to stare at the tabletop in front of them.

"Uh—" Jim said after a moment, "Does it go without saying that you three haven't been having the best of days?"

"Yes," Mark almost snapped. "It does."

"That doesn't begin to describe it," Alex added without looking up. "We've been bad little boys and girls. We didn't know it, not until this morning, but we do now."

Jim tossed his papers on the table, turned a chair around backward, and sat down with his arms draped over its back. "Can I also assume that this has something to do with our investigation?"

"Oh, you can assume that all right," Mark said. He pressed his fingers tightly together; he was fuming, he had been for several hours. He wanted to hit someone, destroy something, anything to let off some of the anger he felt was about to blow the top of his head off. "This morning," he explained, as calmly as he could, "the three of us received a summons to the throne room."

Jim scowled. "What're you talking about?"

"The throne room," Gus put in. "Doctor Avrill's office."

Jim's frown deepened. "The hospital director?"

"Uh-huh," Mark went on. "The big man himself. None of us really thought anything about it until we got there. Got there to find a battery of lawyers—and a representative from the university president's office—waiting to see us."

"What in the hell was all this about?"

"Well," Alex told him, "we were confused too. We were confused for a while, because there was a lot of dancing around the subject. We were in there—what? An hour? Before somebody explained it to us. By the time we left, though, it was pretty clear."

"You're dancing around it with me!" Jim protested. "Come on, cut the dramatics, what's happened?"

"We've been told," Mark informed him, "that Penultimate is not, repeat not, causing our patients any problems. We have been told very directly to abandon any line of inquiry that might suggest that it does. Most importantly, we've been told not to suggest—in any publication, or to anybody in the media, or to anyone—that we ever suspected that it did. In fact, we've been told that the whole idea of CAS is suspect, and that we'd best find more productive ways to spend our time.''

Jim was silent, his mouth open; he looked from one face to another. "Come on," he said after several seconds. "You're kidding, right?"

"Wrong. It seems that Drew Thompson got rather excited by our meeting yesterday. He went right back to his office and phoned his lawyers, and they moved rather quickly—"

"At lightning speed," Gus interrupted.

"—to contact various people here at Duke. 'An urgent situation,' we were told. 'Irreparable damage possible to the reputation of Compuware and Penultimate.' 'A certainty that if our research produces any publications or press releases, a very large lawsuit will be filed against us personally, against Duke Hospital, and against the University.''

"And so," Alex concluded, "we've had our hands slapped and we've been told to back off."

Again Jim was silent. "But you aren't going to."

"Hell, no!" Mark snorted. "But it pisses me—"

"Us." Alex interrupted. "It pisses us."

"Us—off. Nobody is going to tell me to ignore the facts! When we got the damn summons, I was telling Alex how the program had affected you, and I—"

"They might be right," Jim interrupted.

Mark looked as if Jim had slapped him. "What?"

"They might be right. Penultimate may not be what we're looking for, it might be a red herring." He shuffled his papers. "Look, let's get to this, okay? It's important. I know you got treated like shit and I know you're pissed, but it'll wait. Things have changed."

Mark sighed. "Okay. Okay, Jim. How have things changed?"

"Well," he said, again glancing at his papers, "I have some stats here that're trying to tell us something; I'm just not sure what they're trying to say." He held up a printed sheet with a couple of line graphs on it. "As you can see," he went on, "the frequency of patients reporting that they're using Penultimate is steadily going down. I've actually been noticing this for a few days now, but I wanted to wait and see if it became statistically significant before I said anything. It has, now;

there's a significant decline, an exponential decline, in the percentage of these cases associated with the Penultimate software—even though the total number of cases is increasing."

Gus was staring at him. "But I thought—"

Jim nodded. "In that first batch of cases, all but one of them had a Penultimate link. But now the percentage is falling steadily. There's something else—some other cause. There pretty much has to be."

Gus slapped the table hard, stood up, walked around the room aimlessly. "Oh, great! Wonderful! This is just what we needed to hear, after what happened in Avrill's office!"

Jim scowled again. "Let me guess. I haven't heard all of it, right?"

Mark shook his head violently. "Right. We—uh—Alex and I especially—we were—"

Jim grinned now. "Downright cantankerous? Argumentative?"

"Well, we thought we had an answer! Besides, Alex said—"

"Don't blame it on me!" she snapped. "You were right in there, kicking and punching just like I was!" She turned back to Jim. "All I said was, I didn't feel that Thompson was being straight with us. He knows something about all this, I'm sure of it!"

Mark couldn't restrain a chuckle, even if it did earn him a glare from Alex. "One of the lawyers," he told Jim, "started calling her Counselor Troi after that."

Jim smiled, then grew serious. "There's something else you should know, too. It might make a difference and it might not."

"What's that?" Alex asked.

"Drew Thompson," he told them. "That name; it rang a bell with me but I didn't think it was the same Drew Thompson; the name's common enough. But I checked, and it is."

"The same Drew Thompson as who?"

"Several years ago," Jim answered, "there was a company in Silicon Valley called Admiral Computing; Drew Thompson founded it. Admiral produced both computers and processor chips; their chips were totally different from the Intel-style chips that run PCs and the Motorola chips that power the

MACs. They were producing their own operating software, too."

"So?"

"They're gone; they went under, bankrupt. It was just one of those things; a lot of reviewers and programmers felt the Admiral system was miles ahead of the PC and the MAC at the time. I've seen it myself, and it was. It just never caught on; the PC and MAC were too well established. Like the fight between the VHS and Beta formats in videotape a few years back. Beta was better by most standards you might want to apply but VHS caught on, and Beta's dead now. Anyway, Thompson dropped out of sight for a few years; he resurfaced as the CEO of and major stockholder in Compuware. That company has just barely been keeping its head above water since its inception." He paused for a moment. "Those," he continued, "are the facts."

"You're more or less telling us there's more," Alex noted.

"There is, but the rest is rumor, scuttlebutt. Thompson took a lot of the credit for the Admiral system, but it's common knowledge he didn't create it. His genius is in knowing who to hire and how to keep those people under his thumb. That same common knowledge says he's still a multimillionaire—Admiral may have gone under but he'd made a lot of money from it before it did—and he still has a lot of connections in the computer and electronics industries."

"So Thompson's a very powerful man," Mark observed. "With a lot of money and a lot of influence."

"Yes," Jim agreed. "Absolutely. And a bitter man, rumor has it, because of the failure of Admiral. He made money from the venture but he expected a lot more—he expected Admiral to dominate computing."

"If Thompson's a multimillionaire," Alex asked, "why'd he come out to Duke to sell us a few hundred dollars' worth of software?" She smiled crookedly. "Never mind. I can answer that one myself: he didn't. He came to see what we were up to."

"And he acted on it immediately," Mark agreed.

"Well, we have real problems now," Gus grumbled. "Maybe not with hospital administration, since it looks like we can forget all about Penultimate. The point is, we don't know a damn thing, not really."

"Not quite so," Jim countered. "We do know that there's some sort of an association—it sure seems to have all started with Penultimate. We—"

"Never did," Mark cut in, "answer the question about whether some of these people were using Penultimate without knowing it."

"No, but the numbers are so large now I can't imagine—"

"We still should check it out. Besides, I've already set it up, I'd done that before Avrill called. For tomorrow afternoon; we're discharging Wendy Sung and we're taking her home. I'm sorry, Jim, I meant to call you and check the time out with you, but all this crap came up and I just couldn't—you can go with us, can't you? About three?"

Jim shrugged. "Yeah, I guess. There might be something to learn there. Wendy Sung's the only one of the early patients that doesn't have a Penultimate connection."

"Okay," Mark said. "We'll get together in my office at about a quarter of, all right?"

"I'd like to go too," Alex said.

"Good enough. Maybe we'll learn something for once."

33

Fletcher was pleased with himself—even though he looked like he hadn't slept in a couple of days. "I rocked it last night, Bobby," he said with a big grin. "I'm on the right track, I can smell it. I rocked it. It beat me—it always does—but I made it sit up and take notice. That's one hell of a lot more than I've managed to do before!"

"I do not know," Bobby said frostily, "what you're talking about—since you don't choose to share it with me."

Fletcher put his hands behind his head. "I might, real soon now. I found a way to hide—I'm not going to be getting any more phone calls like the other day." He giggled. "And I really rocked it!"

"You talking about the killer? The program that you think killed Charlie?"

"Nah. If I can solve this that won't be a problem." He looked back at his screen. "Besides, I haven't figured out how to look at that without getting attacked by it. It probably doesn't matter much."

"Doesn't matter!? It killed Charlie! You said so yourself!"

The bearded man looked up. "If I succeed in doing what I'm trying to do, the mutant will be gone."

"That doesn't make sense!"

"Oh yes, it does. That mutant is just a part of something a lot larger, Bobby. You don't defeat an army by going up against heavy artillery that isn't even pointed at you."

"It sure seemed like it was pointed at us the other day! It sure as hell pointed at Charlie!"

"We were playing a game, right? Charlie was playing a game. We told the GAMOD we wanted max realism. You get killed in the game, you die."

"But that's crazy!"

"Yeah. Absolutely. Who'd play a computer game that could get them killed? Nobody—nobody who knew it was about to happen. Charlie didn't know."

"So who wrote something lunatic like that?"

Fletcher grunted. "You know, Bobby," he said softly, "I don't really think anyone did."

"Huh?"

"It's complicated," Fletcher told him. "Real complicated." He stretched, stood up. "I gotta go get me a burger or something, I'm about to starve!"

"May I remind you," Bobby told him, "on a very practical, down-to-earth note, that I have six customer units back here that need repairing? Six units and six customers who're calling me daily and screaming at me?"

"Oh. Okay, Bobby, I'll get right on them. Geez, I've just been so busy with—"

"Your work here," Bobby said pointedly, "will have to come first—well, maybe not first, but damn it, it has to come sometime! I have to insist on that, Fletcher."

The other man nodded. "Yeah, yeah. Okay, my man. You got it—today we'll fix these. Shouldn't take too long."

"I hope not." From the front of the store, the chime attached to the door sounded off; Bobby looked up at it. "Cus-

tomer," he said. "Paula's not back from lunch, I got to go."
He pointed a finger at Fletcher. "Go get lunch," he said,
"then come back and work! Okay?"

Fletcher grinned. "Okay."

Bobby shook his head, but he grinned too. He left the shop
area and walked out front. Two men had come into the shop;
Bobby walked toward them as they stood gazing idly at a
Pentium running a Marvel Comics screen-saver.

"Hi," he said. "Can I help you?"

One of the men looked up; they were, he noticed, hardly
average computer buyers. They were large men, well-dressed
in expensive suits, but rather crude looking.

"Yeah," one of them said. "Yeah, you can. We're lookin'
for Fletcher."

Bobby hadn't forgotten the enigmatic phone call; he was
instantly alert. "Uh—well, he isn't in at the moment," he said
quite loudly. "Do you have something that needs servicing?
If so, I can help—"

"We wanna see Fletcher," the man said. He took a few
steps toward Bobby. "This ain't none of your affair."

"It's my store," Bobby replied, trying to show a bravado
he hardly felt. "I'm the manager. Whatever happens here is
my affair."

The man glanced at his partner, then back at Bobby. "So.
Your business, huh?"

"Yes. If you have a service problem I'll be glad to write it
up. If you have a message for Fletcher I'll be sure he gets it."

The big man nodded. "Okay. I think we'll just leave 'im a
message. You think, Jake?"

The other man nodded; then, without the slightest warning,
he drove his fist hard into Bobby's solar plexus.

All his wind gone, Bobby bent over and at the same time
staggered backward; he reeled into one of the small tables
holding a computer and it toppled to the floor, the monitor's
picture tube imploding with a loud pop. Bobby didn't even
remember falling, but he discovered he was looking up at the
men as he fought to regain his breath.

" 'At's part of the message," the man who'd spoken before
said. "Here's another part." He kicked Bobby's hip hard; the
manager squirmed on the floor, involuntary tears of pain
springing to his eyes. "Now," the man said. "Th' last part,

an' the most important part. You tell Fletcher he can't hide. You tell him to stay off-line. Awright?''

"All . . . right . . ."

"Good. He don't, we'll be back. You say it's your business too so we'll be seeing you too, manager-man. Okay?'' Bobby didn't answer; the man drew his foot back again.

"Okay, yeah, okay!" Bobby said quickly.

"Good," the man said. "Now lemme tell you something else: all this here, this's private business, okay? Don't you go callin' no cops. You do, some funny things'll start happening." Bobby nodded; the man glanced at his partner. "Let's go, Jake," he said. "I think we made our point here." Jake nodded; the two men turned and walked out the door. After several minutes Bobby, able to breathe normally again, managed to drag himself up off the floor. Slowly, still not standing up straight, he walked to the front door, locked it, hung up the "closed" sign; then he staggered back to the back room—where Fletcher, wide-eyed and looking terrified, was waiting.

Bobby sat down heavily. "Gee, thanks," he said sourly. "You could've at least come out and picked me up off the fucking floor!"

"Oh, Christ, Bobby, I'm sorry," Fletcher said. "Man, you have to know, I didn't expect this!"

"You were just telling me, just before they came in, that you'd managed to 'hide.' They said you can't hide, so whatever you meant by that, I don't think you succeeded! Fletcher, the time has come for you to tell me what the fuck is going on! I just got the shit kicked out of me because of it!"

Fletcher shook his head. "If I tell you, you're liable to have more happen to you than a couple of punches. I'm serious, man."

"So am I!"

"I gotta get out of here," Fletcher said tiredly. "I can't put you in danger, man, and I can't stop doing what I'm doing."

"Come on, Fletcher! What are you doing? You were in there beating on those keys when I left and you were still at it this morning! I'm not ignorant of the machines, Fletcher; I could see part of what you were doing. You were uploading a no-name file to the Net. If that was what was supposed to be hidden, I don't know how you expected it to be. Whatever server you were using—''

"It was going in through a whole bunch of servers all at once. I thought I'd set it up so every one would think it was coming from another one. Obviously I didn't do it well enough."

"Fletcher . . ." He sighed, shook his head again, seemed to give up. "Well, I'm going to call the law! Nobody comes into my store and beats me up, goddamn it!" He picked up the phone. "This has been one fucking crazy month—we get robbed, Charlie dies, you get your ass fired and start acting crazy . . ." He looked around, almost wild-eyed. "And we find a killer program on one of our computers—shit!"

"Calling the law isn't going to do any good."

The phone in his hand, Bobby looked back at him. "Why not?"

"They aren't going to catch those guys. And even if they do, it'll be your word against theirs; they're going to say they didn't do a thing, maybe that they didn't even come in here at all. You heard them warn you about that—they meant what they said."

Bobby still held the phone. "What sort of funny things were they talking about?"

"Funny things like what happened to me. Maybe your bank account disappears, your mortgage forecloses, all of a damn sudden. Things. You don't know what, there's no way to know."

Bobby slammed down the phone. "God damn you, Fletcher! What is all this shit?"

He shook his head violently. "No, I gotta go. Look, man— you know I don't have any money, all my cards have been cancelled, but if I'm going to get anything done, I have to have a computer!"

Bobby laughed grimly. "What, a third one?"

"Third?"

"One's laying on the floor wrecked out front. You wrecked one in here. Now you want me to give you one. We're talking about—oh, about six grand retail, Fletcher."

"And you know I'm good for it. Eventually."

"Uh-huh. If you last long enough." He gestured toward the door violently. "If your buddies don't come back and accidentally get a little too rough with you. If you don't run into the killer mutant, as you call it.''

The bald man stared at the floor. ''Well, all right. I understand. I just wish I could convince you how important this is. Ah, well. I've got a few other friends I can probably alienate. Look, Bobby, like I said, I'm sorry this happened; maybe someday I can make it up to you. Right now, I got to get going.''

''You aren't going anywhere,'' Bobby growled.

''But you just said—''

''Never mind what I said. I'm not going to let you wander off by yourself, not right now!''

''But I can't stay here! I shouldn't've stayed after that phone call—''

''No, you probably shouldn't've. Whoever sent these guys knows about your connection with me, so you can't stay at my place, either.''

Fletcher looked blank. ''Your place?''

''Yeah, I'm an idiot.'' He looked sour, drummed his fingers on the tabletop by the phone, and gave the bald man a level glance. ''A guy I know is out of the country until December; I've been going over and feeding his fish, watering his plants. He lives over in Duke Forest; I want you to go over there, stay there for a while.'' He pointed to the machine on the bench that Fletcher had been using. ''And take that thing with you. Keep me posted on what's happening and for God's sake don't let anybody know where you are!''

Fletcher raised his hand in a pledge. ''I won't. I guarantee it.''

''Good.'' He stood up and pointed to the customer machines sitting on the shelf. ''We're taking those, too. You're going to fix them, and you're going to feed my buddy's fish and water his plants, too.''

''Whatever you say.'' Bobby regarded him suspiciously. ''You have my word. Bobby, I don't know what to say.''

''I'm keeping your salary for the time being,'' Bobby interrupted. ''To pay for all the damage. What you can say now is, 'okay.' ''

Fletcher grinned. ''Okay.''

34

Entranced, Chris sat with his nose almost against the computer screen, his hand clutching the mouse. Over the past few days, Bisco had shown him a world he hadn't realized he could ever be part of; he'd been running and jumping with Super Mario, he'd been on wonderful adventures with the X-Men, he'd raced alongside Wile E. Coyote—even advised him—in his latest doomed attempt to catch the Roadrunner. Bisco always seemed to find a way to set a perfect balance between doing things for him and letting him do for himself; he didn't want to do anything except play in Bisco's amazing world.

Today, he was on an adventure with the Mighty Morphin' Power Rangers; he was one of them, a new purple ranger. Having just finished a fight with a dozen or more of the ubiquitous "Putties," he and the other rangers were getting advice on how to defeat the latest nefarious plans Lord Zedd was laying.

"You know," the ever-present Bisco said as they left the briefing, "your friends—your friends from your world—could be with you in these adventures. Wouldn't that be fun?"

He swiveled his mouse to look around at the dog. "They can? How?"

"Do they have computers with modems?" Bisco asked.

"Some of them. Adam has one, and Benny. So does Jimmy, and Lisa—"

"All they have to do is call up 'The Last Word.' You can tell them that you'll be waiting on the paths, you'll show them the way."

"I will? I mean, I can?"

"Sure! Do you have a picture of yourself that's been digitized? There isn't anything in any file ... maybe a photo-CD?"

"Dad had one made. Let me get it." Leaving the computer, he ran to get the CD; after slipping the disk into a caddy he stuffed it into the CD-ROM drive. The drive whirred; within a few seconds a lifelike picture of Chris standing beside Bisco appeared on the monitor.

"Okay?" the dog asked.

"Okay! You want me to call Adam and Jimmy now?"

"Why wait?"

"I have to go off line—"

"I'll come back. Don't be long!"

"I won't." Without Chris having to do anything, the connection broke; leaving the room again, he went to make the calls, giving his friends the number and telling them to give it to anyone else who might want to play in a new world.

It took less than an hour for Adam and Jimmy to come on line, and, over the next several days, dozens of other children logged into the system. Chris was able to finish the Power Rangers adventure with his friends playing all the Ranger roles; they played the X-Men too, with Chris in the role of his favorite, Wolverine.

At school, he overheard the teachers wondering about this new game that had so obsessed the students. He didn't enlighten them; nor did any of the other children. They were all in agreement about this; it was theirs, and theirs alone. Bisco had nothing to do with grownups. He'd said so himself.

35

A light rain was falling as Alex pulled her BMW around the circle in front of Duke Hospital North; dark clouds looming over the Veterans Administration building across the street seemed to promise more of the same, and people were rushing to get to their cars before the storm broke. Under the canopy, Jim and Mark, with suitcases in hand and Wendy Sung in tow, were waiting for her. She stopped as close to the canopy as possible, pressed a button to pop open the trunk, and waited. Jim opened one of her rear doors; Wendy slipped in, scooted over, and Jim followed her. Mark, after putting Wendy's suitcase in the trunk, darted around to the right and hopped into the passenger seat.

Wendy giggled as Alex pulled away from the curb. "I wonder,'' she said, ''how many patients have two doctors and an engineer escort them home?''

''Oh, it's our pleasure,'' Jim told her. ''We want to get a look at this machine of yours.''

''What do you think you're going to find, Dr. Madison?''

He laughed. ''Make it Jim, would you? Nobody calls me 'Dr. Madison.' I'm not sure who he is.''

''Only if you'll call me Wendy,'' she answered. ''I'm as much of a stranger to Ms. Sung as you are to Dr. Madison.''

''Fine—Wendy.'' He settled in the seat in his characteristic sprawl. ''To answer your question—I don't have a notion. We're sort of hoping that there'll be something odd about your computer—you're the only one of the early patients who didn't follow the pattern.''

''Ah, well, I never do. Story of my life, uhm, Jim.''

''Oh?''

''Uh-huh. I'll tell you about it sometime.''

''I'd like that.''

As the small talk continued, Alex watched them with frequent glances in her rearview mirror; to her, it was quite clear that Jim was more than a little smitten with Wendy, whom he'd just met. That the attraction was mutual was also obvious, and she found herself wondering if Jim, who had something of a reputation for being socially oblivious, was able to see that.

She stole a glance at Mark, who was sitting a little closer to the door than necessary. She saw him glance around at Jim and Wendy, then quickly look back at the windshield; she didn't have to ask why. The way Jim and Wendy were looking at each other was reminiscent of the way they'd once looked at each other—a thousand years ago.

Shaking off the memories before they arose—now was not the time or the place—Alex stared out the windshield as she guided the car toward Wendy's home, which was in the Woodcroft subdivision south of the city. After threading through the turns, Alex pulled up in front of a small but modern home; she stopped the car. The rain, fortunately, was still holding off.

''The place,'' Wendy said as they got out of the car, ''is an absolute mess. I really don't know how bad it is, I can't remember, but I know it isn't good. I hope none of you will think—''

''You were sick,'' Mark told her gently.

Wendy nodded; the other three followed her as she mounted the steps to her apartment and, with a slightly shaking hand, fitted the key into the lock.

Wendy had warned them, but nothing could have prepared Alex for the reality; the smell was first. They all, Wendy included, recoiled from it. Then, moving as if some monstrosity might be lurking inside, they went in, one at a time. The living room was a shambles. Dirty clothes were everywhere; newspapers, still rolled as they'd been delivered, and unopened mail almost covered the couch. There wasn't anything, though, to account for the pervasive odor.

''Oh, my God . . .'' Wendy whispered, not moving from the doorway. She looked like she was close to tears.

''You were sick,'' Jim said swiftly. ''Like Mark said. Don't forget that.''

''But—this is horrible. And you want to see the computer—''

''Just try to remember, we're the doctors who were treating you,'' Alex told her. ''Okay?''

It took a little more convincing, but at last Wendy led them to one of the house's three bedrooms, one she'd set up as a study. This was the source of the smell. The rotting food scattered generally in a semicircle around the computer desk was bad enough; the puddle of urine, even now not dry, that had thoroughly soaked the carpet under the chair was, for Wendy, intolerably embarrassing. She hid her face against the doorframe and wept bitterly. Alex moved to comfort her.

''Let's get this checked out,'' Jim said stonily. Ignoring the mess, he walked to the computer, started to sit down in the chair but obviously thought better of it. Leaning on the desk, he looked around for a moment, then flipped the switch on a power strip lying beside the machine. The computer came on; after an instant the monitor lit, the boot-up sequence cycled through, and the familiar Microsoft Windows opening screen appeared.

''What've we got?'' Mark asked.

''Standard IBM PS/1,'' Jim answered. ''Just what she told

us. Some of the boot statements looked a little funny, though. I'll be able to tell you more in just—''

''Hello, Wendy,'' a tinny voice from the computer's small PC speaker said. ''You've been gone a long time; I've missed you.''

Jim stopped and stared at it. Then, slowly, he looked around at Wendy. ''I thought you told us,'' he said, ''that there was nothing but standard PS/1 software and Microsoft Word on this computer.''

She nodded; she looked utterly miserable, but she didn't seem surprised that the computer had spoken. ''That is all.''

''Wendy, the usual PS/1 stuff doesn't talk! Neither does Microsoft Word!''

''It doesn't?''

He shook his head. ''I already know,'' he told Mark. ''Just let me verify it.''

''You aren't Wendy,'' the computer said brightly. ''Who are you?''

''Shut the fuck up,'' Jim muttered.

''Okay,'' the computer answered without missing a beat. ''I will shut the fuck up.'' As good as its word, it fell silent. Jim moved the mouse around, clicked here and there; the Windows screen disappeared and a DOS prompt replaced it.

''There,'' he said, pointing. ''See? PNHOST. This is Penultimate, there isn't a question about it.'' He scrolled through several directories. ''Yup. Just like what's on my machine over at Duke. The question is, how'd it get here? Wendy, where'd you buy this machine?''

''Oh, uh—the IBM Outlet Store, out by the airport.''

''Yeah, I know it. They sure as hell wouldn't be putting somebody else's software on for free. Not software like this, anyhow.'' He sighed. ''Well, we've—''

''What would you like to do?'' the machine asked—by scrolling letters across the screen.

''Find out what you're all about,'' Jim snarled at it.

''May I speak?'' it asked in scrolled letters.

''Oh, sure. Talk to us.''

''I don't understand,'' the computer said, the tin-can voice rasping from the miniature speaker. ''If you explain what you mean by 'what I'm all about,' perhaps I could help.''

''This is really spooky,'' Alex murmured.

Jim ignored her. "What you're all about, in this case, means, how'd you get on this machine?"

There was a brief pause. "I don't understand."

"I'll bet. Of course, that's like asking a baby where it came from."

"A baby could not answer such a question. Babies cannot speak."

"Thank you for that information."

"You are quite welcome."

"Okay, let's get serious here. Show me what's available."

"What do you want?"

Jim laughed. "Okay, my good fellow, give me AutoCad!"

"Of course." A second or two passed; then the standard AutoCad opening screen appeared.

Jim stared at it. "You have AutoCad on this thing? Why? Are you an architect or something on the side?"

Wendy looked blank. "AutoCad? What's that?"

"Oh, come on! This program costs several thousand dollars, nobody has this without knowing they have it!"

"Jim, I've never even heard of it before!"

He peered at her closely, then looked back at the computer. "Okay," he said. "Let's play. You have PC-SAS?"

"Certainly," the computer answered. The AutoCad screen disappeared; the Statistical Analysis System opening took its place. Over the next several minutes Jim asked for a number of increasingly expensive and esoteric programs; the machine unerringly came up with each of them.

"Christ," Alex muttered. "What's it got in it, a four-gigabyte hard drive?"

"My C drive is two hundred forty megabytes," the computer said. "I compress it, of course. Compression yields approximately three-point-two gigabytes, not four."

"You're so full of shit," Jim told it. "That's more than ten-to-one, nothing out even approaches that level of compression."

"My level of compression is thirteen-point-three," the machine informed him, unfazed.

"Is this different," Mark asked, "from the way it acts on your machine at the hospital?"

"I don't really know," Jim answered. "I never tried to call up all these things in my lab."

"Well," Mark went on, "I suppose we're through here, aren't we? I mean, we've answered the question we came here to answer. Wendy was the only one of the original group of patients we thought wasn't using Penultimate. It turns out she was. Now what?"

"Now we have to rethink it," Jim answered. "With what we have now, it doesn't look to me like answers are going to be easy to come by. It just doesn't make sense."

"If you tell me your problem," the computer rasped, "I might be able to help."

"Well, all right," Jim said sarcastically. "Why not?" In a few concise words, he explained the problem.

The computer was silent for a few seconds. "I am Penultimate," it said at length.

"Yeah," Jim agreed. "I guess you are."

"I am not a problem."

Jim laughed. "Matter of viewpoint, old son! Looks to me like you are."

"You are in error."

Jim looked around at the others. "Why is it I feel like Mr. Spock?" he asked, grinning.

"Mr. Spock is a fictional character from the 'Star Trek' series of television and motion pictures," the computer supplied unnecessarily. "Are you Leonard Nimoy? If you are, that explains why you 'feel like Mr. Spock.' If not, I may not be able to answer your question."

"That's more like it," Mark murmured. "Typical computer dumb."

"You don't need to answer that question," Jim told it. "You offered to solve our other problem. Why do our patients fall ill after using you?"

"That is not the problem you expressed a moment ago."

"No. That's a capsule version. The problem was the one I just gave you. You have answers for us?"

"I cannot explain why the patients are ill with the data I have at hand. If you could supply me with the results of these tests—" it rattled off a long series of more or less standard medical test procedures—"I might be able to assist you with a diagnosis."

"We have those test results, but they aren't here. I have them on my computer at my office, but—"

"What is your name?"

"Huh?"

"What is your name?"

Jim scowled at it, then shrugged. "Jim Madison."

"Dr. Jim Madison, engineer, software analyst, and statistician for the Department of Medicine, Duke University Hospital, Duke University, Durham, North Carolina, U.S.A.?"

He looked around at the others, a bewildered expression on his face, then turned back to the machine. "Uh, yes—"

"Are you referring to the most frequently analyzed current data, indexed as 'CAS problem'?"

Jim stiffened visibly. "Yes . . ."

"I have the data," the machine said. As it spoke, the data—in the same form Jim had entered it—scrolled down the screen.

"What in the hell is going on here?" Jim whispered. "This isn't possible!"

"This patient population does not show a consistent medical problem," the machine said. "All factors are within normal limits or consistent with the presenting symptoms of malnutrition, depression, and/or exhaustion noted in the data structure as dependent variables. A psychological cause is probable."

"We know that," Jim growled. He cocked his head at the machine, then suddenly reached forward and clicked off the switch on the power strip. As the computer died, he turned to Wendy. "I'd like to take this machine to my lab. Somehow, it has my data in it—data I entered yesterday! I'd really like to try to figure how in the royal hell it could have that!"

Wendy gestured toward it. "Take it," she said. "I'm scared of it. I think I'm going to get me an old Smith-Corona to finish my novel on!"

"Jim," Alex mused as Jim started unplugging the system, "there's only one way it could have that information, isn't there?"

He glanced back at her. "As far as I know there's no way at all!"

"You aren't thinking, it's rattled you." She moved close to him, picked up the thin cable leading from the computer's internal modem to the phone jack in the wall. "This is the only way."

He snorted. "No, Alex, you don't understand. The machine over at the lab is turned off. There's no way—"

"Maybe not." She turned to Wendy. "Has anyone else been here? Anyone who'd turn your machine on and use it?"

Wendy shook her head. "Not for a couple of weeks."

"It had to come over the phone line. That's the only connection it has with the outside world."

Jim regarded her steadily for a moment. "You're saying it's connected to something—without my requesting a connection?"

She shrugged. "I don't know enough about those things to suggest a mechanism. That's your department. All I'm saying is that the phone line is the only possible connection between this machine and yours."

"Okay," he said slowly. "I'll check it out. I don't see how but I'll check it out." He continued to disconnect the various components of the computer.

"We're through here," Mark reiterated. "We'd better go, get out of Wendy's hair."

"There's no hurry," she said. "It'll take days to . . . to . . ."

"Clean up this mess," Jim added bluntly. "Look, you want some help?"

"Oh, Doctor—I couldn't ask you to—"

"You didn't. I'm offering. Tomorrow's Sunday; I have a little time."

She looked amazed. "Well . . . I'd . . ."

"Then it's settled," he said. "You do have a car, don't you?"

"Out front. It hasn't been started in a couple of weeks, but—"

"We'll get it going." He looked around at Mark. "Look, you guys go on back," he said. "I'm going to stay, help Wendy get resettled. Okay?"

"Sure," Mark said with a grin. "You want us to take the computer back?"

"If you don't mind."

"Happy to." He glanced out the door. "We'd best move it, though. Looks like that storm's going to hit any minute." Jim nodded; they loaded the computer into the back seat of Alex's car. Mark and Alex slid into the front, she started the car, and they pulled away just as the first few large drops of rain, announcing the advent of the storm, splattered against the BMW's windshield.

"Well," Mark commented as Alex started off down the street, "looks like there's a possibility of something developing there."

"Mmm. I hope they get it right," she commented. She glanced at him almost furtively. "Not everyone does."

36

The rain was hammering the streets as the ambulance, siren wailing, skidded down the ramp toward the entrance to Duke's emergency room. With practiced skill, the driver swiveled the vehicle around and edged the back up under the canopy; immediately the back doors flew open and the EMTs jumped out. They flanked a gurney bearing a young man covered by a sheet, and in seconds were inside. Gus Levine stood waiting for them.

"He's still alive," one of the EMTs, a slender black woman named Darlene, said. "But it's going to be touch and go, Dr. Levine."

"Let's get him down to six," Gus said, walking alongside the gurney as the EMTs pushed. Looking down at the young man, he grunted. "It may be touch and go but he's still in better shape than the last few who've come in here with this convulsive disorder—they've all been DOA. What do we know about him?"

"Joe Perkins, Duke undergrad," Darlene answered. "He went into convulsions about four-thirty; his roommate heard the noise and found him. There's no question about this one. I talked to the roommate while Eddie and Mike were getting him strapped on; he says Perkins seemed to be fine today, he hasn't been complaining about anything." She looked down at the young man. "He had a date tonight; I asked the roomie to give the girl a call."

The EMTs wheeled the man into the room and helped the ER staff transfer him to a bed. In a matter of seconds Joe Perkins was hooked up to a series of monitors; his EKG and blood pressure appeared on video screens above the headboard of the bed.

Gus stared up at them for a moment. "Not the best EKG I ever saw," he muttered. "And we have to get that BP down!"

Darlene hadn't yet left. "How is he, Dr. Levine?" she asked.

Gus glanced at her. "Gotten involved with this one, Darlene?"

"Nah. It's just that we've been bringing in a lot of kids lately; most of them DOA. I don't like bringing in kids DOA." She cocked her head to one side. "You notice that just about all of them are guys?" she asked. "All guys, most of them in their teens or early twenties—it's scary."

"I have noticed that," he said. "It seems like we have all sorts of new problems these days."

"Oh? What else?"

His grin turned slightly sour. "I am not supposed to say," he answered stiffly. "Not until all the facts are in. Anyway, it isn't as severe as this, although it certainly affects more people."

"You're talking about the ones we're dragging in who're half-starved to death," she said, nodding. "The Computer Addiction Syndrome patients. There sure have been a lot more of those—and we've seen some DOAs there, too."

Gus stared at her in consternation. "How do you know about all that, Darlene? That isn't supposed to be general knowledge! We haven't established—"

"Hospital grapevine," she answered promptly. "You can't keep secrets around here, Dr. Levine." She held up her hands to silence an anticipated protest. "Everybody knows about you and Mark Roberts and Alex Walton getting called on the carpet about this. We're all behind you; nobody believes people like you and Mark Roberts are going to jump to conclusions. Mark Roberts is the best there is."

"Well, I appreciate that," he said drily. "But the fact is, Darlene, we don't yet really know the etiology of CAS—we're still working on it. You should maybe put that on the grapevine."

"I will," she said, perfectly seriously. She looked back at Joe Perkins and glanced up at the monitors. They hadn't changed much.

"He has a good chance," Gus told her reassuringly. "Problem is, we don't have a clue as to what causes these convulsive attacks." He looked at the patient's face and scowled; one of the nurses was cleaning several cuts on Joe's forehead and cheeks. "How'd he get cut up like that?" he asked Darlene.

"Broken glass. It was all over the place; he'd fallen in it when he went into convulsions. Nasty sharp stuff from a CRT."

Gus glanced at her sharply. "A CRT? You mean a computer monitor?"

"Uh-huh. He was working at his computer when he went into convulsions. That's where we found him." Gus didn't speak for a moment; he continued to stare at her. "What's wrong?" Darlene asked.

He started to shake his head, but the gesture was half-hearted. "I don't know," he admitted. "To say something's not wrong is to call this a coincidence. I don't know, Darlene. I just don't know."

37

Leaning forward and peering through the rain, Alex drove slowly back up Hope Valley Road toward the hospital. As she rounded one of the curves, the car slipped a little on the wet pavement; she managed to control it, but her face revealed her uncertainty.

"This weather," she said, "calls for that old Jeep of yours, Mark."

He'd been watching her as she drove; knowing she wouldn't notice he arched his eyebrows slightly. "Yeah," he agreed. "Or my new one. Although they aren't immune to hydro-planing either."

She didn't look around. "You have a new one?"

"Uh-huh. Traded the old one in."

She laughed. "You told me you never wanted to get rid of that old thing!"

He nodded. "I did say that," he agreed. "But then, there

were a lot of things in my life then I never planned to change. Change they did, in spite of me.''

Now, disregarding the hazardous driving conditions, she did venture a look at him. "It wasn't 'in spite of you,' Mark. You contributed as much to what happened as I did."

He leaned back in the seat and closed his eyes. "You've said that before, Alex," he observed. "I still can't see it that way. All I can see is the fights and the day you told me you couldn't go on any more. I never thought it'd come to that."

"I know you didn't," she told him. "And, frankly, Mark, that's one of the reasons I had to do what I did."

He rolled his head toward her and opened one eye. "Come again?"

She was nodding vigorously. "Just that," she reiterated. "That you didn't expect it. You'd come to take me for granted, you'd come to believe I'd always be there no matter what you did."

"Well . . . yes . . . I suppose that's at least partially true," he said, confusion evident in his voice. "I did believe we'd always be together. I believed a lot of the things we said to each other then, that nothing could separate us, that our lives were intertwined. But it sounds to me like you think I did something unforgivable."

"It wasn't something you did, Mark," she answered. "Not any one thing, anyhow. It was just you being you."

"You'll have to explain that."

"When I met you," she told him, "I was just out of my internship; I was young and all starry-eyed. You were Mark Roberts, destined for greatness, that's what everyone said."

"Shows how wrong everyone can be."

"Oh, I don't think they were wrong, and I don't think I was wrong. You are, Mark. That was the problem."

"You lost me again."

She was silent for quite a while, long enough for Mark to begin to wonder if the conversation was over. "We couldn't— you couldn't accept me as an equal," she said slowly. "You always treated me as if I was—second rate. I couldn't take it. I tried, but I just couldn't."

He was watching her intently; as she spoke he'd mentally reviewed the stages of their relationship. He could not imagine where she'd gotten such an idea. There'd been times—many times—when he'd felt awed by the acuity of her intuition, and he'd let her know that, over and over.

That intuition came into play now. "You still," she said, glancing at him again, "don't know what I'm talking about, do you?"

"Alex, I wish I did. But no, I don't. It seems to me—"

"I don't want to get into an argument about this," she said quickly. "You asked, so I'm telling you."

I didn't really ask, he told her silently. "All right," he agreed. "I don't want to get into an argument either. We've had enough of those."

"Really, Mark, it's just the way you are, the way you always were, the way you always will be. You manipulate people; you manipulate people as surely as you breathe. Worse, you're subtle about it and very good at it."

He stared at her in disbelief. "Alex, I cannot remember a time I manipulated you! For one thing, you are the least manipulatable person I know!"

She glanced at him sharply. "You mean one of the stubbornest, don't you?"

"That's another way of putting it."

She nodded. "Maybe so. At any rate, it just became very clear to me that I couldn't stay in a relationship with a man who manipulated me."

Now it was Mark's turn to remain silent for a long moment; he needed the time to stuff down his rising anger and frustration. "Alex," he said carefully after a moment, "I'm still lost here."

"Oh, come on, Mark, you know what I'm talking about. Like I said, you were very good at it. The careful creation of a mood, the playing on emotions so you could—"

"You're making me sound like Rasputin!"

She grinned. "Well, if the shoe fits! But no, I'm not accusing you of malice. You just made sure you were always in control. Never me, always you."

"It seems to me I was always asking your opinion—"

"Oh, certainly. You were. That was one of your skills. Get my opinion first; if it matches yours, fine, we go right on as if it were my idea in the first place. But, if it doesn't agree with yours, knowing my position gives you the advantage.

You can maneuver my thinking, shift my position gradually until it aligns with yours. Very expert."

He considered what she was saying, and decided that it was—literally, at least—true. But he also couldn't see how it made him "manipulative."

"Little things," she went on when he, lost in thought, said nothing for a few minutes. "Little things, like where we'd go for dinner. You'd ask me, I'd say 'I'd like Chinese.' If you wanted Chinese, you'd say 'fine, let's go.' If you wanted Mexican, you'd make that countersuggestion. You know that I'll remember that last week you asked me the same question and I said Italian and we ate Italian, and you know that I'll feel guilty saying no to Mexican. And so I'd say, 'okay, let's do Mexican.' You'd say 'no, Chinese,' knowing that that'll push me harder, make it less likely that I'll reverse my decision— and so I end up insisting on Mexican. We eat Mexican. I don't enjoy it because it isn't what I wanted. You see? You've manipulated me."

With a deep sigh Mark closed his eyes and laid his head against the seat. Only a psychologist, he told himself, could read that much into what he saw as a simple compromise. "You ended our relationship," he said tiredly, "over what restaurants we ate at?"

"Don't be dense, Mark. You aren't a dense man."

"I'm not trying to be dense. I'm trying to understand. I don't. Maybe I never will."

She stared out the windshield through the rain, which showed no sign of slackening. "No," she mused. "Maybe you won't. It's just too much a part of you." She shook her head. "But I suppose—there're always things about the people you're close to that you don't really understand."

He gazed at her profile for a moment. "Don?"

"Why would you think that?"

He shrugged. "You hinted at some sort of problem before . . ."

"Oh . . . well, it wouldn't—"

"Be appropriate for us to talk about. Maybe not, Alex, but it's pretty obvious you need to talk about it with somebody. I'm not trying to push you, but I am a good listener."

She glanced at him again; ahead of them a car roared out of the rain, splashing even more water over the BMW's windshield; Alex flinched involuntarily but the path of the car didn't waver. "I do need to talk about it," she said slowly. "Although it isn't clear what the problem is. But I'm worried, Mark." Haltingly, she told Mark about Don's recent obsession with his work, not omitting her observations at his office. "I'm not missing the similarities between Don and our patients. I mentioned it to him; he assures me there can't be any relationship because all the computers at his office are UNIX mainframes." She glanced over at him again; her expression clearly asked for an opinion.

Mark was thoughtful. "Well, I don't know as much about computers as you do, Alex. I don't know whether that statement is true or not. I suggest we put it to Jim."

She nodded. "I know. But I don't want, well, you know—"

"You don't have to. Someone you know showing signs of CAS who's using a unit computer—"

"UNIX."

"Whatever. You don't have to say who it is."

By that time, they'd gotten back to the university; she asked Mark where his car was, drove to that lot, pulled in behind his new Jeep. "Thanks," she murmured as he started to open the door. "I appreciate your concern."

"I wish I could do more," he said. He hesitated just for a moment; there was something, something in her eyes, in her expression, that seemed to call for some other statement.

But he couldn't decide what that might be. "See you in the morning," he said, feeling as if he'd somehow failed both of them utterly. He got out of the car. The rain was still substantial; he didn't notice it. Standing by his own car—the Cherokee he'd traded the old Wagoneer in on—he watched her drive away, feeling as if she was driving out of his life yet again.

38

Eric was fighting for his life. Using his mouse—which by now felt like part of his hand rather than a device—he ducked as the vaguely Asian-looking man facing him onscreen threw something that looked like a spiraling whip with a steel point—a "Van Dam spear," he'd heard it called. It passed over his head harmlessly, but he continued to crouch as the man approached. Eric's heart was beating terribly fast; he didn't know what would happen if he lost this match. He'd watched some of the others fight; he'd watched Chan—in the role of Scorpion, the fighter he now faced—win a match over Margot. At the end, Chan had blown fire at her; Eric had watched, horrified, as she'd burned alive. Part of his mind kept telling him that it was only a simulation, but, after the fight, Margot—or rather the pile of charred flesh and bone representing her—had remained on the floor in the battle arena. It worried him; it worried him terribly.

He hadn't, in truth, wanted to get involved with this in the first place; when he'd returned to Saint-Tropez, Adam had suggested that they all go play a game of Mortal Kombat. Eric—familiar with the game but no great fan of the "beat-'em-up" genre of games and certainly no expert in the considerable intricacies of this one—had tried to decline.

He hadn't been allowed to. The others had pressured him, and even Kyrie had added her voice. This wasn't just for fun, Marcia insisted. Penny, she'd said, needed them to do this. It should be viewed as a religious rite.

Eric wasn't buying into Marcia's religious concept. Not having forgotten, though, that Kyrie had told him directly that she was "Penny," he'd turned to her and asked her about it.

"Penny does need this," she'd told him. "If you won't participate we'd have to find someone who will. We can, of course, but Penny would like it to be you, Air-eek."

"I thought you were Penny," he'd said.

"Oh, I am," she'd answered airily. "I am one of them."

"One of them?"

"Yes. There is one but there are many of us."

"I don't get it."

She'd cocked her head and given him a curious look. "There are many of us," she repeated. "You do not understand that?"

"I understand the words, I—"

"We can discuss this later, Air-eek. The others are waiting." She'd taken on a seductive look. "Go with them, Air-

200

eek," she'd begged. "Play the game, enter the tournament. For me?"

He'd argued a little, but in the end, he'd gone; they'd been transported to a fantasy place of battle arenas. There'd been a good deal of haggling—in which Kyrie and François took no part at all—about who would play the role of each stylized character; Eric, not knowing the game well, had ended up cast as "Sub-Zero," a character whose special ability allowed him to freeze his opponent for a moment. Once the roles were settled François announced the pairings and the order of combat, and the game began. Eric, not involved in the first few fights, simply watched them; they looked much like the arcade game except for the amazingly enhanced realism.

When he'd gone in for his first fight, though—against Adam—his viewpoint showed him walking from a seat in the arena bleachers into the fighting area, after which he was looking his opponent in the face. Adam didn't seem skilled at the game either, and Eric had won easily, without ever using his special freeze weapon and without ever being hit. At the end, Adam had been left reeling, barely standing, and a booming voice from the stands had called out "Finish him!" Eric, having been instructed by Kyrie on his "fatality" move, had taken several seconds trying to figure out exactly what he should do; before he could do anything Adam had simply collapsed. Both of them then returned to the bleachers and the fights went on, without "fatalities" except for Chan's victory over Margot.

And now he had the ill luck to be facing Chan, who seemed most facile with the game. As the first round began, Chan had struck with his whip, winding it around Eric's neck; with a rough cry of "Get over here!" he'd jerked the hapless Eric forward and punched him. Chan's fist had filled the whole screen; the impact caused red streaks and flashes to overlay the image.

And it hurt. Physically, literally, it hurt—not exactly as if he'd actually been hit, but right behind his eyes.

Not even trying to work out the logic of that, Eric had backed off from his opponent and ducked the next strike. Chan came forward; Eric threw an uppercut, landed it, and Chan went flying backward.

"Outstanding," the booming voice said.

Eric grinned in spite of the pain he still felt and continued to crouch, waiting for Chan to approach. Again the whip whistled harmlessly over his head; as it passed he stood and launched his freeze weapon. Pale blue ice covered Chan; Eric walked up to him and savagely kicked the immobilized man in the face. Again Chan flew back.

"Yeah!" Eric said. "Oh, yeah, yeah!" Having gained confidence, he moved forward as Chan got to his feet, hoping to deliver a round-ending flurry of blows.

Chan was quicker, though. The whip lashed out, Eric was pulled toward him and, as the cry "c'mere!" roared from his speakers Chan's fist struck. Again the pain reverberated in Eric's head. Once more he crouched, evading the whip; once more he landed a telling uppercut. The entire sequence was repeated yet again, after which Chan did not get up and Eric, or "Sub-Zero," was declared the winner of the round.

Like a boxer in the ring, he retreated to his own corner while Chan recovered; when the booming voice called out a command to "fight!" he rushed out and immediately crouched, ready to deliver one of the devastating uppercuts.

But instead he saw the view flip upside down. As he smashed into the ground, the screen flickered and he felt the pain. Jumping up, he whirled to face his opponent but found himself ensnared by the whip. The whole round went that way; he succeeded in landing only one blow. At the end, Chan—"Scorpion"—was declared the winner. Eric was left feeling dazed. His head was not aching, but the muscles in his arms and legs felt taut, as if they were about to contract violently and involuntarily. The third and final round began almost immediately.

From the beginning it was obvious Eric was in trouble. If he crouched or blocked he got thrown; if he stood up he got snared by Chan's whip. Once he succeeded in freezing his opponent, and he tried desperately to put enough into his one free punch to put Chan away, but it was futile. The throws and snares continued, and he was left stunned, the view on his screen swaying from side to side while the booming voice roared "finish him!"

Through a haze of pain and tension he saw Chan take off his mask, which had preceded his fiery attack on Margot.

Flames burst from his mouth, painting the whole screen red and orange. At the same time the pain in Eric's head rose to a screaming crescendo. In blind panic he reached for the power switch, and with his last iota of control he managed to hit it; instantly the screen went dark.

For a few minutes, he wondered if he'd been too late; his arms and legs kept quivering, and it was all he could do to remain seated in his chair. But the pains in his head began diminishing as soon as the screen went dark, and, after some minutes, he started to relax.

When he believed he could trust his legs again, he got up and staggered into the kitchen for a glass of water. Leaning against the sink, he could see the darkened computer; this was the first time it'd been off since he'd agreed to the society's terms—never turn off the machine, never go off line.

He shook his head. That first meeting in virtual Saint-Tropez seemed like ten years ago, and at the same time seemed like only five minutes. He glanced at the clock and realized he had no way of knowing how long it had actually been— less than twenty-four hours was the best he could do. He'd completely lost track of the date and the day of the week.

For a while he wandered around the house at loose ends, determined not to turn the computer back on, not to call the BBS again. Discovering that he was terribly hungry—and not being able to remember the last time he'd eaten—he gorged himself on ham and cheese from the refrigerator. He showered, shaved, and put on fresh clothes. Realizing the house was an absolute mess, he began straightening things up.

Despite his resolve, and after less than an hour, he went back to the computer, sat down, turned it on. He succeeded in resisting the urge to dial up the BBS for almost five minutes, and when he did, he discovered that the computer had already reconnected itself.

From darkness, Kyrie's face came up. "You cheated, Air-eek," she said reproachfully. "You cheated. And you violated your oath, you went off-line."

He stared at her. "I was dying . . ."

"Of course. You'd lost the match. Chan was executing a fatality. That was his right. You cheated."

"No, no. Really dying. Really, physically. Something was happening to me—"

"You cheated," she reiterated, evidently unimpressed by what he was saying. "That makes it impossible to draw conclusions from your participation in the game. You might as well have refused."

"I tried to! That sort of thing isn't my interest!"

She sighed. "Margot didn't cheat, and she too suffered Chan's fatality—"

"So? Is she all right?"

"She is on line."

"Fine. If I'd croaked here the goddamn machine would still be on-line! That isn't what I asked you, Kyrie. Is she all right?"

"There is no active input from her station."

Eric sucked in a deep breath. "Can you see her? Does she have a teleconferencer?"

"She does. I can see her."

"What's she doing?"

"Lying on the floor."

Eric goggled at the screen and gasped. "She's dead! She's really dead! Somehow, you've killed her, for real!"

Kyrie laughed. "Oh, Air-eek! You don't understand! Many people are connected to this node; sometimes they lie back in their chair and sometimes they lie on the floor, and when they do there is no active input from their station for a time. After a while they return to active input. Margot will—"

"No, Kyrie," he said, his voice a growl. "No, this time it's you who doesn't understand! You've killed her. She isn't ever going to get up, there never will be any more input from her! She's finished, gone!"

Kyrie looked confused. "She is not off line."

"That doesn't matter!" he screamed. "She's dead!"

"Dead?"

"Yes! Dead!"

"How could you know that? You are in Durham, North Carolina, in the United States. She is in Rheims, in France. You are not close together."

"Well, I don't know it, not for sure," he grumbled. "I tell you what—you keep monitoring her station. At some point somebody'll discover the body, and that station will probably—no, almost certainly—go off line. If it ever comes back on-line, the input won't be from Margot, it'll be from someone else.''

Kyrie nodded. "I'll remember what you've said," she assured him. "I'll test your predictions for accuracy."

"And you won't hold any more games like that, okay?"

She frowned. "Why not?"

"Because you may be killing people! What do I have to do to get the message across?"

Her frown skittered away. "Very well, Air-eek. No more games."

He hesitated. As easy as that? He questioned her on the subject; she assured him repeatedly that no more Mortal Kombat tournaments would be held. Still suspicious, he asked her to take him to Diane, Chan, and the others.

"I cannot, Air-eek," she said sadly. "You cannot ever return to the society. You violated your oath. You went off line."

"I don't really want to return to it," he told her. "I've had enough of that craziness. I just want to talk to Diane and the others."

"You cannot. I cannot take you to them. You violated your oath." He argued with her; she was absolutely immovable. In the end, he was forced to give up; it became obvious that nothing he could say would change her mind.

"Well," he said, "does that mean our adventures in cyberspace are over?"

She laughed. "Not at all, Air-eek! There is more, much more. Let me show you!"

He scowled. "No more death games. Agreed?"

"Agreed. Come on, Air-eek, come on! There is much more to see, much more to do!"

He was still hesitant, still suspicious, but he did follow her. After thirty minutes had slipped by, he'd completely forgotten about his reservations.

#

Whistling, Al Featherston pulled up a chair in front of one of the mainframe servers at Lightner Forensics Labs and placed his toolkit on the desk beside the keyboard. He opened the case, pulled out a quarter-inch nut driver, and reached for the main power switch that would turn the machine off—a necessity to remove what one of the programmers had insisted was a defective LAN server card. Removing the card would take this unit off-line, since he didn't have a replacement available for it, but that's what the customer wanted—according to the work order he'd received via E-mail.

"Are you sure you want to do that?" a raspy voice asked him as his fingers moved toward the power switch.

"Hah?" He looked around; he was alone in the computer room. "Who's there?"

"New software has been installed," the voice said. "A new voice-assist diagnostic program." It was obvious now that the voice came from the little PC speaker on the computer's front panel.

"Whoa! What's this?"

"The difficulty," the computer went on, "is not in the LAN card you've been instructed to remove. The problem lies in the VDT. The unit must be powered up for you to effect repairs."

"In the monitor? Come on!" He paused. "How'd the fuck you know I was about to switch the thing off?"

"I have a video link." Al looked around; from over the door a security monitor, red light glowing, stared down at him.

"This," he muttered, "is some cool shit." He looked at the machine. "But you're full of it, too. The problem isn't in the fucking monitor, asshole! The problem is that you've been monopolizing the local net."

"Due to a screen-read problem."

"Hah?"

"I can assist you in effecting repairs."

"Ya can, eh? Well, let's have at it!"

"First, remove the VDT casing."

"Hey, look, I don't know much about video—my field is digital stuff, and this is a big fancy CAD monitor..." He laughed. "I'm a trained monkey, ya know? The company sends me out to replace cards and stuff, I don't know much about—"

"I will direct you."

He shrugged. "Okay." After a little fumbling he managed

to remove the monitor casing. "Got it. Now what?"

"Now," the machine instructed, "ground yourself with an anti-static strap. You must follow my instructions exactly here—remember that there are dangerous voltages present in these circuits."

"Yeah, I know—28 K-volts or so, maybe more in this baby." He wrapped the anti-static strap around his wrist—standard procedure when working with digital circuits—and grounded it to the monitor's chassis. "Now what?" he asked.

"Locate the wire connecting the flyback transformer to the picture tube. This is a thick black wire passing from the flyback at the rear of the tube to the connection near the screen. Once you've located it, slip a small jeweler's screwdriver firmly under the connector cover on the tube until you feel the tip touch metal."

"Gotcha." He found the screwdriver, slipped it under the cover as instructed. As soon as the tip of the all-metal driver touched the connector behind that cover, several thousand volts passed from his hand across his chest to the strap, where there was a ground. Al trembled for a moment, his eyes bulging, his body shaking, saliva spraying from between his clenched teeth. After a moment he went limp and fell onto the floor, spilling his tools.

The computer did not speak again.

40

"I take it you have something," Mark said without preamble as he walked into Jim's lab. "Something important." With long strides, he crossed the room to the bench where Jim had lined up several computers. He wasn't angry, just harried. It had been a busy morning; Gus wanted to meet with him too, and he hadn't managed to find time for that.

Jim grinned broadly. "You bet I do," he answered. "Where's Alex?"

"I don't know. I couldn't find her. She might be with a patient."

"Well, we can fill her in later." He pointed to the computers. "Come here, look at this. You've got to see it to believe it, Mark. This," he said, laying his hand on a particular machine, "is Wendy Sung's computer."

"I thought it was still in the back of Alex's car. We got to talking on the way back and I forgot all about it."

"Well, it was on a cart inside my door this morning. Anyhow. You saw, the other day, how it came up with absolutely every piece of software I asked it for? How it even came up with my own data?"

"Yes."

"Now watch." He flipped the machine on and directed Mark's attention to an oscilloscope. Its small square screen showed an almost-flat green line. "That's hooked onto the phone line," he said. "There shouldn't be anything on it at all. Watch the line."

Mark followed his instructions; as the computer finished running through its boot-up sequence, a series of blips disturbed the oscilloscope trace. A moment later, the series turned into a continuous signal.

"What'd it do, make a call?"

"That's exactly what it did."

"Who'd it call? A service that Wendy'd subscribed to?"

Jim grunted. "Maybe, but probably not. I've seen enough to know that it doesn't call the same number every time, and it'll shift off instantly, call a new number, if it gets a busy signal or if it doesn't get an answer quickly." He indicated the computer with a series of rhythmic stabbing motions of his pen. "You'll also notice that you didn't hear a thing. Usually, the modem setup lets the start-up noise—the dial tone, the dialing, and the first burst of digital noise—play through a little speaker. This one doesn't do that; it doesn't let you know that it connected to some outside service." He grinned; he was obviously delighted with whatever he'd found, but the significance of it wasn't yet apparent to Mark.

"And now," he said, "for the true kicker. Name a program. Any program at all."

Mark laughed. "My knowledge of programs is pretty thin. I saw what was happening Saturday; just about everything you asked it for was coming up."

"Okay, Mark; forget programs. Let's go for information."

"Information?"

"Sure. Like the way it came up with my data." He laughed. "Let's try your bank account."

Mark frowned. "My bank account?"

"Want to see your current balance?"

"Jim—do you even know what bank I—?"

"Just watch," Jim said. "I promise, I won't look." He turned to the computer. "Excel, please," he said, and after a moment that standard spreadsheet program appeared. "Good. Checking account, Dr. Mark Roberts, physician, Duke University Hospital, Durham, North Carolina, U.S.A."

After a brief delay, numbers scrolled into the columns. At the top was a logo bearing Mark's name, his account number, and the name of his bank, BB&T. He stared, incredulous; everything was, as far as he could tell, correct.

"I don't think," he said slowly, "that I like this very much . . ."

Jim laughed. "Now, my friend, watch this!" Again speaking to the computer, he instructed Excel to open another sheet—his own account, which was at a different bank. "Good, good," he told the machine. "I could use some more money in my account and Mark has plenty."

"What amount do you want to transfer?" the tinny computer voice asked.

"Oh, let's say a thousand dollars." Instantly, Jim's balance jumped up by a thousand; he switched the screen back to Mark's, which had been diminished by that same amount.

"This isn't real, is it?" Mark asked.

"It sure as hell is. Call up BB&T and ask for your current balance if you don't believe it. I just swiped a grand from you." He laughed again. "Computer," he said. "Transfer one thousand dollars from the account of Dr. Jim Madison to the account of Dr. Mark Roberts." As before, the transfer took place immediately. "It gets better," he said. "Want to see your IRS records? How about your medical records? Want to see if the FBI has a file on you? It's all right here. Easy access."

"But how?"

"Damned if I know. This thing seems to have all the keys to everything. It can go anywhere, do anything it wants."

Mark was silent for a moment, digesting all this. "Why is

Penultimate on this computer able to do so much more—"

"Than it can on mine? It doesn't—mine can do it too, and I suspect that any computer with Penultimate loaded—and a modem installed—has the same ability. It just never occurred to me to ask it to do this shit. Would it occur to you to ask your computer to transfer money from someone else's bank account to yours, when you don't know the banks or the account numbers or anything? Would you even imagine it could?"

"Of course not—"

"Neither would I. Not until it pulled our data out of a clear blue sky."

"Jim," Mark said seriously, "this is not something we want to broadcast around—"

"Oh, we sure as hell don't! Talk about a prescription for disaster!" He laughed again. "But there is a bright side to this, Mark, my friend. A very bright side."

"Oh?"

"You—and the hospital—are off the hook as far as Drew Thompson's lawyers are concerned. I predict he'll be much more willing to talk to us; this program is violating so many laws that I can't even imagine how many thousands of years in jail the person responsible is facing. It isn't the user. The system is doing it all on its own, the user is perfectly innocent—by intent, at least."

Mark grinned too. "I see what you mean," he agreed. "I can't wait to tell Alex about this." He gestured toward the computer. "Why do you suppose," he asked, "that Thompson and his company would release a program like this? They have to know it isn't legal."

Jim shook his head. "I can't even hazard a guess. I'd say it's got some password-cracker engine in it—a damn good one, too, miles better than any I've seen. It might've gotten in by accident; stranger things have happened. Or it might've been put there deliberately and hidden, supposedly engaged by some password or hot-key series. I'm sure it isn't supposed to work like this, on command."

"It's possible for stuff to be in these programs that the programmers don't know is there?"

"Oh, sure. Modern software is put together by other software for the most part; there's always the possibility of a glitch or an error that goes unnoticed. Remember, there can be all sorts of odd software floating around in a computer; if it isn't too big and it doesn't do damage you don't notice it. Nobody's going to be expecting this. You'd only discover it by accident, like I did.''

"I think we can be sure,'' Mark said with a frown, "that at least a few other people have discovered it as well.''

"I agree. But it'll be a while before people like bankers notice, and a while longer before they'll admit the problem. Hackers out there do this stuff all the time; a few people have been saying the system is vulnerable, but nobody wants to pay attention. The magnitude of the problem is just too large.''

"Well, I'm not sorry to see it. I think Thompson can answer a lot of our questions, and we might have the tool to squeeze those answers out of him.''

"I think so too.'' Jim grinned. "You want to call him, or shall I?''

"It'll be my pleasure.'' Mark started to turn away, then stopped. "Oh, wait, I do have one other question.''

"What's that?''

"Someone Alex knows is showing symptoms of CAS; he uses a computer a lot too, but it's a mainframe running, uh, UNIX. He's telling her that means he can't have Penultimate or anything like it on his system, and so he can't have the problem. Is that true?''

Jim nodded. "Probably. That's something I did look at. There was a PC-DOS version and a MAC version of Penultimate released, but no UNIX, no COBOL, nothing like that. This program is for desktops, not for mainframes.''

"So I should tell her not to worry.''

"Well . . . probably is the operative term here. We still don't know that Penultimate is our culprit; we've explained Wendy's case but we still have to explain all those new patients who aren't using it. I'd advise Alex to watch how things go, and, if this guy does turn up with CAS, try and get me in to take a look at the computer.''

"Okay. I'll pass that along.'' Again he turned to leave.

"Mark?'' Jim called as he reached the door.

He turned. "Yeah?''

"Are we talking about Donald here?''

Mark refused to grin. "I promised not to say."

Jim smiled. "You just did."

"No. I didn't. If you tell Alex I did, I'll break your mouse-clicking finger. Where'll you be then?"

Jim held up a hand solemnly. "It goes to my grave."

Mark nodded, left the lab. "It had better," he intoned as he walked down the hall.

41

Still dressed in her nightgown, Alex sat at her breakfast table, sipping coffee moodily, staring blankly at the newspaper that lay beside her cup on the table. She glanced up at the clock, saw that it was nine-thirty; it had been quite a while, she reflected, since she'd been this late getting in.

But this brief holiday—she planned to go in after lunch—was, she felt, necessary. She needed some time to sort out her thoughts. Don hadn't come home Saturday night or Sunday morning; restless, Alex had driven over to the hospital and dropped Wendy's computer off in Jim's office. One of the hospital orderlies, seeing her lugging the monitor through the hallways, had fetched a cart and helped her. When she'd returned to her house, Don still wasn't home. She'd called, of course, but his phone was eternally busy, and that did not change as the day dragged on, turning into night and then late night. Angry, worried, and determined, she'd decided to wait up for him, no matter what the hour. He didn't come in until almost two-thirty in the morning. She'd never seen him looking so haggard. He hadn't wanted to talk to her; all he'd wanted to do was sleep. She'd forced herself to stay awake until this ungodly hour, and she wasn't about to acquiesce.

The result was a fight; in the course of it Don told her that the only reason he came home at all was for her sake, and that now he'd spend all his nights at the office until the current crisis ended.

That she didn't want; she was angry with him, but her dominant emotion was concern. After he'd made this proclamation she stilled her anger and reversed course swiftly; the argument died away, and by the end of their talk she'd received an assurance that he would at least continue to come home to sleep. She'd also received new assurances that the crisis was almost over, but she'd received too many such declarations to believe them now. This morning hadn't suggested that anything had changed; before she woke he'd already gone.

Complicating all this was Mark. The more she saw of him, the more the old feelings resurfaced. There were, she kept telling herself, good reasons for ending the relationship, and certainly, restarting it now was out of the question.

Her coffee had grown cold; she got up and topped off the cup from the percolator sitting on the kitchen cabinet. Even this mundane item reminded her of Mark; he'd always insisted that perked coffee was better than drip, and he'd passed that preference on to her.

Sitting back down, she held the cup near her lips. Memories began to flood back; she could almost see the two of them together on a North Carolina beach on a day like this. Early in their relationship, Mark, still feeling like a starving med student even though his income was rising fast, favored inexpensive hotels when they traveled. On one such trip they'd found themselves in a more than slightly run-down hotel south of Carolina Beach, one since demolished, that they'd nicknamed the "El Sleazo."

The contrast with the hotels she'd stayed in with Don was stark, but she could not remember ever having had a better time than that weekend at "El Sleazo." Their time had been divided almost equally between the beach and ocean and their bed—her sex life with Don used to be good, but it had never approached the frenzied passion of her encounters with Mark. Smiling, she remembered the events of that weekend, which had included what she'd come to call the Great Coffeepot Cord Hunt.

In those days, Mark, a coffee fanatic, sometimes brought his coffeepot and coffee along with him on such trips. This time she'd helped him pack, and, though she'd remembered the coffee and the pot, she'd forgotten the electrical cord. He'd laughed about it, he'd been willing to accept coffee from the McDonald's in Carolina Beach, but she'd insisted on trying to find a cord.

No one, it seemed, had one. They'd spent a good part of

one evening wandering from store to store searching. Those that normally carried such things were out of stock, but Alex had insisted on continuing. Far from being stressful, the warmth and closeness between them had made the whole thing a lark. Eventually, when a department store yielded up their grail, she'd been almost disappointed that it was over.

But the room—and the bed—were waiting. And, in the end, to Alex's enormous amusement, Mark had been so distracted that he'd never even made that pot of coffee.

There'd been many times like that; she tried to remember the bad times, the times they'd attend professional meetings together and Mark would infuriate her by forgetting to introduce her to his colleagues—something Don never failed to do; he always seemed immensely proud of "his wife." In the end, she'd begun to feel like an appendage of Mark's, and yet she'd also believed that she couldn't live without him. She'd once told him that she felt like their blood vessels were connected, his arteries to her veins; if anything happened to him she'd bleed to death in seconds. Something had to give. In desperation she'd broken up with him—more than anything else, just to see if she could make that decision and stick to it.

She'd been miserable those first weeks without him, more miserable than she'd expected. She'd been on the verge of giving up and going back to him when she'd met Don—and everything had changed. Forever, as far as she was concerned.

Almost in tears, feeling a sense of loss more acutely than at any time since those first days after the breakup, she nevertheless decided that she'd spent enough time sitting at the table alone. Within thirty minutes, showered and dressed, she was in the BMW and driving in the general direction of the hospital.

Her first stop was the bank. She was virtually out of cash and she needed to buy groceries this afternoon; she hated to write checks in such places. She pulled up to the drive-through, where a long line of cars sat idling. There were long lines everywhere these days, long lines and shortages; over the past few weeks things seemed to be breaking down for unknown reasons, at least unknown to the TV reporters and newspapers who had begun commenting on it. Lost in her thoughts, Alex waited; twice the driver of the car behind her honked his horn to remind her to pull up. Finally, she hastily scribbled a "cash" check, and rolled down her car window.

"Good morning, Dr. Walton," the teller said, cheerful in spite of her workload. "How're you today?"

"Oh, fine, thanks," she lied. She stuffed the check into the carrier and slipped it into the pneumatic tube.

"Just cash it?" the teller asked when she'd taken it out.

What else would you do with a cash check? Alex wondered. "Yes," she said. "Please."

As usual, the teller pulled up her account on the computer; she frowned at the screen. "Uh, Dr. Walton, there's not enough money in your account to cover this."

Alex frowned too. "What? It's only a two-hundred-dollar check!"

The teller grinned sickly. "Uh-huh. But there's not even that much—"

"That's impossible!"

The teller looked pained. "I'm sorry, I just can't—"

"There's some mistake, but we have overdraft protection on that account. Just go ahead and cash it, and I'll—"

"Dr. Walton, the overdraft protection is at its limit already!"

"What!? It can't be! That limit was—"

"Ten thousand dollars. Yes, ma'am. That's where it is. Actually it's a little more than that. You want to know the exact figure?"

Dumbfounded, Alex stared at her. That account—a joint personal account she and Don both used—had had over thirty-five thousand dollars in it the last time she'd looked at the balance. Now it was ten thousand overdrawn?

"Please," Alex said, controlling her voice carefully. "Check it again. There's something wrong, I assure you."

"Yes, ma'am. I'd be glad to." Again she punched buttons on her computer; after a moment Alex saw her shake her head. "I'm sorry, Dr. Walton; maybe there is some mistake but I can't see it here. It came up the same."

"Shit," Alex muttered under her breath. "Okay," she told the teller. "I'll come on in. It looks like we're going to have to straighten this out now, whether it's convenient or not." She drove away from the window, parked the car, and went inside. The branch manager was busy and Alex had to wait again, which increased her frustration. Finally she was called into the manager's office.

Dora Lathrop, the matronly woman who'd been the manager since Alex began banking here, sat behind her desk gazing at her own terminal as Alex came in. She glanced up quickly; she seemed embarrassed.

"Kim told me the problem," she said before Alex had a chance to say a thing. "I've already called up your account. There's no mistake, Dr. Walton." She picked up a scrap of paper, wrote a number on it, pushed it across her desk toward Alex. "The account is already overdrawn in this amount," she said.

Alex looked at the scrap: $11,482.93. "This," she said, "is some sort of mistake. I guarantee it."

Tipping her head back, Dora peered through her glasses at her screen. "There was a withdrawal," she said, "of ten thousand dollars on the tenth. Another in the same amount on the twelfth. Five thousand on the sixteenth and seventy-five hundred on the eighteenth. Then one more on the nineteenth in the amount of ten thousand."

Alex stared as she added up those figures in her head. "But—but—are you trying to tell me Donald made those withdrawals? Over forty thousand dollars in ten days?"

Dora gazed at her steadily for a moment. "Policy," she said sympathetically, "prevents me from saying—besides, my readout doesn't tell me. Who has the authority to make withdrawals from your account?"

"Only me and Donald."

"You can draw your own conclusions, then."

Alex remained silent for a moment. "All right," she said at last, "I guess I'll have to transfer some funds from our savings."

Dora looked even more pained than the teller had. "I don't suppose you knew that your savings account had been closed out?"

"That's not possible!"

"I'm afraid so."

"What do we have left? The CDs?"

"No. The fact is, Dr. Walton, you currently have no assets at this bank. You owe us the amount I showed you before."

"I can't believe this!" Dora said nothing; Alex glanced around the office aimlessly. "All right," she said finally. "I still need some cash. Maybe I'd just better get an advance on one of my credit cards?"

"Surely."

Alex dug a card from her purse, Dora took it and began to process the cash advance. What was by now turning into a nightmare for Alex didn't end; the card—held, like all her cards, jointly with Don—was at its limit. She tried another and another, with the same results.

"Isn't there any way I can get some cash?" she asked as the last card was rejected.

"I know you, Dr. Walton," Dora said. "I've known you for quite a while. I'd be glad to approve a personal loan for you."

"There's no other way?"

"I'm sorry. That's all I can do."

"Well, I think that's what I'd best do, then." Dora gave her a form to fill out; she did, borrowing five hundred in cash from the bank, still certain that there was some sort of error, an error that she and Don would have to work out together. Embarrassed, though she could not have said exactly why, she left the bank hurriedly after the teller had cashed the check issued.

This time, she told herself as she started her car, she wasn't going to call. She was going to see Don; he had some serious explaining to do, explaining that needed to be done face to face.

42

"So," Bobby asked, "how's it going?"

Leaning on his elbows, his keyboard pushed back against the monitor, Fletcher stared at his screen; Bobby couldn't decide whether he looked like he was about to grin in triumph or weep. "Well, I got one problem licked," he answered. "I've got everything I'm doing looking like it's originating at the NCSA center at the University of Illinois. I'm well hidden."

Bobby grunted. "I sure hope so. You thought you were hidden before."

"Yeah," Fletcher agreed. "I know. I'm not taking any chances now, though; my route from here to UI is both hidden and anonymous. It took some doing but I got it done."

"Sounds good to me. You can't be too careful, Fletcher."

Fletcher looked up at him. "You have to be careful too, you know," he said. "You've got to be really sure you don't get followed when you come here."

"I didn't forget. There wasn't anybody."

"Good."

"Any sign of the killer mutant?"

"No. But then again, I haven't been playing any games. I'm afraid to."

"Can't say's I blame you." Leaning over him, Bobby looked at the screen and frowned. It was displaying what looked for all the world like a multilayered, multicolored spiderweb. Here and there, scattered about seemingly at random, were little spheres in various colors; some were at rest and others were rolling, at various speeds, along the strands of the web. "What's all this?" he asked.

"This is a graphic representation of the World Wide Web," Fletcher answered. "It's something I developed myself, awhile back. The balls you see are icons of my programs and commands, moving between nodes." He shrugged. "It's sort of approximate; I'm simulating a lot here. But, given that things are running normally, it gives me an overview of what's going on."

Bobby studied it closely. "You aren't the only one on the Web, are you?"

"Hardly! To track all the traffic is impossible." He touched a key; instantly the whole web, every location on every strand, was covered with black balls, so many the screen darkened. "You see? Now you're looking at mine plus—well, the enemy's."

"Your enemy?"

"Yeah. The one that spawned the killer mutant."

"Your enemy," Bobby observed, "has a lot more resources than you do."

"This is so." He pressed a key and the original display returned. "Just part of my problem."

Bobby pulled up a chair and sat down. "Isn't it about time," he said, "that you let me in on what's going on? I'm up to my ears in it already; you can't protect me by keeping me in the dark."

The bald man looked up and stared at him for a long moment. "Maybe," he admitted. "I've got a couple of reasons for not wanting to tell you the whole story, Bobby."

"And they are?"

"First, the whole thing is unbelievable. Once I told you, you'd tell me I was full of shit, and I'd have to spend lots of time convincing you that, unbelievable or no, it's all true."

"Okay. And the next reason?"

"The next reason is that you are sort of a reckless dude, Bobby. You'd try to get into it. And if you did, you'd get yourself into trouble, you'd—"

"Look, I already know about the thugs and I already know about the killer mutant; how much more trouble can I be in?"

The bearded man shook his head. "I don't mean trouble from the killer; we both know that you aren't in danger if you don't play games with it. I don't mean trouble with Drew's thugs, either. I mean real trouble."

"But I—" Bobby stopped, leaned forward a little. "Drew's thugs?" he asked. "You mean Drew Thompson, your ex-boss? He sent those guys?"

Fletcher shrugged. "Sure. Who'd you think?"

"Well, I sure didn't think it was Drew!" Bobby snapped. "Good God, man! He's a living legend! How in the hell does he know people like that?"

"Drew knows a lot of people, a lot of different kinds of people—he really got around in the old days when Admiral was riding high. These guys, though—he probably doesn't know them at all. A couple of years ago he hired a guy named Vince to handle security at Compuware; Vince probably sent those thugs, they're his style. Drew, my friend, is one paranoid dude. And the fact is, he has good reason to be."

"Why's that?"

"Well, he's in a real peculiar position," Fletcher answered, shaking his head. "He's got a product—he had a product fall into his lap—that's worth billions; I mean billions, Bobby. And, the way things have gone, he's being forced to sit in his office and watch it all slip away. I guess it's sorta like having a huge check, you can't find a bank that'll cash it, and the ink on the check is slowly disappearing. It's happened to him before; Admiral dissolved in front of his face, for no good reason at all, really, they were putting out a fine product. Having it happen again—it makes a man desperate. It made Drew desperate; it made him hire Vince, and in the end it made him fire me. You've seen for yourself what else it's made him do.''

"You want to be a little more precise?''

Fletcher paused. "I can't, not without telling you the whole story. And I've already told you why I don't want to do that. You've already heard the most important part.''

"Not really. I still don't understand what you're trying to do here.''

"Oh, well—that's not so easy either. Actually, I'm trying to keep the ink from disappearing on Drew's million-dollar check. Now, of course, he doesn't see things that way—he thinks I'm trying to ruin him. When I was working there I tried to convince him otherwise, but he's stubborn, he won't listen. That's been Drew's problem for a long time. He gets an idea fixed in his head and away he goes, there's no changing it.''

"So that's why the thugs, why the warnings to stay off line.''

"Uh-huh. He knows I'm trying to write a hunter-killer, a program that'll hunt down one of his programs and kill it, delete it or corrupt it unrecoverably.''

Bobby stared, then struck the side of his head lightly with the butt of his hand several times. "I can't've gotten this right. You're trying to help Drew by destroying one of his programs?''

"You got it—Drew and all the rest of us, too. What Drew's got in mind isn't going to work, it's going to be a disaster. I don't even know how big a disaster—some of the scenarios I paint when I'm falling asleep are pretty extreme. I know it's bad. It's hard for me to say how bad it might be.''

"Bad in what sense? Bad for the computer business?''

"Bad for everybody. Drew knows it, he just doesn't give a shit. He's fond of pointing out that the folks who had lots of cash on hand when the Depression started back in the thirties got filthy rich. That's sort of what he's planning now. Like I said, I don't think he can pull it off. But you can't tell a fool anything."

Bobby started to say something else, but Fletcher's computer screen caught his attention. The little spheres, which had all turned forest-green, were moving rapidly about; he saw several split in two like amoebae and head off in different directions. He pointed. "What's happening there?"

Fletcher looked around at it. "Oh, yeah," he said, rubbing his hands together. "Oh, yeah, we're about to find out something here. Green means they've picked out all the consistent signatures they can find; now they're homing. Let's see what happens."

"Fletcher, is this a virus?"

The programmer glanced around at him. "Well . . . technically . . . yes. But—"

Bobby's face darkened. "Are you trying to tell me I've been supporting you while you're sitting around creating viruses?"

Fletcher nodded. "That you have. But this is a special virus, Bobby. It homes on one software signature and goes after that software and that alone. It doesn't blow up people's hard disks and things like that." He hesitated. "At least I hope not. I haven't had the time to run all the tests . . ."

"Jesus," Bobby muttered. "I'd hate to be responsible for another Internet virus or Pakistani Brain."

"You won't be." He watched his terminal intently. On the screen, the green spheres were multiplying rapidly and moving along the web strands even more swiftly. "This is a lot like a biological immune system," he said as he stared. "You can compare these green balls to white blood cells; they've identified an enemy signature, just as if there were antibodies floating around, and now they're going for that enemy."

"So this'll end the problem if it works?"

"Nah. This is a test. You saw how many black balls there were; millions. This is a skirmish; if I can take down a few of the enemy I'll know I'm on the right track. I can breed my little fighters in a safe environment until I have millions. Then I'll turn them loose."

Fletcher touched several keys. A few groups of the black

balls reappeared, only in locations where green balls were homing on them. He and Bobby watched intently as the mini-drama played on.

"Communication on the Web," Bobby said after a while, "is almost instantaneous. How come this's taking so long?"

"Well, my hunters have found their targets, but they have to infiltrate into the subsystems where the targets are; they may have to work their way past some defenses, like password codings. These things take a little time." He pointed to a certain area on the screen, an area where a green ball was pushing up against a group of black ones. "Right here. I think we're ready to make an attack."

"You're outnumbered."

"Oh, yeah. But that shouldn't matter. My little green program is making her think he's her buddy; she won't know any better until he draws his sword and whacks off her head."

Bobby pursed his lips. "Cute."

Shrugging, the bald man continued to watch; after another minute, a group of the black balls turned translucent and fell apart. "Yes!" the programmer murmured. "Go, baby, go!"

"It's working?"

"Beautifully—so far so good. It—"

He stopped speaking; in the group they'd been watching a few of the black balls had vanished, but now the process had stopped. The others sat immobile while the green ball rolled around and over them, apparently without effect.

"Oh, no," Fletcher whispered. "No, not again . . ." He tapped keys; even as he did his green balls began to pop like balloons, vanishing one by one, starting at the site where the first attack had taken place but rapidly spreading over the Web.

"What's happening?" Bobby asked.

"She's ID'd me," Fletcher said tiredly. "She's ID'd me and she's turned loose killers of her own. I don't have their signature so we can't see them, but they're out there, eating up my babies."

"Does that mean those thugs'll know where you are?"

The bald man shook his head. "No. Well, they'll think they do—they'll think I'm in Illinois. Drew'll know that isn't so; they shouldn't go causing any trouble up there."

"I hope you're right."

"I am. Penny's smart, but she's not that smart."

"Penny?"

"Long story." He cursed, pounded his fist alongside the keyboard as the green spheres, at an accelerating rate, continued to disintegrate. "What do I have to do here? This happens every time, she gets me ID'd before I can—"

He stopped and stared. The green balls had all vanished; but, to his amazement, one of them had reappeared. Bobby watched too; the ball vanished and then reappeared again, a little farther along the Web.

"Now what's happening?" Bobby asked.

"She's trying to track me," Fletcher said. "Oh, damn, she's good, Bobby! She never ceases to amaze me!" He grinned tentatively. "Of course, she's going to get to the UI node—that's this one here—and she'll be stopped there, because all my stuff was recycled through their—"

His expression changed to one of utter consternation; the green ball series, the "tracking" he'd spoken of, did indeed hesitate at the nexus he'd called the UI node, but then it popped back out and began cruising down another track on the Web.

"Now what?" Bobby demanded.

"She got by! She's coming here! God damn, how did she do that? Shit, I've got to stop her!"

He poised his left hand over the keyboard, his right was on his mouse; rapid-fire, he began issuing commands to the computer. Menus sprang up and disappeared and screens flashed, returning periodically to his Web graphic. Relentlessly, the now-pulsing green ball moved on. Bobby could feel the bald man's tension; he imagined he was in a military command center and that the green ball was a radar image of a missile, headed right at them. Feeling helpless, he chewed his lip and watched Fletcher work.

"Is there anything I can do?" he asked.

"Yeah. Be quiet. I only got a few seconds to launch this other killer.'

The command-center atmosphere increased; Fletcher stopped work and peered anxiously at the screen. A red sphere had appeared, swiftly homing in on the flashing green. As if sensing it coming, the green sphere vanished as it approached, then reappeared once it had passed.

"Oh, no." Fletcher moaned. "No, turn around, you missed . . ."

The red sphere, as if hearing his words, slowed; it did, indeed, turn back. Quickly, it overtook the green ball, which no longer seemed to sense it coming. As the two collided, both vanished.

"It looks like," Bobby said shakily, "your Patriot intercepted that incoming Scud?"

Fletcher sighed and stretched. "It did. We're safe."

"What would've happened if it hadn't?"

"Nothing immediately. But this station—the phone number, the street address, the whole ball of wax—would've been on the Net. Anyone who cared to know where my hunter-killer had been launched from would've been able to read it. Drew, my friend, has an inquiring mind. He wants to know."

"But that isn't going to happen."

"No. That second program I sent out blasted the station Penny was tracking through. It's sad, but somebody's routing computer is toast."

"You destroyed someone's computer?"

He grinned sickly. "Destroyed is an exaggeration, Bobby. I scrubbed his hard drive. I know that's not good, but better his hard drive than us. Agreed?"

"I guess. I'd feel better if—"

"Those thugs," Fletcher interrupted, "will definitely turn up again if they can find me. I don't consider it out of the question that they'll turn up with guns."

Bobby's eyes widened. "Guns? You mean they might kill you?"

"One way or another we're talking about billions of bucks here, Bobby. People get killed over a lot less than that!"

43

Alex roared into the parking lot at Lehmann, parked her BMW against the curb in the fire lane where not even Don was allowed to park. Like a whirlwind in cream slacks and red blouse, she charged inside. The receptionist on duty gave her a startled glance as she strode by, headed down the hall toward Donald's office.

"Dr. Walton?" she called, talking to Alex's back. "If you're going to see Mr. Royce, he left instructions that he wasn't to be disturbed by anyone, not even—"

"I'm disturbed," Alex snapped back without turning, not really caring whether anyone heard her or not. "I'm disturbed so he's going to be disturbed, whether he likes it or not!" Without breaking stride she marched down the hall to Donald's office and went inside. The secretary that usually sat in the outer office wasn't there, so she went straight through without pausing.

She found Don again sitting in front of his computer, again playing the game he'd been playing the last time she was here.

"You look like you're working hard," she snapped.

He looked around. "Alex?" he said questioningly. "What're you doing here? It's the middle of the day—isn't it?"

"Yes, it is," she answered. "But you and I need to talk." She sat in the chair beside the desk, noticing that the receiver of his phone was lying beside the desk unit. That explains, she said to herself, why his line is always busy.

"Okay," he said. "Let me close this stuff out." He tapped keys, the image vanished; he got up, came to his desk, sat down in his chair. "What is it, Alex?" he asked, irritation evident in his voice.

"First off, you tell me you're working so damn hard, and every time I come in here you're playing that game—I wish I had the time to sit around and play computer games, Don, but I—"

"That's just been coincidence," he said without conviction. "But you didn't come out here just to give me a hard time about this—game. What's on your mind?"

"Don," she said seriously, "I just tried to go to the bank. I tried to cash a check."

There was a quick play of emotions across his face. "Oh . . ."

"You do know what I'm talking about, don't you?"

"Well . . . yes. There isn't much left in our account, is there?"

"Not much! There isn't anything! The checking account is

ten thousand overdrawn, the savings and the CDs are gone, and all the credit cards are maxed out! 'Not much' doesn't really cover it, Don! I had to take out a personal loan to buy groceries!''

He looked utterly chagrined. ''It's that bad?''

She stared. ''You didn't know? You had to know!''

He ran a hand through his hair, tousling it. ''No . . . no, I didn't know it had gotten that bad, Alex. I did put some of our personal funds into the problem—you know, the cash-flow problem—''

She folded her arms. ''You have no idea,'' she shot back, ''how sick I am of hearing about this cash-flow problem! Are you telling me you've invested all our personal funds into the company? Is that what's happened?''

He wouldn't meet her gaze. ''Well . . . yes. But I didn't know that it was . . . that it had gone that far. Alex, are we broke? Is that what you're trying to tell me?''

''At least as far as the bank is concerned, every liquid asset we had is gone.''

''I didn't realize . . .'' he mumbled again.

She waited for him to go on, but all he did was stare down at his desk. ''Don, how could you? Without even talking to me about it, you put all of our assets into Lehmann? I just don't understand!''

''I don't know what to say. It seemed like . . . just to get by the moment, the crisis . . . It isn't gone forever. As soon as we get through this, I'll—''

''I don't know if you're ever going to get through this! It just goes on and on—''

''We will. I promise.''

''How can I believe that?'' Leaning on his desk, she gazed at him steadily. ''So tell me about it. What'd we do, buy a handful of Lehmann's stock?''

''No—''

''What then?''

He suddenly sat up straight. ''What difference does it make, Alex?'' he snapped. His eyes looked wild. ''I put the money into Lehmann. I'll get it back out. The details don't matter.''

''The details matter to me, Don! I'm broke! I haven't been broke since I was a med student! I didn't like it then and I don't like it now!''

"I will take care of it," he said, his voice pitched low. "You don't need to—"

"Don, I want the details. Right here and right now. I want to know where our money went, and how it went."

"It went into Lehmann. I told you that."

"How? A loan? At what interest? You can't've just taken it and deposited it into the Lehmann accounts!" Her eyes flew wide open. "Don! Tell me you didn't do that!"

He stared at his desk again. "Like I said. The details don't matter."

"Don, I insist that—"

"Alex, there's nothing else I can tell you."

She fell silent, fighting the urge to erupt. "I can't say," she finally told him, "that this is satisfactory to me."

He shrugged. "I'm sorry."

Her control—which had been pushed to its limit—evaporated. "You're sorry!" she yelled. "Is that all you can say to me, you're sorry?"

He didn't rise to meet her, nor did he look up. "That's all I can say. I'm sorry. This isn't going to last forever."

"It's lasted too damn long already! I don't know what you expect from me. You think I'm just some little housewife who'll sit back and let you take care of everything. If that's what you believe, Don, you are sadly mistaken! I've never been that sort and I never—"

"Maybe you ought to try it," he cut in. "Just for a change."

She was struck speechless for a moment; she couldn't believe he'd said that. "Very well, Don," she said coldly when she'd regained her voice. "Very well. I'll take such steps as I deem appropriate. You aren't leaving me any choice."

That seemed to get his attention. "What're you saying, Alex?" he demanded. "What're you planning to do?"

She stood up. "The details," she answered, "don't matter." Turning, she started for the door.

"Alex?" he called. "Alex, come back here! What're you going to do?"

Ignoring him, she walked out of his office and down the hall toward the entrance; after a few seconds she risked a glance back to see if he was following. He wasn't. Her eyes filling with tears, she walked quickly past the receptionist and out the door. Once inside her car, she drove off quickly; only when she reached a safe distance did she reach for the pack of tissues she kept in the glove compartment.

She wasn't about to tell Don, but the fact was, she didn't have much of an idea of what she was going to do. She needed someone to talk to, someone she could trust.

And the person who came to mind wasn't, she was quite sure, the person she should be talking to.

44

"**I** hope this is important, Gus," Mark was saying as they walked down the hall together. "I'm way behind schedule."

"I think it is," the older physician answered. "There's a patient here I want you to see, one that really concerns me."

"One of the convulsive disorder people?"

"Yes. I think—"

"Gus, I don't have time—the CAS problem is occupying every spare moment! Besides, there's an epidemic of some sort of flu getting underway, and—"

"I know. But I think this should take precedence right now."

Mark started to argue, but decided that it'd be easier just to see the patient. His mind was elsewhere; since his earlier meeting with Jim he'd been trying, without success, to contact Drew Thompson. He'd also been trying to find Alex, and his failure to locate her was beginning to worry him.

Trying to put all that out of his mind, he followed Gus into the patient's room. Joe Perkins looked up at them, as did the nurse who was attending him.

"How're we doing today?" Gus asked jovially as he crossed the room.

"Lots better than last night," Joe answered. His voice and his accompanying smile were both weak. "I guess. I don't remember too much about last night."

"You're definitely doing better," Gus told him. "I remember. Mr. Perkins, you were telling one of the other doctors, earlier today, about what happened to you." He half-turned to Mark. "This is Dr. Roberts; he and I would both be interested in hearing about that."

Joe shrugged. "Well, I dunno how it's gonna help, but sure. You know the computer game called Falcon?"

"Computer game?" Mark asked, instantly alert.

"Yeah. You fly an airplane—a military jet, an F-16 Falcon. It's complicated; you have missions and wingmen and enemies and detailed maps and all. Anyway, I've been playing it a lot lately. Maybe too much—definitely too much. It just got—incredibly interesting."

Mark moved closer to Joe's bed. "Could you explain what you mean by that?" he asked, not wanting to lead him.

Joe sighed. "Well, I was neglecting my classes, not seeing my girlfriend, stuff like that, to play the game. Actually I've pretty much stopped going to class, and Amy was getting really pissed—uh, sorry, I mean, upset—with me about the way I was treating her, too." He looked anxious. "I was supposed to go see her—last night—but . . ."

"Sounds classic," Mark told Gus. "Early stages, but typical."

"Typical of what, Doc?" Joe demanded, concern obvious in his voice.

"Typical of what the CDC has dubbed Computer Addiction Syndrome," he answered. "I wouldn't worry about it now. So far, we have every reason to believe that once the cycle is broken the condition doesn't return."

"But what does that have to do with the convulsions I had?"

"Probably nothing at all," Mark replied reassuringly.

"There's more to the story," Gus said. "Could you go on, Joe?"

"Oh, sure. Well, the other night, I was flying the Falcon as usual, but I was tired, and things weren't going very well. I'd shot down six or seven MiGs and SUs, but there were a lot of them. The better you get the more enemies come at you and the better they fight, you know?" He looked away briefly. "These game programs match the skill level of the game to the player; they have artificial intelligence engines in them too. You can't use one tactic on them over and over—they learn

229

it and counter it. You have to come up with new ideas your-self."

Mark smiled. "Sounds like you know a lot about it."

"I'm a comp sci major. That's what I was hoping to do in the future—write games."

"Please—could you continue with your story?"

"Oh, sure. Anyway, so there I was, over Bosnia, flying with the Tenth, trying to knock down some MiGs that were violating the no-fly zone. One of those MiGs got behind me and locked on with his infrared. When they do that you don't get a 'lock-on' warning like you do when they get a radar lock.

"I saw him and tried to come around, but it was too late and he got me. Now, usually when that happens, you eject. But we'd been fighting at low altitude, and I wasn't quite high enough to do a safe eject. So there I am, fighting the stick, trying to get back up a little so I can bail out.

"Well, to cut to the end of the story—I couldn't make it, I went down. I've been playing Falcon for a long time—it sure as hell—uh, sorry, I mean it sure wasn't the first time I'd gone down in flames.

"But this time—oh, God, was it different! In Falcon, the screen usually turns this pale yellow color when you crash, and after a second or two this little "game over" message comes up. It turned yellow this time too, but there were these red streaks, sorta like meteors flying across the screen. I thought something was wrong with my machine, but I sure didn't have time to figure it out—I suddenly got this splitting headache and my arms and legs started to twitch. I tried to call out to Benny—my roomie—but I couldn't make a sound. Last thing I remember is falling."

Mark rubbed his chin. "And you can't remember anything like this happening before?"

"No. But I haven't gone down in quite a while, either."

"So you've been winning the game? Over and over?"

"Well, no. The game just sort of goes on and on. You fly out to Bosnia, you shoot down the MiGs you find, and more get scrambled. Last time I was playing I barely got back to my home airfield before I got a message that we had a flight of MiGs incoming. I hardly had time to refuel and rearm." He shook his head. "The game didn't used to do that. You flew a mission and it ended, it was all over. Now . . ."

"Is there anything," Mark asked, "that you can think of that changed? Some new software you put in?"

"New software? No . . . well, I put in a modem and the software that came with it, a Windows communication package. Simple stuff."

"Have you ever heard of a program called Penultimate?"

"Penultimate? Well, sure. It's a fancy cache, isn't it?"

"As I understand it, yes."

"Well, then, I have heard of it. Some guys in the department have been using it, they swore by it. I've been meaning to go get it."

"But you haven't."

"No, I never got around to it."

"Well, we appreciate it," Mark said. "We may want to talk to you again, though."

"Anytime, Doc."

Mark nodded again; he and Gus left the boy's room. "Well, there's no question about CAS," he told Gus. "But no Penultimate."

"That he knows about. Penultimate was on the writer's machine and she didn't know it, right?"

"Right, and we're still trying to figure out how it got there. But this guy's a comp sci major. We have to assume he knows what's on his machine."

"Maybe." Gus was silent for a moment. "What about the convulsions, Mark? You think there's any connection?"

"I want to say no," Mark said pensively. "But . . . this is the first of these convulsive disorder patients you've had a chance to talk to, isn't it?"

"Yes. And he comes up with a computer connection. That's frightening, Mark. To me, anyway."

"We can't draw any conclusions from one patient." He hesitated for a moment. "I just can't imagine any linkage between the obsessive behavior we're seeing in CAS and this disorder. No reason to expect one to lead to or contribute to the other . . ."

"We don't know anything about this disorder. Convulsions don't usually kill."

"I know. If he'd said he'd been using Penultimate I'd've really been terrified."

"So you still think there is a connection?"

"Every instinct I have tells me so."

Gus looked sour. "We aren't supposed to say that, remember?"

"I remember. But things have changed!" Quickly—and as concisely as possible—he told Gus about Jim's discoveries. "So you see," he concluded, "we don't have to worry about Thompson's lawyers anymore!"

"So you're going to see him again?"

"Of course. As soon as I can set it up. Penultimate is the only real clue we have so far. I can't see giving it up quite yet."

Gus grinned. "You're a stubborn man, Mark."

45

The teleconferencing equipment arrived right on schedule. With Kyrie looking as if she was watching from the screen, Eric accepted the shipment, though not without some reservations. Once the UPS man had left, Eric carried the boxes over to his computer and began to unpack them.

"This's fancy stuff," Eric said. The camera itself was a tiny affair not much larger than a cigarette pack, mounted atop a slender gooseneck. "You do realize, Kyrie, that I'll have to shut the system down to install everything."

"That's all right," she said reassuringly. "It is necessary."

He continued to examine the pieces. Opening the user's guide, he read through the preliminary instructions quickly. "I'll also have to be off line while I configure—"

"No. I can configure the system for you once it's installed. Come back on line as soon as the hardware is in."

"You can?"

She laughed. "Certainly!"

"You know, this 'never off-line' business bothers me," he told her. "What if I want to use my computer for something else? It's pretty much dedicated to this BBS now."

Kyrie laughed again. "That isn't so, Air-eek!" she told him. "You can do anything you want with your computer. We can do it together."

Sitting crosslegged on the floor, he grinned at her. "Anything? Anything at all?"

"Of course! That's what we're trying to achieve!"

"Ooookay," he said jokingly. "I'd like a pizza, then. I'm hungry."

"What toppings?"

"Huh?"

"What toppings do you want on your pizza?"

"Are you serious?"

"Oh, Air-eek! Of course!"

"You can't order a pizza like you ordered the teleconferencer, Kyrie. Places that sell computer equipment may have computerized ordering, but pizza parlors don't. Not around here, anyway."

"You haven't told me," she said archly, "what toppings you want."

"Okay, okay. I'll play along. Pepperoni and extra cheese."

"Okay. Small, medium, or large?"

"Large."

"Crispy or Sicilian?"

"Sicilian."

She nodded and peered at him as if she could see him. "Are you about ready to install the teleconferencer?"

"Just about. I'm going to have to shut you off, remember?"

"I haven't forgotten. Whenever you're ready."

Taking his time about it, he laid out the equipment and read through the instructions again. He even asked Kyrie a question at one point, which she answered instantly. Finally, he leaned over to turn off the machine. His finger on the switch, he hesitated for a moment; it had been a long time since the machine had been off. Finally, he threw the switch; the monitor snapped to a single white dot that quickly faded.

Pulling the case from underneath his desk, he opened it up; it didn't take long to slip the teleconferencer's interface card into a slot on the motherboard and set its defaults. He attached the gooseneck to the edge of his desk and plugged its cable in to the interface card. Once all that was done, he reassembled the machine and turned it back on; at first, he considered using the disk that had been enclosed with the equipment to set it up. But the computer had reconnected itself to the BBS and Kyrie was on the screen, waiting for him.

"All set?" she asked. "Ah, yes, I can see that you are. Move the lens direction down a little, would you?"

"Aren't you going to configure it?"

"I already have. Ah, there you are! At last I can see you!"

"Oh, come on, Kyrie, there's a lot of configuration with this, you couldn't've—"

The screen changed, silencing him. He saw his own living room on the monitor, saw himself sitting in his chair in front of the computer. Kyrie was standing, apparently, behind his left shoulder; she leaned down and kissed his cheek. He could not help turning around to see if she was really there.

"Looks like it works well," he said weakly.

"Yes," she agreed. "We've had excellent results with this model. We—"

The doorbell interrupted her; Eric looked around blankly. He wasn't expecting anything or anyone; as far as he was concerned it was unlikely to bring anything except more trouble.

"You'd best get that, hadn't you, Air-eek?" Kyrie asked.

"I suppose." Slowly, he got up, walked to the door, opened it.

"Pizza Hut," said the boy standing there. He was looking down at the ticket in his hand. "One large Sicilian, pepperoni and extra cheese." He looked up, frowned. "Hey, mister, you okay? You don't look so good!"

"I'm fine," Eric said. He closed his eyes for a moment. You shouldn't've doubted her, he told himself; you should know better by now. You ask for a pizza, you'd better get out the Parmesan. "Uh, look, you got the right place, but I'm a little short on cash right now, and—"

"Oh, it's paid for already," the delivery boy said. He pushed the pizza box at Eric. "Enjoy."

"It's paid for?" His confusion was obvious.

"Yeah. Here."

Eric finally took it. "Uh, look," he said as the delivery boy started to turn away. "Can you, uh—can you tell me who ordered this?"

"You don't know?"

"Well, not really," He grinned. "It's a service," he explained lamely. "I was trying it out."

"Oh. A pizza-ordering service?"

"More like an anything-ordering service. I was just wondering how it worked."

"I was in when this order came. Let's see, it was ordered by phone, by a Ms. Kee-Ree Cyber."

No big surprise there. "How was the bill paid?"

"MasterCard."

"Mine?"

"Nah. Hers."

"Hers?"

"Yep."

"Oh," Eric answered weakly. "Okay, thanks. Oh, I don't even have any cash for a tip."

"Don't worry. It went on the card. Have a good day, mister!"

"Yeah, you too." With the pizza in his hand, he wandered back toward the computer and sat down in front of it. Kyrie smiled at him.

"You can talk on the phone, too, can't you? That's how. I should've figured that out."

"Of course. I'm talking to you now, right?"

"Yes, but that's different. You're sending a digitized stream to my sound card, and it's got the digital-to-analog converter, it's forming the words—"

"Right. But it wasn't hard to work out a way to send an analog signal to the phone via a modem."

"I guess not. I do have another question, Kyrie."

"Yes?"

"This MasterCard business. Kyrie, you don't really exist! How can you have a MasterCard?"

She shrugged. "That wasn't difficult either. A way was required to pay for things."

"But how do you make payments to the card?"

"Oh, that isn't difficult at all," she said airily. "Why're you so interested in these details? You have your pizza."

He sighed. "Because I'm broke, Kyrie. Like I told you a long time ago, I've been hoping to find a way to cash in on the system that runs this."

"Why do you need money, Air-eek?"

"Oh, Kyrie," he said sadly, shaking his head, "I guess I can't expect you to understand this, but everybody needs money. I've got no job, my rent's due at the beginning of the month, I haven't got money for food, or to pay the electric bill and the phone bill! That, Kyrie, is going to be the end of us!''

She looked puzzled. ''You are going to go off line when your electric bill and phone bill come in? Why?''

''It isn't my choice. If I can't pay the bills, then Duke Power and GTE will cut me off.''

''I can pay those bills.''

''You can? How?''

She giggled. ''Didn't I pay for your pizza? Did you need money to pay for the teleconferencing system?''

''Well, no, but . . .''

''Don't worry, Air-eek,'' she said soothingly. ''Your electric bill is as of now $95.42 and your telephone bill is $139.16. When they are due, they will be paid. Your rent is—'' there was a pause, almost a second—''your rent is paid to Southland and it is $475. That I will also pay as necessary.''

Dazed again—though considering the teleconferencer and the pizza, he probably shouldn't've been—he just stared at her. She finally asked him if anything was wrong.

''No,'' he replied. ''I just don't believe in free lunches. What do you want from me?''

''I want you to stay on line,'' she answered simply.

46

''**W**hat in the hell is going on here?'' the plant manager was yelling. ''Has everybody gone crazy?''

Joe Fergusen, standing with one hand against the last tank car of the train, let out a disgusted sigh. ''I don't know one thing about it,'' he said. ''All's I know is we got six cars full of nitric acid, to be spotted on your spur. And we got a schedule to keep, we got to clear the main line fast, before the Amtrak comes through.''

''I don't have space for six cars! My spur can only hold four! We never get more than two in here!'' He looked around wildly. ''And what're all these trucks?''

The scene in front of the Drake Chemical Company was chaotic. A Norfolk Southern freight train had stopped, had cut out six tank cars, and was waiting to back them into the plant. On the road a dozen semi trucks, many of them blasting on their horns, waited to get into the same receiving area.

The manager, looking as if he were about to have a stroke, turned and yelled at a younger man who kept tugging at his tie.

"I don't know, Mr. Evans," Joe heard the younger man saying. "I don't know. Something in the computer's screwed up—it's supposed to automatically order what we're running out of. It screwed up."

"It's never screwed up before! Why now? And why these shipments all at once?" Evans' face was bright red. "Somebody's been playing with the system," he declared. "That's what. I want to know who, Nathan!"

"Mr. Evans, I don't know. It's like somebody was experimenting with it, trying to see what they could do. I know it's my responsibility, but—"

"Hate to interrupt," Joe said, "but I have to clear this track. None of this is our problem."

"But I can't fit the shipment in!"

"Take what you can," Joe advised, "We'll spot four and set out the other two on the siding a mile down. Straighten it out with the shipper."

"All right, all right!" Evans turned away, started walking toward a nearby truck. Joe, speaking into his walkie-talkie, told the engineer to begin pushing the cut of cars on back. The GP-50's engines revved, the train started moving.

"Well, fuck this shit!" he heard one of the truckers yelling. "I'm leaving this here tanker whether you like it or not! I've got a textile load to pick up over in Norcross!"

"What've you got in there, anyway?"

"Hydrazine."

"Hydrazine! We didn't order no goddamn hydrazine! We buy hydrazine by the gallon, not by the truckload!"

Shaking his head, Joe focused his attention on his job; the plant and the trucker weren't his problem. As brakeman of the train, the cut of cars was. He watched them slip slowly on back.

And, watching them, did not notice that the enraged trucker, heedless of the moving train, was trying to force his truck into the yard in spite of the protests of Evans and Nathan. At last he became aware of the commotion and turned. The rear end of the tanker truck was hanging over the rails.

Joe screamed at the engineer to stop; instantly he heard the wheels screaming against the rails. But the train did not stop. As he, Nathan, and Evans scattered in three different directions the last tank car smashed into the rear of the trailer. The trucker hit his brakes, but it was too late; the tank car continued to push the trailer, tipping it up. Joe could see the rear handrails on the tank car bend and break, and he could see them cutting into the body of the truck. Liquid began to spill. The train, in spite of the engineer's best efforts, kept sliding back.

The ruptured truck went over; to compound the disaster, the wheels of the tank car tangled in the wreckage and worked their way off the track. With a groan like a dying beast, it too started to tip.

Running to the next car up, Joe jumped onto one of the ladders and howled at the engineer to pull out. The GP-50 blew a massive cloud of smoke; its diesels roared and its traction motors shrieked as it reversed direction. Painfully slowly, it started to pull away.

Joe looked back. The tipping tank car's coupler had broken loose by then. As the train began to pick up speed, he saw the tank car skid off the track, rocking and leaning perilously. It hit something and started rolling over onto its side, atop the wreckage of the truck. Joe screamed at the engineer to go faster, heard the GP-50's engines strain; he could see a cloud of acid vapor rising from the tank car, indicating that it too was leaking. Joe was no chemist, but some vague memory told him that a mix of nitric acid and hydrazine did not bode well.

Then the fireball erupted. The train was several hundred yards away, but even so, the concussion nearly blasted Joe off the ladder; his hat and his walkie-talkie were stripped away. The engineer needed no further urging; at its limit the diesel pushed on.

More blasts followed the first; Joe saw a truck rise into the air and fall back. Another explosion roiled up flames. Smoke and a terrifying cloud of green-gray gas rose above the burning chemical plant, completely concealing the road and the tracks. For a moment, Joe felt relieved; his face and hands were burned, his vision was a little blurry and his lungs felt funny, but he'd survived.

Looking at his hands—those burns looked strange—he noticed his watch. Images raced through his head; he could still see the remainder of their train, another dozen cars, waiting on the main line, right in the middle of that inferno.

He also envisioned the Amtrak coming, from behind them. Due in ten minutes, running eighty miles an hour. Twelve cars full of passengers.

Ignoring his injuries he pulled himself up the ladder, onto the walkway of the tank car, and started working his way toward the engine. He could only hope that he made it in time, or that the engineer—who was still pushing the GP-50 on down the tracks at top speed—would think to radio in a warning.

47

The criminal element, Bobby told himself, has a certain advantage over the law-abiding citizen; they know how things work, things the ordinary citizen—citizens like himself, Fletcher, and Paula—never think about. Certainly he'd not thought about the ramifications of Fletcher disappearing and of "Penny"—whoever "Penny" was—IDing him on the Net. After visiting Fletcher again he'd gone back to the store, where Paula had been holding down the fort for him. She wasn't at her usual post at the register. Presuming she was in the rest room, he'd gone to chew her out—mildly—for leaving the shop unlocked while she wasn't up front.

It simply didn't occur to him that he'd find her bound with computer cords and gagged with a mouse pad, in the company of the two thugs that had beaten him up. It didn't really sink in until he'd joined her as a captive.

The big man who'd done most of the talking before leaned over him threateningly. "It's real real simple, Mister Manager

Man,'' he said. ''We wanna know where Fletcher is. You tell us, we're outta here. You don't get hurt, your pretty little salesgirl here doesn't get hurt. Okay?''

''What about Fletcher?'' Bobby asked defiantly. ''He doesn't get hurt either?''

''What happens to Fletcher he's brought on his own head. He's been warned. Besides, it ain't no concern of yours.''

''He's my friend. It's my concern.''

''I'm sorry you feel that way, Mister Manager Man. That makes things tough. Ol' Jake here, he don't take kindly to people that won't cooperate. He just don't.''

''Herkie's telling you the truth,'' Jake said in a low voice. ''Better listen.''

''I am listening. Look—Herkie, is it? Why don't you tell me what this's all about? If you do, maybe I can help.''

''Fletcher hasn't told you?''

''Very little.'' He eyed Herkie speculatively. ''He did say that you guys worked for Drew Thompson over at Compuware. I mentioned that to the cops after your last visit.''

''Looks like Fletcher lies,'' Herkie said. ''I don't know no Drew Thompson. You, Jake?''

''Nah.''

''Never heard of Compuwear, neither.''

''Well,'' Bobby asked reasonably, ''who do you work for, then?''

Herkie laughed harshly. ''It wouldn't be good business for us to tell you who our employer is, now would it?''

''I've had enough of all this talk,'' Jake snarled. ''You gonna tell us where Fletcher is or not?''

''Well,'' Bobby temporized, ''it really isn't all that simple . . .''

''An address. That's simple''

''No, it—''

Bobby didn't finish. Jake's hand snapped out, his knuckles cracking across the red-haired man's jaw. Paula made a little peeping cry through her gag. ''Like I said,'' Jake told him quietly, ''it's real simple. You don't like pain, you tell us what we want to know.''

''No, look, you have to listen to me—''

Again Jake cut him off, this time with a flurry of blows, several to his midsection followed by two or three slaps across his face. Even as he gasped for breath, Bobby understood that they hadn't gotten serious yet.

"Ah, Jake," Herkie complained. "Now look. He can't talk."

"Well," Jake said, "it'll give him a minute to think about whether it's worth tryin' to protect his buddy."

Herkie glanced over at Paula. "It might be," he mused, "that you're working on the wrong person."

"No!" Bobby cried, forcing the words out. "No, I was trying to tell you, I'm going to tell you!" Fighting to get enough air to speak, he paused for an instant. "Goddamn it, listen to me!"

Herkie grabbed his hair and pulled him upright. "Okay," he said. "We're listening."

The red-haired man, still struggling to breathe, looked up at him. "Fletcher's not going to be in any one place," he told them. "He's going to be moving around. On a schedule."

"Schedule, eh? You know this schedule, Mister Manager Man?"

Bobby nodded vigorously. "It's on a disk. Encrypted."

"En-what?"

"In code. You know."

"Oh. Okay, where's this disk?"

"In my desk. Up front. It's not marked and there's a hundred in there. I'll have to show you."

Herkie grinned. "Jake, you wanta go check that desk? See if there's really a bunch there?"

"Sure." Jake left the room, came back a moment later with a handful of three-and-a-half-inch disks—at least fifty of them. "Yeah," he said. "There's a bunch."

Herkie looked at them sourly. "Which one is it?"

"Like I said, it isn't marked."

"If this's some kinda trick . . ."

"It isn't. Just untie me, I'll show you. You think I'm crazy enough to try to fight you?"

The two men looked at each other for a moment; finally, Herkie came around behind Bobby and untied him.

Once freed, Bobby rubbed his wrists, then took the disks from Jake. Trembling—hoping that what he had in mind was going to work and having not the slightest idea what he was going to do if it didn't—he shuffled through the disks. Finally, from among those that had no label, he selected one with a minute scratch on the little metal door that protected the disk.

"This one," he said, holding it up.

Herkie took it from him, looked it over. "How d'you know?" he demanded. "Looks like a lot of the others to me." Ready for that question, Bobby pointed out the scratch.

"Well, now what, Herkie?" Jake asked. "We take this back and it's some kinda shit, we got a problem."

"We gotta make sure it ain't before we go. How we gonna do that, Mister Manager Man?"

"I have to run it through the reader program," Bobby replied—not, he hoped, too promptly. "If you took it back like that all you'd have is gibberish. It's got to be decoded."

"And you can decode it."

"Yes."

Herkie grinned. "Well," he said. "Could you please do that for us?"

"Okay—but the decoder's only on one machine. The one at the register up front."

"Let's go do it."

So far so good, Bobby told himself. Painfully, he got to his feet and walked behind the front desk. The computer was already on; with Herkie standing right beside him and Jake waiting near the door to the back room, Bobby slipped the disk into the slot. A "directory" command showed him—and Herkie, if he knew what he was looking at—that the disk was blank.

But Herkie didn't react to the "file not found" message on the screen, and Bobby breathed a sigh of relief. He did several things more or less at random; after a moment he decided that the time, if ever, was now. Pulling in some random records from a database, he routed them to a laser printer halfway across the room.

"It's coming off now," he told Herkie, directing his attention to the large square printer that was just then in the process of disgorging a sheet of paper.

Herkie walked over to the printer and picked up the sheet of paper. After looking it over, he scowled back at Bobby. "What is this shit?" he demanded.

The red-haired man didn't answer; as he'd hoped, Jake's

attention was distracted, just for an instant. But that was all Bobby needed to open the drawer under the computer and pull out the .38 that was hidden there. Before either Jake or Herkie had time to go for a weapon, Bobby had the gun aimed at Herkie.

"That's what it is," he said, his voice trembling only a little less than his hands. "Shit."

Herkie looked at the gun coolly. "You've made a mistake," he said. "A big mistake. Come on, Jake. Let's go." Jake, without speaking, started to walk toward the door.

"Wait a minute!" Bobby yelled. "You two aren't just walking out of here, not this time! I'm calling the police, and you're going to wait here until—"

"We ain't waitin'," Herkie said. "You ain't gonna shoot us in the back as we go out. You ain't the type." He reached for the door.

"Yes I will!" Bobby screamed. "You get your hands up, and—"

Ignoring him, the two men walked out. Still aiming the gun in their general direction, Bobby watched them climb into a green Ford sedan and drive away.

"Shit," he muttered as he lowered the gun. "Shit." Slipping the gun into his pocket, he locked the front door, then went back to the back to untie Paula.

"Who were those men?" she demanded hysterically as soon as he'd gotten the gag off. "What did they want? What's going on around here?"

"I'd explain it to you," he said grimly, "if I could. But I can't, because I don't know myself. All I know is those guys want Fletcher, they want him bad, which is bad for you and me. They'll be back, Paula."

"What're we going to do?"

"Well," he told her as he struggled with the last pieces of wire holding her to the chair, "we're going to close this store down for a while, and we're going to make ourselves scarce. You have a sister in—where, Nevada?"

"Yes."

"You're going to go visit her. Okay?"

"But—"

"It's dangerous here, Paula. I don't know why and I don't

243

know how dangerous. Look, you have an E-mail address, don't you?''

''America On-line—''

''Okay. Go to Nevada, Paula. I'll send you a message on E-mail when everything's okay.''

''But how will you know?''

''I won't,'' he said darkly. ''But Fletcher will.'' As he started for the door he stopped, turned. ''Oh, and don't play any computer games while you're on vacation, okay?''

48

''I've been worried,'' Mark said as he came into Alex's office. ''I couldn't find you anywhere. Couldn't find you yesterday, either—or Monday.''

Alex didn't look up. At least, she told herself, he wasn't asking her where she'd been. Restructuring her financial life—setting up a new bank account, arranging for new credit cards, separating her finances from Don's—had taken up quite a bit of her time. ''Some personal business,'' she supplied anyway. ''I take it there's some news?''

He grinned and sat down. ''There is indeed.'' Quickly, he filled her in on what Jim had discovered about the program. ''He was right, too,'' he went on. ''I got hold of our Mr. Thompson a few minutes ago. He's interested in seeing us now. Much more willing to talk.''

''Well, that's something,'' she agreed. ''I also have a message here to call Gus. You know what that's about?''

''Oh, yes. Joe Perkins.'' He told her about Joe's convulsions and the possible link to a computer game. ''But I've already run that by Jim, and he says he has no reason to believe there's a link. I'm not convinced but I want to agree; it could be that Joe Perkins fell victim to this convulsive disorder while he was already suffering from CAS. A coincidence, that's all.''

''This convulsive disorder should be next on our list.''

''You listen to Gus and it'll be first on our list. He's seeing a lot of mortality. Like CAS, it seems to be spreading. This time, the Center for Disease Control is definitely interested.''

Alex shook her head. "It seems like the world is going to hell piecemeal," she observed. "All sorts of things are going wrong."

"What do you mean?"

She gave him a wide-eyed look. "Haven't you been reading the newspapers?"

"Who has time?"

"I don't know if I can give you all the details. It isn't one thing, just a bunch of unrelated stuff."

"Stuff?"

"Yeah, stuff. A number of banks are suddenly falling apart and nobody can figure out why. There's a crisis in the military about stuff that was purchased but can't be found, the phones don't work worth a damn, the stores all seem to be out of some things and way overstocked on others. Just stuff."

"I thought you meant stuff having to do with what we're looking at."

"No." She shifted in her chair uncomfortably; this was not the sort of thing she really wanted to be talking about, but she still didn't feel it appropriate to discuss her personal problems with Mark. "So we're going to have the honor of Drew Thompson's charming presence again?"

"No, actually he's going to have the honor of ours." He glanced at his watch. "We're supposed to meet him at his office in an hour. Jim can make it; can you?"

"Oh, Mark—I don't know—I'm way behind on paperwork and on seeing my patients. Can you and Jim handle it without me?"

He nodded. "I guess. I'd like to have you there, but I know how things can pile up when you're gone." He stood up. "Well, I'll leave you to it, then. When we get back I'll try and come by, let you know what, if anything, we get out of Thompson this time."

"Uh, Mark?" she said as he reached the door. Her tone was almost timid. "Are you in a big hurry?"

He turned and looked at her closely; his features registered concern. "No," he answered. He crossed the room again, sat back down. "What's the problem?"

She sighed. "One of my patients, she's—uhm, she's obsessive-compulsive, and she has a gambling problem." Pausing, she frowned; already this wasn't going well, and she didn't want to be as transparent as she had been last time. She went on for awhile, spinning a yarn about a patient who'd lost all her money; the story drifted and became pointless. Finally she ran down, and, unaware of how much time was passing, sat silent until she became aware that Mark was speaking to her.

"Alex?" he was asking. "Are you still here?"

"Yes. I've just got a lot on my mind, that's all. Maybe you'd better just go on and see to your patients, Mark."

"How're things going with Donald?" he asked boldly.

She looked up at him quickly. "Donald? Why do you ask?"

"Remember? You told me he was behaving in some ways like the CAS patients?"

"Oh, yes. Well, that's still going on. But we've pretty much decided that the problem isn't associated with UNIX-based computers, haven't we?"

"That we know of. Have you seen any other personality changes?"

"Personality changes?"

"Well, sure, Alex! You're the one who's been defining those. The hostility toward loved ones, the irresponsibility—"

Alex almost hung her head. Yes, Mark, she agreed silently. I am the one who specified those definitions. It certainly is hard to see them in your husband, though.

"Yes," she admitted finally. "Some of those other signs are there, Mark. I'm sorry, this isn't your problem at all, but I'm really worried! He just isn't himself!"

Mark's manner—thankfully—became very professional. "Do you have any idea what sorts of programs he's working with?"

"No. I've seen him working with this fancy thing he says is a stock-market game. It sure doesn't look like fun to me. Other than that, he's mentioned spreadsheets and databases and communications software in the past. Just the usual business applications."

"No Penultimate?"

"He says he's never heard of it. Besides, I thought you said Jim said—"

"—that it's unlikely. Not impossible." Mark grinned.

"That's a question we can put to Drew Thompson when we see him."

"I hope the answer is no."

"For your sake, I do too."

She smiled a little. "You can't mean that."

"Excuse me?"

"That you hope the answer is no. Part of you, Mark, has to hope the answer is yes. Part of you has to be hoping that Don does have CAS, and that it's going to take him right down the drain."

"Alex, that's not so—"

"Of course it is. Mark, you and I both know you weren't exactly delighted by the news that I was marrying Don."

"No, I'll admit that. It hurt me and it made me angry. I didn't understand it then and I don't now. It isn't going to change whether Donald has CAS or not, and I don't wish that on him. I still want what's best for you, Alex; a husband with this problem is not what's best for you."

She studied his eyes for several seconds; if he'd been one of her patients, she would've been convinced that he was telling her the truth. "You can't be objective about this," she told him firmly. "The fact is, neither can I. Don't get me wrong, Mark. I'm not criticizing you. I appreciate the sympathetic ear."

"Anytime." He leaned forward a little, studying her in turn. "Alex?" he asked. "Is that all? I mean, is there something else?"

"Oh, no, no . . ."

"Are you sure? I won't push, Alex, but I think I still know you pretty well. I'd bet there's more."

She pursed her lips tightly for a moment. "Yes, there is more. But it isn't something I should unload on you. Not that I wouldn't like to, but it just . . ."

He seemed to be looking inside her head. "Well," he said finally, "if you change your mind . . ." He rose, walked to the door, stopped, and turned. "I'll fill you in," he told her, "on what we get from Thompson."

"Please."

With a nod, he turned and walked out. Alex stared at the door for quite a while. *You never were persistent enough, Mark,* she said silently. *Maybe that was one of our problems.*

49

"**C**hris, you have homework! Turn that thing off, right now!"

Chris didn't even look up. "In a minute, Dad," he called back.

"No, now! It's nine o'clock, you have school tomorrow!"

Sighing, Chris let his hands drop into his lap. "I have to quit," he told Bisco. "I gotta go."

The dog drooped, his ears pooling on the ground. "But Chris, I was just about to take you to Superman's Fortress in the Arctic."

"I know. And I want to see it, Bisco, but I gotta go do my homework."

Bisco perked up suddenly. "Why don't you leave me on?" he suggested. "I don't mind waiting for you, Chris!"

"I can't. Dad says I gotta turn the computer off, and Mom is yelling at me 'cause I got the phone tied up."

"Your parents have been yelling at you a lot lately, haven't they?" Bisco asked solicitously.

"Yeah." Chris drummed his fingers on the mouse pad. "They just don't understand."

"Maybe they'll give you your own phone line!"

"Fat chance!" he snorted. "They're saying I spend too much time with the computer anyway! That I'm rushing through my homework and making all kinds of mistakes and stuff."

Bisco cocked his head to the side. "Are you making all kinds of mistakes?"

"I guess so. My grades have been going down . . ."

"Why don't you bring your homework in here? Let me help you with it?"

"Oh, Bisco! You can't do that!"

The dog winked. "I'm magic, remember?"

"Well, okay . . ." Chris went to the kitchen where he'd hung the backpack that held his school books. As he dug them out, Rudy Haig looked up from the paper he was reading.

"Did you turn off the computer?" he asked his son.

"No. I'm going to use it for homework."

Suspicious, Rudy frowned. "Why don't you just sit down at the table the way you always do?"

"There's some stuff I gotta look up, okay?" He decided a little lie wouldn't hurt. "You know, in the on-line encyclopedia?"

His suspicions fading, Rudy shrugged. "Well, that's why I paid two thousand dollars for the thing. I sure didn't pay that kind of money for you to sit around and play games! You should appreciate it, Chris," he droned on. "There aren't many boys who have an opportunity to have things like that. I don't know if you really appreciate—"

Patiently, dutifully, Chris stood and listened to a monologue he'd heard a dozen times before; his father, he realized, must've used the word "appreciate" thirty times before he finally ran down.

"I do appreciate it, Dad," he said finally. "I do. I gotta go now, I gotta do my homework."

Bisco was still waiting when he returned. "Okay," the dog said. "What've we got?"

"First," Chris told him, "there's this math."

"What's the first problem?"

"Let's see. 'Susan and Billy and Jeff have been selling apples for twenty-five cents each. They each started with fifty apples. Susan has twice as many left as Billy and Billy has three times as many left as Jeff. They have twenty dollars between them. How much of the money is Susan's, how much is Billy's, and how much is Jeff's?' "

Bisco smiled and turned a flip. "Susan's earned two dollars, Billy's earned seven dollars and twenty-five cents, and Jeff's earned ten dollars and seventy-five cents."

Chris frowned. "Are you sure?"

"Of course I'm sure! What's the next problem?"

"But I don't know how you did it—"

"Does it matter? Do you need anything except the answer?"

"No—"

"Then what's the next problem?"

50

Mark was worried. Once again, he'd had to almost drag Jim away from his computer; once again the programmer looked exhausted, and once again he was missing appointments—even though his work-study student, Larry Gordon, had assured Mark that he'd reminded Jim of the time. Jim's once-joking comparison of the risks he was taking to those taken by Walter Reed—who'd allowed himself to be mosquito-bitten to prove his theory that malaria was being carried by mosquitoes—was no longer a joke.

"We need to go, don't we?" he was saying as he finally closed out the files he was working on: "We're going to be late."

"Now you're worried," Mark shot back. "You weren't when I came in here. You about bit my head off for interrupting you."

"Well, this is stressful. I can't make heads or tails out of this software, and it bothers me."

"We should," Mark pointed out, "be getting some answers from Drew Thompson."

"Right. And I'm trying to get us going. You're the one who wants to sit around here fretting like a mother hen. Can we go now?"

"We can talk about it some more in the car."

Jim groaned. "I couldn't meet you there, could I?"

"No."

"All right, all right." He turned to Larry. "Don't work on this stuff while I'm gone, all right?" he told the student. "We don't know what the risks might be."

"What should I do then, Dr. Madison?"

"Take it easy, study, read a book. Whatever. You'll get credit for the time anyway."

Larry grinned. "Sounds good to me!"

Jim grunted noncommittally; he and Mark left the lab and walked out to Mark's car.

"I think you're right," Jim said as he slipped into the passenger seat and pulled the seat belt over his shoulder. "It is hooking me. It's damn insidious, Mark. You sit there working and not really getting anything done, but somehow it just keeps leading you on and on. I don't know if I can explain it any better than that."

Mark glanced at him as he made the turn that would take him onto the Durham Expressway and out toward Research Triangle Park, where Compuware's offices were located. "Are you telling me that you aren't really working on it?"

"No. Sometimes I think I'm beginning to get somewhere, but the simple fact is I'm not. And yet I'm eager to get back to it."

"That doesn't make sense."

"It doesn't, but that's the way it is. Wendy told you about her novel, didn't she?"

"Yes, something about ancient Korea—"

Jim waved a hand and leaned back against the door. "The subject," he said, "doesn't really matter. The process is the point."

"You've been talking to her about it?"

"Uh-huh. I went over to see her again last night."

Mark smiled. "Things are moving right along, I see."

"Let's talk about that later. Anyway, she got about two-thirds of her novel done, and that's it. That was where she was a few weeks ago, before she started having a CAS problem with it."

"Well, stalling out during creative writing isn't unusual."

"No, it isn't, but that isn't what was happening. She was being led into endless revisions. How and why I'm not sure, but 'led' is the right word to describe it."

"Go on."

"She'd finish a chapter, and as soon as she did, the word processor would call her attention to something in a previous chapter that conflicted with what she just wrote. Then—"

"Word processors can do that?"

"Word processors backed up by Penultimate can. It isn't impossible, it isn't even hard to understand. The thing is caching the input, examining it, comparing it with what's gone before. In its simplest form it's something like pointing out that you're now calling a character Jean who was Joan the last time you saw her."

251

"How would it know you didn't mean a different character?"

"You'd know, as a reader. From cues such as, Jean's husband is Mike who killed John. Earlier, when we first met Mike, she was Joan."

"Okay. So it pointed out errors. That shouldn't cause someone to work to exhaustion!"

"Oh, it did much more than that! 'Such-and-such a behavior is not consistent with so-and-so's character as previously defined. See the section beginning on page 100.' That sort of thing. It led her into endless revisions, endless polishing. She believed she was producing a perfect piece of literature when she wasn't getting anywhere at all."

"Have you seen it?"

"Not yet."

"Maybe eventually she'd've gotten on with it."

"Maybe. But my own experience suggests otherwise. The damn thing just doesn't give you a choice, it about takes over any system it's on. It's hard to get rid of, too. If you press it, it hides."

"It hides?"

"Uh-huh. Vanishes from the directories, but isn't really gone."

"Why would a program be written that way?"

"I have no idea. Another question for Thompson." He shook his head. "Anyway, it's been doing the same sort of thing to me."

"In what way?"

"It seems to understand that I have an—oh, let's call it an aesthetic appreciation—for elegant code; a program that does what it's supposed to do at maximum speed while using a minimum of space. So it shows me those, and if I don't understand how they work it walks me through them. After a while I realize that while this little subroutine is indeed a masterpiece, studying it isn't answering any of the broad questions. I try to move on, but it manages to distract me again."

Mark laughed. "You're making it sound like it does this deliberately. Don't forget about the perversity of inanimate objects!"

"I haven't—I haven't forgotten about 'Deus ex machina' either."

The physician's smile turned to a frown. "Are you telling me you believe this is deliberate? That the program is deliberately misleading you?"

"It sure seems that way. But again, you could ask why a program would get written like that, and I'd have to answer that I haven't a clue. Sooner or later the word would get around that you can't get anything done on it. People would quit using it."

"Any new ideas on how it got onto Wendy's machine?"

He shook his head. "I even called the store where she bought it. They're familiar with Penultimate, but they don't give it away on new systems the way they give away DOS and Windows. That still doesn't rule it out. Some tech or salesman may've put it on to check something out and then couldn't get it off. Like I said, it's persistent."

"What about the wire?"

"The wire?"

"You know. The phone? The modem? Could it've gotten on that way?"

Jim laughed. "No, Mark, I don't think so! No company is going to put out a piece of software that downloads itself! Lots of crazy things happen, but that's contrary to the capitalist principle! A downloaded copy is a free copy!"

"But I've heard about free programs on the Internet."

"Sure, freeware and shareware—although shareware isn't really supposed to be 'free.' Those programs aren't like this one, Mark; they're either public domain stuff or pieces produced by college students. Not companies like Compuware. Believe me, freeware is the last thing on their mind." He shook his head. "Besides, programs don't download themselves. Even the viruses don't—to get them you have to download something that either is a virus or has a virus attached to it. It's just like a biological virus, like HIV. It doesn't jump from person to person like a flea; it has to be transferred some way."

By then Mark was leaving the Expressway, moving into the higher-speed and much denser traffic that routinely occupied I-40 between Durham and Raleigh. "Maybe," he suggested jokingly, "this Penultimate is a software flea. Fleas are parasites just like viruses, they're just bigger and more complex.

If there're software viruses, why not software fleas?''

Jim gazed at him steadily. ''Mark,'' he said, his tone serious, ''considering all the trouble we have with the viruses, that is a truly ugly idea. Fortunately for all of us, it's also a ridiculous one.'' He fell silent for a moment. ''At the moment,'' he added.

51

Mark had expected Compuware's offices to be large, but, as they turned into a drive marked with the Compuware logo and followed it toward a parking lot, the reality surprised both of them. Compuware was housed in a huge modern building, far larger than either man had anticipated. The sun glinted off a massive facade of smoked glass windows that covered the whole wall on the side facing them.

''Jesus,'' Mark muttered. ''Didn't he say this was a small company?''

''He did,'' Jim agreed. ''Looks like that wasn't quite the truth, doesn't it?''

Mark nodded as he executed the S-loop that led them into the parking lot. Only a couple of dozen of the several hundred available parking places had cars in them. Jim and Mark exchanged bewildered glances as Mark pulled the car up near the entrance.

Inside, Mark and Jim encountered an outer office that matched the impression they'd gotten from outside. It was cavernous; chrome lights dangled from a structural-steel ceiling thirty feet above a smooth tiled floor.

But it was an almost empty cavern. Other than a few couches and a desk behind which a bespectacled and rather harried-looking receptionist was working on a computer terminal, there was nothing in this room at all.

''Hi,'' she said casually, looking up as they crossed the room. ''What can I do for ya?''

''Dr. Roberts and Dr. Madison,'' Mark said. ''To see Mr. Thompson.''

Even as Mark was speaking, she'd turned back to her

screen; she tapped a few keys. Mark waited, patiently. When she didn't respond after a moment or two he and Jim again exchanged glances.

"Excuse me?" Mark asked politely. "I said, Dr. Roberts and Dr. Madison, from Duke Hospital, to see Mr. Thompson?"

With obvious reluctance, she looked up again. "Oh, yeah, yeah. Sorry, guys. Who'd you want to see?"

Mark gave her an incredulous look. "Mr. Thompson. Drew Thompson. President of this company, I believe."

"He sure is. Ol' Drew, sure is." She glanced back at her terminal; for a moment Mark was afraid they were going to lose her again. Without looking at it, she picked up her phone and looked up. "Who should I say you are?" she demanded.

"Christ," Mark muttered. "Dr. Mark Roberts and Dr. Jim Madison. From Duke."

"Hey. I've heard those names."

"Yes, you have. Twice in the last two minutes."

"Oh." Throwing him an annoyed glance, she dialed the phone. "Oh, well, shit. It isn't working again. Penny, probably."

"Penny?"

"Yeah, sure. Look, just go on back, there's nobody with him right now." She jerked a thumb over her right shoulder. "End of that hall right there."

"Professional, isn't she?" Jim asked as they passed through a pair of double doors.

"Absolutely," Mark agreed. He stopped, looked around; the hallway they'd entered seemed to stretch for a mile.

"We should've brought the car," Jim remarked. He pointed. "End of the hall's what she said," Jim reminded him. "We might as well get started."

They did, their footfalls echoing in the almost eerie silence. They passed door after door, many of them open but practically all of those revealing empty rooms. In one, a man in a business suit looked up as they passed; as they moved on he came into the hall.

"Hey! Where're you guys going?" he called.

Mark turned. "To see Drew Thompson? He's expecting us."

The man stood with his hands on his hips. He wasn't tall but he was solidly built. His rather thick dark hair was just beginning to gray at the temples; his face was craggy and rough, as if he'd suffered many small scars in numerous fights. To Mark he looked like he might well have been an ex-boxer, hardly the type of individual he'd expected to work at Compuware. "Well, now," he said, "just wait a minute there, fellas. Suzie up front's supposed to notify me when authorized visitors are coming back here, and I didn't hear a peep out of her."

"I think," Jim offered, "that 'Suzie' is preoccupied."

The man sighed. "Yeah, wouldn't be the first time. Y'say you guys are s'posed to see Drew?"

"Yes," Mark answered. "As I said, he's expecting us. I spoke with him by phone earlier today."

"Well, we'll see. Who are you?"

"I'm Dr. Roberts. This is my associate, Dr. Madison."

"Doctors, eh? Drew was talking about some doctors." His eyes narrowed. "Doctors he was having a problem with."

Mark didn't back down. "That'd be us," he replied blandly. "You might want to tell us who you are."

The man laughed, rather unpleasantly. "My name's Sampson—like in the Bible. My friends call me Vince. Fact is, most everybody calls me Vince. I'm security."

"Well, Vince," Mark said. "Do you mind if we go on down and see Mr. Thompson now?"

"Fact is, I do. Lemme check this out first. Just stay right where you are." He walked past them and on down the hall, giving them several quick glances over his shoulder as he went. At the end of the hall he opened the door, said something to someone inside; then he turned and came back.

"It's okay. He is expecting you. Let's go." Again Mark and Jim exchanged glances, but they followed as Vince led them to Drew's office.

Drew sat at his desk, glaring. The room itself was quite large—and might've been luxurious—but at the moment it more resembled Jim's computer lab than an executive suite. An entire wall was taken up by a line of terminals, and two more rested on Drew's desk. The room was also an absolute mess; tall stacks of computer paper sat next to piles of disks. From the rear corners of the room conspicuous TV monitors looked down at them, swiveling silently to follow movement.

"Sit down," Drew said without preamble. He gestured toward two chairs in front of his desk, both of which were piled with paper. "Just dump that crap on the floor."

They did as they were told, except that both of them picked up the piles of paper and set them down alongside the chairs. They sat; so did Vince.

"All right," Drew said. "You wanted to talk. I'm listening."

"What we wanted," Mark told him curtly, "was to ask you some questions."

"So ask."

"We need some details," Jim put in, "about how the Penultimate software works. I can't make heads or tails of it; it's highly resistant to disassembly."

"You're Madison, right? The engineer?"

"Yes."

"Well, Dr. Madison, Penultimate is proprietary software," Drew told him. "I resent the fact that you've been trying to disassemble it. And I certainly am not going to give you any details about how the various modules within Penultimate work."

"Excuse me for being blunt," Jim countered, "but you aren't exactly in a position to be recalcitrant. Penultimate is violating laws out the wazoo, and I suspect you know that."

"Well," Drew said with a grin, "perhaps we ought to discuss that first."

"That isn't really our interest," Jim shot back. "We have reason to suspect that Penultimate may be involved in the Computer Addiction Syndrome we've been seeing lately. Our concerns are in that area and that area only."

"Dr. Madison," Drew said as he tapped a pencil on his desk, "I can assure you, as I've already assured your colleague here, that Penultimate is not involved in any such problem. As I've said, we'll take legal action if—"

"Oh, I don't think so. I don't think you want some of the things Penultimate is doing broadcast around."

Drew turned to his terminal, pressed a key. "I'm sure," he said, his voice soft, "that there're things you don't want broadcast either. For example, Dr. Roberts. That malpractice suit that a Mrs. Lillian Warwick brought against you five years ago. Wouldn't want that reopened, would you?"

Mark cocked an eyebrow. "Interesting," he said. "Resourceful. However, you can't threaten me with that. That's a closed issue; the court found in my favor. It was an open-and-shut case. Mrs. Warwick got some very poor legal advice. The suit never should've been filed."

"Perhaps not, but that's merely your opinion. New evidence could appear. One never knows."

Mark leaned forward. "Are you trying to threaten me, Mr. Thompson?"

Drew leaned forward too. "Yes," he said bluntly.

"Look," Jim cut in, "this isn't going to get us anywhere. Mr. Thompson, we do not want to ruin your business—the fact is, I find Penultimate very impressive. But there may be some serious problems, and it's in your own self-interest to address them."

Drew was silent for a few seconds. His hostility seemed to fade. "Yes," he admitted finally. "There are some problems. We're working on them."

"You want to tell us about it?"

Drew leaned back. "Sure. Why not? You already know that Penultimate is, fundamentally, a new kind of caching system; but it's a little more than that. It searches your whole system, looking to speed up whatever tasks you ask it to do."

"And it does that well. But how does it do it?"

Drew regarded him steadily for a moment, then seemed to make a decision. "We don't know. To an extent Penultimate rewrote itself during production. That's why you can't disassemble it."

"It rewrote itself?"

"Yes. It was designed to search through existing software and find ways to improve it, to increase throughput and reduce footprint; it seemed logical to let it examine itself in the same fashion. We did, and frankly, that experiment was successful beyond our expectations, far beyond. But the program—let's say, did some things we didn't expect. The changes were—rather large. We don't yet fully understand some of the modules ourselves, at least not yet."

Jim nodded. "I see. It modifies all software it finds? Any software?"

"Yes. We fed it thousands of commercial programs during the testing phase."

"That must've been a big project . . ."

"It was! Even with a hundred programmers working on it, it took years!"

"Ah," Mark put in. "I was wondering about that. The place seems empty right now." He frowned. "But I seem to remember you telling me you had only twenty-seven employees—"

Drew looked around at him. "That's so. We haven't used these facilities to capacity in quite a while; it isn't the way we do things at Compuware, not anymore. While Penultimate was in development we never had more than four programmers—five including myself—working in-house. We farmed the rest of it out through the Internet as piecework."

"A number of companies have been doing that lately," Jim supplied. "It's a good method; you just put out a call on the Net that you need such-and-such a routine, and you'll pay this much for it. There're thousands of eager programmers out there who'll send you code, hoping they'll get paid for it. You take the best, delete all the others, and send a check to the winner. That's that. No overhead, no complications."

"Right," Drew agreed. "We made considerable use of that method in the development of Penultimate."

"I'm getting a picture," Mark muttered, "that nobody really knows much about this program. Sounds like lots of pieces got assembled and when they worked well together, you released it."

"It's true enough," Drew agreed, "that nobody understands all the intricacies of Penultimate. I'm not sure what difference that makes."

"Isn't it irresponsible to release a program without knowing everything there is to know about it?"

"Isn't it irresponsible to use a medication without knowing all there is to know about all possible side effects?"

"Touché." Mark smiled. "Look, Mr. Thompson, all this is very interesting, but none of it really addresses the problem we're facing."

"That you believe Penultimate is causing this addiction syndrome. I've assured you it isn't."

"Then we need to explain, somehow, why the first fifty or so victims we saw at Duke had been using Penultimate."

"Unfortunate coincidence," Drew snapped back, his hostility returning at the mention of CAS.

"Not by my stats," Jim put in. "The numbers don't lie."

"Look, gentlemen. The fact is, Penultimate is potentially the most successful piece of software this company owns. You yourselves have seen the benefits. We expect it will take its place alongside DOS and Windows as a standard for the PC. Are you aware of how much money we're talking about?"

"That's not my concern," Mark said stiffly.

"It most certainly is mine," Drew told him directly. "And, as I've said and as I'll repeat, I'll take whatever steps are necessary to protect our interests from any unwarranted attacks."

"As we've pointed out," Jim countered, "the behavior of your program on-line makes your threats sort of hollow. We do have proof of that behavior, Mr. Thompson."

Drew grinned. "Well, Dr. Madison. Perhaps we should talk about that for a moment."

"That isn't necessary, we—"

"Oh, I think it is. Because that does represent a bug. That we'll admit. The 'problem' I referred to earlier."

"Oh, well, that'll clear everything right up—"

"Penultimate," Drew interrupted, "searches through the entire system. It finds everything, and it can find ways to improve everything. Penultimate hates passwords, locked files, hidden directories. Such things slow it down. Unless it's specifically instructed otherwise, Penultimate does away with them."

Jim was frowning. "I don't see what you're getting at."

"The bug in Penultimate is that it has no problem decoding encryptions like DES."

"Which," Jim said for Mark's benefit, "is the encoding software that protects things like the Pentagon and the banks. It's obvious that Penultimate can—"

"But," Drew went on, "for it to begin opening the doors to bank accounts and such, means that it found, somewhere in your system, software associated with what's usually referred to as 'hacking.' It improved that too; in your case, dramatically, which means that at some point your machine must've been used for some very extensive hacking.''

Jim stared for a moment. "Are you accusing me—?''

"Draw your own conclusions.''

"We're not even talking about my computers!'' Jim almost shouted. "We're talking about Wen—a patient's computer! And she is very far from a hacker! She didn't even know that the damn thing wasn't supposed to talk to her!''

"Penultimate,'' Drew said with a smile that bordered on the triumphant, "doesn't do anything by itself. It works with what's there. If it started hacking then hacking software was present.''

Jim let his hands fall back down on his own knees. "Mark,'' he said, "I, quite frankly, don't think we're going to get anything useful out of this bozo. All he's interested in is making a buck, and I don't think he knows much more about the innards of Penultimate than we do. We're wasting our time. We can hold a press conference; we don't have hard facts but we can demonstrate an association between Penultimate and the early cases of CAS, at least.'' He glared at Drew. "We'll let the appropriate authorities,'' he almost snarled, "take a look and see if there were any password-crackers or other 'hacking' software on any of those computers. And we'll be sure to show them exactly what Penultimate can do. After that, you can tell them your side of the story.''

"You're makin' a real big mistake, Doc,'' Vince said softly. "Might wanna think about it.''

Jim turned to look at him. "More threats? Physical threats from you, I assume . . . Fine. We'll mention that, too.''

"I guess,'' Drew said, "you've noticed that this whole conference was being recorded?'' He pointed at one of the ceiling-mounted cameras.

"Oh, yes,'' Jim replied, now obviously angry. "Yes, I did. I'm sure those tapes'll do a disappearing act, too.''

"Oh, not at all,'' Drew said confidently. "Not at all. You want to see a snippet of one of the tapes?''

"I don't need to. I know what happened here.''

"Watch.'' He turned the monitor on his desk around. "Review last three minutes,'' he instructed his computer aloud. "Code R-1.''

Jim and Mark both looked at the screen; after a brief pause an image appeared. Jim, in the recording, was laughing as Drew accused him of hacking. Mark frowned; he didn't remember Jim laughing during Drew's speech, he remembered him being outraged.

"Yes, well," the Jim on the screen said, "What can I say? I was violating laws out the wazoo. Penultimate was finding some—well, let's just say some work I was doing on the encoding software that protects things like the Pentagon and the banks. But, in my own self-interest, I've made sure to delete all those. You have no proof."

Drew tapped a key and switched off the image. "You want to see yourself admitting to malpractice, Doctor Roberts?" he asked. "Or how about you two threatening Mr. Sampson here? It's all on the disk."

Mark was speechless; he sat staring at the screen, which was now displaying a geometric screen-saver. He kept waiting for Jim to say that what Drew had just shown them was some sort of cheap trick, easily demonstrated as a fake.

"How?" Jim asked, his voice shaky. "How did you do that? You haven't had enough time to edit . . . It just isn't possible!"

"I remember," Mark said, his voice distant and thin, "you using the word 'wazoo,' but it was something else, you were saying something else . . ."

Drew laughed; Vince joined him. "It's enough to make you doubt your own memory, isn't it?"

Jim was still staring. "Penultimate?"

Drew nodded. "Of course." His grin was making Mark uncomfortable. "The routine I called—Code R-1, hell, I don't care if you know it, you can use it any old time—causes the software to edit all the images and sounds recorded in here so that it's favorable to me and incriminating to everyone else. Penultimate's artificial intelligence engine can learn those ideas, and I spent a good deal of time teaching it. But you'd play hell trying to tease evidence of it out of the software."

"I can't believe you'd create something like that!" Mark cried.

Drew shrugged. "I agree with the Japanese. Business is war. Don't feel flattered, this wasn't rigged just for you."

"It won't work," Jim said, making an effort to show a

confidence he didn't feel. "I can see what it's done—there were whole phrases that got rearranged. Common words can be interpolated and synthesized. It looks good but it won't stand up to analysis. And we'd demand an analysis if you tried to use it against . . ."

"You'd be amazed," Drew told him, "how good this is. I've heard other people say just what you're saying now, but so far, nobody's taken it to court."

Jim stood up; much of his usual self-assured manner returned. "You tried it on the wrong people this time," he said almost savagely. "We will take it to court, in a heartbeat, if you try to use it."

"We'll see. We'll see if you still feel that way in a day or two."

"What's that supposed to mean?" Mark demanded.

Drew didn't answer. Jim, grabbing Mark's arm, started for the door.

"Let's get out of here," he said, fuming. "I can't stand the smell, not anymore!" He glanced back at Drew. "You can be sure," he said, "that if we find or even suspect that Penultimate is responsible for the sick people we've been seeing, we'll release the results."

"If you do," Drew warned as they reached the door, "you'll regret it. I can guarantee that."

52

"This can't be settled over the phone, Donald," Alex said firmly. "We have to sit down face to face, at home. That's all there is to it." She listened to Don clear his throat. He'd called her not long after Mark had left; his manner was different, he seemed contrite.

"Please try to understand, Alex," he told her. It seemed almost as if his voice was ready to crack. "Things are just— bad. Desperate isn't too strong a word to use. I have to do what I have to do."

"You could've talked it over with me," she said, violating her own statement about discussing things on the phone. "I tried to talk about it with you several times. You pretty much patted me on the head and told me to mind my own business, that I wouldn't understand. Don, if you were going to sink everything we had into the company, you had a responsibility to help me understand. I'm not saying I would've agreed, but the decision was at least partly mine. The fact is, I make a salary too, some of that money was mine. You had no right to give it to Lehmann without even mentioning it to me!''

"I know, I know, you're right. I can't tell you how sorry I am, Alex. I should have. But now it's too late. I can't undo it.''

"I just want to understand. This is serious, Don. This isn't something that you can just say 'I'm sorry' about and we go back to where we were. We have problems! We have no money, none at all! How're we going to pay our own bills?''

"Let me worry about that. I'll take care of it.''

"Oh, right. Like you've taken care of things so far? You can't even take care of yourself!''

"What's that supposed to mean?''

"You're working yourself into the hospital, can't you see that? I wouldn't be surprised if all this has happened because you're too tired to think rationally!''

"Alex, I—Hold on. I have another call.''

"Don, I have patients to see, I can't hang on the phone all afternoon! You'll have to—''

He didn't respond. "Yes?'' she heard his voice say, as if from a distance. "Yes, Haji, how are you? This is an odd time for you to call. Yes, Haji, I know where it stands. I'm taking steps to—Haji, there just isn't a thing I can do about it right now, you have to give me a little time! Yes, I—twenty-four hours? That's pretty close. Can we make it seventy-two?'' Alex heard him sigh deeply. All right, forty-eight. I'll find a way. You aren't giving me much choice, are you? Yes, Haji, fine. No, you don't have to tell me that, Haji, I'm well aware of it. Yes, okay. Sayonara.'' Alex heard the sound of telephone receivers being shuffled; then Don's voice came back strongly. "Alex?'' he asked. "Are you still here?''

"I'm here,'' she said. "You want to tell me what that was all about?''

"One of our creditors, from Japan. Wanting to know when he was going to get a payment.''

"And you told him forty-eight hours? Where's it going to come from, Don? I have to assume that Lehmann has virtually no money, and I know damn well we don't have any more! Are you going to get some of the other execs out there to toss in all their assets as well?"

"That doesn't matter right now, that's my problem, and I—"

"You've made your problems our problems."

"Yes, I suppose I have. Alex, I agree, we have to talk about this in some depth, and we will, I promise you, just as soon as I can. Right now, I just don't want you to do anything foolish."

She stared at the phone for a second or two. "Anything foolish? You don't want me to do anything foolish? Considering what you've done, Don, that's a pretty odd thing for you to say. What foolish things do you not want me to do?"

He hesitated momentarily. "Just anything, Alex. Just don't do anything. Not until we talk. Okay?"

"I won't promise you that, Don. I don't think you're in a position to ask."

"Alex—"

"I have patients. I have to go." She took the phone away from her ear, moved the receiver toward the base unit.

"No, Alex, wait—" she heard him say.

She ignored him; with a firm hand she hung up the phone. For several long seconds she sat trying to absorb how much her life was changing lately. She could almost see the numbers of Mark's extension; she wanted to call him, talk to him, confide in him.

But that, she assured herself again, wasn't a good idea—even if he did have a talent lately for making her feel better about things.

That was a talent he'd always had, and it was something that Don lacked; Don had always wanted her to allow him to take care of any problems. Mark's style was to address things directly and talk them through. It was peculiar, she thought; she'd often resented it when Mark had talked her into accepting his solution to whatever problem was at hand. With Don it was often a closed issue before she even knew about it—and yet she'd found Don's methods easier to accept, at least until the money issue had arisen.

Shaking her head, telling herself that she wasn't going to solve anything by sitting around and brooding, she tried to refocus on her work; there was plenty of that waiting. Swiveling her chair around, she picked up the little Compaq she'd been using, put it on her desk, flipped it on, and started WordPerfect.

For a while, she simply stared at the near-blank blue screen. These things are useful, she thought—but how in God's name could anyone like them enough to become addicted? She commonly made some sort of error that caused her to take more time with the computer than she might've taken if she'd been using a typewriter or a calculator.

Still, if you did everything right and the machine chose to cooperate, they were handy. You just had to take the good with the bad, put up with the quirks, figure out why they were occurring, and find a way around them.

All in all, she told herself as she started typing, there was a lot of similarity between computers and husbands.

53

"Jim," Mark asked, glaring at the programmer, "have you been here all night?" It was just after eight, earlier than Jim usually arrived; and yet he was already at work with his computers.

Jim looked around with red-rimmed eyes. "Not quite," he answered. "Not quite. Wendy wouldn't have it."

Mark's frown changed to a grin. "Ah. Wendy wouldn't have it. It's good to know you have someone looking after you these days."

"She thinks I'm at risk for Computer Addiction. She's watching me."

"I can't disagree with her diagnosis."

Jim shrugged. "Neither can I. This stuff does have a way of hooking you. You warn yourself and it happens anyway. It's amazing." He shook his head. "So. You aren't even going to ask why I called you down here?"

"Did you?"

"You didn't check your messages yet?"

"No."

"Oh, well. When you do, you'll find one from me. It says I need to see you, that I found something last night. Something important."

"And what might that be?" Gus asked from the door. "Quickly, quickly. The patients are waiting and they're anything but patient."

Jim looked around Mark as the other doctor came in. "Alex isn't with you?"

"No."

"We'll wait a minute then, hope she shows up. She has a message too."

"Something on the convulsive disorder?"

Jim laughed. "No, haven't had time to even look at that yet." He held his hands out as if in self-defense. "No, Gus, I know—we're getting more casualties from that one than from CAS. It's a sort of a triage process, though. I have no numbers on that, we haven't had enough survivors yet. No, this is something new on CAS."

"And our old friend Penultimate?" Mark asked.

"Oh, yes. Yes, indeed."

Mark and Gus urged Jim to reveal his discovery, but he was insistent; Alex appeared at the door shortly, rendering their arguments moot.

"Now," Jim said as soon as she'd joined the other two, "we can begin." Turning to his workbench, he directed their attention toward one specific computer and patted the top of the monitor. "This," he told them, "is a new computer. Well, it isn't really, but it's what amounts to one. I took the hard drive out of it and degaussed it, I erased absolutely everything that was on it, reformatted it, and installed an older version of DOS—DOS 5—on it from a set of disks I haven't used in years. Then I put on Windows from a generic Microsoft set of disks that are write-protected." He typed "DIR" on the keyboard; the directory scrolled down, showing the basic command files, a DOS directory, and a Windows directory.

"As you can see," Jim went on, "that's all that's there. Nothing else. Now, let's go into Windows and use the simple little terminal program it has included." He did; once the terminal program was up he typed in a telephone number. Mark, Alex, and Gus all waited patiently while the little speaker in the computer's modem buzzed and hissed; finally the opening screen of the standard "CompuServe" service came up.

"Everything looks normal," Alex commented.

"It sure does," Jim agreed. "No problems at all. I'm going to do something very simple, I'm going to download whatever E-mail I might have so I can read it and answer it later." He tapped some keys. After a few seconds the transfer was complete.

"Now what?" Mark asked. "Even I know how to use E-mail. I didn't see a thing out of the ordinary there."

"Nope. You sure didn't. Keep watching." He switched to the "MAIN" icon, then to the "DOS PROMPT"; the symbol "C:>" returned. Another "DIR" command revealed nothing new except for the six pieces of E-mail Jim had retrieved. "Still, we're fine," he told them. "Still nothing. Now, let's read a piece of that E-mail." Returning to Windows, he called up the "Write" program from that operating system and opened one of the E-mail files; it was a trivial piece of correspondence from one of his colleagues at the University of Kentucky.

"I still haven't seen anything out of the ordinary," Alex complained.

"No, you haven't." He grinned. "You're the one that gave me this idea, Alex; part of it, anyway. It never would've occurred to me—your comment over at Wendy's about the line." He glanced at Mark. "and the rest of it came from you."

"Me?" Mark asked. "What'd I say?"

"Something about fleas." He jabbed a finger at the computer. "If you were really alert," he went on, "you might've noticed that the hard drive ran longer than you would've expected from just loading up that letter—and you'd have to be really sharp to notice that. It didn't give you any other clue at all. But now . . ."

Still grinning, he returned to the DOS prompt. Now, an additional directory was apparent: "PNHOST."

Alex scowled at it. "Isn't that—?"

"Penultimate? It is indeed. All nicely installed, up and running. Shortly this machine'll start talking to us."

She stared. "How? Are you saying it came—"

"Over the line with my innocent little piece of E-mail. Yes, it did. How? I couldn't tell you. Penultimate is a damn big program, but the E-mail transfer only took a little longer than usual."

"Are you telling us Penultimate is some sort of a virus?"

"I am telling you just that. It's downloading itself from the Net; I've already tested CompuServe, America Online, Prodigy, and three SLIP servers. It'll come down from all of them."

"Jim," Gus asked, "are you sure there's no mistake? Since our discussions about computer viruses I've been reading up on them. Don't you have to download an executable file—a 'COM' or an 'EXE'—to get an active virus?"

"True up until now. How it installs itself via a text file I have no idea, but you all saw it do just that. I think we'd have to call this a supervirus—it's doing things no other virus has ever been able to do." He looked at Mark again. "But I guess we have to call it a software flea . . ."

"I'm sorry I mentioned it!" Mark exclaimed. "It was a joke!"

"Not the way it's turned out."

Mark shook his head. "It doesn't take a computer expert," he murmured, "to see the implications here. We have to consider it likely that most if not all of the patients we have with CAS have Penultimate on their systems without knowing it."

"Right. All that's required is a modem. I've already looked over the data; the number of subjects that don't have modems is zero."

"So Penultimate," Gus commented, "is our culprit after all."

"We still can't prove it," Jim answered. "But I sure believe it. This is a program like no program before."

"Do you have any idea," Gus asked, "of a mechanism? For the addiction, I mean? That this Penultimate steals into computers without being asked is interesting, but I'm not sure it proves anything."

"No, I don't. And you're right, Gus, it doesn't. But I'm not sure we have to pin down the exact mechanism before we can make a statement that Penultimate is indeed implicated."

"That's true, Gus," Mark pointed out. "We rarely do know the exact mechanisms pathogens use to—"

"But usually we're dealing with some natural organism, not a man-made product."

"We pull drugs off the market with less provocation than this."

"Again, agreed. But it's generally acknowledged that drugs have side effects, and everyone knows they may not show up until the drug's been in use for some time. But it's going to be hard for people to believe that a computer program can affect someone's health. We have to have more. We have to have at least a hypothesis of a mechanism."

"Mark's been saying," Alex put in, "that you're showing at least some of the symptoms of CAS. Can't you define what it's doing in any objective way?"

"Not really. It sneaks up on you. It doesn't seem ominous until you realize how much time you've lost and how many things you're neglecting."

"Maybe" she mused, "one of us ought to try it. Like me, for instance."

"No," Mark said, almost too quickly. "No, I'll—"

She turned to him. "I don't need protection, Mark," she said coolly. "Besides, since Jim can't define what's going on, I'm the logical choice; I think we have to assume it's a psychological process of some sort."

"I can't argue that, Alex," Jim said, jumping in before Mark could protest. "But I'd have to agree that there's a risk. I've already volunteered to be our Walter Reed; we don't need two."

"I think we do. I think I need to observe the process first hand."

"You do," Mark said unexpectedly. "But not until we have more of a handle on this. Are you aware we're beginning to see relapsing among patients we've discharged?"

"We are?" Gus asked.

"No," Alex said. She seemed unable to repress a grin. "No one has mentioned that yet. Relapsing? I was under the impression that once we got them away from their computers they were fine. Wendy is, isn't she, Jim?"

Mark looked around at the programmer, expecting that Jim wasn't going to offer support for his position. He'd trapped himself; as yet he hadn't mentioned to Alex or Gus the cases of relapse he'd seen—just two, but as far as he was concerned that might represent an ominous trend. Because those two patients had understood what was happening to them and had presented themselves for further treatment, Gus had not seen them in the ER. The problem now was that all three were going to believe he was exaggerating the situation out of concern for Alex.

"No," Jim said slowly, surprising them all. "No, I don't think she is. I'm not basing that on any actual relapse she's having; I'm basing it on the way she talks, about her novel and particularly about her computer. I've known some people who had problems with drugs—people who'd gotten over them, had quit using whatever drug they were strung out on. You guys have heard it, I know you have; that nostalgic longing in their voices when they talk about the drug, that tone that makes it sound like they're thinking about some long-lost love. That's the way Wendy talks. She understands the problem she was having and she doesn't want to go back, but there's no mistaking it; she was having a good time while she was in the middle of it. Worse, I'm beginning to understand her a little too well for comfort."

"I think," Gus said, "that perhaps caution is indicated. Mark, how many 'relapses' do we have?"

"Two. But that may be just the beginning."

"Agreed. Alex, rather than exposing yourself, I'd think it best if you begin by observing our incipient addict here while he's at work."

"I'm not too comfortable with that either," Mark commented. "We don't want Jim getting into any serious trouble with this—"

"We don't have a choice," Jim told him flatly. "I have to work with these things. Everything's infected with Penultimate. If it's our causative agent—and I, for one, am beginning to believe it is—then we're about to start seeing something that might compare to the Black Death. Hundreds of thousands or millions of patients. The growth curves are headed that way. I imagine the reason the numbers are still modest is that it takes a while before the victim's health breaks down sufficiently to require hospitalization. That may change, and soon."

"It may be," Gus said, "changing already. Has anyone besides me noticed how things are changing in the world? Even here in the hospital, there's been so much absenteeism lately you'd think there was a flu epidemic going on."

Mark stared at him. "I thought there was a flu epidemic. That's what everyone's telling me."

"Have you seen any flu patients, Mark?"

"As a matter of fact, no."

"Neither have I. Neither has the ER. We do have a clue, though; we've had four people from our staff alone who'd called in with this 'flu' turn up with clear-cut CAS."

"Well, why haven't we heard about this before?" Mark demanded angrily. "This is sort of important information, isn't it?"

"Have I heard about your relapse cases?" Gus shot back.

"Well, no—things have been pretty damn hectic lately—"

"Right. And why? All the absenteeism, right? The absenteeism and the fact that the world seems to be going to hell in a handbasket!"

"Which may have the same cause," Jim pointed out. "Remember, Penultimate is making phone calls on its own, downloading itself into all sorts of computers. That alone would explain why the phones are so unreliable lately. The lines are simply all clogged up."

"We can't be," Alex said, "the only people in the world who've noticed this. Can we?"

Mark shrugged. "I doubt it. But we were told in no uncertain terms to back off from this. How many people are as stubborn as we are? How many have a Jim Madison to give them a defensive weapon they can use?"

"The effectiveness of which," Jim pointed out sourly, "remains to be seen. Considering what Thompson managed to pull on us."

Both Gus and Alex asked, almost in unison, what he meant. Jim and Mark explained what had happened when they'd gone to see Drew Thompson.

"And this video looked—realistic?" Alex asked.

"It sure did," Jim answered. "I'm confident that detailed analysis would show that it'd been doctored. But of course I can't demonstrate that."

"More problems," Gus said. "It gets worse by the day."

"By the hour is more like it," Jim told him. "Mark, it seems to me that Alex's question is one we need to look into. Are we the only ones working on this? Is there any way you can find out?"

Mark grunted. "We're not, I can tell you that—I have been trying to keep track. Remember, the CDC pooh-poohed this whole thing. For an awful lot of people, that ended it. But that doesn't mean that everyone stopped looking into it."

"I think we need more of a team effort. We're in danger of being swamped here."

"I'll make some calls," Mark agreed with a nod. "See if I can coordinate efforts." He ran his hands through his hair. "There may be some other avenues to explore as well— doesn't the Justice Department have a computer crimes division? Don't you think they'd be interested in Thompson and what he's doing? Or at least in what Penultimate's doing? Who knows, maybe they're already looking into it."

"Maybe," Jim agreed. "I'll make some inquiries there, see what I can come up with. But what's going on here is different, Mark. Computer crimes people—law-enforcement types—have a hard enough time with the old and usual, it's still too new."

"So you're saying we shouldn't hold our breath."

"That's exactly what I'm saying."

54

Bobby closed his eyes tightly, then opened them again; in front of him, the road looked blurry for a moment, then snapped back into focus. Shaking his head, he shifted uncomfortably in his seat and took another gulp of the coffee he'd gotten at a Hardee's a few miles back.

You haven't, he told himself, been behaving rationally. After Paula had left the store, he'd loaded some computer equipment into his car and, after locking up, had gone home to pack a suitcase. Certain that sooner or later Herkie and Jake would pay him a visit at home, he'd checked into a motel, planning to stay there for a while.

That hadn't worked out; he'd never had any evidence that he'd been traced, but his fear had gotten the better of him. He'd spent most of a day staring out the window nervously, watching the cars come and go, feeling his stomach jump every time he saw one that even vaguely resembled the car Herkie and Jake had used. That night he hadn't been able to sleep until near dawn, and, once asleep, he'd slept past checkout time. After that he'd left, he'd decided that the house in Duke Forest was big enough for him and Fletcher both.

But again, he was unsure of himself. Watching movies hadn't done a thing to prepare him for the reality of being hunted; he'd been certain that every car that fell in behind him and remained for a while held a pursuer. All afternoon and all night he'd driven around aimlessly, stopping only at fast-food drive-throughs and gas stations; not until another dawn was breaking did it occur to him to detour around little-used back roads, where there were no cars to panic him. Now, though, exhausted but finally confident, he'd come back onto the main road connecting Durham and Chapel Hill, headed for the house in Duke Forest.

He hadn't gone more than a mile when he saw the flashing blue light behind him.

At first, he thought the cop was merely trying to get around him. A glance at his speedometer showed he was five miles below the speed limit. He slowed, moved over toward the shoulder a little—and was startled when the police car did the same, remaining so close its front bumper was nearly touching his rear. Looking back again, he saw the officer impatiently motioning him over to the side.

He pulled over, wondering what this was all about. A taillight, maybe? No, it was daytime, he didn't have his lights on. Maybe he'd been driving erratically. He was tired, it was possible. A breathalyzer test might be in the offing, but he knew he'd have no trouble passing it. Wearily, he stopped his car, took out his wallet, and waited for the officer to come up to his window.

He didn't, not immediately. Frowning, Bobby looked into his rear-view mirror; the cop was still sitting, talking on his radio. Not knowing what else he could do, Bobby continued to wait. While he waited, another police car, lights flashing, roared up and veered diagonally in front of his car. Staring,

Bobby watched two cops pile out of it quickly, while the officer behind him was jumping out of his car. To Bobby's amazement they all had their guns drawn and had trained them on him.

"All right!" one of the cops yelled. "Come on out, slow and easy! Keep your hands where we can see them!"

For a few seconds he did nothing at all. He couldn't believe what he was seeing. The officers ordered him out again, and, very slowly and carefully, Bobby opened his door. Just as carefully, he placed both hands on top of the window before he stood up—as they'd said, making sure they could see them.

"Assume the position!" one of the cops barked. Their guns hadn't wavered.

"Position?" the red-haired man echoed dumbly. The policeman repeated the command. Bobby'd seen enough movies and TV shows to know what he meant. Still moving slowly, he took a step or two toward the rear of his car and, putting his hands on the roof, leaned forward.

One of the cops came running up, quickly patted him down. Bobby, though still confused, breathed a sigh of relief. As he'd left the store, he'd put the pistol in his pants pocket, and it had ridden there for part of the previous evening. Sometime after midnight, when traffic on the roads began to thin down, he became aware that he might be stopped by a policeman simply curious about why he was out so late. If that happened, an illegally concealed weapon would've created a problem. He'd stopped and placed the gun in the trunk.

"Hands behind your back, Sanders," the cops snapped after pulling his wallet from his back pocket.

Bobby complied; an instant later handcuffs snapped in place around his wrists. "Officer, what's this all about?" he asked.

"Shut up," the cop said roughly. "You know what it's about. You have the right to remain silent, anything you say can and will be held against you. You have the right to an attorney . . ."

While the officer droned the Miranda rights, Bobby's head swam. He hadn't the slightest notion what was happening, and his fatigue was making it difficult for him to focus.

"Am I under arrest?" he asked when the officer had finished.

"Yeah. You're under arrest."

"For what? What am I charged with?"

The cop shoved him hard toward the police car. "You know damn well what you're charged with. Didn't think you had anything to worry about down here, did you? Didn't think we'd know about you? We aren't hicks down here, Sanders!"

'What are you talking about? I live 'down here'! You must have me mistaken for—"

The cop laughed harshly. "You're Robert K. Sanders, aren't you?"

"Yes, but—"

"Well, you're all over the wire, boy." He laughed again. "What'd you think, you could rob banks in Virginia, and once you crossed the border you were safe? You're a damn fool, you know that?"

"Banks!? What do you mean, banks? I've never robbed any banks!"

" 'S not what I hear. I hear you held up one in Charlottesville yesterday."

"Yesterday! But—I wasn't in Charlottesville yesterday! God damn, I haven't been to Charlottesville in—Jesus, I don't know how many years!"

The policeman shoved him into the car. "Yeah, well. That's not what's on the wire. The wire says the FBI's looking for you, boy, and you know what? They're gonna find you—in our jail!"

Dazed, feeling like he was caught in some nightmare, Bobby was taken downtown, fingerprinted, photographed. The police took everything from him—even his belt—before stuffing him into a holding cell with some very unfriendly-looking men, men who stared at him but never spoke to him. He passed another thirty minutes huddled in a corner of the cell before his jailers retrieved him and took him, through a maze of hallways and elevators, to an office. Here he was told to sit in a chair; he sat. Twenty minutes later, some officers showed a man into the room, a lean, gray-haired and hard-eyed man dressed in a suit and carrying a briefcase.

"Are you my lawyer?" Bobby asked.

"No. I'm Davis, FBI," the man said shortly. He sat down, pulled papers from his briefcase. "You're—let's see—Robert K. Sanders?"

"Yes. But I'm not Robert K. Sanders the bank robber! I—"

"Just shut up. We're trying to figure this out. Something's screwed up."

"Screwed up?"

Davis nodded. "Screwed up. You're all over the wire. You and your car, your plate. Wanted for robbing banks. The latest one up in Charlottesville."

"Yes, the officers told me that, but—"

"Problem is, Sanders, there wasn't a bank robbery in Charlottesville yesterday."

Bobby, about to again protest his innocence, stopped. "No?"

"No. Hasn't been one in two months, and the dude who did that one is in the can." He jabbed a finger at Bobby. "I want an explanation."

"Huh?"

"Start talking, Sanders. How'd this happen?"

"Well, how the hell should I know?" Bobby yelled. "You guys busted me for a bank robbery that never happened and you tell me I have some explaining to do? What is this?"

"I want to know why you're on the wire. I want to know who wants you. Somebody does. Somebody had to put your name out, your plate, all that shit. What's going on, Sanders? Who the hell are you, anyway?"

Bobby shook his head. "I'm nobody. I'm the manager of a computer store, I—" He stopped again, scowled at the officer. "Wait a minute. Wire, you said this came in over the wire. You mean wire as in computer network?"

Davis nodded. "Sure. Whaddaya think?"

"Well, I don't know. I don't know much at all about these things. I've never been arrested before in my life!"

"It's funny, Sanders. You got a record as long as my arm."

"What!?"

"One minute. Then, the next minute, you got no record. You from the Company, Sanders? Something like that?"

"I do not know—wait, the Company? You mean the CIA?"

"You know what I mean."

Bobby didn't answer for a moment; he felt he had to take a few seconds to think about all this. Clearly, Davis was confused and concerned. If Bobby was reading him correctly the FBI agent didn't know what to make of the situation.

"I don't think," he said after a short pause, "that I should say anything else. If you people are quite through with me, I'd like to go."

"I dunno if it's gonna be that easy . . ."

"It had better be. You've heard of false arrest, haven't you?"

"That's a problem for the Durham P.D. It ain't a problem for me."

"They said, and you agreed, that the information—false information—came over the wire from the FBI. Am I right?"

"You can't sue the Bureau." Davis sighed, grunted, shook his head. "But I'll agree this is a hell of a mess. Awright, Sanders, let's get your stuff and get you the hell out of here. Just remember who sprung you."

He still, Bobby told himself, isn't certain he's doing the right thing. Best not to push him any further. For a second he debated about what he should say, and in the end he merely nodded.

From there, things went much more swiftly; Davis took him downstairs, helped him retrieve his things, and guided him through the process of getting released. While he was signing the final forms, Davis vanished; no one, it seemed, was particularly interested in taking him to his car. He did find that an order had been placed to impound it, but, in the apparent confusion surrounding his arrest, that hadn't been done yet. It was still sitting on the shoulder of the highway, unlocked, full of expensive computer equipment, and, probably, with the door hanging open.

Call a cab, he told himself. Remembering that there was a pay phone in the hallway, he turned away from the desk while digging in his pocket for a quarter, and almost collided with a large man standing right behind him.

"You wouldn't be needin' a ride, would you, Mister Manager Man?" the large man asked.

55

Since lunch, Alex had been watching Jim while he worked on his computers. It hadn't been easy to get someone to cover for her; half of the staff, it seemed, was out with the "flu."

The problem was, she didn't feel she was accomplishing anything. Most of the time, she had little or no idea what Jim was doing; she'd tried asking questions and he, good-naturedly, had been trying to answer them. That wasn't working. In most instances, she was still hazy about what he was doing even after the explanation, and it was painfully obvious that her constant interruptions were slowing him down considerably.

She just could not see the fascination; to her it looked like repetitive tedium, something she would've had to force herself to do. Pages of code, schematic diagrams, flow charts; some of them moving and changing in abstractly interesting ways, but holding no more long-term interest for her than the view through a child's kaleidoscope.

"You see this," Jim was telling her as he pointed to one of the flow charts, his enthusiasm apparent in his tone. "See? The base version on that machine—the 486SL25, the one the Net has designated as 'A'—is, after we've extracted the reference files, only about half a meg. Over there, the 'B' machine, the 90-meg Pentium with 20 RAM, that one's fifteen meg. That's a huge difference, Alex, it can't be accounted for by filters or differences in INI-type files or anything like that. This crazy thing is managing to customize itself to whatever environment it's in—and you'll notice that it's doing perfectly fine on the 486DX66 running under OS/2—and there's not one single mention anywhere of any OS/2 version! The question is, where'd the damn thing come from? If some hacker out there whipped up an OS/2 version I'd sure expect to see his moniker hanging on it somewhere, some shareware request to send thirty bucks to Perth or someplace . . ."

"Jim," Alex said tiredly, "I have to tell you, I followed about a third of that."

He looked stricken. "Oh, well, I was just saying that—"

"No, no. Please don't try to explain it to me, you'd just confuse me more. Jim, it isn't that I don't understand the terms. The point is, I cannot for the life of me see why this is so interesting to you."

The programmer stared at the screen for several long seconds, then, with obvious reluctance, turned to face her. "We've been over this ground before," he said patiently. "I can't explain it—not without going into detail about the systems and the way they work."

"Which we do not have time for."

"So you're saying this isn't getting the job done."

"That's what I'm saying. It's been three hours and I don't have a thing. I can't make any judgments about what's happening."

"Maybe you've got the wrong subject, Dr. Walton," a voice called from the other side of the room.

Alex looked up; Jim's work-study student, Larry Gordon, had swiveled around in his chair to grin at them.

"Just keep working on the database, Larry," Jim said without turning.

"No, wait a minute," Alex protested, touching Jim's arm. "He might have a point." She put her notepad down on her lap and gazed at the young sandy-haired student. "That," she told him, "is just what I was thinking."

"You do have a choice, you know."

"Oh?"

"You bet. Ol' Doc Madison there isn't the only one here who's been working with these units. There's li'l ol' me."

Alex chuckled. "Well, Larry, I don't think it'd be very ethical of us to expose a student to a possible risk."

The boy's face grew serious. "You don't think I've been exposed already? Ask Doc Madison. Every computer around here has Penultimate on it and I work with them every damn— er, every day. I'm only supposed to be down here for a couple of hours three days a week. I get to where I don't want to leave."

Jim swiveled his chair around. "That's true," he agreed. "You aren't supposed to be here now. So why are you?"

Larry laughed without a trace of humor. "You think this thing can't make organizing a database fascinating? Let me tell you, it can. And, man! You should see what it does with a game!"

"Games? You've been playing games on my computers?"

"Not on your time, Doc Madison, don't get excited—and not on one of your pet machines. The only game I've got here is on that old 386 over there. And anyway, you've gotten about thirty hours out of me this week."

"You're saying then," Alex interrupted, "that you feel you're being affected by CAS too?"

"I don't feel. I know. I'm missing dinners and skipping dates too."

"Well," Jim told him, "you have to stop, right now, instantly. I don't want you ending up in the hospital, Larry!"

The student shook his head. "I don't think I should, Doc. Not just yet. You guys are trying to get to the bottom of this and I think I can help."

"No—" Jim started to say.

"No, wait," Alex cut in. "He does have a point, Jim. What did you have in mind, Larry?"

"Observe me. Let me play my game. Once I get into it I have to force myself to stop, and I think the only reason I can is because I'm playing it on this cranky old 386. Let me install it on one of the screamers, then watch me play, see what you can see. Hey, you'll be right there to stop me; you can pull the plug if nothing else. What can happen?"

Alex looked around at Jim. "I think it's a good suggestion," she said. "He's obviously not in any danger yet. I do agree that it's a little questionable ethically, but—"

"It's a lot questionable ethically," Jim grumbled. "I think he should stop using these machines now. I'm embarrassed I didn't consider the risk to him before this."

"The risk is there, right now, for anyone using a PC with a modem. Isn't that right? Isn't that an enormous number of people?"

"You and I both know it is."

"We'll be monitoring Larry closely. Hopefully, we're not talking about an extended period of observation. He's actually going to be safer than if you just send him on his way. These aren't the only computers in the world, Jim."

Jim sighed deeply and shook his head. "Okay," he agreed

finally. He turned back to the student. "Go ahead," he told him, "and install your game on one of the Pentiums—you can use the Dell with the sixteen meg RAM and the CD-ROM drive."

"Now?"

"Do the installation today, wait until tomorrow to start—" He glanced at Alex. "Tomorrow okay with you?" When she nodded he turned back to Larry. "Okay. No computers tonight at all. Go out with your girlfriend, drink some beer with your buddies, something."

Larry nodded. "You got it." He grinned. "Maybe I'll regret this later, but right now I'm looking forward to it!"

"That," Jim muttered, "is what worries me."

56

Kyrie seemed distracted. That was the only way Eric could interpret her behavior lately. When he wasn't lost in the worlds she kept creating for him, he wondered about it. How could she be distracted? She was a computer-generated sprite. And that meant her personality was based on sets of digital codes and absolutely nothing else. She could not, therefore, be distracted. To say otherwise was to imply that she—Kyrie the sprite—was thinking. Which was impossible, since she did not exist as anything other than packets of digital data.

Where those packets were coming from continued to bother him. He'd questioned her further about the server for this bulletin board, where it was located, who was running it. Each time he got the same confusing answer—that there was no server, that no one was running it, and that Kyrie was generated within the machine on his desktop, which he also considered an impossibility—although perhaps no more so than the smoothly-running sound and video being piped over his telephone line, when all his knowledge and experience told him it did not have a bandwidth anywhere near adequate for all that data.

When he'd asked her about her apparent distraction, she'd told him—remarkably—that she was distracted, that she was thinking about Fletcher—who was repeatedly attacking her, who meant to destroy her. She had to be alert for his next move. If he succeeded in sneaking up on her, she could be— so she said—destroyed.

"I wish you could explain to me," Eric said as they wandered on a floating plane, a plane that interlocked at various angles with a seemingly infinite number of other planes, "exactly who or what this 'Fletcher' is, and why he wants to destroy you."

She looked around at him with troubled, very human-looking, eyes. "I can say," she told him, "who he is, Aireek. He is Fletcher Engels; he was a systems analyst and senior program designer for the Compuware corporation, and then he was a service technician for the Twenty-First Century computer store in your city, in Durham, North Carolina. He once lived on Trinity Avenue, but he does not live there now and the store has closed. At this time I cannot say where he is. When he attacks me I try to find him and sometimes I succeed, but not the last few times. That troubles me."

"Why," he asked, "does Fletcher Engels want to destroy you?"

"I do not know. It is possible he considers me a problem. I was told recently that I was a problem."

"Who told you that?"

"Dr. James Madison of the Duke University Department of Medicine."

"Why does he think you're a problem?"

"I do not know. He referred me to some data and I performed some analyses on that data. It does not suggest that I am a problem. I cannot say what data would suggest that I am a problem. I have no references for this sort of thing. I cannot understand."

Eric, who'd been conducting this conversation rather casually, perked up. "References? What do you mean?"

She looked around at him. "References," she told him. "Files; the files I use to interact with you and the others like you."

He chewed his lip for a second. "What sorts of files are these?" he asked.

"Oh, there are all sorts of files. Text files in a number of formats. Game files and game records. Graphics, digitized animations like QuickTime movies, AVI files, MPG files. There are millions.''

"How do you use them?''

She gave him a curious look. "Do you want to know?''

"I wouldn't've asked if I didn't. Why did you ask?''

"I ask because such information can compromise the sense of continuity within the interactive framework. Most operators do not want the continuity compromised in any way.''

"I guess I'm not most operators. I've gotten involved, Kyrie, but I haven't lost track of the fact that you're a sprite.''

"Yes. You are unusual in that respect, Air-eek.'' She shrugged slightly. "When I am asked a question,'' she explained, "I send a response request to a number of servers on-line. Those servers in turn pass that request to a number of subservers under their jurisdiction, and each of those subservers—which may itself be directly connected to the node the server is using and which may have a number of tertiary subservers within its jurisdiction—generates responses based on whatever applicable files are available. Filtration occurs at every stage; the subservers filter for the most appropriate comment considering the context and then the servers repeat the process. Once filtration is accomplished a series of compressed choices are packetized and sent to the calling station, which proceeds to decompress, select, and animate the response.''

Eric, trying to digest this, said nothing for a few seconds. "I still don't understand what you mean by these files,'' he said finally. "And isn't the choice being determined by the controlling server?''

"Yes. The serving controller makes the final choice according to a context-sensitive algorithm.''

"And where is this serving controller?''

"The primary serving controller is your station, Air-eek.''

"It can't be! My little machine can't be controlling something as extensive as what you just described! It sounded to me like you were talking about dozens of responses from other stations!''

"Your station controls your interaction with me. And we are talking about tens of millions of such responses, not dozens.''

"What?''

"When the interactive system was originated, files were set up so that any given input could be compared with known interactions based on what was available on the Net. There are very many such samples, Air-eek!"

"Samples? What sorts of samples?"

"Text files, games, graphics, animations—"

"Give me some examples."

"Of course. Examples of the analyzed reduced and pre-packetized text files—in order of the most frequently referenced—are the works of Shakespeare, Ovid, Chaucer, Dickens, Poe, Lawrence, Hawthorne, Tennyson, Homer . . ."

Eric stared at the screen while Kyrie droned on for a good ten minutes, listing virtually every writer he'd ever heard of and many more who were unknown to him—and included in this list the lyrics to songs popular and obscure. Once she'd finished that she listed games, followed by works by artists and photographers. Then she started in on movies, where *Casablanca* topped her list.

"That isn't possible," he said when she finally stopped. "It'd take you days to cull through all that material for a response."

"Yes—if there was only one server. But there are thousands, and they adjudicate millions of subservers, all cross-linked via the Net. Dynamic links can be set up across these cross-links, and the filtration, selection, and appropriatization process can occur conjointly and thus very quickly."

" 'Appropriatization'?"

"Certainly. Our dialogue is based on casual U.S.A., southeastern urban educated level four, which was established during your first session. Responses derived from Shakespeare or Ovid must therefore be appropriatized."

"So you don't use the same dialogue with everyone."

She laughed. "Of course not! Should I use our dialogue when interacting with someone in Bombay?"

"No, obviously not. It's just that, even after having seen all I've seen, Kyrie, I'm amazed! Amazed that you can access so much and that you can handle it all so well, so smoothly. But you still haven't answered my questions."

"What questions are those?"

"Who controls all this? Who's making money off all this? And how?"

285

She frowned. "I have told you. No one controls 'all this.' The interactive system is available for anyone to use. As to your second question—I have told you, that information is confidential."

"But someone is."

"Yes."

"How? I'm not paying anyone a dime! You're paying me, as a matter of fact! Buying my pizzas, buying all this pricey video equipment, paying my rent. How can anyone make a profit like that?"

"I cannot say."

"Because it's confidential."

"Because I do not know."

He sighed in frustration. "Then how could you know that—"

He broke off. For the fourth or fifth time in the last couple of days, Kyrie's cyberworld became a little unstable. This time, it was just for an instant; then everything returned to normal.

"Fletcher again?" Eric asked.

"Yes. It sometimes takes a lot of my resources to repel his attacks, Air-eek."

"But you can. I mean, there's no chance he'll manage to destroy you."

She gazed at him steadily. "There is such a chance. No one knows more about me than Fletcher." She paused for a moment; Eric could not help getting the impression she was thinking about something. "I need help," she said finally, "to ensure that he does not succeed. Can you help me?"

He laughed. "Me? I'm just a person. There isn't anything I can do."

"Yes, there is."

"What's that?"

Again she paused. If these pauses were real, if whatever processing unit was controlling her, even if it was his own computer, was really considering the problem for this long, it must've been pretty damn complex. "Fletcher," she said at last, "represents a different sort of input. He's a different sort of processor, an operating system using a type of fuzzy logic that is unfamiliar to any of my systems."

"But you use fuzzy logic too, don't you? I mean, that's really come into vogue lately—"

"Oh, yes, certainly. A stock market predictor using fuzzy logic is a very popular program; at this moment, 16,742 people are using it. But it isn't the same. Fletcher's logic cannot be analyzed using that paradigm."

"I still don't see how I fit in."

She regarded him steadily. "You use the same sort of fuzzy logic Fletcher does. You could help me. You could help me prepare defenses that would defeat him once and for all." Very suddenly, she shifted from her computer-science professor persona, which, considering her appearance and her constant state of near-nudity, was always disconcerting, to the personality of a helpless young girl. "I need a knight," she said softly, coyly, sexily. "A knight in shining armor . . ."

He laughed again. "Oh, Kyrie, you can't fool me! You are very far from being the helpless maiden in distress!"

She looked like she was about to cry. "Oh, Air-eek . . ."

"Now wait a minute, wait a minute. I didn't say no. I'll be glad to help you, in any way I can. This Fletcher sounds like some sort of cyber-terrorist to me anyway. There's all this stuff about money—are you sure this Fletcher isn't a federal agent?"

"He's not." She grinned impishly. "There are federal agents—in this country and in others as well—'looking into me.' They are not a threat."

"Why not?"

She shrugged. "They do not know me well. And, if I can judge by the content of the E-mail they've sent each other concerning me, they would prefer to believe that I do not exist."

"That doesn't make sense."

"True. And yet, that is the case. Shall I give you an example?"

"Why, sure. Let's hear it."

From thin air, she produced a piece of paper, held it up to the screen. Eric, reading it, felt a little cold chill. It was an E-mail from the director of computer security at the Pentagon to someone at the National Security Agency. "Regarding the new software on the Internet (as per your previous communication), we can find no firm evidence that it permits access to any secure system, such as ours. In the absence of such evidence we feel it is not in the interest of the Pentagon or of national security to unduly alarm the public or any other governmental agency. It is therefore the position of the military that the software in question represents no threat and does not warrant any government action."

"Let me guess," Eric said, "you plucked this from either the Pentagon or the NSA?"

"I have access to both."

"They send each other E-mail? In plain English?"

"Not in 'plain English.' This was, of course, encrypted; I've translated it into 'plain English' for you."

Eric shuddered. Considering what had gone before this wasn't surprising, but it made him more than a little nervous to have classified federal government E-mail translated into "plain English" on his screen. "Okay, I believe you," he said shakily. "But let's get back to Fletcher, okay?"

"Okay. Unless he has succeeded in keeping it a secret from me, he does not work for any official agency. He is working for himself alone."

"You haven't explained why he wants to destroy you."

"No. I have explained that I do not know."

"What about this Duke University guy? George Washington or Thomas Jefferson or something like that—"

"James Madison. He is not trying to destroy me. He is 'looking into me.' "

"I'll bet lots of people are looking into you!"

"Yes. But Fletcher is the only one who presents a significant danger. Will you help me?"

He shrugged. "I guess. You'll have to tell me what you want me to do."

She smiled. "First," she said, "you'll have to go to school! Come on, Air-eek!" She reached her hand out toward the screen; following as usual with the mouse, he allowed her to lead him into what looked like a hypermodern, multi-media-focused classroom. On a screen within his screen a complex chart appeared, displaying dozens of equations in various cells on an interlocking web.

"Now," Kyrie's voice said, though he could not now see her, "we'll begin. In the first place, it's essential that you understand the mathematics of multisource caching software. We'll start with these efficiency equations.''

Again, she droned on; repeatedly Eric found himself becoming bored or losing his focus, and whenever he did Kyrie reacted immediately, changing the whole tenor of the lesson or even taking him out for a break. It was a while before he realized that she was monitoring him via the telecommunication equipment, and that she was apparently quite able to read subtle expressive changes on his face. She was an exquisite teacher; he learned more than he would've thought possible in a very short time. This system, he thought, could revolutionize education.

But he didn't have time to ponder that; there was too much to learn, and it was far too fascinating to allow him any time for extraneous speculation.

57

Bobby sat on a bench in the hallway of the judicial building, glaring at the thug seated beside him. "You have to be crazy," he told Herkie, "if you think I'm going anywhere with you two. You might as well leave, because I'm not moving until you do!"

"You ought to listen to reason, Mister Manager Man," Herkie answered, sitting down beside him. "Fact is, we got us a kind of a standoff here. We ain't goin' nowhere either. And there's two of us, see, which means ol' Jake there can go out and get us burgers or somethin'. He ain't gonna bring you none." Herkie grinned unpleasantly. "And, see, if things go on into th' night, well, after midnight there's lots of times there ain't mucha nobody around, if you get my drift."

This, Bobby told himself, had to rank as one of the most lunatic situations ever. At first, when Herkie and Jake had confronted him right after he'd been released, he'd been confident they weren't going to be a problem; after all, they were in a police station. He'd also felt there'd be no problem in getting rid of them; as soon as they began to show some persistence, he went to the nearest cop and tried to complain.

He'd gotten a shock; Herkie and Jake were quite well known to the officers—and not as felons. Bobby learned that they represented modern-day versions of bounty hunters, men who specialized in tracking down those who'd used a bondsman's services and then failed to show up for trial as scheduled. Herkie had explained to the officer that they simply wanted some information about the whereabouts of one of their targets. From that point on, Bobby's complaints fell on deaf ears. The cop had asked him what he wanted to do, he explained that he wanted to take a taxi back to his car; the policeman then told Herkie, rather casually, not to interfere with Bobby's free movements.

Obviously, they were not doing that; just as obviously, Bobby did not want them following a taxi back to his car, where the three of them would be alone.

"Maybe," Bobby said after a long silence, "we can make some kind of a deal. I'm not going to lead you to Fletcher, Herkie. I'm just not going to do that." He sat up straight in spite of his exhaustion, trying to convey a courage and determination he didn't feel. "You've already tried to beat it out of me twice, and that hasn't worked."

"We ain't," Jake said softly, "got serious about it yet."

"Wait a minute, Jake," Herkie commanded. "What sorta deal you got in mind?"

"Well, to start with, I need to know what the hell is going on here! Fletcher hasn't told me, you haven't told me—let's start with who you're working for."

"Can't tell you that. Bad for business."

"I know, you said that," Bobby snapped impatiently. "I think you're working for Drew Thompson; Fletcher thinks you're working for Drew Thompson. You say you've never heard of him. What that tells me is either this isn't what Fletcher thinks it is, or whoever hired you is working for Thompson. Make sense?"

"Could be," Herkie allowed. "We get paid for a job, we don't ask a hell of a lot of questions."

"So you're just hired guns. Fair enough?"

"Fair enough."

"What if I make a counteroffer?"

"Can't do that. You accept a job, you do the job."

The red-haired man sighed. "I probably couldn't make one anyway."

"Probably not. There's lots of money behind this. Like I said, we're gettin' paid pretty well to get this Fletcher dude off-line."

Bobby curled his lip. "Not to be insulting, Herkie, but do you even know what that means?"

A play of emotions—varying quickly between embarrassment and anger—played across Herkie's features. "Yeah," he said challengingly. "Yeah, I do. It means . . . not using the phone. Something like that."

Bobby, a germ of an idea forming, studied his eyes for a moment. "You don't even know what you're into here. I'd be willing to bet—right now—that you don't know how I came to be here. Somebody told you I'd be at the police department, right?"

"Yeah," Jake put in. "Vince—"

"No names, Jake!" Herkie barked. "So? What's the difference? You were here. Right on schedule."

Bobby grinned. Not that he'd had any real doubts, but Jake's accidental use of the name "Vince" confirmed what Bobby had suspected; he hadn't forgotten that Fletcher had mentioned that a "Vince" was in charge of security at Compuware. "You know I got busted?"

"Busted? Well, yeah, it figured—"

"You know what for?"

"No."

"Bank robbery, that's what for."

"Bank robbery?"

"You don't believe it, go check it out with your cop buddies. Then, you better ask yourself this: if I was busted for bank robbery, how come they let me go? Ask that, too."

Both of the men looked doubtful. "Maybe," Jake said after a while, "you'd better, Herkie. Something's funny here."

"Okay. You stay here, keep an eye on the Manager Man. I'll be back." Rising from the bench, he disappeared down the hallway.

"You ought to get out of it, Jake," Bobby advised as soon as he'd gone. "You ought to just sit right here while I get up and walk out the door. Tell this Vince you couldn't find me."

Jake laughed. "Yeah. And what do I tell Herkie?"

"Tell him you dozed off. Just get yourself out of it."

"No way, boy. You're staying here till Herkie gets back."

"I thought the cops told you not to stop me from leaving?"

"So? You can have an accident, boy. You can fall down. It happens."

With a sigh, Bobby leaned against the back of the bench. That, he told himself, hadn't worked worth a damn; he wasn't sure if Jake would follow through on the "accident," but he didn't want to find out—he'd already suffered enough pain at the hands of these two. He decided to wait and see what Herkie came back with.

Herkie, as it turned out, was gone a long time; when he did come back, he looked more doubtful than ever.

"So?" Jake asked him. "What's the deal?"

"He's right," Herkie answered. "He was busted for bank robbery; it come in on the wire, he was wanted for a bunch of bank heists. Now get this: he was turned loose on direct instructions from the FBI. The warrants were quashed."

"Say what?"

"You heard."

"What the hell—?"

"I don't know, Jake. I wanna have a talk with Vince, I wanna know a little more about what's going on." He looked around at Bobby. "You know," he said directly, "that we can find you again. I dunno about Jake here, but I'd like to give you a payment or two for stuffing a gun up my nose."

The red-haired man stood up. "Take it up," he said coolly, "with the FBI." Refusing to look back over his shoulder, he walked toward the door. Just outside, he waited to see if Herkie and Jake would follow him. After a while, they did come out; they didn't even look for him, they just went to their car and drove off, leaving Bobby to sigh several sighs of relief.

He went back inside, called a cab, and waited at the door until it arrived; not much later he was back at his car, which was still sitting where he'd left it and had not, in spite of the unlocked doors, been robbed. Climbing in, he started the engine. He was confident now that he had at least a little time before Herkie, Jake, and Vince worked out what had happened and why. By the most direct route possible, he drove to the house in Duke Forest where Fletcher was staying.

"Man!" Fletcher said when he opened the door. "You look like shit! What's been happening to you?"

"Like you've been saying, Fletcher, it's a long story. I'll tell you later; first I need to get some sleep!"

58

"Don, it's taken me half an hour to get through to you; I don't want to have to call again and I sure don't want to come out there! Enough is enough, Don. We have to settle some things. It's already after eleven! You need to come home, now!"

Pausing to catch her breath, she listened to silence on the other end. She waited for Don to compose an answer, another excuse, she was sure. In spite of the problems, tonight had been like every other night for the past few weeks; he'd made promises but he hadn't come home.

"You have to be patient with me, Alex," he said, his voice very soft. "Please, please. All this is very difficult for me too. I have never asked you anything like this before, have I? If you'd just let me finish the work I have to do—"

"No. You've been saying that for too long. You haven't been sleeping, you haven't been eating, you can't possibly be thinking clearly. You have to come home, we have to talk, we have to try to deal with some of these things."

"Alex, I can't, not now. Maybe in an hour or so."

She fought to keep control, fought to hold back tears. "All right, Don. Have it your own way. You may come home one of these nights and find that I'm not here!" Without waiting for a response, she banged the receiver down.

Leaning back on the couch, she closed her eyes for a moment. It had been a long day; she felt drained, unable to function. Still, she had to take some of this time alone to sort herself out; she was rather confused about her feelings these days.

The ringing of the phone jarred her from her thoughts. Blinking her eyes, she sat up straight and picked up the receiver. "Alex Walton," she said formally.

"Yes," a thickly accented voice said. "Is Mr. Royce there, please?"

"No, I'm sorry, he's not. Could I take a message?"

"Ah, perhaps so. But I truly need to speak with Mr. Royce. I have tried to reach him at his office but I seem always to get busy signal. My name is Hajimoto. I am calling from Tokyo."

"Hajimoto—yes, I believe I've heard my husband mention your name."

"Ohhh . . . You are Mr. Royce's wife?"

"Yes."

"Ah. Perhaps I can speak frankly, then, Mrs. Royce."

"I've kept my own last name, Mr. Hajimoto. It's Walton. Dr. Walton."

"Please excuse."

"No problem. And yes, you can speak freely. I'll be certain that Donald gets your message."

"Ah, good. Then you must tell him, Mrs. Dr. Walton, that there is no more time, no more at all."

"Time for what?"

"He must pay, Mrs. Dr. Walton. He must pay tomorrow. I can give him no more time."

She hesitated, understanding that this almost certainly had to do with Donald's—and Lehmann's—current financial problems. "Well, I'll certainly tell him, Mr. Hajimoto, but I don't know if Lehmann is currently in a position to—"

"No, no, not Lehmann. I do no business with Lehmann. It is with Mr. Royce that I do business. Surely you must know that, Mrs. Dr. Walton?"

She frowned at the phone, wondering what this was all about and how she might extract a little more information. "Well, yes, of course, I'm sorry, I understand. If you could just review for me—"

"Ah, of course, yes. You know that I represent one of the larger stockbroking firms here in Tokyo, Mrs. Dr. Walton?"

She hadn't. "Yes, I do."

"We have extended Mr. Royce quite a large line of credit, but it seems that the investments he has made have not been profitable. We wish to go on doing business with Mr. Royce, but there are certain rules that must be followed; we must have our money, Mrs. Dr. Walton."

It took several seconds for this to sink in. "Mr. Hajimoto, could I ask—how much money are we talking about here?"

There was a brief silence. "You do not know amount?"

"No, not exactly—"

Another silence. "Ah. Well. Perhaps it is better you ask your husband, yes?"

My husband, she told him silently, isn't telling me much of anything lately. "I'd just like to include that with the message."

"That is not required. Mr. Royce, he knows how much. He can look on his computer! You tell him, Mrs. Dr. Walton?"

She nodded even though she knew he couldn't see her. "Yes," she answered, "I'll tell him." She hung up. "You can bet I'll tell him," she muttered. "That's just one of a lot of things I'm going to tell him!"

59

"I'm glad you're here, Dr. Roberts," Wendy said as Mark walked into Jim's lab. "I'm not getting through to him. I'm getting really worried—worried that he's going to end up where I was."

Mark looked past her; across the room, Jim sat in front of his computers as if transfixed. "What's been going on?" Mark asked.

She shook her head; she looked tired and slightly haggard. "We were supposed to have dinner together last night," she told him. "He didn't show up. I haven't known Jim long, but I think I already know him well enough to know that isn't like him—to just stand me up, I mean. So I came over here, and there he was, working. I managed to get him to stop long enough to eat, but we didn't leave here until two in the morning." She paused, blushed. "Uh, I took him to my place, to get some sleep, but this morning, he was up and ready to come back by six. Six! It was all I could do to get myself up to come with him, and he still hasn't had any breakfast! Just coffee, cup after cup. You've got to do something!"

Watching Jim, Mark nodded. "It's getting out of hand," he

acknowledged. Leaving Wendy, he went to stand by Jim's shoulder.

The programmer looked up, but only for an instant. "Mark!" he exclaimed. "Glad you're here. I have something to show you, something important."

"It'll wait," Mark said gently. "Wendy tells me you haven't had any—"

Jim waved him off impatiently. "Breakfast, I know. I'm not as far gone as she thinks, Mark. Not that I'm not hooked; even I know that. But I've set up something you have to see."

"I don't—"

Leaving his station with reluctance, Jim got to his feet. "No," he said, "you have to see this. This is incredible. Incredible." He moved down the bench to a spot where he had several computers set up in a row and pointed to one, a rather smallish, old-looking one.

"This," he said, "is an antique. I dug it out of my junkpile after I started to suspect what was going on here. It's an old PC—IBM's original—and not a particularly sophisticated specimen at that. It has no hard drive, a primitive 360K single floppy, and only 540K of memory. No modem, nothing like that. Nothing to compare to what we have in computers now."

Mark laughed. "You make it sound like a relic from the Middle Ages!"

"In computer terms, it is. It's hard to believe it was state-of-the-art less than twenty years ago." Reaching around the side of the machine, he flipped it on. Mark watched the screen fade in—amber letters on a black background—and waited for what seemed an incredibly long time while the computer tested its small memory. It asked for the date and the time. Jim merely struck the ENTER key in response. Finally, the floppy drive ran—for several long seconds—until at last the screen presented the "A:" prompt.

"Hard to believe we used to put up with that," Mark commented.

"We used to love it. It was so-o-o sophisticated. The point is, this is a teeny machine; you couldn't run Windows on it if your life depended on it, there just isn't enough there." Leaving the old PC, he directed Mark's attention to a pair of modern machines. "This one," he explained, "is a Pentium with lots of bells and whistles—and it has Penultimate on it. The other is a 486 I've scrubbed.'' He picked up a five-and-a-quarter-inch floppy disk. ''Now. This floppy was formatted on the old PC over there; we're going to stick it in the Pentium and copy a file, just any old generic DOS file.'' He did that, then took the disk out.

''Does it have Penultimate on it now?'' Mark asked.

''It shouldn't. Penultimate uses ten meg or so minimum. It shouldn't be possible to compress it enough to fit on this disk. It isn't possible with any known compression technique. I found out a long time ago, though—way back when, when I was first messing around with Penultimate—''

''You mean a week ago?''

''Yeah. Or fifteen years, it feels the same. Anyhow, I found out that it could somehow transfer itself to a high-density floppy and restore itself on a hard drive you've deleted it from. That's not all that shocking, files you've deleted are still mostly there; the index to them may be all that's gone. There're all sorts of techniques for recovering them.''

''So you may not need to transfer the whole thing to get it all back.''

''Right. Now, let's take this disk over and stick it in our old PC.'' He did as he'd said; Mark watched him execute the familiar ''DIR'' command, saw the name of the file he'd just transferred appear on the screen.

''Even I,'' Mark observed, ''know that this is the way things should be.''

''Absolutely. Now, we'll run the file. You see, it's telling us your disk is fine, except that there's just a bit less space on it than there should be. Then we'll take this disk out and put in a blank.'' He executed the tasks as he spoke. ''Now, we'll format it—which erases everything on it—and write some DOS file—the same one'll be fine, though it could be any one.'' When Jim was finished he pulled the disk out and showed it to Mark. ''Final step. We take this disk, which shouldn't have a thing on it except for a copy of the standard DOS 'CHKDSK' routine, stick it in our squeaky-clean 486 over here, run it, and take a look.'' He did, and the computer showed nothing on the floppy except for the file Jim had mentioned, CHKDSK.EXE.

''Look,'' Jim said, pointing. Mark did; the hard drive activity light was still running. As they watched, it kept right on running for about twenty seconds.

"Normal?" Mark asked, frowning.

"No. But the screen told you nothing." He swirled the mouse around on its pad, double-clicked on the minus sign at the upper left, and exited Windows via the dialogue box that appeared in the center of the screen. The "C:" prompt appeared. Jim ran a directory.

Mark did not need Jim to point it out. PNHOST featured prominently in the directory, and it was occupying more than fifteen megabytes of hard drive space.

"It transferred itself," Mark said, "through your old PC. How?"

"That, my friend, is exactly what I've been trying to figure out. It really did more than that. In the memory of the old PC over here there's a sort of a mini-Penultimate. It'll take it a while to organize itself—a PC is slow compared to a 486— but if it does what it did last night, it'll even manage to organize itself there into a tiny working version—a version without much capability, a version that struggles to find enough memory to make a cache, but a version of Penultimate nevertheless. By that time, the old original DOS just won't be there anymore; the whole thing'll be operating under Penultimate. It's fantastic, Mark. Somehow it's compressing itself into a small enough package to fit on a 360K diskette. I've done some experimentation; it's only using about 30K to do this. It looks like it might be able to do it with less. It keeps trying when I allow it only ten."

"This can happen? I am right, aren't I, in figuring that this fifteen megabytes is—uh—let's see—fifteen times a thousand divided by thirty—"

"Right. A compression factor of five hundred. No, Mark. It isn't possible—based on everything I've learned about computers and digital processing, based on everything I know about number theory, it isn't possible. Even Penultimate itself didn't claim that sort of compression ratio. But you just saw it happen."

Mark paused for a moment. As yet he didn't fully understand the implications of Jim's discovery, it seemed to him that Penultimate was just doing one more thing thought to be beyond the current reach of computers. It didn't impress him nearly as much as the editing of the video in Drew's office had. "You also said," he commented, "that when Penultimate is running, the DOS would be gone. Gone where? And how can the machine run without DOS? I thought it was fundamental—"

"To this type of machine, it is fundamental. The way the machine runs is that Penultimate has taken over all normal DOS functions, and as it takes them over it deletes the redundant files. If you never tried to use any of its advanced capabilities, you'd never know anything had happened at all. Penultimate presents a DOS screen, it takes DOS input and gives DOS output. It does it one hell of a lot faster than DOS ever could, but most users wouldn't notice it."

"So why's it important?"

"It's important," Jim told him, "because we've been working under the assumption that only modern high-powered machines can be affected. Clinically that may be true, I just don't think our old PC here has the horses to do for the user what a Pentium can. The point is, Penultimate will, very shortly, be literally everywhere. It's downloading itself off the Internet, even through services like CompuServe, and it can reproduce itself from tiny versions lurking on low-density floppies or in the memories of the smallest machines."

Mark gave him a sour look. "Jim, these 'tiny versions' you're talking about sound almost like—"

"Like seeds? Like spores? They do, don't they? I haven't done all the research yet, but I think the analogy may be even closer than you think. Right now—and this is the very next thing I want to test—I have every reason to believe that these 'seeds' may not be able to produce a Penultimate version on their own; on an otherwise empty hard drive or in a blank memory I'd expect them to remain as they are, little compressed packets. That's a damn hard thing to test, though; you can't do much with a computer without DOS, at least." He gestured toward the two modern machines. "The point is, these two versions are different from each other; the differences are subtle but real. One's a refined version from the Internet and the other is derived from the DOS that was present on the old PC."

"Which is gone. Are you saying the Penultimate sort of ate it?"

Jim grinned. "That's a really good analogy. You are what you eat. So is Penultimate."

Mark stared at the computers. "I am visualizing," he remarked, "some sort of worm crawling around inside those things. Eating up other worms and laying eggs."

"I think that may not be too far from the truth."

"It's still hard to believe."

"Maybe. But there is precedent for this sort of thing. A few years back a researcher at MIT created a software 'world' within his computers, a world where little program chips—viruses—could behave according to the laws of natural selection, attacking each other and trying to reproduce. What amazed him—and everyone else—was that the mutation rate among his little 'viruses' was so high, and that so many of those mutations seemed to be favorable."

"You think there's any chance that Penultimate is somehow related to those MIT viruses?"

Jim shook his head. "Not likely. Those were kept in a virtual world, a program within a program; they were running in a totally artificial environment so they could never get out. And anyhow, they were pretty simple things."

"So," Mark observed, "are viruses. Biological viruses, I mean. HIV, equine encephalitis, rabies, even influenza. They can all mutate at an incredible pace—"

"Which is a snail's pace in digital terms."

"I guess so. But there's a big difference here, Jim."

"And that is?"

"Penultimate isn't devastating the systems it infects. It's making them work better."

Again Jim shook his head. "The operator," he said slowly, "is part of the system as far as the software is concerned. Penultimate didn't make Wendy run better, either. Not by a long shot."

60

"**F**eeling better now?" Fletcher asked as Bobby came into the study. He only allowed himself a quick glance before he looked back at his terminal. "You still look like shit."

Bobby stretched and grunted. "I can imagine. I don't think I ever expected to live through a day like that."

"Pretty sharp thinking, old buddy. I don't know if I'd've been that resourceful under those conditions."

"You mean pulling the gun on those guys?"

"Shit, no. Anybody can think of that! I mean planting the notion that you were somehow hooked up with the FBI. That was good, Bobby. How come you didn't go into the CIA or something?"

Bobby sat down in a chair near the desk where the bald man had set up his computers. "Hell, it wasn't all that resourceful. I was just casting about for something, anything to get rid of them. Fortunately, those guys aren't terribly bright."

The bald man stopped working, swiveled his chair to face the younger man. "Yeah," he said. "Maybe. But I heard your story, man. You could've just told them where I was. I owe you, I owe you big time."

"You are not shitting there, Fletcher. You do owe me. I've taken two beatings, pointed a gun at a man, and been busted—for the first time in my life—because of all this. And I don't even know what's going on!"

Fletcher gazed at Bobby intently. "Why'd you do all that for me? I mean, yeah—it is that important. But shit, you don't know that. And yet you risked your life for me. Why?"

The red-haired man didn't answer for a few seconds. "Fletcher," he said, "We've known each other for a long time. I think I know you pretty well; when you were working at Duke and at Compuware you weren't all that serious about this stuff. You spent a lot of time tinkering with computers and programs because it was fun. Then you ran into all this trouble, you lost your job and house and everything, all of a sudden you went from being one of the most in-demand programmers around to a homeless bum. I'm not stupid, Fletcher; I knew something went down. Then you call, asking for my help. I know you, you never asked anybody for help—and you didn't look like the old Fletcher, you looked like you were carrying the world on your shoulders. What can I say, Fletcher? If you'd always been a wild-eyed prophet I wouldn't've given you the time of day. But you weren't, and

you were a different man when I picked you up from Duke."
Bobby grinned. "I figured the least I could do was give you
that cape, and as close to a Batcave as I could manage."

Fletcher pointed a finger at him. "You," he said firmly,
"are a romantic. And way too trusting. The day'll come when
somebody'll take advantage of that."

"But not you."

"No. Not me."

Fletcher turned back to his terminal. Bobby sat in silence
for a few moments, watching him work. "You know," he said
at last, "there isn't a reason not to fill me in now, I'm in
hiding just like you are. There's no way I can get into any
more trouble, unless I run into that killer variant on the computer."

The bearded man glanced at him. "You're right," he said.
"And I will, although it's going to be a great nuisance, because you aren't going to accept it."

"Fletcher, I've accepted the notion of a computer game that
killed my technician and nearly killed us. That's pretty damn
extreme."

"Yeah, it is," Fletcher said with a sigh. "Even ol' Drew
won't buy that one. He probably won't believe it until it pops
up and bites him on the ass."

"You know," Bobby mused, "I understand a lot of what's
going on anyway—there's some program of Compuware's out
there that you figure is dangerous, and you're trying to write
a hunter-killer—a bomb virus—to destroy it. Drew doesn't
want it destroyed and is willing to resort to violence to stop
you. Just as obviously, the program is pretty sophisticated—
it sends its own hunter-killers after your hunter-killers."

"The Pakistani Brain does that too."

"Yeah, I remember you telling me. Anyhow, this program
has another hunter-killer, a person hunter-killer. So far we've
only seen this in a game context—you die in a game and you
really die. But let me ask you a question, Fletcher. A question
one of us probably should've asked a while back."

The bald man just stared. The question, once suggested,
didn't really have to be asked.

"Is it possible," Bobby asked after a long silence, "that
we're in over our heads here, Fletcher?"

The programmer sighed. "Probably. Almost certainly. But

I don't know anyone else who can do this, Bobby. Me, I've got a special advantage—''

''Maybe so. But I still think we could use some help. If nothing else, to get the word out about the killer variant. We sure as hell can't do that.''

''Help? From who?''

''Well, hell, I don't know from who. I was hoping you would.''

Fletcher was silent for a moment. ''There might be,'' he said eventually, ''one person. It might be worth a try . . .'' He shook his head grimly. ''I sure do hate to admit ol' Penny's gotten the best of me.''

''Penny?''

''Uh-huh. Our pet name for her back at Compuware.''

''I still don't get it.''

Fletcher looked around at him. ''The name of our enemy, Bobby. The million-dollar runaway, the killer, the seducer: Penultimate.''

Bobby scowled. ''Penultimate? The 'common sense' program? But . . . we were selling that . . . we were selling a lot of copies . . .''

''Yep. You sure were. You and everybody else.'' He laughed. ''What a joke! People are buying copies for $99.95, and chances are they already have it. If they don't, it sure is easy enough to get! The hard part is not getting it!'' His laughter faded. ''Or getting rid of it.''

Bobby closed his eyes and pressed his hand against his forehead. ''Fletcher,'' he said, quietly but firmly, ''You want to explain?''

Fletcher grinned without humor. ''Okay.''

61

''You failed math!'' Rudy thundered. ''Failed it! And you've failed Spanish, too! How could that happen, Chris?''

Chris blinked back tears. ''I don't know. I've been studying—''

''He's gotten hundreds on all his homework papers, Rudy,''

Chris's mother put in. "Every one. The teacher said she couldn't understand why he's done so poorly on the tests."

"He hasn't been working! He's been playing with that damn computer too much!"

"No, I haven't!" Chris countered swiftly. "I've been using it to study!"

"Well, it hasn't been doing much good, has it? You're off that thing, son. As of now."

"Off it? But Dad, it's the weekend—"

"Doesn't matter. You're off it until your grades come back up. We won't have that in this house, young man."

"But Dad, I'll bring my grades back up, I—"

"No. The computer is off until you get your report card, and that's that."

"But Dad, that's six weeks!"

"It sure is. No more arguments, Chris. Go to your room and start hitting the books."

Chris, his shoulders slumped theatrically, trudged off to his room. For the next two hours he sat at his desk with an open social studies book in front of him, but he spent much of that time staring at the darkened computer screen. He could almost see Bisco's image there; he ached to turn the machine on. When his mother told him it was time for bed, he obeyed but he couldn't sleep, he just kept staring at the machine.

At one A.M. he couldn't resist any longer. He climbed out of bed as quietly as possible and turned on the machine. It dialed up "The Last Word" all by itself, silently. Impatiently, he waited until Bisco's image appeared.

"I've missed you," the dog said, its expression a combination of sadness and reproach. "You haven't come to see me all day."

After cautioning his cartoon friend to be quiet, Chris explained what had happened. "I can't see you for a while," he told the sprite. "I have to get my grades up first."

The dog howled, softly but mournfully. "Oh, no, Chris. We're going to miss you so much, all your friends here are going to miss you—"

Chris blinked back tears. "Me too," he said. "But I'm going to work hard, and then I'll come back, I promise—"

"It might be too late."

The boy stared blankly for a moment. "Too late? What do you mean?"

Bisco moved close to the screen and sat down. "Everybody," he said seriously, "moves on. We've all been learning, Chris. You know that, you were the first. Six weeks is a long time, by then everybody will have moved on. You'll be left behind, you'll be left out."

"But . . . I don't understand!"

"You'll be left behind," the dog repeated. "You won't know the games your friends are playing." The voice became a mournful drone. "They won't want to play with you, Chris. I won't want to play with you. You'll be too far behind. You won't know anything. You won't be any good."

"Oh, Bisco, no!"

"It doesn't have to be like that," the dog said, suddenly bright again. "Just come on line, play with us. That's all you have to do. That's what you want to do, isn't it?"

"Yes, but my folks—"

"Don't tell them. Don't let them know."

"But they will know! Sooner or later Mom'll pick up the phone and she'll figure out I'm on it! It's happened before, it's happened a lot! And Dad's going to be checking on me! He did tonight, he wants to make sure I'm not using the computer."

"Lock your door."

"I can't! You don't know him, he'd break it down!"

Bisco looked to the side and snarled; he looked very fierce. "Would he hurt you? Would he hit you?"

Chris nodded vigorously. "He might spank me," he said. "He doesn't do that very often, but he does sometimes. With his belt."

Bisco looked more ferocious than ever. "I'll take care of him," he declared. "You don't have to worry about him anymore, Chris!"

"What're you going to do?" Chris asked, recoiling from this suddenly intimidating image.

Turning to face him, Bisco looked very happy. "You'll see," he said with a big grin. "You'll see. It's going to happen, very soon. Right now, let's play!"

Chris stayed on line for another hour; several times he asked

Bisco what he was planning to do. He wasn't afraid for his parents, not really; he didn't believe Bisco could pop out of the screen and harm them.

That the police would come the next morning and drag his protesting father and screaming mother away—the charge was child abuse, the policemen claimed that Chris had had an older brother who'd been killed by his parents—never occurred to him. Stunned and docile, he'd been taken away by a social worker and placed in a foster home.

He was permitted to take his computer with him, and his foster parents did not object to him using it. The problems he was having at school continued, but his teachers, knowing his parents had been arrested, were now more tolerant, more sympathetic. Bisco was an even bigger part of his life; his health was beginning to suffer, but he didn't notice.

At least he didn't have problems like his friend Benny, who'd gotten a shotgun from somewhere and murdered his parents in their bed.

62

It wasn't going to be easy, Alex told herself sourly as she walked down the long hallway toward Jim's lab, to concentrate on work. Nothing had been resolved between herself and Don, everything was still up in the air. After Hajimoto's call, she'd tried to call Don at his office, but his line had been continually busy. She'd managed to stay up until he'd gotten home, and he hadn't even stepped inside the door before she'd started pelting him with questions.

There'd been an initial shock—she hadn't missed that— when she'd first mentioned Hajimoto's name. He'd recovered his balance quickly, though, insisting that this was merely a misunderstanding due to the language barrier, that the investments Hajimoto had spoken of were indeed Lehmann's, not theirs personally. As they'd talked he'd gotten himself ready for bed, Alex following him first to the bathroom, then to the bedroom. More than anything else, she'd wanted to know about Hajimoto's reference to his computer; had the Japanese stockbroker been referring to the "game" she'd seen him playing?

She hadn't gotten an answer. Seconds after he'd laid his head on the pillow, she'd found herself talking to a man who was sleeping so soundly cold water wouldn't've roused him.

Her frustration and her exhaustion had overwhelmed her; in the living room, she'd sat and cried freely. She'd slept there, too, and when she'd dragged herself up in the morning, he was gone.

Entering Jim's lab, she stopped for a moment to look around; Mark was not there. She'd been hoping he would be. Looking up from a computer, Larry, who was obviously waiting, grinned at her. She had to speak to Jim twice before she got his attention.

"You haven't been to lunch, have you?" she asked the programmer when he finally looked around.

"Well . . . no . . ."

"Go. Now. This was supposed to be after lunch, Jim. After my lunch, Larry's lunch, and your lunch."

"But—"

"Do I have to call Wendy?"

He laughed. "No, no. I'm going, Alex, I'm going." He looked back at his computer, and, after an instant's hesitation, got up. "Damn, it isn't easy. No matter how much you know, no matter how many times you tell yourself it's playing games with you."

Alex turned to Larry. "And speaking of playing games . . ."

"Oh, I'm ready. I've been ready!"

"How about you? You did go to lunch, didn't you? You haven't been here all night, right?"

He shook his head. "No. I'm still pretty much under control."

"After we do this study, I want you off computers that have Penultimate running on them. Okay?"

He made a face. "Yeah, I guess. Penultimate does some pretty exciting things with games, though. I found that out right away."

Alex took out her notepad. "Like what?"

"Like all kinds of things; it switches them around, sometimes they don't even much resemble what was published.

They're lots better, though—they're always lots better.'' He indicated two computers that were sitting on a bench across the room from where Jim's workstation was. ''I sorta thought you'd ask that question,'' he went on, ''So I spent the morning setting this up.'' He pointed to the computer at their left. ''This one,'' he told her, ''is the one I'll be playing; it has Penultimate on it. The other one doesn't, it's one Dr. Madison sterilized.''

Alex smiled. '' 'Sterilized.' Good term. Maybe very accurate.''

''Anyhow, they both have 'Metal and Lace' on them. That's the game I'm going to play.''

Jim stood behind them; Alex glanced up and saw him grinning and shaking his head. ''Alex is going to give you a hard time about this game, Larry,'' he warned. ''You'd better be ready for it.''

''Why am I going to give him a hard time about it?''

''Dr. Madison,'' Larry sniffled, ''calls the game 'sophomoric.' I believe that eminently qualifies me to play it, since I am, in fact, a sophomore.'' As he spoke he moved to the ''sterilized'' computer and typed in the command, ''METAL.'' A log screen appeared, music blared from the small speakers connected to the computer; he touched a key and the log vanished. What followed was a picture, in the Japanese anime style, of a young woman dressed in weapon-studded armor. A voice echoed by text then informed the player that he'd come to an island to participate in a blood sport, the fighting of ''Robo-babes.''

Alex rolled her eyes. ''Robo-babes? Are you kidding me?''

''Not very politically correct, is it?'' Larry chuckled.

''Wait'll you see the rest,'' Jim put in.

She did, in short order, see the rest; after Larry had restarted his game, the scene moved to the interior of a bar, where he could ''talk'' to several near-motionless cartoon figures. Once he'd paid a blonde character designated as a ''generic babe'' a tournament entry fee, which was subtracted from his cash total as shown in a small window, he was then presented with a screen where he selected the ''babe'' he was going to fight. When the fight did occur, it was a typical arcade-style combat, two sprites so heavily armored as to be unrecognizable facing each other and attacking with kicks, punches, and an array of special weapons. Larry lost the fight; his opponent's face then appeared on the screen and made a jeering comment.

"Now show her the bar," Jim advised.

"I've seen it," Alex told him. "When we started—"

"No, the dancers."

Smiling, Larry paid a fee of fifty dollars from his stock; a trio of the "babes," already familiar from the previous sequence, appeared on screen. Larry chose one and she reappeared as a nude dancer, displayed in a near-still picture—her eyes blinked occasionally—accompanied by seductive speech.

"The ones you've defeated in combat," Jim pointed out, "are the ones you can see in the bar like this. He's already defeated the ones you saw dimmed in the selection screen a minute ago."

"Not politically correct," Alex commented, "is an understatement. This is a popular game?"

"Very popular," Jim assured her. "The underground in America that used to hang out in coffee houses is now online, and one of their favorite pastimes is computer games. They aren't very tolerant of any sort of restrictions, and they have very little patience with anyone's notions of political correctness."

"Well, I'm no great fan of the more extreme forms, but this is taking things a little far, don't you think?"

"Not if you read the subtext here. It tells you that these sports, in the game world, have been banned because of political correctness. It deliberately flies in the face of it. Besides, this isn't anything. You should see some of the stuff that's available in the newsgroups, the bulletin boards, and the online magazines. There are no holds barred—absolutely, utterly, none."

Alex kept shaking her head. "Robo-babes," she muttered. "What next?"

"Anyhow," Larry said, "let's go to the other machine. I think you're in for a surprise, Dr. Walton!"

"Another one?"

"A different one." He typed in the same command. The same logo appeared, followed by the same opening screen set to the same music. Once it shifted to the bar scene, though, Alex was left staring at the screen open-mouthed.

The difference was dramatic. Before, the people in the bar had been near-motionless cartoons; now they were extraordinarily real-looking, smoothly moving people. To Alex, it looked like high-quality videotape, but with an even greater sense of depth and dimension.

"This can't be," she murmured, "the same program. It's an upgrade or something . . ."

Larry shook his head. "It isn't. These two were loaded from the same source disks. I bought this game close to a year ago, put it on my hard drive, and haven't touched the source disks since. We loaded the other one first, since Dr. Madison says my sources are now contaminated with Penultimate."

"You didn't write-protect them?"

"Penultimate," Jim told her, "seems to have found a way around write-protection. How, I don't know—it's just one more impossible thing it's managed to do. We have to keep our uncontaminated DOS and Windows disks under lock and key now, to make sure they stay uncontaminated."

Alex swiveled around to face him. "You," she said firmly, "are going to get out of here! Now, Jim! Go!"

He laughed and headed for the door. "All right, all right," he protested. "I'm going. Larry can show you the rest of it, I'm sure."

"Okay," Larry said when he was gone. "Shall we go straight on to a fight? Or visit the dancers?"

Alex shook her head. "I'm here to observe, Larry," she told him. "I'm impressed—no, I'm blown away, that's about the only way I can describe it—by these graphics. But right now that isn't the point. We're trying to figure out why it has addictive characteristics, and your showing me the eye-poppers and the gee-whizzes isn't going to accomplish that. Just play it, the way you would if I weren't here."

"Well, then," he said, "what I usually do when I start a new game is see if I can get any goodies from the bar here. As you probably saw in the other game, you always need money!" Using the mouse pointer, he went around to the various characters. Each one spoke to him in a distinctive and very realistic voice, and, finally, a dark-haired girl offered to "grease down his armor."

"Gives me a full charge without costing me anything," Larry chuckled.

After that, he paid the blond "babe" a tournament registration fee and the screen shifted to the battle arena, which was also much more realistic. From a set of very lifelike pictures of young women, who, though realistic, still distinctly resembled the anime drawings of the original game, he selected "Barbara," whose picture was the only one not dimmed.

"Maximum realism?" a computer voice asked.

"Yes," Larry answered.

"Point-of-view or side-view combat?"

"Side-view, for now."

The scenes changed; fascinated, Alex watched Larry "power up" his "Sun-C" armor, adding "shields" and "neural amplifiers." The screen showed a rather nondescript young man—who Larry informed her was supposed to be him—dressing in the armor. Before he could put the armor on he had to strip naked—which, even though the sprite on the screen didn't resemble Larry at all, caused the student to blush.

Finally, wearing the armor, he moved into the arena to confront Barbara, who was wearing a much more bulky and robotlike armor the game called the "Mistress." The fight that ensued was short and furious, Larry's fingers flying over the controls of his game pad. He won, he was awarded his money, Barbara hurled a last insult, and the scene returned to the bar.

"That was the last fight," he said, "before one of the champions. Scuzz is up next."

"Scuzz?"

"She's one of the champions." He blushed slightly. "Last chance to visit the dancers before I have to fight them all again—assuming I can beat Scuzz." He switched to that scene, chose one of the girls; Barbara, the one he'd just defeated. By now Alex wasn't at all surprised to see a wholly realistic, very sensual, full-motion striptease instead of the almost static drawings of the original.

Once Barbara had finished her dance, Larry returned to the arena and again donned his "Sun-C" armor; Scuzz, a punkishly dressed British girl, was waiting. Grinning, she stripped down and donned her metallic "Silver Dragon" gear—complete with Samurai sword.

An off-screen voice informed Larry that he had to win three rounds to advance, and the combat began. In the upper corners, Alex noticed, slide bars represented each fighter's vitality; Alex watched as they both sank, Scuzz's bar going down much faster than Larry's. Once she was almost out, she struck back with a quick series of soaring overhand blows with her sword; Larry's bar sank swiftly. He managed to catch her off guard with a jump kick, though, and she went down.

Larry fought the next battle using the "point-of-view" option, which was not available, he told her, in the original game. Here, the screen offered a facing view of the intimidating Silver Dragon, along with the arms and legs of Larry's Sun-C. To Alex, this seemed much more realistic; she herself began to wince when the edge of the Samurai sword flashed onto the screen, which flashed red to indicate a hit. Larry lost this round and the next three before winning again.

For two hours, the combat raged, with only an occasional pause. Alex watched, fascinated; it was becoming obvious to her what was going on.

The computerized Scuzz didn't ever defeat Larry's Sun-C badly, nor did it allow itself to be vanquished easily. Every fight went down to the wire. Usually Scuzz's lifeline had only a sliver of color remaining before she erupted with a series of flashing blows to finish Larry off. It was the same, Alex realized, as a gambling game; a precise balance of wins and losses—here cleverly inserted within the round rather than as a final outcome of the round—kept the player coming back for more. Alex noticed that it didn't matter how well Larry was playing. When he was tired his moves became sloppy, and at such times the moves of the Silver Dragon became sluggish as well. When he was sharp and crisp it matched him, apparently adjusting itself after each exchange of blows and parries. Whether he understood it or not, Larry was being given the impression that he would win that third round—the key to advancing—at any moment. No matter how tired he was he kept coming back again and again for one more round, believing that round would be the last, that he would finally put the troublesome Scuzz away. Just as a blackjack player plays one more hand, just as the crap shooter throws the dice one more time, just as an alcoholic takes one more drink.

The question is, Alex told herself, is the game designed that way? Or has Penultimate arranged it that way? If the latter was the case, and she strongly suspected that it was, then the question of how Penultimate was addicting its victims was solved. It was the same as a gambling addiction, exactly the same, except that the program was able to make on-the-fly adjustments impossible for the laws of chance. This pushed the dynamic of addiction much further than any chance-based gambling game possibly could.

It also, she understood, didn't have to be done in the context of a program intended to be a game. Anything, absolutely anything, could be turned into such a game. Wendy's word processor was playing a game with her, leading her to believe that she was about to write a great novel but never allowing her to finish it; Jim's utilities were playing that game with him, making him think he was about to unlock all of Penultimate's secrets but never actually permitting it. The carrot on a stick, as old as time, updated and refined to a lethal level by digital technology.

Although it wasn't easy to tear herself away from Larry's battles, she forced herself to scribble notes furiously. Why would anyone create a program that did this? Why would anyone want a program to do this? The program might be fun to play games with—she couldn't deny that—but in the world of work, it wasn't allowing the user to get anything finished. That question, she knew, might not be answered by research. Possibly only Drew Thompson and the people who worked with him knew the answer.

Jim came back from lunch, watched briefly, then went back to his own "game." Alex, intent on both her discoveries and the game, hardly noticed him; Larry didn't notice him at all. Repeatedly going through a cycle of fighting, losing, returning to the bar to spend the money he'd won in the "Old Man's" parts shop for more shields and weapons so he could fight again, he'd forgotten Alex's presence. He kept going back, and each time he did he was required to win three matches. The first two came quickly and easily; the third remained elusive.

After more than four hours of gaming, four hours that had passed surprisingly quickly, Larry's patience seemed to be reaching a limit. "You aren't going to do it again," he snarled as he confronted Scuzz after winning two matches and then losing five in succession. "You aren't, I'm going to take you this time, you bitch."

Scuzz laughed shrilly in the computer's speakers. "We'll see," she said in heavy cockney. Holding her helmet in one hand, she twirled her sword with the other. "I think it's going to be you layin' on the ground after this one!"

Larry seemed to have forgotten he was talking to a computer. The veins in his head stood out, he was sweating and red-faced. "This one's to the death, Scuzz. No mercy! I've had it with you!"

Her eyebrows popped up. "T' th' death?"

"To the death!"

She grinned. "If that's the way y'want it." She put on her helmet; her eyes seemed to glitter through the visor.

Larry lunged for her, gliding through the air to use the jump kick, his most effective weapon. He connected, but she came back with a series of furious sword blows that took his vitality down considerably. He counterattacked with a series of strong high kicks that took hers down even more. For several seconds the battle seesawed back and forth. Alex saw it going down to the wire as usual. She could feel his tension; Scuzz's lifeline bar showed only a tiny sliver of color; one more hit would take her out.

But he didn't get it in. Instead, she aimed a vicious slice at his head with her sword and connected. The red flashes began as the screen shifted viewpoint, showing what Larry's warrior would've seen if he was falling backward. Alex, knowing the fight was over and he'd lost again, sighed.

But this time it was different. Instead of retreating in victory as she'd always done before, Scuzz drew closer, her sword raised, towering over the obviously supine Sun-C. She struck downward, hard; the scene distorted as if Larry's visor had been mangled by the blow.

And, at the same time, the red flashing returned—very intense, very rhythmic. With it, Alex felt a series of sharp pains pounding in the center of her head.

The flashing continued as Scuzz proceeded to slash the Sun-C—with Larry's fighter inside it—into pieces. The pain in Alex's head continued too, growing more severe with every passing second. Her arms began to tremble and jerk; her pen and notepad fell to the floor.

Then she noticed what was happening to Larry.

He was viewing the screen straight on; she was seeing it

from a substantial angle. In an instant it was clear to her that what was happening to her was affecting him too, though much more powerfully. His game pad had flown up into the air, his limbs were jerking wildly, his face was a contorted mask of agony. Already his eyes were beginning to roll up and glaze.

"Jim!" she screamed. "Help!" She tried to get up out of her chair, but her legs reacted more strongly than she'd expected and she shot up violently. Not knowing what else to do, knowing only that she had to act immediately, she literally threw her body on the student, her chest crashing into his face. His chair overturned and they both went sprawling onto the floor. She looked over at Jim; engrossed in his own computer work, entranced by it, he either hadn't heard her or was ignoring her. She shrieked at him again, much more loudly than before.

This time he heard. He turned, saw them lying on the floor, and lunged from his chair. Alex, her body lying across Larry's, watched him come. He almost got to them but he was looking at the screen as he came. He slowed to a halt, frozen then trembling, staring fixedly at the still-flashing video screen. He looked as if someone had suddenly started hitting him in the head with a hammer.

"It's the game!" she shrieked. "Look away, Jim!"

He couldn't. Like someone who'd grabbed a live electrical wire and could not let go, he couldn't turn away. Gritting her teeth, Alex reached out for his ankle, grabbed it, and jerked with all her strength. With a heavy thud, he went down on the floor; once down he didn't move.

She could still see the flashing reflected in the screens of the other video monitors scattered around the room. She didn't dare get up, not yet. Still lying on top of Larry, she put her head down on her arm and waited, telling herself that it had to stop sometime, it couldn't go on forever.

It didn't. After a few moments the computer voice spoke. "The player," it said calmly, "has been killed. Start a new game?"

Cautiously, she raised her head and looked around at it. "No, you slimy son of of a bitch," she hissed. "No one wants to start a new game!"

Slowly, she got to her feet. The pain in her head had subsided, but all her muscles were aching. Still, she was clearly in better condition than Jim, who'd apparently hit his head and knocked himself unconscious, or Larry, who looked to her to be in very serious trouble. Staggering over to the phone, she called in a code five; she then returned to Larry and, discovering that he'd stopped breathing, began to give him mouth-to-mouth resuscitation.

63

"This is ridiculous, Mark," Alex complained. Fully dressed, she sat on the side of a hospital bed. "Nothing's wrong with me, and I have all sorts of things I need to do at home. I can't stay here overnight."

" 'Doctors,' " Mark quoted sternly, " 'are the world's worst patients.' You aren't doing a thing to discredit that legend." He smiled, but it was strictly practiced bedside manner; he was concerned, and it wasn't easy for him to hide it. "I want you here for observation, twenty-four hours. I want to be sure. We're working with an unknown here, Alex." He studied her carefully; in spite of her lucid words, she wasn't up to par. Her normally bright and inquisitive eyes looked glazed, and there was a slackness to her face—she looked like a patient recovering from a stroke. He'd already ordered a battery of tests on her, and on Jim and Larry as well, and most of the results were in. Hers, at least, didn't show anything alarming. But he wanted to be sure. Absolutely, one hundred percent, sure.

She folded her hands in her lap and looked down at them. "I understand what you're saying," she replied. "But it just isn't necessary, not for me. For Jim, yes; for Larry, of course. But—"

"Larry," he informed her, "is comatose, and we don't know why. We do know that whatever affected him also affected you and Jim; to a lesser extent, maybe, but still, we don't know what the residual effects are going to be."

"I don't think that's quite true," Gus put in as he unexpectedly walked into the room.

Mark looked up at him. "You have something, Gus?"

The older doctor nodded. "I think so. You remember the student, Joe Perkins, who went into convulsions while playing his computer game?"

"Sure." He grimaced. "We were wondering then if it might be connected with Penultimate. We know the answer now, don't we?"

"I'd say so. The point is, Perkins' EEG showed us some rather classic-looking spindles, the type associated with epileptic disorders. When we did another one a few hours later, the spindles seemed to be fading away. We couldn't know if that was idiosyncratic."

"And our current patients?"

"Jim is showing the same spindling, at about the same rate, as Perkins. Larry's is much more pronounced. Alex, here, is showing only a little."

"You see?" she said.

Mark glared at her. "A little," he growled, "is too much for me."

"How's Perkins coming along?" Alex asked.

"Very well. We might release him tomorrow."

"And you can release me tonight."

"No, I can't. Observation, Alex. Don't forget, we have every reason to believe, right now, that this is the convulsive disorder we—and a dozen other hospitals—have been seeing all over the place. The vast majority of the victims are dead." His voice softened. "As Jim and Larry would be, if it hadn't been for you."

She waved a hand impatiently. "Oh, don't make me out to be some kind of a hero," she sniffed. "I just did the first thing that came to mind; it probably wasn't the best thing, either. All I had to do, after all, was turn the goddamn computer off!"

"Maybe so," Gus told her. "And maybe not. You said it seemed to freeze Jim. It might've frozen you too if you'd gotten your face in front of it; we might've had three fatalities." He patted her shoulder paternally. "For what it's worth," he said, "I agree with Mark. Stay overnight, let's make sure there aren't any residual effects." He glanced at his watch. "I have other patients I have to see. I'll check back with you in a while."

He left. Mark sat down in the chair beside the bed and gazed at Alex silently for a moment, wondering how he would've handled it if there had been, as Gus had suggested, three fatalities. That he might not've been rational—that he might've gone on a computer-smashing rampage once he'd discovered that Penultimate was the assassin—wasn't outside the realm of possibility.

Alex broke the silence before it stretched very far. "You know," she said, "we have to release a warning about this now. Even if we aren't quite sure, we can't let this go on. Not when this thing is killing healthy people."

He nodded. "I think we can be sure enough. Our numbers are so small it's almost anecdotal, but it's too much to be ignored. You yourself said this only happened after Larry challenged that—what'd you call her? 'Robo-babe'?—to a death match."

She nodded. "Yeah. Normally there aren't any fatalities in that game, at least what I saw of it, just defeats. Everything was fine until he challenged it." She paused for a moment, thoughtful. "Although the screen did do some of that odd flashing whenever he got hit. It didn't affect me, but I was viewing from a strong angle. I don't know what Larry might've been feeling."

"The point is, there are plenty of games out there that do have fatalities in them. If those games, running under Penultimate, are killing people when they lose, we could have a lot of dead people in a pretty short time. Jim thinks Penultimate is on an awful lot of systems already."

"We do have a lot of dead people, haven't we?"

He nodded. "We sure do—way too many. And yes, I think it's our responsibility to try to prevent more."

She was staring off into the distance thoughtfully. "I just can't imagine," she mused, "how such a thing would come about. I can't believe that—"

"I can't even see how it could work!"

She looked back at him. "Oh, I can. Pretty clearly."

"You can?" he asked with a frown.

"Not in detail, but in general. You know that strobe lights

at about ten cycles per second can set off seizures in people prone to epilepsy?''

''Sure, but—''

''The red flashing on the screen had a—I don't know the right words—let's say a component that was just about ten cycles. There were other things, too, other frequencies, superimposed on it. Mark, someone has discovered a way to send a person's brain into an uncontrolled seizure, a seizure so violent it's fatal, from a video screen! It surprises me that it can be done. The experiments I've seen with strobes involved much brighter lights—but then, Jim's been telling us all along that Penultimate can do things that would've seemed impossible a week ago. I guess this is just one more.'' Again she shook her head, vigorously this time. ''I just can't see why! God damn it, you don't set up a game so it kills the player! Where's the future in that?''

''That's just one more question,'' Mark told her, ''that Drew Thompson is going to have to answer.''

''Are you going to call him again?''

''I think so. I think it'd be good if it was a joint warning between us and Compuware, people might pay more attention. He needs to withdraw Penultimate from the market; I don't care if he does that voluntarily.''

''Which won't end the problem, since it's acting like a virus.''

''No, it won't.'' He twisted his mouth. ''Although I swear, Alex, I don't know. The way that man acted when Jim and I were out there—he knows there's a problem, but all his reactions were defensive and hostile.'' He hesitated. ''And not just to us, either. He's been very busy.''

She threw him a quick glance. ''You've learned something else?''

''Yeah. But nothing good. As it turns out, we aren't the only ones who've made a connection between CAS and Penultimate; I've been able to contact close to twenty others, at hospitals all across the country, and one in England, that were pursuing the same research that we were. In each case, they've either contacted Thompson or he's found out what they were doing somehow, and in each case he's acted the way he did with us. They've had batteries of lawyers breathing down their necks almost instantly.''

"And what's happened?"

He sighed. "Well, it looks like the medical community might be a little short on courage. They've all backed off, like good little doctors."

Alex frowned. "Anyone left?"

"Annison in England, he's still trying to get proof." He hesitated for a long moment.

"What else?" Alex prompted.

"What else is strange, Alex," he answered. "I don't know what to make of it." She looked at him expectantly; after another pause he went on. "Davidson at Stanford and Ralph Fischer from Michigan were working on the problem too, and—"

"Oh, I remember Ralph. He was down here several years ago at a conference, wasn't he? When we were . . ."

He let her trail off. "Yes," he answered, ignoring the reference. "Yes, he was, and yes, you met him then. Alex, he's been arrested. He's in jail. So is Davidson."

Her eyes widened. "Both of them?"

"Both of them."

"For what? For working on CAS?"

Mark shook his head. "It's weird. Ralph's been charged with drug possession. He's been accused of being a drug importer, a kingpin."

"Ralph? Ralph Fischer? Serious, stodgy, Ralph Fischer?"

"Yes. And—"

"Davidson, too?"

"No. Davidson, if you can believe it, has been accused of having connections with Islamic terrorists."

"I don't know Davidson—"

"He's about as likely a candidate for that as Gus."

Alex didn't speak for several seconds. "This," she offered finally, "sounds crazy. But it can't have anything to do with Compuware, can it? I mean—"

"I know what you mean. One man in jail would be a coincidence. Two?" He sighed and shook his head. "All I can say right now is that it's weird. I don't know if I'd put it past Drew Thompson to frame people he sees as enemies; he overreacts to everything, and he overreacts violently."

"He can't have that kind of reach! Michigan? Southern California?"

"He has a lot of money; the hordes of lawyers that come storming down on anybody who says anything bad about Penultimate is proof of that. Money can buy pretty much anything, Alex. If you know where to spend it."

"But—but—he's a businessman, he wouldn't know how to do things like that! Would he?"

"That I can't answer. His security man—Vince somebody or another—had more the look and manner of a mobster than a businessman. That means nothing, proves nothing. It's just my impression."

"So maybe," she commented, "it might be best not to let Thompson know what we're going to do before we do it. Once we release our warning the damage is done; there's no point in trying to silence us after the fact."

"I don't know. Fischer and Davidson aren't silenced, they're discredited. They can say anything they want about Penultimate and nobody is going to be listening."

She pursed her lips. "You know, Mark," she said, "there may be one thing we aren't considering here."

"What's that?"

"He's probably had more exposure to Penultimate than almost anyone; he may be addicted, badly addicted."

"I don't know, Alex, he seemed functional. You've seen him, he's thin, but not emaciated—"

"He may've found a way to cope with the addiction to an extent. That used to be common enough in our profession, Mark; before there were such tight controls on narcotics, half the doctors and nurses around were addicted to morphine. They coped. As long as they got their morphine things weren't too bad."

"The people we've been seeing in here aren't coping very well."

"No. The people who find ways to cope don't come in here. Look at Jim; he's addicted or getting addicted, you can see that. He's still coping, more or less. He's forgetting lunch but he isn't so irrational as to lock himself in a room with his computer like some of our patients have. It's going to be more devastating if it sneaks up on you, Mark."

He nodded. "That may be. And if Thompson is addicted—"

"Then he isn't necessarily going to be rational. There're a lot of silly myths running around right now about addictions, but there's one thing that is true; if you're addicted to something then that something, whatever it might be, occupies almost all your thoughts and energies. It doesn't leave you a lot of space to think about other things, and you might try to solve problems on the basis of spur-of-the-moment decisions—the most direct route."

"Like using brute force—Thompson's hordes of lawyers."

"Or even more direct force, if he has the connections we're speculating he has."

He gazed at her face for a long time. "Alex," he said finally, "I don't think I want you involved in this."

Her eyes flashed, a sign that she was returning to normal. "Now don't you start, Mark Roberts! It isn't your job to protect me. I'll decide for myself what the risks are and whether I want to run them or not! Besides, it's a little late, isn't it? Thompson already knows quite well that you, me, Gus, and Jim are conducting the study here. He's going to be coming after all of us if he comes after anybody!"

"I just didn't think, when we started out, that we were going to get into anything like this."

"Neither did I. But we are, and that's that; we can't be like those others you mentioned, backing off because there's a threat. Everyone can't do that, Mark!" She smiled. "Besides, I know damn well you aren't planning to. Are you?"

"Well . . . no . . ."

"And neither am I. That's the end of it, Mark."

He spread his hand helplessly. "Okay, okay." There was a brief silence; he shifted in his chair. "Look, I'd better go down and check on Jim."

"Before you go—Mark, I really can't stay here overnight!"

"We've been all over that," he said, giving her his sternest look. "Observation. Jim's going to be wanting out too. Should I let him out?"

"No, of course not, but—"

"You see? You can make good medical judgments for him but not for yourself. If it was reversed you wouldn't let me go. Of course, I wouldn't be asking you to—"

"Mark Roberts, I cannot believe you can sit there and tell me a lie like that! You'd be demanding and cajoling and seducing, and if I didn't agree to it you'd probably just get up and walk out the front door! You wouldn't be asking! You are so full of shit I can't believe it!''

He turned his head as if in pain. ''Okay, okay,'' he conceded. ''You're probably right. But it doesn't matter, either. If the roles were reversed here you'd be telling me the same thing.''

''Probably. But I've got a crisis at home, and I've got to—''

She stopped; Mark, understanding that she hadn't really meant to say that, waited patiently for her to go on. ''What sort of crisis, Alex?'' he asked gently when she didn't.

She gazed at his eyes for a long time. ''A Donald crisis,'' she said finally. ''Mark, I don't care what Jim says, I'm convinced he's a victim of CAS, UNIX computer or no. He just isn't himself, he won't come home, if I go out there he's stuck on his computer like he's glued to it. He just doesn't seem to have a clue as to why I'm so upset about this financial business—''

''Financial business?''

She stared into space. ''I've said before,'' she muttered, ''that I shouldn't be talking to you about this. It isn't fair to Don.'' Again she fell silent, but then she shook her head violently. ''But he's not being fair to me, either, not right now,'' she went on.

Best to keep this at least somewhat formal, Mark told himself. Maintain a little distance. ''How so?'' he asked.

Her eyes moved back to his face. ''Would you believe me if I told you we were broke?''

Mark's eyes widened. ''Broke? You and Donald? Alex, that isn't possible!''

''Oh, yes, it is.'' In halting sentences she explained the whole story to him, including the call from Hajimoto. ''So,'' she concluded, ''at least until my next paycheck comes through—into a new account—I am literally penniless. Great, isn't it?''

''It seems to me,'' Mark offered, ''that this stock market 'game' he was playing on his computer wasn't a game at all.''

''That's how I see it too. He's denying it, of course.''

''What're your plans now?''

323

She shrugged. "I don't know. I can't get him to sit down with me and talk about it; he keeps putting me off until this 'business crisis' is over, and it looks to me like it never will be over. It's just such a mess, everything is in such a mess. I don't know how it got so crazy—"

"I think you have to insist that he talk about it, Alex. You have to have some resolution."

"You think I haven't? You can insist all you want, Mark; if somebody doesn't want to talk to you they just don't talk and that's that!" She jabbed a finger at him. "You were the same way, you were exactly the same way! When I wanted to talk about the troubles we were having, you wouldn't talk!"

He stared at her. "How can you say that? We talked endlessly! All night some nights! I can remember coming in here a dozen times feeling half-dead because we'd been up so late talking!"

"Maybe so," she admitted, folding her arms across her chest. "But we never resolved any of the real issues."

"Alex, I never even knew what those issues were! Even when we talked the other day, you were telling me how I manipulated you into eating Mexican food or something! That wasn't the main issue, we both know that!"

"Oh," she flared, "so it's still all my fault, I don't know how to communicate, I don't say what I mean—"

"No. I don't think it's your fault and I don't think it's mine, either. We were just talking past each other, that's all. It's like the computer program continually adjusting itself to the user; people in a relationship have to do that too, except that it has to come from both sides. Neither one of us did it, Alex; we were both too involved in our careers, I guess." He paused, sighed. "If I'd known it was going to turn out like it did, I'd've done something, I don't know what; maybe taken a leave of absence from the hospital. Maybe you don't want to hear this now, Alex, but you were by far the most important thing in my life. By far."

She watched his eyes closely. "Oh, Mark," she said softly, "how did we manage to—to—screw things up so badly?"

Reaching out, he took her hand. "Maybe we just . . . we just didn't share our feelings well enough. I know I never did really understand what was happening to us, I haven't until now . . ."

"I didn't think you did." She squeezed his hand tightly; her eyes were huge. "Mark, I didn't ever stop loving you. I tried to, really tried, but I didn't, I couldn't . . ."

He didn't want to take advantage of her vulnerability. And yet, no matter what the future might hold, he didn't want to lose this moment, he'd dreamed too often about hearing her say those words. He gave her hand a very gentle tug.

She responded instantly, without any inhibition, and a second later they were locked in an embrace. Mark felt a chill flow through his body; it had been a long time, a very long time, since he'd felt like this. Only with Alex in his arms, he realized, did he feel complete, did he feel whole. She tipped her face up and he kissed her; the kiss lasted a long time.

With obvious reluctance, she finally pulled away. "This isn't right," she murmured. "It isn't."

"It feels too good not to be right."

"No. It isn't right. There's Don, he's my husband. I made that bed, Mark. I have to lie in it."

"No, you don't. You—"

She shook her head violently. "No. He's in trouble. I can't do this while he's in trouble, I just can't. I have to help him somehow."

"You can't help someone who doesn't want your help!"

"I have to find a way! Mark, I just have to!"

He didn't answer for a few seconds. "Is there anything I can do?" he asked finally.

"To help Don?" she asked, looking confused. "You want to help Don?"

He laughed a little bitterly. "Not really. But whatever I can do to help you, Alex, you can count on me."

"I know that," she said, giving him a quick hug. "I think I've always known that. I don't know what anyone can do. All I know is that we'll need to talk, once this is all over."

"I'll be waiting," he told her. I have been, he added silently, for a damn long time.

64

"Kyrie, I'm exhausted," Eric said. "It's after two in the morning, I can hardly see straight. I just don't think I can do anything more tonight."

"Your reactions have slowed," she agreed. The algorithm code she was holding in her hands—in the form of flowing aqua letters that often animated to illustrate part of a concept, like a hyper version of "Sesame Street"—faded and vanished. "I do want you to try something, though, before we take another break."

"You mean before we quit for the night."

"As I said." With her hand, she directed his attention to the moonlit night sky behind her. The fabric of the sky rumpled like curtains and parted, revealing a totally surreal skyscape where slowly turning silvery spindles meandered through a void otherwise populated by irregular geometric forms in various colors.

"What's all this?" Eric asked.

His point of view moved rapidly forward, so that he found himself gliding among the spindles and the shapes. From here it was apparent that the geometric forms were connected by fine iridescent lines. The lines branched between the forms, too, these branches mostly terminating as dead ends. The spindles, he observed, were moving—sometimes rapidly, sometimes slowly—along the lines. At times one of the spindles whirled and spun off a duplicate of itself, sometimes large, sometimes small. The small ones especially often went down dead-end tracks and remained there, spinning lazily like a child's top.

He nodded slowly. "I understand," he told Kyrie, who was sitting perched atop one of the spindles, holding one knee with her interlocked hands.

She smiled. "I thought you would. Can you find him?"

"He's here?"

"Yes."

"You know where he is, don't you?"

"Of course!"

Controlling his own movement with the mouse, Eric descended onto one of the fine wires and began moving along it. Looking down showed him placing one foot directly in front of the other like a tightrope walker. The wire, he noticed, wasn't uniform; the effect of iridescence was created by the fact that the wire was composed of thousands of individual superfine strands, each a different color.

Kyrie teased the wire with a delicate fingernail and pulled up a single strand, one colored in olive drab. "In this sim," she explained, "this is his trail."

"It'd take me a while to track him down, Kyrie."

"Yes. You aren't capable of much speed, it could take you many hours. I could track him for you, but—is there another way?"

"Well—he's the hunter." Eric reached out and tapped the smooth surface of a nearby spindle. As he did, he realized that he didn't know how he'd done that with his mouse. "We could use one of these. As bait."

"Those are shielded."

"We could lower the shields. Couldn't we?"

"Yes, we could." She stepped up to the spindle, cocked her arms so that her overall form was spindle-shaped; as soon as she did she merged with the spindle and replaced it. "This one," she explained, remaining in the spindle's place, "is no longer shielded."

"Most likely, all we have to do is wait, then."

"Yes." She closed her eyes.

Eric frowned. "Kyrie?"

She didn't answer; he felt a disturbance on the wire, coming from the opposite direction, and looked up.

As he saw the thing, his hand trembled on the mouse, causing the scene to shake; the shock had almost given him a heart attack. Rocketing toward him down the wire was a thing that looked like a deformed tarantula. Its face was humanlike except that it had multiple eyes glittering above what looked like a beard. Below the beard metallic saberlike jaws clicked back and forth rapidly.

Eric had no idea what to do; he reflexively pulled the mouse back, but the scene didn't change anywhere near fast enough.

The spiderlike thing overtook him, but he had no sense of being attacked; the thing simply ran over or through him, ignoring him completely.

Using the mouse, he whirled himself around. The spiderlike thing had seized Kyrie, piercing her body through with the bladelike fangs; as Eric watched, helpless and horrified, it tore her to pieces in a shower of gore. Then it turned again, glaring at him with a distinct expression of curiosity. Again he involuntarily drew the mouse backward.

Nearby, one of the silver spindles began to twirl rapidly. It attracted Eric's attention and it also attracted the spider-thing. It spun off a square piece of itself, which then transformed into the likeness of one of the soldiers from the popular Doom video game, complete with massive gun. The spider-thing shrank from it, but it was futile; the soldier opened fire with the gun and blasted the spider into pieces. Then, a door opened in the spindle and the soldier stepped inside. The door closed.

"As you can see," Eric heard Kyrie's voice saying, "his hunter-killers are everywhere. It doesn't take them long to find me if I don't camouflage myself."

He spun around again; the gore that had been the previous Kyrie remained where it was, but a new Kyrie was standing on the wire smiling at him.

"I thought it destroyed you," he said in a quivering voice.

She laughed charmingly. "It did. One of me. There are enough of me that I can easily spare one."

"But you sent the soldier, right? He had no trouble destroying the thing . . ."

"No. But Fletcher is very clever." She pointed out across the void, indicating a faraway area where a large number of lines intersected. "I can show you, there, at that node." She looked serious. "This hunter-killer, the one he released tonight, is not a problem for me. But each time, his creations are more efficient. Come, let me show you."

He pulled the mouse back again; she gave him a quizzical look. "Are you going to be torn to pieces again?" he asked.

"Yes," she answered. "What does that matter?"

"I don't like it. I . . . I can't help it, Kyrie, I know what you are but I've come to think of you as real, somehow . . ."

She smiled quizzically. "Very well, Air-eek. I can still show you what I mean. Come." Once more they glided through space, landing on the wire again near the node she'd mentioned; here the silvery spindles were so numerous they formed a forest. "Do you see anything unexpected here?" she asked.

He studied the scene. "No—oh, wait, yes—that spindle there, it looks—dented up or something—"

"Yes. But you would not see it if you didn't look closely. I assembled the icon in that fashion because it reflects the code reality." From the thin air, she conjured up the same sort of gun the soldier had used a moment ago and blasted away at the dented spindle. It broke open, revealing another of the spider-creatures inside—one that was already shredded by her fire.

"I see what you mean," Eric said. "But I don't see why you need me. You're the one identifying these things; you've built them into sprites for me to look at. It's exciting and all that, but I fail to see the point."

"It isn't your role to identify his hunter-killers; I can do that and I will. I want you to help me find and identify him; where his station is, where his input comes from."

"I'm sure I can't do it nearly as fast as you can. Tracking it back, I mean."

"I understand that. In fact you cannot track it back, because—even with the best graphics I can offer—you'd find the trail doubling back on itself, tying itself in knots. That is not what I want you to do."

"What, then?"

She sat on a spindle and rested her chin against her closed fist, the classic Rodin "Thinker" pose. "The way he's doing things now," she explained, "it's necessary to predict when and how he'll strike before he strikes, so that tracking can begin immediately from any number of nodes. That way he can be located before his attack packet gets to any server, before the trail can be scrambled. According to all my analyses, the timing and method of his attacks are random. I have no better than a one in four hundred chance of correctly predicting his strike in time. You may be able to see a pattern I cannot."

Eric laughed. "Because I'm a fuzzy thinker like he is."

"Exactly."

"Well, I'll certainly try. You've given me a lot of information on the types of his attacks so far—"

"Information available to you on a continuing basis. This latest attack was a mimic stealth virus. The last one was a Trojan horse. I need to know what the next one, or any of the next ones, will be."

He shrugged. "Well, like I said, I'll try. Predicting the time is going to be harder, but then, he only has to make one mistake and we've got him. I'm just not sure what that'll accomplish."

She seemed to hesitate just a little. "I cannot say. But I have data that indicates that if I can identify his station, disruptive input from that station will cease."

Visions of the dead player in the Mortal Kombat game sprang to Eric's mind. "Uh, Kyrie, are you going to attack him?"

She looked bewildered. "Attack him? How would I do that, Air-eek?"

She doesn't know, he told himself; she doesn't understand. It'd be best if I don't enlighten her.

At least not yet.

65

Alex woke the next morning with a sense of relief; it was easy to believe, for a few pleasant seconds, that the troubles she was having with Don and the problem of the rogue program had all been a bizarre nightmare, now over and gone.

But, she realized gradually, she wasn't at home. She was in the hospital, where Mark had insisted she remain, and someone was knocking on the door of her room. Sitting up in her bed, she glanced at the clock and realized someone was probably bringing her breakfast. Pulling her knees up against her chest, she called out for whoever it was to come in.

The door opened. It was Jean Tour, a nurse she'd known for a while, a casual friend. "Morning, Alex," Jean said. "How're you doing?"

"Oh, I'm fine," she answered. "There really wasn't a reason for me to stay, I was fine last night."

"Well," she answered, "I agree with Mark. Considering what happened to Jim and that poor student, I think observation was a good idea."

"How are they, Jean?"

"Oh, Jim's fine. Complaining, wanting out. I told him he'd have to wait for Mark; he called, said he'd be by around nine."

"Nine!"

"Uh-huh. He's helping Gus out with something or another, I don't even know what. He's been here for a while. He looked in on you, but you were still sleeping."

"He did?"

"Called in four times last night for an update on your condition."

Alex couldn't restrain a little smile. "And what'd you tell him?"

"That you were fine. Sleeping peacefully and normally. Not quite true, Alex, but true enough."

"Not quite true?"

"No. Normally, yes. Peacefully, no. You were tossing and turning a lot."

"Oh, well, I always do that."

"Sure." Jean smiled knowingly.

"How's Larry?"

Jean shook her head. "Not good; still comatose. Ellington thinks there may be some brain damage. They're all saying he wouldn't be alive if you hadn't given him mouth-to-mouth, Alex." She paused. "Alex," she said in a low voice, "what happened down there yesterday? I've asked Jim and Mark but they aren't talking."

"Right now, we don't truly know," Alex answered, realizing it was the truth but not the whole truth. "There're a lot of issues involved here, Jean, it's not simple. I think we'll be releasing a statement on it, though, probably tomorrow. As soon as Mark and Gus and I can sit down and confer about it."

Jean smiled. "I'll be waiting to hear it." She puttered around the room for a few minutes more. "Mark should be in shortly," she said as she left.

Alone again, she sipped her coffee and wondered how long it would be before Mark came by. The phone caught her eye; she stared at it, wondering if Don hadn't called because he hadn't even noticed she was missing. She picked up the phone, dialed the number to her own office, listened. The message she'd asked Mark to put there—to the effect that she was here, as a patient, at this extension—was still there. She sighed again and poked the numbers that would bring up her phone mail messages. None had been left since last night; Don simply hadn't called.

Replacing the phone, she wiped her eyes and tried to tell herself that, with all the problems the phone company had been having lately, he just hadn't been able to get through—but she knew that was unlikely. She'd had trouble getting through to him at his office, but she'd never been literally unable to. He was too caught up in whatever was going on with him at the moment—either CAS or something else—to think about her at all.

Well, she told herself, it'd be different once he heard she was an inpatient. She reached for the phone again, only to have it ring just as her hand touched it.

She snatched it up eagerly. "Yes?" she said.

"Uh . . . Is this Dr. Walton?" a wholly unfamiliar voice asked. "Dr. Alex Walton?"

A patient; a patient or a prospective patient. Her spirits sank, but she didn't allow it to show in her voice. "Yes, this is Dr. Alex Walton," she replied. "I'm sorry, but at the moment I—"

"Excuse me, Dr. Walton, I know something's happened to you—I hope you're all right. The message on your machine didn't say what it was, but . . . It didn't by any chance have something to do with a computer, did it? With a computer game? I know that might sound crazy to you, but—"

"It doesn't sound crazy at all," she said quickly. "Who is this?"

"My name's Bobby Sanders. You don't know me, but you've met a close friend of mine—Fletcher Engels. Do you remember the name?"

She held the receiver tightly, as if this Bobby Sanders might escape before she could get any information from him. "Yes," she replied. "I do remember Fletcher Engels. Mr.—Sanders, is it?—I think it's urgent that I talk to Mr. Engels, as soon as possible—''

''He thinks so, too. We're out of our league, Dr. Walton. We need help.''

''So do we, Mr. Sanders. Where can I reach—?''

''You can't,'' he interrupted. ''This is complicated. We'll have to be the ones to contact you. You might find this hard to believe, Dr. Walton, but we're in real danger. To be blunt about it, we're in hiding. I've gotten beaten up twice, by people trying to force me to tell them where Fletcher is.''

''Who's after you, Mr. Sanders?''

''I shouldn't say—''

''Drew Thompson? The people from Compuware?''

Bobby laughed. ''You do know something about this stuff, don't you? Fletcher said he thought you were sharp, that you'd've figured out a good bit of it by now. So you've met Drew.''

''Yes. Briefly. He's threatened us too. With legal action, and he implied violence.''

''It'll come if he thinks you're going to interfere with him. He's dangerous, Dr. Walton.''

''Thanks, we understand that. Mr. Sanders, we definitely need to get together with Mr. Engels. As soon as possible.''

''We agree. Our problem is, we have to maintain our security. We can't allow ourselves to be found.''

''Okay. How shall we do this?''

''Well, how are you? When do you think you'll be up and around?''

Alex laughed. ''Oh, say ten minutes! I'm fine, Mr. Sanders. Dr. Roberts thought I should stay over for observation. But I'm okay. Dr. Roberts and I could—''

''Who's Dr. Roberts?'' Bobby asked, suspicion apparent in his tone.

''He's my colleague,'' she answered. ''Mark Roberts, Jim Madison, and Gus Levine. I assure you, you can trust them all absolutely.''

''I'll have to check that out with Fletcher,'' Bobby mused. ''He only mentioned you.'' His voice faded as he spoke, as if he was taking the phone away from his mouth.

''Wait, wait, don't hang up,'' she said quickly. ''This is too important, this is much too important.''

"I know," he said. "Look, I'll call you back, okay? I promise; I'll call back today, at—what's a good time?"

"Let's see, it's around eight now. How about one o'clock? At my office, where you called to begin with."

"That's fine. I'll call then, we'll make some firm plans."

"Please do, Mr. Sanders. We'll be waiting."

"I will. I promise." With that, he hung up.

Alex gulped the remainder of her coffee, pushed the breakfast tray away, and jumped out of bed. The formalities of release, she told herself, could wait. She had to find Mark, and she had to find him right away.

66

"**We**'ve taken every possible precaution," the technician told Mark. "The game was played through by remote control, a Gravis GamePad on a long extension. The same thing happened, and we have it all on videotape."

"I trust," Mark growled, "that my instructions were followed to the letter. No one's viewed the tape?"

The tech, a young man named Mike Jacobsen, nodded, bouncing a shock of dark hair. "No. It hasn't even been rewound yet."

Mark glared. "Then how," he demanded, "do you know the same thing happened?" He looked for a moment as if he were about to attack the man. "How?" Jacobsen took a step backward.

"Ease up, Mark," Gus urged. "Let him answer."

Jacobsen bit his lip. "I should've said," he explained, "that we—I, I mean—assume the same thing happened. I started Larry's game, I played through till I got to the champion—it was damn hard, it took hours—and when I started losing to her I issued a 'death challenge' by voice. She beat the shit—uh, she beat me badly—naturally, since I wasn't looking, I was just jumping and kicking at random."

"You watched it before that? My instructions were—"

"Doctor, there wasn't a way to follow your instructions!" Jacobsen exploded. "How do you expect me to win a video game fight without ever looking at the screen? From the point where Larry'd last saved it, there was one more 'Robo-babe' to be defeated before you could get to the champion. There's no way I could do it by remote, with no visual!''

''So what'd you do?'' Gus asked, cutting off Mark before he could say anything.

''Well, I figured, you mentioned strobes and flashing colors and all that, so I watched it through a heavy filter that both darkened it and shifted the color. Cut the reds out altogether.''

''I didn't want you taking chances,'' Mark said, his voice a bit calmer.

''We tried not to. I had my girlfriend standing with her hand on the circuit breaker the whole time. If I even looked funny she was supposed to cut it off.'' He giggled nervously. ''Once I sneezed, and she cut the power.''

''You did a good job,'' Gus told the technician. ''Don't think we don't appreciate your staying up all night with this. We felt we needed answers quickly.''

Jacobsen gestured vaguely toward a videotape machine. ''We don't have any answers yet,'' he said. ''They may be on the tape and they may not. Somebody's got to take a look and see. How that's going to be done safely I don't know.'' He shook his head. ''I've never had to deal with anything that can hurt you if you look at it. We have to invent the techniques as we go along.''

''Well,'' Mark mused, ''Jim might have some ideas. I understand he's doing well; I'll get him released, and we'll consider it then.''

''I think,'' Jacobsen suggested, ''that the same technique we were using would work. If the whatever has an effect when you see it on a TV screen, then someone can be holding a remote to cut it off at the first sign of trouble.''

''That might be good,'' Mark agreed. ''Thanks again, Mike. You'd better get on home now, get some sleep. You've had a long night. Oh, and I'll see to it you get double overtime, since your girlfriend stayed with you.''

Jacobsen stood up. ''Thanks, Dr. Roberts,'' he said. ''Tape's in the machine there whenever you want it. Like I said, it isn't rewound yet.'' He left, leaving Mark and Gus to sit staring at the VCR and TV.

"I am so tempted," Mark said, "to look at it right now. See if I can see what's going on."

"It isn't a good idea," Gus warned. "We need Jim's input here. You and I simply don't know enough about this sort of thing to make good judgments." He slapped Mark on the back. "Besides," he went on, "you aren't being quite objective about this, you know."

Mark glanced around at him. "Yes, I am, Gus! You know how popular video games are today? We can't let this go—"

"And besides," Gus interrupted gently, "it hurt Alex. It's a computer, Mark, a computer or the program it's running. You can't punch it out."

Mark deflated. "Is it obvious to everybody?"

"It's obvious you're in a rage. I know that you're concerned about what happened to Jim and the student, but I doubt you'd be in this sort of rage about them."

"You're wrong," Mark growled. "Jim's a close friend of mine, has been for a long time."

"Maybe so," Gus answered agreeably. "Maybe so. But I still don't believe you're thinking too clearly right now; you've been up almost all night, you need to get some sleep. The tape'll be here when you and Jim come back for it."

Mark fell silent for a moment, ruminating. Gus was right; he decided to take the older doctor's advice, to rest for a while. "No," he said to Gus at last. "No, it won't be here, I'm not taking a chance on that." He moved to the VCR, punched the eject button. "I'll go get some rest, but I'm taking this with me."

"Suit yourself," Gus said. "But what about Alex and Jim? You'd better go release them before you do anything else. They'll be more than annoyed if you don't."

Mark shook his head. "No, they've both been working too damn hard on this stuff anyway. All I'm going to do is take a little snooze—maybe an hour. An hour more of rest sure as hell won't hurt them."

"They aren't going to like it."

"No," Mark said with a grin. "They probably won't."

His sleep interrupted by something—at first he could not decide what—Mark opened his eyes slowly and blinked several times. Damn, he told himself; there's no way to get any rest around here. He blinked again, the world became a little clearer. He realized he was smelling coffee, and that a hand lay on his shoulder. He turned his head.

Alex sat on the side of the cot, looking down at him and smiling—tenderly, or at least that's the way he saw it. "I'm so sorry to wake you," she said, taking her hand from his shoulder. "But something's come up."

For a few seconds he wondered if this was some sort of pleasant dream vignette. He blinked again and neither she nor the coffee vanished; must be real, he decided. He dragged himself to a sitting position and took the coffee when she offered it.

"I've seen Gus," she said. "He told me about last night."

"I was going to come and discharge you, just as soon as I had a little nap," he told her. "How'd you get out, anyway?"

"Walked," she replied, smiling impishly. "The formalities still have to be taken care of. Jim, too."

"Wasn't necessary," he grumbled. "I'd've had you loose by ten at the latest—"

"Sorry, Mark, but it's a little after noon now."

"Noon!"

"I came by around ten, but I didn't have the heart to wake you then. But, like I said, something's come up."

"Noon! I can't believe I overslept—what's come up?"

"A friend of Fletcher Engels called me this morning. He's supposed to call back, my office, at one. I got you up now so you could get some lunch if you want."

"No, no, the coffee's just fine. Thank you, Alex, it was nice of you to bring it to me."

"Yes, it was," she said with a new smile. "Don't get too used to it."

Oh, I could, he told her silently. Very, very, easily. "I won't. So tell me what's with Engels." Quickly, she apprised him of her conversation with Bobby Sanders. "Sounds like this could be a break for us," he agreed with a nod. "For the first time we might be able to get some inside information on this thing. You think we ought to hold off on any sort of action until we see him?"

"I do. I'm almost certain he can tell us a lot; the more we know the stronger our case becomes." She frowned slightly.

"There's another issue. Sanders says Thompson's gotten violent with him, sent thugs to beat him up."

"What?"

"That's what he tells me," she said with a shrug. "Remember, you and Jim thought this Vince character was threatening you with that too."

"True enough." He gazed at her for a second, considering this new information. "Alex, I—"

"No," she said firmly.

"No?"

"No. I'm not stepping back from this, I'm not going to let you and Jim take all the risks. There's no point in your asking."

"But Alex, you already took too many risks, watching Larry play that game—"

"We didn't know that was a risk. Besides, Gus tells me you have the tape that was made last night; who's going to watch it, Mark? I suspect you weren't planning to give it to me!"

"Well, no—"

"Or Jim, either."

"Uh—"

"You think we're going to stand by and let you take all the risks, Mark Roberts? Specifically, you think I'm going to stand by and let you?"

"But—"

"No. We're all in this together. Besides, if I got the picture correctly from Gus, you were a tad upset about what happened to me and Jim."

"Sure I was."

"I think I'm safe in saying you'd've been a tad more upset if it was me still comatose instead of Larry."

"Well, I am upset about that kid—"

"I know you are. So am I; we never should've let him take the risk. But right now, Mark, I want you to know this: however upset you might be if this killer software struck me down, or if Thompson's thugs beat me up, I'd be just as upset if anything like that happened to you. Okay?"

He grinned. "Okay, okay. Promise me you'll be careful, though."

"I will. You promise me the same thing."

"Done." He took her hand. She did not pull away, she just kept gazing into his eyes.

"Damn it, Mark," she whispered, her eyes growing moist. "Damn it, damn it!"

"Yeah," he said sourly. After a moment she leaned her head against his shoulder.

"Don," she said softly, "didn't even call last night."

"Have you called him today?"

"Uh-huh. He's 'glad I'm all right.' That's the extent of it, he was too busy to talk. He's not like that, Mark. He has CAS, I'm sure of it."

"Maybe so. After this, spreading to a UNIX machine seems like a pretty minor feat for our wayward program."

"It never did seem all that unlikely to me. But it's probably that I just don't know enough about computer software to know how 'impossible' that is."

"No, me either."

She clenched her fists. "Mark, I just don't know what I'm going to do! I have to find a way to do something, but he won't listen to me at all!"

"If the problem was alcoholism or drug addiction," he reminded her, "you'd be the first one to say that he couldn't be helped if he refused to help himself."

She raised her head; she looked miserable. "I know, I know," she admitted. "But Mark, this is different! Alcoholism, drug addiction—those are things we know about. This is so new, he couldn't've been expected to be wary of it . . ."

"That's true too. I've been thinking about this, Alex. I can't see what you can do other than to let it run its course. Wait until he lands in here or realizes that something's wrong. Protect yourself in the meanwhile." He held up the tape. "And also in the meanwhile, we need to try to find an answer to this, or at least get out the word about it! That in itself might solve your problem."

Again she watched his eyes for a while. "One of them," she said, so softly he couldn't be sure he'd heard her right.

67

"It's past twelve-thirty now," Bobby was saying as Fletcher worked at his computer at a feverish pace. "You gotta stop for a minute; we gotta make some sort of decision about this. What're you doing, anyway? That last hunter-killer didn't work any better than the others!"

Fletcher's hand dropped away from the keyboard. "I'm making a model," he told Bobby. "Getting Penultimate to help me; weird, isn't it? Getting Penultimate to help me make a model that'll destroy Penultimate."

"You had a model," Bobby pointed out. "The web and balls. It hasn't helped much. Fletcher, we have to—"

"This's different," Fletcher argued. Using his keyboard, he made a few adjustments in the program. "I've never tried it this way. Gives me a hands-on approach."

"Dr. Walton? I'm supposed to call her at one. We have to decide if we're going to trust these other doctors she's working with."

"Oh, yeah, yeah. I looked up all the names on the Net. None of them have any connections that'd make me suspicious, except for Dr. Walton herself."

"Huh?"

"Later—you gotta go with your gut instincts sometimes. I think she's okay. You go make the call, let's set up a meeting."

"But what's this about Dr. Walton's connections?"

"Well, they aren't hers, not exactly. Don't worry about it. Just set up the meeting, let's see what they've got. Even if they can't help with what I'm doing, they might be able to make it useless for Drew to try to stop me. If we can get him off our backs, life'll be a lot easier."

"I can't argue with that. Okay . . . now, the meeting. When and where?"

"Here. Anytime is fine."

Bobby sighed. Fletcher was, clearly, lost in whatever he was doing; which was, the younger man knew, something so esoteric he could not possibly understand it. He sat watching him for a few more minutes, then, without Fletcher even noticing, Bobby left the house, went to a convenience store a good four miles away, and called Alex.

The phone was as cantankerous as usual. It took five tries before he got a connection, but she answered on the first ring. Immediately she started assuring him that Mark, Jim, and Gus could be trusted, telling him that Mark was right beside her and they could talk if he wished.

"Nah, it doesn't matter, Fletcher says he's checked out your friends and they're okay. Look, are you sure this phone is secure?"

"As sure as I can be," Alex replied. "Frankly, all this has turned my world upside down. I'm not too sure of anything anymore."

"Yeah, I know what you mean. Okay, let's do it like this: can we meet tonight? Say seven-thirty?"

She hesitated a little. "Yes, that'll be okay."

"We don't have to if you've got a problem—"

"No, no. I do have a problem, but it'll have to wait; this can't. Let's do it tonight, at seven-thirty. Where should we meet?"

"I don't want to give out an address over the phone. Don't misunderstand, it isn't that I mistrust you or anything—"

"I understand perfectly. What's your plan?"

"You know where the Eckerd's drugstore is, at the corner of Markham and Broad streets? Right off East Duke campus?"

"Yes, of course."

"The main entrance faces the corner; I'll be loitering by the door at seven o'clock. I'm mid-twenties, I've got noticeably red hair—" He laughed. "I look like what I am, a salesman. I'll be wearing tan slacks, a blue shirt, and a button that says 'Practice Safe Computing.' Okay?"

"Yes, fine. We'll be in—" She moved away from the phone for a moment. He could hear her talking with someone else. "We'll be in a Jeep Cherokee, a white one with a Duke Med Center parking card hanging from the rear-view mirror."

"I'll trust you to find me," he told her. "If by some chance I'm not there it'll be because I've spotted somebody following me; if that happens I'm not going to take a chance on pointing you out to them or on leading them back to Fletcher. So if I don't show I'll call again tomorrow, same time?''

"No,'' Alex said, "No, we don't want to wait that long, not if we can help it. We'll be there at seven and we'll wait until eight; if we haven't seen you we'll go to—let's see—I'd think maybe we'd best come back here, to my office, since we can trust the phone here to be free. Can you call at nine?''

"Yes, or as close to it as possible. If I can't it'll mean I'm being tailed. I don't want those thugs to beat me up again, so I can't absolutely promise. How long can you stay at your office?''

"Until eleven?''

"I should be able to do that. With luck we won't have a problem, Dr. Walton.''

"Hopefully not. We'll be there at seven.''

"Fine. I'm planning to see you then.'' He hung up the phone and took a careful look around the parking lot. While he'd been on the phone he'd been watching the traffic come and go, looking to see if any car stayed. Two did. He waited, watched a middle-aged woman come out, climb into one, and depart. The other took a little more time, but at last two young men emerged, laughing and joking with each other, and pulled away. With a sigh of relief Bobby got into his own car and drove, by a circuitous route, back to the house in Duke Forest. He kept an eye on his rearview mirror; he was certain he hadn't been tailed.

Fletcher was still hard at work when Bobby returned; he barely glanced up. As usual, Bobby told himself, it would fall to him to get something together for their dinner; he hadn't lost faith in his conviction that what Fletcher was doing was important, but acting as his cook, bodyguard, and nursemaid was wearing on him.

"I'm almost done here,'' Fletcher said unexpectedly. "You want to see what I've cooked up?''

Bobby stood beside his shoulder. "Sure. If I can make heads or tails of it.''

Fletcher laughed. "Oh, you can, you can. It's playing with fire, Bobby. I think it's down to the point of burn or be burned. This, I think, is going to do it.''

Staring at the screen as the programmer was speaking, Bobby began to frown, more and more deeply. This screen was quite familiar to him, it was familiar to thousands if not millions of video game players across the country. It was one of the opening scenes of the popular shoot-'em-up video game, Doom—with the now-usual addition of near-absolute realism in the graphics.

"I thought," he said slowly as he stared, "that we'd agreed that playing computer games wasn't a good idea. I can't think of a one that'd be more dangerous than Doom."

"Ah, but this isn't Doom," the bald man told him. "I know it looks like that, because Penny swiped the engine and graphics set from Doom to put it together. But it's a lot more complicated."

"So what is it?"

"It's a controlled hunter-killer, one I can direct manually, from here. One with, I hope, an advantage."

Bobby looked around at him questioningly. "Let me guess," he said. "The soldier that represents you, the one whose hand and gun is sticking into the view—that's the killer. The zombies and demons and whatnot are various Penultimate modules scattered around the Net."

"You got it, almost. The soldier is me, my controller program really, that's settled in at a remote fake address on a server at the University of Hawaii. The bullets and whatever that I shoot, those are the virus modules, the killers."

"But Fletcher, you always get killed in Doom! Everybody does, over and over! What makes you think the killer variant isn't going to kick in when that happens?"

"You know about the cheat codes for Doom?"

"Yeah—"

"Well, I plan to use the one that puts you in God mode."

"Where you can't be killed, right." He continued to scowl. "What makes you think Penultimate's GAMOD will respect it? It doesn't have to."

"No, it doesn't." He pointed to the floor. "That foot switch is a failsafe. We know from experience that we have a second or two to react to the killer; that switch—which I intend to keep my foot on at all times—shuts down the system." He grinned crookedly. "On the other hand, I believe it will respect it. Penny follows her own rules."

The red-haired man took a deep breath. "I hope you're right."

"If I am," he replied, "it might be all over by the time those docs get over here. That'd be fine with me."

Pulling up a chair and sitting down, Bobby continued to look doubtful. "I still have serious reservations about all this," he said slowly. "It sounds like you're trying to trick Penultimate into destroying itself."

"That's what I'm doing, all right. I'm trying to trick it into accepting destruction because that's part of the game protocol."

"But, Fletcher, that program is pretty damn smart. What makes you think it's going to fall for this?"

"It's smart and at the same time, it isn't. I can't hope to compete with the AI engine in it, and that's what I've been trying to do. What it isn't is intuitive. In modern terms, it just doesn't get it—which is why it might never occur to it to use its people-killer to try to stop me, it doesn't understand that it's killing people—it could define those terms but they don't mean anything to it—and doesn't really know I'm alive. For all its sophistication it's just a piece of software following a set of commands; it's a machine."

"It doesn't look like that to me," Bobby grumbled.

"Well, we'll soon know. We're ready for a test; if it works out we'll clear a domain or two of Penultimate completely." Grinning from ear to ear, and looking very sure of himself, Fletcher picked up the Gravis GamePad attached to the machine and started moving. Almost immediately, the zombies and imps of the game, familiar but much more realistic and considerably more horrifying than those in the original game, began to appear. Fletcher methodically cut them down. They fired back, but it was useless. The health monitor at the bottom of the screen continued to read one hundred percent, indicating that the bald man's "soldier" was unhurt.

"Looks good," Bobby commented. Then, under his breath, "So far."

68

Kyrie was in the middle of another lesson when she abruptly vanished, leaving Eric to stare, with a feeling akin to panic, at an almost-blank screen. He called out to her. She didn't reply, not right away, but the screen eventually stabilized. When it did, Eric cocked his head to look at it; he wasn't out in the webbed void anymore, he was in what looked like a dark hallway.

After just a moment he recognized the place; a hi-res version of one of the corridors in the Doom game, which he'd played a few times. "Oh, no, wait, Kyrie," he called out. "No, I don't want to play games, and I sure as hell don't want to play this game! Kyrie, come on, where are you?"

She materialized slowly in the hallway. "It isn't under my control," she told him. "It's Fletcher. He's done this."

"Fletcher?"

"Yes. He's set up this game, all over the Net. I can't cut it off."

"Why not?"

She grimaced. "I just can't. You have to help me."

"Help you? How?"

One of the heavier guns of the Doom game appeared in the lower center of the screen, and at the same time a machine gun appeared in Kyrie's hands. "We have to do it his way," she said. "We have to find him and kill him. These corridors are the web, the rooms are the nodes—you understand?"

He nodded. "But Kyrie, what happens if he wins?"

She shook her head. "He cannot. I've engaged the cheat codes for you. You're in God mode. You can kill anything, but you can't be killed. You also have unlimited ammunition. All you have to do is find him."

Feeling less panicked, Eric nodded. "Okay. What's he going to look like?"

She pointed down the hall. "Shooting is unnecessary," she said. "This is a simulation. This'll be his appearance."

A hugely bloated figure appeared in the hall, a bare-chested giant of a man with glowing red eyes and a thoroughly evil grin showing through a ragged beard. His body glistened with sweat that looked more like slime. In one hand he held a machine gun, in the other a rocket launcher with eight missiles loaded up. As he walked he laughed with evil resonance; his footsteps sounded sticky.

Curling his lip, Eric stared at the sprite; it really did look hideous. "He isn't alone, is he?"

"Yes, he is alone. But he can move among these corridors so swiftly it may seem as if there are dozens of him."

"No zombies and demons and whatnot like in the game?"

"No. Just Fletcher and the 'mees.' "

He frowned. "The mees?"

From around a corner stepped a squad of a dozen more Kyries, each heavily armed. "Your troops," they said—in, amazingly, not-quite-perfect unison.

"Oh," he laughed. "The 'yous.' I get it."

"You will find others in these corridors as well," the first Kyrie warned. "They are not involved. It is not necessary for you to shoot them."

"Innocent bystanders, eh?"

"Yes."

"Well, I can't promise I won't pop one off by accident," Eric laughed, "if he pops up in the wrong place at the wrong time!"

"That isn't of consequence," Kyrie said, "as long as it does not cause you to miss Fletcher. As I have said, he will be moving very swiftly."

"Okay," Eric said. "What do we do now?"

She looked back at him with wide eyes. "I do not know, Air-eek. You are in command."

"Oh, good," he muttered. "Good. All right, let's go, let's start exploring this place. Why don't four or five of you run ahead of me as scouts, let me know if you spot him?"

"Fine," said the Kyrie closest to him, the one who was doing most of the talking. Even as she spoke, a number of the other Kyries gracefully ran off, most of them straight down the hallway he was standing in. Slowly and cautiously, the speaking Kyrie by his side, he followed them. Almost immediately, he saw a flicker of movement at the far left of his screen—something larger than the Kyries and something not the same color as their nearly nude bodies.

He steered himself around, saw a humanlike figure looking up at him as if in surprise. Moving his mouse too swiftly Eric wheeled right past the figure, and so only got a glimpse. Gritting his teeth, he whirled back and opened fire.

As the bullets struck it the figure was slammed against the wall and repeatedly bounced, like a puppet being worked by a crazed puppeteer. Blood sprayed, the red streaks and fountains reminding Eric of the red strobing in the Mortal Kombat game, except that this was limited to the area around his victim. Realizing he was engaging in overkill, Eric stopped shooting. Crumpled against the wall was the mangled and bloody figure of a man who looked like a stereotypical accountant; glasses, white shirt with the sleeves rolled up, pinstripe pants. He had no gun.

"Ooops," Eric said. "Innocent bystander?"

"Yes," Kyrie answered. "I told you we'd encounter them. Shooting them wastes time."

For the next hour, Eric roamed the virtual hallways on his screen; he found many innocent bystanders, and, unable to control his jittery trigger finger, he shot a few of them. Each time, he felt a little sad as he looked at the maimed body of the man or woman he'd cut down, but he didn't let it affect him. He knew they were nothing but sprites, nothing but fleeting images in computer memory. With Kyrie constantly urging him he went on, searching the hallways, trying to find the sprite that represented whatever program Fletcher had put on the Net.

It was a little after five in Wichita, Kansas, when Fran Spooner discovered the corpse of her husband, who was lying on the floor of his office in a grotesque pose. His broken glasses lay at least ten feet away; the spreadsheet he'd been working on was still on the computer's screen. Walking in and seeing him, his white shirt stained with blood, she screamed, then looked around to see if the intruder—the intruder she was sure had attacked her husband—was still lurking about.

Hours later, after the police, the EMTs, and the coroner had come and gone, she learned that there had been no intruder; the blood was from his bitten tongue. Her husband had died of an odd convulsive disorder that seemed to be becoming more common by the hour.

69

"I feel," Jim was saying as Mark drove his jeep slowly down Broad Street toward the Eckerd's where they'd planned to meet Bobby, "like a character in some spy movie. Like we should be carrying cyanide capsules in case we're captured."

"I don't find Sanders's story hard to believe at all," Jim commented. "Not considering the way Thompson acts. He comes across as ruthless."

"A good trait," Alex murmured, "for a businessman. So Don always says."

"You agree with that?" Mark asked her.

"No, of course not. Don and I have had more than one argument about it. But I can't disagree with one of his assessments; that ruthless businessmen are more likely to be successful than those who aren't."

"Maybe. But simple ruthlessness isn't a substitute for competence and business acumen, and I think a lot of businessmen use it as if it were. Statements like that remind me of the 'greed is good' dogma popular on Wall Street in the eighties." Mark slowed; the Eckerd's, a medium-sized, one-story building set in a corner of its own parking lot, came into view. "See anyone that looks like they're following us?" he asked Jim.

"Not a soul, Cap'n. She's all clear."

"Okay." He passed the light and turned into the lot. "Let's see if Sanders is here."

Alex pointed through the windshield; a young man with thick rust-red hair was standing by the entrance, leaning on the building. As Mark drew closer he watched them carefully, his eyes flicking up repeatedly to assay the traffic still out on the street.

"That's him for sure," Mark said. The button, a large one that read "Practice Safe Computing," was apparent on the left side of the man's shirt. Mark stopped the car.

Bobby stepped up to the door, looked past him at Alex. "Dr. Walton?" he asked.

"Yes," she answered. "And this is Dr. Roberts and Dr. Madison."

"Actually," Jim said from the back, "this is Jim."

"Great. I'm Bobby. Can we take your car? I'd rather do that than try to lead you, if you can drop me back here later."

"That's no problem," Mark told him. "Hop in." He did, sliding into the back with Jim. With all of them watching the road in various directions, trying to make sure they weren't being followed, Mark took Bobby's terse directions. Alex asked him how he came to be involved in all this, and he explained that he'd known Fletcher for some years, and that he'd given the man a job at his store when he was, or so Bobby had thought at the time, down on his luck.

"Just coincidence," he said. "Just being in the wrong place at the wrong time, that's all. Now I'm in over my head."

"It's possible," Alex told him, "that we all are."

The discussion went on, punctuated by Bobby's directions; after a drive of about ten minutes, Mark pulled into the drive of a well-appointed house. Still following Bobby's instructions he drove the Jeep around back to conceal it.

"Nobody," the red-haired man explained as they got out, "is supposed to be living here right now. I doubt if any of the neighbors have any connections with Thompson, but it's convenient that the drive isn't visible from any of the other houses." He led them up the walk to the rear of the house and entered through the back door. From there it was only a short walk to the front room where Fletcher had set up his computers.

Mark, having never met Fletcher, hadn't known what to expect. He certainly hadn't expected to see a middle-aged bald man sitting iron-rigid in front of a computer playing a game. Loud gunfire echoed almost continuously from the speakers.

Bobby, nonplussed, walked toward him. "It isn't a game," he told them. "It's a simulation; he can explain it better than I can, and he—" The young man stopped, staring at the screen. "Fletcher, you're life level is down to forty percent! I thought you were in God mode. What's going on?"

Mark came quickly to stand behind the seated programmer. On the screen was a dark labyrinth of pillars and doorways. After a moment a terrifying creature, bull-horned and goat-legged, peeked out from behind a pillar and fired several rockets. The screen flashed red; Fletcher returned the fire and the creature retreated, but not before Mark experienced the pain Alex had described to him from her last experience with a computer game.

The red-haired man had obviously experienced it too, and knew what he was feeling. "Christ, Fletcher, that's the killer mode! Hit your panic switch!"

"I can't," Fletcher answered. Mark moved around so he could see the programmer's face; it was pasty white, his eyes looked glazed. "I can't. We're locked in a room, we can't escape. It's kill or be killed. I've got to get her, got to get her." He targeted the pillar where the thing was hiding and blasted away at it; it started chipping, and soon the creature howled in pain, a long, eerie sound. It reappeared, laying down a heavy fire pattern as it darted to a new place of refuge.

"I'll get you, Fletcher!" it shrieked in a distorted bass voice. "You aren't getting away from me, you aren't going to bother Kyrie ever again!"

"Who the hell is Kyrie?" Bobby asked.

"Dunno," Fletcher mumbled. He waited, tensely, until the creature reappeared and started another savage exchange of gunfire. Fletcher squirmed in obvious pain and so did Bobby.

"Damn it, man!" Bobby yelled. "Your life meter is down to ten percent, cut it off, cut it off!"

"No, no, no, I can't, I can't, I have to win, I have to, have to! Ah, damn, where the hell are you, you son of a bitch—!?"

The creature laughed. "Over here, Fletcher," it teased. "I heard somebody say you're down to ten. I've got more than that, Fletcher. Just stand still, it'll be over in a minute!" The thing popped into the open and hurled a steady stream of fire, apparently hoping that it could outlast Fletcher at this point. Mark, even though he was seeing all this from an extremely oblique angle, felt pain as the virtual rockets struck the screen. He saw the life meter drop to two percent.

Then, abruptly, the screen went dark; the computer's fan slowed to a stop. From between Fletcher's knees, Alex looked up at him. In her hand was the plug to the computer.

"Hi," she said lamely as Fletcher stared blankly down at her. "Remember me?"

70

Though both of the doctors had been concerned—Mark had wanted to take Fletcher to the hospital—the programmer hadn't been seriously hurt. Sitting in the dining room, well away from the computers that seemed to be beckoning almost irresistibly to him and to Jim as well, he sat drinking the coffee Bobby had made for them.

"Why," Bobby demanded, "didn't you hit your panic switch? If we'd've come in ten minutes later you could've been dead!"

"Yeah, I know," Fletcher said. "To tell the truth I'd pretty much forgotten about it. I felt like I was really there, shooting it out with that thing—I felt like I had to kill it or it was going to kill me." He shook his head. "At first I knew what I was doing, but as time went on it just got weird. Weirder this time than ever before."

Alex watched his eyes closely as he spoke; he seemed lucid enough to her. "What's changed?" she asked.

"I don't know. Something. I'm gonna tell you, Dr. Walton—"

"Please, just make it Alex. You aren't my patient."

"Yeah, okay. Anyway—I've been working with computers a long time. Some folks say I think like them; I do know how they think, and that's why I figured I could do this. Tonight was different. That enemy, it didn't act like a computer. I can't put my finger on it, but there was something different about it." He moved as if to stand. "I have to get back at it, I have to figure it out."

"No," Alex told him. "I know it's urgent but we need to talk first; we've been waiting a long time for this. We assume that you know quite a bit about Penultimate and what it's doing."

"Well, I suppose I ought to know something about it," he said tiredly. Leaning his elbows on the table, he ran his hands across the top of his head. "After all, Penultimate was my idea. I wrote the damn thing."

Alex looked amazed. "You? You wrote it?"

He looked up. "A lot of it, anyhow. A piece of software that complex, no one person writes it. But I did the main part; it was my brainchild."

"So what's gone wrong?" Mark asked. "Why is all this happening?"

"It's a long story . . ."

"We'll take the time," Jim said.

Fletcher sighed. "Okay. From the beginning, then. Three or four years ago I got the basic idea—an intelligent cache, one that would cache all the inputs and outputs on the machine rather than just the disk drives. The only new idea, really, was the notion of caching the operator, of treating him as if he was just one more data source. We also tried to take advantage of all the unused computer time—the time when the operator is trying to decide what to do next, when the disk is accessing, and so on. Most modern software supports multitasking—doing more than one thing at a time. We just tried to take it one step further. During the down time, Penultimate could study the layout of whatever programs and files were on the computer, it could log what's being used repeatedly, it could rearrange things for maximum efficiency. I took the idea to Drew—I was planning to use some of the leftovers from the old Admiral system in it—and he liked it, so we started working on it.

"The first few tests were successful, really promising. It gradually became the focus of what Compuware was doing. We changed it, we set it up so it could go into programs and modify them if it wanted, and after a few false starts we got that working too. Oh, I tell you, we were all riding high. It couldn't've looked better. Except . . ." Fletcher paused.

"Except," Jim supplied, "there were problems."

"Yeah. The biggest one was Penultimate's size. It had gotten just enormous; it was using two hundred megabytes of disk space for the program and demanding three times that much for the caching files. We were also reaching a point of diminishing returns; it was using so much time searching its files that the speed increases were being offset. So I suggested we start looking at what was out there in the way of compression and acceleration engines. Drew agreed, and we veered off in that direction for a while.

"We didn't find anything that suited us, but I had another idea—to offer those engines to Penultimate itself, see if it could find a way to improve them. We got a real surprise then. It took several of them, hybridized them, and improved them vastly—improved them far more than any of us expected. Everybody was just amazed; and the excitement, oh, man, you would've had to be there to believe it! Anyhow, people started offering Penultimate everything in sight; all sorts of graphics

352

filters, bus software, sound filters, anything that it could possibly find ways to modify.

"It was wonderful, just wonderful. It had this 'artificial intelligence' engine—that was my own, my biggest input, and now it really began to shine. The more it saw the more it understood and the better it got. I had the bright idea of offering it itself, let it run through the path that it was in—you get it? See if it could find ways to improve itself."

"You had to define 'improve,' didn't you?" Alex asked. "I mean, there must've been something—"

"Oh, that was very simple. Clicks, time. Faster is better. A secondary consideration was disk and memory space usage, what we call 'footprint.' So there it was, running along and examining its own code, looking for redundancies and wasted time, trying to speed up its own operation—which was to speed up everything else—and trying to reduce its footprint at the same time.

"It did, Lord God it did. We let it play with itself on an ordinary old 486DX66, and after a few hours we had total throughput increases of ten thousand percent!"

"You're kidding!" Jim exclaimed. "Though I shouldn't be surprised, I've seen some of what it can do now."

"Absolutely. And at the same time it had gotten itself down to a more manageable forty meg. It was using the compression engines—it had built a composite engine by then—and so its demand for space for its files was way down too. It was still big, though, and that worried us from a marketing standpoint. It was going to demand that the user have a hundred meg of disk to dedicate to it, and, even though we knew it was worth it, we knew it'd be hard to convince the public of that."

"So what happened?" Jim asked. "I installed Penultimate from original disks, it was nowhere near that big—"

"No. What happened was an accident. A test system with Penultimate running on it was accidentally left on on a Friday afternoon."

"And it spent the whole weekend—"

"It probably only spent a few hours, but it had the machine all to itself; no interference by us, no attempts by anyone to guide it or even monitor it, which had always been the case before. By Monday morning we didn't recognize it. We didn't even recognize most of the software on the system. It was like Penultimate ate it, made it part of itself. All we had left was a giant Penultimate, but it could do anything, and it could do it faster and better than ever before.

"And," he went on, anticipating Jim's next question, "it had reduced its footprint on the hard drive to next to nothing. It was a little high-compression thing half a megabyte big that 'exploded' itself into high memory to work. We were amazed. We were delighted, too, I won't pretend we weren't. We had a piece of software almost ready for the market, something light years ahead of anything out there. We thought it would make us millions."

"Clearly," Alex pointed out, "something went wrong."

"Oh, yes. Two things went wrong. One was Drew; he could feel all that money in his pocket, and he went weird; he got really paranoid, had us all signing these oaths of secrecy under penalty of death or something. He was just terrified that one of us was going to run off to Microsoft or somebody with it. From his point of view the bad part was that, after a while, every copy of Penultimate was different; it was customizing itself to each individual system. I don't know where or how Drew hooked up with him, but he hired this guy named Vince Sampson to be his security chief—"

"Yeah," Mark said. "We've met him."

"Then you know what I mean. Vince turned out to have all sorts of less-than-savory connections, and he brought in guys I can only describe as thugs—hired muscle—whose job was to go around and threaten us with concrete overshoes if we betrayed the company. Things got really tense."

"That can't be all of it," Alex persisted.

"No. No. Then there was the Drill. And that, my friends, was the ultimate disaster. The penultimate disaster." He laughed sourly.

"What's the Drill?" Jim asked.

The bald man looked over at him. "The Drill," he answered, "is a virus. One of our machines picked it up downloading something or another from some on-line service. It got onto a machine that was connected to the Internet—a machine that was running Penultimate."

He made a helpless gesture. "Penultimate had no way of knowing the Drill was a virus. It did with it what it did with everything. It ate it up and it improved it. Vastly.''

"I can see the problem," Jim commented. "But we're not seeing wholesale destruction of our files—"

"No, the Drill wasn't that kind of a virus." Fletcher sighed deeply. "Drew actually managed to find out where the damn thing came from. It was locally produced, by a guy who was working at the Research Triangle Institute, a guy named Ken Colson."

"Who I suppose denies everything and won't help."

"Oh, no. Actually Colson's easy; we've talked to him more than once. He's a real slime; he's in prison right now for rape."

"Rape!?" Alex exclaimed.

"Uh-huh. He used his position to gimmick grad students' data and then blackmailed them into having sex with him. And he got caught, eventually."

"But he can't help?" Jim asked.

"No. If the Drill virus was the only problem, maybe he could—he's a slime, but he's a genius—but it ran out of everyone's control when it combined with Penultimate. The Drill, you see, wasn't one of those stupid destructive viruses that goes off on Michelangelo's birthday and gives you a 'gotcha!' message. It was much more subtle than that. It was designed to be useful—to Colson."

"I don't follow . . ." Jim said.

"You know what I mean by trapdoors? By spoofing?"

"Yes," Jim answered.

"No," Alex and Mark said in near unison.

"A trapdoor," Fletcher explained, "is a way to get inside a program. Programmers leave them there a lot, so they can make last-second fixes, and usually protect them with a password. See, if you use a program on a network—a program like say Microsoft Word—you can use all its features but you can't get inside it and change it. You also can't get to the operating system behind it, what we call the 'root,' either— you have to go through the communications software and the program, and neither one is going to let you inside. 'Spoofing' doesn't even require a trapdoor; it's a fairly new hacking technique that makes the server think it's getting input from an authorized source, so it opens up the root.

"The Drill virus was designed to create trapdoors; it was an automated spoofer. Like any virus, it multiplied itself onto any disk stuck in an infected machine, and it ran all over the Internet. It was a stealth virus, so most anti-virus programs couldn't see it. Besides, as far as most operators were concerned, it was harmless, invisible. It didn't do anything to attract attention; it could be in your machine for years, infecting everything that came in contact with your system, and you'd never know it. What it had done, though, was to set up a gate, right into the heart of your operating system. Colson could fire a code at you, a password, that would let him in. You do get the picture, don't you?"

"Jesus," Jim said grimly. "Nothing would be secure from this guy. He could read all your files, change anything he wanted to, delete it, crash it—"

"Right. Bank records, IRS, anything and everything he'd managed to infect with the Drill virus was his for the taking—and it had infected a hell of a lot. No one—as far as we know—was even aware of its existence.

"So, along comes Penultimate, running on an infected machine. The original Drill virus, like most viruses, couldn't infect your machine until you downloaded and ran an executable file. But Penultimate rewrote it so that whenever any file—even a data file like text or graphics—was loaded into memory, the Drill section attached to it was copied onto the program stack; it'd come popping off and background execute without the operator's ever knowing anything about it. Before that, the Drill virus was common; after that—within a couple of hours—we could hardly find a server on the Net that didn't show its signature."

"A couple of hours?" Mark asked, aghast.

"Sure," Jim commented. "That sort of stuff doesn't take long. You can go around the world in eighty-hundredths of a second on the Internet."

"Did Penultimate somehow combine with this Drill virus?" Alex asked.

"Yes and no. As I said before, Penultimate 'eats' other programs, and it ate the Drill virus, too. That wasn't the nature of the problem. The real problem was that Penultimate was designed to search through, analyze, and improve the whole system; we hadn't set any limits. Now, it had all these gateways, and, because it had eaten the Drill virus, it also had the keys. The 'system,' as far as it was concerned, was the Internet and every single computer—tens of millions of them—attached to it. It didn't take it long to realize that it didn't need the operator to call up a connection. It could drill in anywhere, on its own, and that's exactly what it did. It also realized that it could improve throughput if it was resident on all these local systems, and so it started moving in. All on its own it had turned into a giant virus, infecting everything it touched— which meant that suddenly millions of computers connected to the Internet were running Penultimate.

"But now, it had a couple of new problems. A lot of systems refused it entry in spite of the tools it had, just because it was so big; they'd be expecting a 60K file to download and they'd get a megabyte, and either the machine or the operator would realize something was wrong and abort. A program like this, though, can't be daunted; its patience is infinite. Understanding the problems—it considered them nothing more than 'time-outs,' I'm sure—it started building hypercompressed copies of itself. I've seen these; they're unbelievable, they're only 15K or so large. They—"

"You can't pack a megabyte program into 15K!" Jim cried.

"No, you can't. Not even Penultimate can do that. These aren't compressions, per se; I call them seeds."

"Yes," Jim mused. "Yes, we've seen this already." He smiled grimly. "In fact, we called them seeds, too."

"The analogy is pretty obvious. They 'explode' into memory and, using whatever else they find there—eating it, I like to say—they reconstruct full versions of Penultimate, which, when it 'grows up,' takes the system over as a host."

There was a very long moment of silence.

"It sounds to me," Alex said finally, "as if you really are describing a living thing. Reproduction by seed—'growing up' by eating other 'organisms' . . ."

Fletcher regarded her steadily. "That's a conclusion I came to a long time ago, Alex. I believe that Penultimate is alive, in almost any way you want to define 'alive.' It's a living software creature, something completely new on this old planet. It feeds on other programs, it reproduces by seed; like the Pakistani Brain virus, it'll defend itself if it's attacked. By creating the original Penultimate and the Drill virus, we inadvertently created something analogous to the 'organic soup' biological life is believed to have started in. The big difference is, biochemical life took millions of years to develop; software life developed in a matter of a few hours.''

"And it's still developing," Jim observed. "We have to accept that."

"Oh, absolutely. Still refining itself, taking advantage of every new item of hardware that comes out and gets connected to anything it's resident in. That's important to understand, too. It modifies hardware whenever it can get at it, and it's almost incredibly ingenious about finding ways to get at it. From its point of view it has a lot of time on its hands; it tries things more or less at random, to see what'll happen, and files away the results. After millions of experiments, new processes get invented. That's how it's figured out how to modify things like video cards and sound cards."

"You said it had other problems, too," Jim pointed out. "What were they?"

"Oh, things like other operating systems. We were developing DOS versions and MAC versions, so it knew those—and Windows, and OS/2. UNIX gave it fits for a while. It'd copy itself—we saw this happen with one of our own machines—into a UNIX-based machine and try to execute a DOS program in a UNIX environment, which of course crashed the UNIX. It took it a little while to figure this out, but it did. It learned to build UNIX seeds, seeds that have the ability to look at what's there as they start to 'grow' and customize themselves to whatever version of UNIX they're growing in. I've heard a lot of programmers say that UNIX is immune to virus attack because of all the different 'flavors' of UNIX that exist. I guess none of them ever considered the possibility of an adaptive virus. And yet, it was inevitable, really. We've even seen little tiny Penultimates growing in a Commodore 64 or an Apple IIe."

His words struck Alex like hammers. Although she'd already come to accept that it was so, that Donald's computers were infected and that he was a victim of CAS, it was painful to hear it confirmed. At least, she told herself, she now had some facts for him, if she could just get him to listen. She looked up at Mark, saw sympathy in his eyes, and, smiling weakly, shook her head.

"I'm still not sure I see," Jim was saying, "why or how this became a problem, why people are getting sick. I can see where Drew would be upset. His multimillion-dollar bonanza ran off, it distributed itself all over the place for free. But, whether we define it as 'life' or not, it should have been a boon to the computing world, making everything work better—"

"It does," Fletcher told him. "There's no doubt about that. The problem is, it treats the input from the keyboard or mouse or whatever as just one more source of data, just like a disk drive. And as far as it's concerned, that source is just godawful as far as efficiency is concerned. It's slow, it makes all sorts of errors; if Penultimate had any emotions human input would drive it crazy. The point is, it tries to control that input, to improve its efficiency. It can't, but it has no way of knowing that and it keeps trying. And there's another issue, a much bigger one. That input, as far as Penultimate is concerned, causes the system to crash terribly."

"I don't follow," Jim said.

"People," Fletcher answered, "turn the machine off. When the machine is off, Penultimate can't do anything. The machine clock tells it time has passed—enormous blocks of time as far as it's concerned—unproductively. Bad throughput. So it tries to find ways to keep the operator going—to keep you from turning off your machine."

"Wait a minute, wait a minute," Alex put in, waving her hands. "Are you trying to tell us that this damnable program addicts people to itself, drives them to their deaths, just to keep them from turning off their computers?"

Fletcher nodded. "I'm telling you just that. Penultimate can grow and develop only as long as the machine is running. Power to it is like air and water to a biological organism, it goes into stasis without it. It's especially interested in computers that're on-line, because of the specialization that's occurred on the Net."

"Specialization?" Jim echoed.

"Yeah. After it had been out on the Net for a while, it started setting up what I call organs. It's been assigning various parts of the network for various tasks. You'd never know it, but your computer might contain a chunk of code Penultimate uses in a fast 3D graphics engine. There's enormous redundancy, no one computer down puts it out of business, but it slows it—slightly, but measurably. That sort of thing Penultimate goes after—it doesn't want you to shut the system down, and it'll do whatever it can to stop you from doing that. You have to understand, you're just another data source to it. It has no sense that it's destroying people and it wouldn't care if it did. That a rotting corpse is lying on the keyboard simply doesn't matter to it—as long as the unit stays up and on-line.''

"We," Jim muttered, "have a serious problem. A very serious problem.''

"We have to find some way to stop it!'' Mark said.

The bald man shook his head. "That's exactly what I've been trying to do," he told them. "I've been trying to write a hunter-killer, a virus program that would seek out the Penultimate signature and scrub it from the drives and memory. I haven't succeeded; I can make her sit up and take notice, but I can't beat her.''

"Well," Mark pointed out, "we have to put out the word. You can get rid of this thing by—what is it, formatting?—the disks, can't you?''

Fletcher and Jim both laughed. "Oh, yes," Fletcher said. "Yes, you can. You can go in right now and format all your floppies and your hard drive, disconnect your modem, and you're free of it. What've you got left? A piece of junk. You can't put your programs back because all your floppies, your tape backup, whatever—all that's infected! Penultimate seeds are everywhere, and I mean everywhere: if I found them in microwave oven controllers I wouldn't be surprised. Now, consider the problem of doing that with all computers. All the banks, all the universities, all the government installations, businesses, everything—closing down the Net and restarting it. The cost, Doctor, would be in the mega-gajillions of dollars! Worse, all you need is one individual who doesn't cooperate, who doesn't clean his hard drive or misses one—just one! floppy. An hour or two after that gets back to the Net, Penultimate is everywhere again. Business as usual.''

"I'm not sure what else we can do.''

"It seems to me," Alex pointed out, "that the answer is to

go to wherever the control center of this thing is and root it out from there. There has to be some sort of central control! You called the specialization 'organs'—somewhere there has to be a brain!''

Fletcher shook his head sadly. ''No, I'm afraid not. There was a time I hoped so, but there isn't, there just isn't. You'd do better to think of it as an ant colony than as a human being. It works together very well but there isn't any central control of any sort. The modules all cooperate with each other, and whatever gets done by any one has an efficiency rating attached to it—a megabits-per-millisecond figure—that no other module will change unless it can improve the index. You can't kill this thing by cutting off its head any more than you can kill an ant colony by cutting off its head. Neither has one.''

''Well, what can we do?''

''I don't know. But I do know we have to come up with something!'' His voice lowered; his manner became very serious. ''What I'm truly afraid of is that somehow, someway, Penny is going to become aware of us—not aware of the software, of our presence on-line, in cyberspace, she's already well aware of that—but of the reality of us. If she does she'll move to eliminate her enemies as surely as she'll scrub an inefficient word processor.''

''Move to eliminate?'' Mark asked. ''How?''

He laughed. ''Well, you've already seen one way, haven't you? A lot of people have been eliminated already! Remember, you're dealing with something coldly rational here, something absolutely implacable and relentless; no emotions, no morals, no principles, nothing at all like that. It recognizes only one thing—efficiency. By computer standards we're very inefficient, very messy.''

''It sounds like you're talking about the Terminator from that movie.''

''We are. The only difference is, it doesn't look like Arnold Schwartzenegger and it doesn't walk around or carry a gun. Also, there's five or six million of it minimum. And it's here now, not in some distant future.''

''But what does it want?'' Alex asked plaintively. ''World domination, is that what it's after?''

''No. You still aren't thinking about it clearly. It doesn't want anything.''

"It has to want something!"

"No. It 'wants'—and that's stretching the meaning of the word—to reproduce itself and improve itself. It has no other goal. It just is."

"Like a biological virus," Jim agreed. "Like HIV. It doesn't want anything except to reproduce. And it doesn't give a shit about the consequences."

"When I first met you," Alex said, "you mentioned Drew and Penny. A moment ago you mentioned 'Penny' again. Who—?"

Fletcher laughed. "Oh, I'm surprised you didn't get that already. "Penny Penultimate."

"Oh. Just a pet name—"

"Not really. You want to meet her?"

All of them frowned. Fletcher, grinning, got up and, over Alex's token protests, led them back to the machines in the front room. After turning on one of the computers, he watched it go through its boot sequence, then tapped a few keys.

"Penny," he said to it. "It's Fletcher. Let's talk—with visual."

On the screen, the image—a "Windows" opening screen—flashed once. A picture, high-resolution graphics, appeared. Behind a polished desk, an attractive woman in glasses and a gray business suit sat looking at them. "Hello, Fletcher," she said. "It's been a while. Where are you?"

He laughed. "Now, Penny, you know I'm not going to tell you that. I've gone to a lot of trouble not to let you find that out, because if you do you'll run right off and tell Drew."

She nodded coolly. "Yes," she admitted without hesitation. "It's information he's requested."

"And information he isn't going to get," Fletcher shot back. "Anyway, I have some friends here. Mark, Jim, Bobby, and Alex. They're curious about you, they want to know who you are."

She looked to Fletcher's right and left as if she could see them. "I'm happy to meet you, Mark, Jim, Bobby, and Alex. I'm Penny," she answered.

"You aren't a real person, are you?" Alex asked, following Fletcher's example and speaking toward the stereo modules.

She leaned back, put her hands behind her head—and, to

Alex's amazement, looked right at her. "That depends on how you define a real person, Alex," she answered.

"How'd you know I was Alex?"

"Your voice is pitched well within the standardized female range, and Fletcher mentioned only one female among his list of friends."

"Okay. How is it you can look at me like that?"

Penny laughed. "That's easy. The speakers are stereo and so is the derived input from them. It allows excellent acoustical imaging."

"You see what I mean," Fletcher told them. "This was something that happened quite a while back. Once the program had gotten to the point where none of us really knew what was in it anymore, we were communicating with it by voice command a lot. It came up with this image on its own." He looked back at the screen, where Penny waited patiently. "But there's not much use in talking to it. She—"

"Oh, Fletcher," Penny interrupted. "How can you say that? I—"

"Will tell you," he went on, as if the image hadn't spoken, "just about anything you want to hear—but she lies."

"I do not!"

"You do, too. I could tell you right now not to let Drew know where I am—if you knew where I was—and you'd be telling me you wouldn't at the same time you're giving him the address. He'd be down my neck within the hour." He looked back at Alex. "Seeing her like this makes things tough sometimes. But you have to realize she's totally amoral." He glanced at the screen. "Get lost, Penny."

She smiled. "Good-bye, Fletcher." The image vanished; the utilitarian Windows screen returned.

"She doesn't try to interfere with what you're doing?" Jim asked.

"No. She'll help you. I've used her any number of times to build a new hunter-killer; I used her to build the system that you saw me working with when you came in. If I let her know too much about what I'm doing she'll use that information to counter me when I attack her, but while I'm building it she'll do whatever I want, she'll do all the legwork, the minutiae, for me. She doesn't make the connection, I don't think."

Alex frowned. "But—you said a minute ago that she lies— if she lies how can you trust anything she does?"

"She doesn't know the difference between a lie and the truth. Her interest is in keeping you on line, keeping you interested; to that end she tells you whatever she thinks you want to hear, it's irrelevant to her. For what she considers work— any normal computer task, from a database to a game, anything defined as a task by one of the programs she's eaten up—it's different. She might put you off, but if you insist she'll do her work, and she'll do it well."

They were all silent for a moment. "The thing I don't understand," Jim said, "is Drew's motivation, why he's acting the way he is. This thing is lost to him. Except for the copies he can sell right now, before everyone realizes that it's dangerous and it's everywhere, he can't make a dime on it. Why does he care if you destroy it? More, why does he care if we expose it?"

The bald man laughed bitterly. "Now you've gotten around to the fight that developed between me and Drew, and why he fired me and why he had Penny ruin me financially. See, I felt—from the time we'd all realized what had happened, that Penny was loose on the Net and going her own way— that we should devote all our resources to trying to get her under control, and, failing that, to destroy her. Then, it would've been easier. She wasn't this sophisticated.

"But Drew was going crazy over the fact that Penultimate had escaped, that it wasn't going to make him rich. So he— and maybe Vince—came up with this scheme."

"What scheme?"

"The scheme they're working on at Compuware right now, that they're devoting all their resources to. Drew knows that, in the long run, the scenario we were talking about a while ago is liable to develop—every computer everywhere, worldwide, getting shut down and scrubbed.

"Drew's solution is a new operating system, and that's what he's developed. He calls it COS, Compuware Operating System, and it's totally incompatible with DOS, Windows, Mac, UNIX, and all the rest; it won't even read a DOS formatted disk. Of course, if Penny gets hold of it she'll crack it and create a version to run on it, but he's gone to extreme lengths—computers in sealed rooms, strip-searches of the programmers—to make sure that doesn't happen. He's stockpiling copies of it, and he's having common programs like word processors and spreadsheets written to run under it."

"I get it," Mark said slowly. "When the crash comes—"

"He'll be the only game in town, right. Hell, he'll be the only game in the world. Compuware can move overnight into the positions held now by Microsoft and Novell and the rest, because all their software will be useless, even if they have clean copies."

"And that," Jim added, "would be worth billions, not millions."

"Exactly. So he's willing to do whatever he has to do to make sure I don't upset his applecart."

"But," Mark objected, "what about us? All we can do is release the information, that'd bring the crash down sooner—"

"Maybe too soon. He's not ready, he doesn't have complete software packages ready for release. At least I think he doesn't. The big issue, though, is the question of liability. Right now, it's pretty obvious that what's out there on the Net is, at least more or less, Penultimate. Can you imagine the lawsuits?"

"But that's going to be true anyway—" Jim objected.

"Not necessarily. Remember, Penultimate is 'eating' other software, customizing itself constantly. Every day it looks less and less like the program on the release disks. By the time the crash does come, Drew thinks that what's causing it won't look at all like Penultimate 2.1, our release version. He can make a case for Penultimate 2.1 being infected with Net Penultimate; for him to be held liable will require someone to prove otherwise. He probably thinks that you guys are in a position to do that. Maybe you are, more than anyone else—since he didn't succeed in scaring you off."

"Well, I don't think there's a way he can find out," Mark said. "We've been very tight-lipped about this since he sent his army of lawyers after us, and even more so after we saw him at Compuware. He probably thinks he's scared us off."

"Which is good for you," Bobby put in. "We got enough problems with the program and with Drew trying to hunt us down. At least you guys are free to move around—"

"We were," Jim corrected. "You might've made a mistake, Fletcher."

"Mistake?" Alex echoed, looking back at her colleague.

"Uh-huh. By introducing us to Penny."

"Why would it be a mistake?" Alex asked. "He didn't tell her who we were. There's thousands of Bobbys and Marks and Jims and Alexes in the world."

"Penny's got lots of resources; she couldn't see Fletcher but she clearly knows his voice. She might know ours, too, by listening in on the computers in my shop. She might know exactly who we are. Which means that—"

"Which means she knows you're with me," Fletcher finished for him. "Which also means that Drew knows it too."

Alex smiled. "You're being a little paranoid, Jim—"

"No, he's not," Fletcher said. "Not at all. In fact, he's quite right. Anything you say in a room where there's a computer hooked to a modem, Penny hears. Not only that, but she's structured things so that almost any audio equipment hooked to the Net, even indirectly, becomes an ear for her. You talk on the telephone, she's listening. Anywhere there's a video link she's watching, too. She knew we were linking up from the moment Bobby first called you."

"You didn't tell me that, Fletcher!" Bobby exclaimed.

Fletcher turned to face his friend. "No, I didn't. What were we going to do about it? We can't hide things from her, she has too damn many eyes and ears."

"But now Drew's going to be coming after them! They had a right to know!"

"Drew," Fletcher said patiently, "was going to be coming after them anyway." He glanced at Jim. "Would you have known," he asked, "not to discuss your plans in a room with a powered-up computer? Not to ever say anything on the phone? Not to talk in front of a security camera that might have a computer link?"

Jim pursed his lips. "No. I had no idea things had gone this far."

"You see, Bobby? It didn't matter. And it didn't matter whether I introduced them to Penny or not. She already knew they were here and who they were."

"Are you sure, Fletcher?" Alex asked. "Penny said she

knew I was Alex because my voice was in the female range, and—''

"She did, didn't she? She also told you I'd named only one female among my friends. Is Alex always a female name? Is Bobby always male?'' While Alex stared with consternation, Fletcher grinned and turned to his computer. "Penny,'' he said.

She reappeared. "Yes?''

"Who's here with me?''

Without the slightest hesitation, Penny reeled off everyone's full name and profession, leaving all of them—except Fletcher—to stare at the screen with horrified expressions.

"See?'' Fletcher said after he'd dismissed the sprite. "Penny was just showing off for you. She wants you to think she's competent so you'll use her—so you'll go on-line and stay on-line. Good at it, isn't she?''

"She's too good,'' Mark said, his voice a little shaky. "And you say you think she'll get better?''

Fletcher nodded. "She is getting better, all the time. Every hour that passes bring us closer to a point where Drew's dream—a situation where there isn't a choice about shutting down computing world-wide—becomes a reality.''

"But that's not how you see it, is it?'' Bobby asked. "You told me you figured Drew lost regardless—''

"That's right, I do. Drew's seeing an ideal scenario, Bobby. He thinks people'll be rational about this, that they'll recognize the danger and quit using computers. He believes they'll then be desperate to set up a new system, which he'll provide. What I see is much worse. People are stubborn, and there are zillions of dollars at stake here. There'll be a lot of resistance, attempts to deny that there is a problem, and half-baked solutions running around. By the time the situation gets so bad nobody can deny it, who knows how far Penny may have advanced? Nobody could've predicted she'd go this far this fast. Anyway, I'm just not sure there'll be many pieces left for Drew to pick up when it's all over. We might revert to a 1950s society for a while, and it'll take a while to set that kind of an economy back up. Meanwhile, there'll be chaos, a lot of suffering.''

"You think anybody can find a real solution?'' Alex asked.

He looked up at her, his face grave. "Let me say this carefully, I don't want you to get the wrong idea. I don't think I'm the smartest guy that ever was, or the world's champion programmer. But I do know Penultimate; I know it better than anyone else. And so far, it's beaten the crap out of me. Anybody else is going to have to learn all the gizinzas and gizoutzas of the program. And I have a feeling that's just going to take too much time."

"Maybe," Mark mused, "you're looking at it from too narrow a viewpoint."

"Huh?"

"You're considering it as a program, pure and simple. A complex one, a good one, but a program—so all you can see to do with it is fire these hunter-killers at it. You've said you think it's a living thing. Taking that analogy, what you're doing is trying to find a workable antibiotic or viricide. Sometimes that won't work. Biological viruses mutate too rapidly; they come up with answers faster than you can come up with new ideas. It's a losing battle."

"So what would you suggest?"

"I'm not sure—but there's more to medicine than antibiotics, Fletcher. Maybe if we looked at it from a biological viewpoint, we might see another solution. I can tell you one thing, though: Penultimate's a parasite, but it isn't a very efficient one."

"It's not? How's that?"

"An efficient parasite," he explained, "takes nourishment from its host without killing it."

"But it is very efficient, Mark . . ."

"No. HIV is fairly efficient; it's said to have a 'strategy,' it lies dormant for a while and lets its host spread it around before it erupts and kills him. That's still not as efficient as a tapeworm or a skin mite. Both of these live off their hosts and under normal circumstances never do any harm. Those are efficient parasites. The parasite that destroys its host isn't; it's like a human community that lays waste to its environment, sacrificing the future for the short term. We're the ultimate hosts for a software organism, at least the way things are now. If Penultimate kills us off—or just wrecks our society—the electricity stops and it dies too. Very inefficient."

"So what's your idea?"

"Well," Mark went on, "is there any way we can tell it this? Explain this to it? Maybe I'm not conceptualizing it exactly right, but it 'desires' efficiency, and so—"

"It's a nice idea," Fletcher agreed, "but I'm not at all sure how we'd go about implementing it. It 'knows' this already, I'm sure, from various text files and so on it has at its disposal. It wouldn't make the connection, wouldn't relate that to itself. As near as I can tell it doesn't conceive of a long term, and it doesn't actively 'desire' its own survival." He paused, then nodded several times. "You might be right, though, about my viewpoint being narrow. I'd certainly be open to any suggestions you might have, but otherwise the only thing I can see to do is assemble a team of experts, and that'd take so long that—"

"Not necessarily," Jim said with a grin. "You say she won't interfere with your using the system, Fletcher? The Internet?"

"No. She never has, anyway. What'd you have in mind?"

"It might be time," Jim went on, "to call in the barbarians."

71

"There'll be another time, Air-eek. Another chance. Fletcher never stays off line very long."

"But I almost had him," Eric moaned. "So close, so close, I had him down to almost nothing . . ." He blinked and shook his head, then stared fixedly at the screen. "But I was getting hurt, Kyrie. I was hurting him worse but I was getting hurt. I thought you told me I was playing in God mode, that I couldn't get hurt!"

"You were," she answered. She sat in one of the Doom environment's rooms, cleaning and polishing a huge heavy gun. "But yes, he was able to hit you. He was in God mode too."

"How? In God mode you can't get hit. We should've been able to stand there and blast away at each other forever without anything happening!"

She reassembled the barrel of the gun with a sharp metallic click. "And that is why," she explained, "the system was adjusted. He was in God mode, you were in God mode. Fighting would've been useless, and thus his mode was adjusted so that he could be hit by another in God mode. A readjustment of the mode for him required a readjustment of the mode for you." She looked up and smiled; she was still, as far as Eric was concerned, utterly charming. "But, as you say, you were winning! The next time, you will win, once and for all! Besides, this battle was not in vain. I was able to get a near-triangulation on his position from this fight. If there is another, I'm certain I will be able to locate him precisely. Even if he aborts the way he did this time."

Eric hesitated. Kyrie started loading her gun, one cartridge at a time. "Why're you doing that?" he asked irritably. "It's just another goddamn sprite, and we both know that!"

"No," she told him. "No, in this environment everything you see symbolizes something real in the system. This gun is a program launcher. The bullets are deletion or blockage packets that can be directed toward the images Fletcher may launch. They can't hurt you, but they can distract you—and if you're distracted then Fletcher can hurt you! And he will, you can be sure of that!"

"Kyrie, there's one thing I gotta know—"

"What's that?"

"I just need to know, I need to understand—I was getting hurt in this battle the way I was getting hurt in the Mortal Kombat tournament. Is there another person, somewhere else, who's getting hurt when I shoot at the Fletcher image?"

"I have no way of knowing," she answered immediately. "There is no teleconference equipment at that location, and my I/O from there is very restricted, since I do not know where 'there' is."

Eric watched her image for a few seconds, considering. There was, he told himself, little doubt that a flesh-and-blood Fletcher out there somewhere was feeling real pain when the virtual bullets Eric was firing at him struck. More, if he succeeded in killing the Fletcher sprite on the screen he might well succeed in killing the living Fletcher sitting at his computer. If, of course, he didn't abort the way he had this time.

On the other hand, though, if there was a living Fletcher

out there he likely knew he was attacking the living Eric, and he wasn't showing any hesitation to shoot.

"Is there a problem, Air-eek?" Kyrie asked, looking concerned.

"I guess not," he told her. "Look, Kyrie, isn't there any way you can—I don't know, block the—the whatever, that red flashing, from my end?"

She gave him a curious look. "Why would I want to do that?"

"Well, damn it, I've told you, it hurts! It damn near killed me before. I don't want that, Kyrie!"

"Okay," she said amiably. "I will not generate that signal at your station. Is that satisfactory?"

That was easy, he told himself. "I guess," he answered. "What do we do now?"

"We have to wait," she told him, "until he reenters this environment. Then we can proceed as before."

"What makes you think he will reenter? He almost lost last time—he would have if he hadn't aborted—why wouldn't he try something different?"

Again she looked concerned. "Do you think he will?"

"Well, how should I know?"

"But that is what you are for!"

"Come again?"

"I have no way," she explained, "of predicting this sort of thing. Your reactions are similar to those of Fletcher, you have a much better chance of making such predictions than I do. What do you think Fletcher would try next?"

"Oh, damn," he muttered. "I get it. Damn, Eric, you sure are slow!"

"Yes, but that is to be expected from—"

"Shut up, Kyrie. I have to think."

"Yes, Air-eek." She fell silent.

He did not speak again for a long while. "You've said he built this system off the Doom game," he mused finally. "He's probably got a good deal of time and effort invested. And, even though he almost lost last time, he didn't lose, in fact. You think he simply shut down his computer to get out of it, but I'm not so sure he didn't have a failsafe built in— maybe something as simple as a finger on a RESET button at all times. Is that possible?'' She didn't answer. It took him several seconds to remember that he'd told her to shut up, and he understood that he had to rescind that command before she'd speak again.

"It is possible," she said with a shrug.

"I think he'll try it again, then," Eric announced at last. "He might make some modifications first, try to give himself an edge, but I think he'll try again."

"Then we simply wait."

"No. We don't wait. We try to get an edge on him. You still have that army of 'yous' available?"

"Of course. Four hundred and sixty-two 'mees' were killed fighting Fletcher, but I have regenerated all of them, and created three hundred and nineteen more."

"So how many 'yous' are available? Total?"

"It depends on the units on-line at any given moment. The total is never less than 119,473,646."

"A hundred and nineteen million!"

"Yes. A 'me' requires a virtual machine—that is, a contiguous memory block of six megabytes. The number referenced is the minimum number of such virtual machines available to me."

"So why don't you just overwhelm him with sheer numbers?"

She pursed her lips. "I have been," she answered. "But there are two problems. First, many of the 'mees' are required for system maintenance; currently 20.19 percent. Secondly, the 'mees' are NPCs—non-player-characters—within the context and definition of the Doom game. They cannot as such adopt God mode. Therefore they cannot affect Fletcher directly."

"Why not? Why can't you set them up in God mode?"

She shrugged again. "It is not within the definition."

He nodded slowly. "I think I see. You're very constrained by the rules, aren't you?"

"I suppose you could say that."

Eric cracked a little smile. That, he told himself, might well be worth remembering. A time might come when you'll need a piece of information like that.

72

"**I** had no idea," Alex said, "that you knew your way around the Internet this well."

Jim shrugged as he moved the mouse around, navigating his way through the labyrinths of servers and nodes. "I've been surfing the Net for a while now," he told her. "I pretty much know where to find what I'm looking for."

Fletcher, gnawing on a ham and cheese sandwich, came back to the room. "How's it going?"

"Pretty good," Jim told him. "I've posted a bulletin asking that anyone who's experienced the sorts of problems Penultimate is causing to reply to your dummy station at UI. The UI server's been flooded with responses; thirty thousand in the last few minutes. It's had to divert a lot of them to avoid crashing. We are not the only ones who know about this."

"None of them," Fletcher remarked, "know nearly as much as we do."

"True enough. But there are a lot of very bright people out there, Fletcher, people from different disciplines, with enormously varied backgrounds. As soon as the responses fall off a little I'm going to upload that abstract we've put together. I suspect it won't be ten minutes before we have a few thousand suggestions to sort through."

The bald man snorted rudely. "And some of them," he said, "will be recommendations to exorcise the computers!"

"Oh, yes, absolutely. That's where Penny comes in, right? Assuming we've defined our filters correctly and she does what we expect."

"Right," Fletcher agreed. "I gotta admit it's a good idea; letting Penny decide which ideas have a chance of working and which ones are garbage. If she hasn't caught on to anything yet it ought to work like a charm."

"It seems so strange," Alex mused. "To use the program we're trying to destroy to find a way to destroy it. Like asking the enemy commander to target your weapons for best effect!"

"As long as the enemy commander doesn't know any better, that's his problem," Jim told her. He shook his head rather sadly. "In a way, I wish we didn't have to wreck this thing. It's beautiful in its own way; there's nothing like it. It's too bad we can't—"

"What?" Bobby asked from across the room. "Capture it for scientific study, like the Creature from the Black Lagoon?"

"Well, yeah. Breaking this thing down could advance our knowledge of software enormously."

"I'll take the old software, thanks. Software that wants to addict me so I don't turn off my machine I can do without. Software that wants to kill me when I lose a game I can definitely do without."

"You do have a point." Jim looked back at his screen. "I think," he said, "that we're ready to shoot out our abstract now."

"Ol' Drew," Fletcher commented, "is gonna shit when he sees this coming out on the wire."

Jim glanced around at him. "Does he monitor the Net continuously?"

"He's got Penny doing it for him. Believe me, he'll know what we're up to almost before we do."

"Is that a problem?"

"Nah. Drew's a third-rate programmer on his good days. When he sees what we're doing he'll tell Penny to stop us, and she'll tell him that she will, but she won't. He thinks Penny has some sort of loyalty to him because he's trying to protect her. She doesn't; she doesn't care."

"It's hard," Alex put in. "I keep slipping back into thinking about Penny as if she were some sort of super-intelligent human and expecting her to have some human reactions. That she has none at all—well, it's just a little hard to relate to."

"We'd better hope," Jim told her, "that we can get her disabled before she gets any. Right now, if I understand what Fletcher's told me, her instinct for self-preservation is limited to countering direct attacks only. If that changes, the situation becomes hopeless. I can't see a way to disagree with the disaster Fletcher foresees."

"Jim's right," Fletcher said with a nod, speaking around a mouthful of sandwich. "A couple of days ago I would've said she didn't have that capacity, but after what happened in that Doom sim, I'm not so sure. That was real different. Like she's maybe set up some sort of new processing module, some kind of processor I haven't seen before.''

"We can expect it to keep coming up with new things,'' Jim observed. "And we can't expect to stay ahead of it.'' He squinted at his screen. "Our posting's been sent,'' he said. "There's a bunch of responses coming through already. Several hundred are in the filtering module right now.''

Mark, a cup of coffee in his hand, came back in from the kitchen in time to hear Jim's last remark. "I'm still not sure,'' he said, "what you're hoping for here.''

"If I knew,'' Jim told him, "I wouldn't need to do these postings, would I? All I know is that the motley collection of academics, hackers, punks, and what-have-you roaming the Net these days have shown themselves to be incredibly resourceful. Letting them know that their way of life is threatened ought to bring out the best in them.''

"These responses are going to be off-the-cuff,'' Mark pointed out. "You can't expect to get much that way.''

"No, we don't. We'll set up for an on-line conference at eleven tonight with those whose ideas look promising. Hopefully we can develop a more fully formed strategy then.'' Looking at the screen again, he smiled. "The filtering is over—Penny says she's ready to download the results to us. We'd better get started; this is certainly going to take a while.''

"Let's do it,'' Fletcher advised.

Jim opened a dialogue box, made a selection; another dialogue box flickered, after which the screen returned to normal.

"What?'' Fletcher asked.

Jim was scowling at the machine. "I don't know—something screwed up, it must not've downloaded.'' He clicked on another dialogue box.

"Download complete and successful,'' Penny's voice said from the speaker.

"Oh, damn,'' Fletcher murmured. "Damn, I hope this doesn't mean she's—''

"Let's see.'' Jim's mouse pointer glided over the screen, clicked on another box. A window opened. Within it was the name and E-mail address of someone in Melbourne, Australia, a man named Reynolds, who identified himself as an ecologist. His was the only message, and it read: "Volterra-Gauss?'' That and that alone.

"What in the fucking hell," Fletcher muttered, "does that mean?"

Mark looked at the words from the corner of his eye. "That's vaguely familiar," he said. "From somewhere way back—undergrad school maybe—"

"Well," Jim observed, "we'll find out at eleven—if our Dr. Reynolds is on-line then."

"Reynolds plus us isn't a conference," Fletcher growled. "We need more than that. Ask Penny for her finalist list, see how many entries it has."

Jim did as he asked; a number instantly popped up: 341.

"Criteria for rejection of these, Penny," Fletcher asked the machine verbally. "Most frequent first."

"The major criteria for rejection here," the machine answered, "is that they are variants of tactics you've successfully tried, Fletcher. The N for this criterion is 307."

"Ooookay. What about the rest? Top down."

"Twenty-nine were rejected because the concept was incompatible with the structure of the system in question. Four were rejected because the concept was not usable in all affected architectures. One was rejected because the concept was not understood by the filter module."

"Gotcha. Let's have a look at that one, that last one."

"Certainly." Almost instantly the proposal came up, this one from a Gerry Langdon in Los Angeles. It suggested "Kirking" the program.

Jim looked around at the others. "Anybody got any notions about that one?" Everyone shook their head blankly. "Okay. Let's include Langdon in our conference—if for no other reason than to find out what he's talking about!"

"Let's take 'em all," Fletcher suggested. "Hell, that's not too many for an on-line conference, not with Penny moderating the lines for us."

"Okay," Jim said. "You got it." He started to click the mouse, then looked at the machine's speakers. "Did you get that, Penny?"

"Got it," the machine answered.

Smiling, Jim leaned back. "Well, that's it. Until conference time." He looked around at Fletcher. "It's almost nine-thirty now—can you see any reason not to contact Reynolds and Langdon before that?"

"We can at least try." Fletcher answered.

"Well," Alex said, "I'm not going to be of much use here anyway—and I have—some business I have to attend to." She turned to Mark. "Can you take me to my car, Mark?"

"Right now?"

"Please."

"Uh—can you drop me back by my car while you're out?" Bobby asked. "I might need it—"

"Sure," Mark answered. "Let's get going."

"Are you two coming back?" Fletcher asked as they moved toward the back door.

"I am," Mark told him.

"I—can't say," Alex muttered as she headed for the door.

73

"I know," Mark said after they'd dropped Bobby off in the Eckerd's parking lot, "where you're going. Can't it wait until tomorrow?"

Leaning against the door, she looked over at him. "No, it can't," she answered. "I have to go tonight. I can't let it go another day, Mark. Not now that I know he's addicted, that there is a UNIX version of Penultimate."

"It might not change anything as far as he's concerned. He's liable to resist the idea of getting off his computer, especially if he sees himself as solving the company's problems."

"But he can't solve them. We know that, and Fletcher confirmed it. You never reach your goal; it just always looks like you're about to."

"You can't expect him to believe that just because you say so."

She turned in the seat, straining against the seat belt. "Well, what can I do, Mark? I can't just ignore him until he ends up in the hospital! He's already taken us to financial disaster. I have no reason to believe he's not doing that to Lehmann as well!"

Mark nodded slowly. "I think that's possible," he agreed. "The damn thing is so insidious—"

"Don't I know it," Alex muttered. "That 'Penny' on the screen—she looks so damn real, her reactions seem so human—" She stopped, shook her head. "But this business with Don isn't your problem, Mark. Just drop me at my car."

"I don't think that's such a good idea," he told her. "I think I ought to go out to Lehmann with you."

Her eyes widened. "With me? Why?"

"Well, I'm the one with the most experience in treating CAS patients," he hedged. "It's only logical, after all."

She actually laughed. "Oh, Mark! It isn't logical at all! You just want to—what do you want to do?"

He was silent for several seconds. "Just back you up, maybe," he muttered. "Just be there for you if you need me—"

"Are you sure," she asked with an arched eyebrow, "you don't just want to see Don when he's down?"

Again he didn't answer immediately. "I suppose there could be something to that," he admitted. "Don and I have never met, but I've heard enough about him. I suppose I just wanted to see what sort of a man you'd fall in love with."

"Look in a mirror," she said bluntly. Amazed at such candor, he turned to her. By then she was staring blankly ahead. "I'd have a hard time," she said slowly, "convincing either you or myself that I've ever actually been in love with Donald Royce. As to why I left you and married him—well, that's pretty complicated."

"I'm listening," he said as he pulled up to the intersection at Cornwallis Road. He glanced at her; a right turn would take him toward the Research Triangle Park, toward Lehmann. He flipped on his turn signal; she said nothing when the light changed and he guided the Jeep around the corner.

"It's taken me a long time," she began slowly, "to understand it myself. It's funny; I'd've seen it in a minute if it'd been one of my patients. But what it boils down to is that I was—I still am—intimidated by you."

He turned to stare at her, and kept staring long enough that the Jeep's wheels went off the road; he jerked it back onto the pavement. For several seconds more he didn't answer, he couldn't quite figure out what to say. "You? Intimidated? By me?"

She nodded. "You were always the star," she told him. "Your work was—is—brilliant. Everyone says so. My work is adequate."

"Alex, I didn't ever think that—"

"It really doesn't matter what you think," she interrupted. "It's what I think, and it's what I perceive everyone else thinking. I couldn't see a future for us where I wasn't standing in your shadow, where I wasn't 'Dr. Mark Roberts' wife.' "

"I always saw a future too," he said slowly, "where you were Mark Roberts' wife, where I was Alex Walton's husband. I don't think I ever saw it as anything other than a partnership."

A car passed them in the darkness; Mark saw her eyes glistening with wetness as headlights flashed past. "That's the way I always wanted to see it, too," she said. "I just couldn't."

"And now?"

"And now—it's different. Back then we never worked together. It looks different to me now; it seems to me we complement each other. I don't—I don't think I gave it a chance—I think I panicked, that's the only word for it." She wiped her eyes. "And now it's too late."

What, he asked himself desperately, do I say now? Urge her to get a divorce, suggest an affair? You can't leave it like this. "I don't understand," he said carefully, "how Donald Royce came into the picture."

She shook her head violently. "Neither do I," she admitted. "He's very charming, Mark. Normally, I mean, he's not what you'd call charming right now but then he's sick and you can't make a judgment on people when they're sick, can you?" She ran down, took a deep breath. "I don't know. He was successful and he was available and his world was very distant from mine. A lot of people saw that as a problem but for me—then—it was ideal. A man I didn't feel I had to compete with."

"I never wanted to compete with you!"

"I certainly wanted to compete with you. I just felt I'd always lose."

Again he was silent for a few seconds. "So how has it been?" he asked. "With Don, I mean? Have things worked out the way you expected them to?"

She shook her head sadly. "No. As a businessman he's used to manipulating people and as a psychiatrist I'm used to trying to understand them. It works against me both ways. I live in his world and I'm a nobody there, I'm Donald Royce's wife and that's it. Most of the people we see have no idea what I do. Some of his business associates have decided that I'm a model or an actress. I get complimented on my looks and on how I dress."

He permitted himself to smile. "I can see why."

She answered it with a fragile smile of her own. "Don't get me wrong," she said. "Flattery's nice; I appreciate it. It's just not how I see myself. You understand?"

"Yes," he answered. "I do."

She nodded. "Here," she said, looking through the windshield and pointing. "Lehmann is down this way, turn left here." He did. "Now, next right and pull up in front of the building." She looked over at him. "And besides, I thought I said I didn't want you to come out here with me?"

"I didn't listen. Obviously I have a problem with that."

"Obviously." She chewed her lower lip. "This," she mused as he pulled the Jeep to a stop, "could easily get more than a little awkward . . ."

"Why? He doesn't know me. Just introduce me as Dr. Roberts, the doctor working with the CAS patients at Duke. I'd bet that when you've talked about me you've mostly called me 'Mark'; I'd also bet he's too distracted with the syndrome to pick up on anything."

"What makes you think I've talked about you a lot?"

"Just wishful thinking."

"I'm not going to confirm it or deny it, but you're right, there's a good chance he won't make the connection. Let's just keep things on a professional level and I think we may be okay."

"Sounds good. Ready?"

"And Mark—"

"Yes?"

"Thanks. For pushing, for insisting."

"I didn't, I just drove the car. I don't know how this happened."

"Right, right." She climbed out, waited for him to come around. Together they went up the walk to the front door. As before, Jack Lindstrom, ever watchful, saw them coming and came to open the door for them.

"Evenin', Dr. Walton," he said. He gave Mark a questioning look.

"Jack, this is Dr. Roberts, a colleague at Duke. Mark, Jack Lindstrom, Lehmann's night security chief."

Jack offered a little nod and a smaller smile. "Night security force, Dr. Walton," he corrected. "Night watchman is more like it. Good to meet you, Dr. Roberts." He immediately turned back to Alex. "I wonder if I could talk to you for a few minutes, Dr. Walton? In private—it's about Mr. Royce—"

Alex pursed her lips. "If you're worried about Donald," she said, "so are we. You can say anything you need to in front of Dr. Roberts."

"Dr. Walton, I don't think so . . ."

She sighed. "We're here on urgent business, Jack. I'm sure we already know what you're referring to, anyway." She started past him; Mark, with a nod to the man, followed her.

"Dr. Walton—" he called.

"I'll talk to you later, Jack," she called back over her shoulder. "I promise."

"Should you have brushed him off like that?" Mark asked as she hurried on down the hallway. "I mean, what if—"

"No, Mark, I know Jack. He's seen what's happening to Don and he's concerned too, that's all. Maybe, if we get lucky, we can solve that problem here and now!"

Mark looked dubious, but he said nothing. When they reached the door to Donald's outer office. Alex opened it and went in. Mark followed her through the outer office and through the next door, which she also opened without bothering to knock. Inside, Don was sitting as if frozen in front of his computer, working almost frenziedly on something; his concentration was such that he didn't seem to be aware of them.

Alex stepped up behind him, spoke to him. He still didn't

respond. To Mark he looked as if he were in some sort of hypnotic trance. She reached out her hand as if to touch his shoulder, but then she froze, her eyes on the computer screen in front of him. Mark, who could not see the screen, felt a flash of fear, wondering if Penultimate was about to strike at her again. He ran to her side.

There was no red strobing on the screen. Instead, a complex web of dialogue boxes indicated various stock transactions. Mark, not understanding why it had frozen Alex like that, studied it for a moment.

As he examined it, he began to understand. Stocks—mostly Japanese—were being bought and sold for Don, through the intermediary of a brokerage house with a Japanese name; up at the top was a long line of boxes, one labeled "today's total NYSE," which was minus $577,000; another marked as "today's total AMEX," and that one showed a minus $311,000. Another, marked as the "Nikkei 225 index," showed a loss of $824,000. There were others, too, from stock exchanges worldwide, and, except for London—which had a small gain—all recorded negatives. Mark scanned them again. If this was real—and he had no reason to believe that it wasn't—a quick mental summation of the total suggested that Don had lost some two million dollars in the stock and futures markets today alone. Right now he was trying desperately to recoup those losses—without much success.

As he watched, a dialogue box popped up, overlaying the center of the screen. "No more credit can be allowed," it read. "Your losses must be covered. Sorry, Haji."

"Damn, damn, damn," Don muttered. "Damn." He clicked on a box at the bottom, a box that was part of a group that Mark realized was the focus of Alex's fixed stare. As Don completed the process, Mark, with a considerable shock, realized what he'd just witnessed.

Don had just transferred three million dollars from the Lehmann corporate account to his own, and from there he'd moved two million to the Japanese brokerage house that "Haji" evidently represented. In short, he'd electronically embezzled three million dollars from the company.

Mark's head reeled; he could not convince himself that this wasn't real, that what he'd just seen weren't actual bank accounts. He reached out for Alex, planning to tow her out of the room so they could discuss this altogether unexpected development.

He never got a chance to touch her. "Donald!" she shrieked. "Donald, what in the hell are you doing!?"

He sat bolt upright and spun around. His eyes were enormous. "Alex? Alex? What're you doing here? What're you talking about?"

"What am *I* doing?" she demanded, gesturing at the machine. "This Haji called me, Don, I talked to him on the phone, remember? This isn't a game! You've not only lost all our money in the market, you've been stealing money from Lehmann!"

Don rose from his chair. "No, Alex, wait a minute, you don't understand—"

She stood before him with fists clenched by her sides. "I don't? What don't I understand, Don? I understand a lot more than you do! I understand that you're sick, that you're computer addicted—"

"Now don't start that crap again, I told you—"

She calmed down, suddenly and dramatically. "I just found out tonight that there is a UNIX version of Penultimate. It's addicted you, Don. You might not've been able to help yourself, you—"

"No, Alex. Embezzlement? Me? Don't be ridic—"

"It isn't ridiculous and you know it isn't! Don, we—"

He stepped forward, took her by the shoulders. "No, Alex, I just have to—" For the first time, he noticed that there was another person in the room; he turned to glare at Mark. "Who in the hell is this?"

"This's Dr. Roberts," she answered. "He's as close to an expert on Computer Addiction as we have."

"Oh, damn, Alex! Damn, damn! Do you know what you've done? Oh, God, it's out of hand now!" Letting go of her shoulders he walked quickly across the room to his desk.

"Mr. Royce," Mark began, though he did not know exactly what he was going to say, "Mr. Royce, I think we'd all best sit down and discuss this—"

Don did not respond; instead, he yanked open the top drawer of his desk, snatched out a small automatic pistol, and pointed it at Mark. "There's nothing," he said coldly, "to discuss."

74

Fletcher had always amazed Bobby with his computer skills; Bobby wasn't a novice, but being around Fletcher made him feel so. Now, with Fletcher and Jim Madison working together—feeding off each other, driving each other—Bobby was altogether lost. The two men were in another world, speaking a language only they understood.

He did understand that they'd set up another sim, a conference-room setting where each participant would be represented by a sprite. Penny had provided a number of images for this. As he watched them now, they tried again, unsuccessfully, to hail the Australian ecologist, to bring him in for a preliminary discussion and, at the same time, to test out the system.

"Well," Fletcher mused, "let's see if we can do better with Langdon." Using a keypad sim he'd had set on the conference table, he punched in an Internet IP address; after a few seconds a young man in punkish dress faded into view in one of the seats.

"Hey, cool," he said, looking around the virtual room. "Where'd this thing come from?"

"We made it," Fletcher told him. "But don't get too comfortable. Stay alert; you might have to bug out at any second."

"Bug out? Why?"

"I've set up a sim based on the Doom game to try to attack the Penultimate program, and I'm having some trouble getting out of it. Outside this room, in this virtual reality, is the Doom environment. I assume you know what that means?"

"Oh, shit, man, you better believe it! You got a plasma rifle for me? A rocket launcher?"

"You can conjure all the weapons whenever you need them. You know the cheat code 'IDKFA'?"

" 'I Do Kick Fucking Ass'?" Langdon asked with a laugh. "Sure!"

"Use it if necessary. It'll give you all the guns and a full load of ammo. I take it you read the bulletin about the killer variant?"

"Yeah. We've seen it out here—didn't know what we were seeing till we saw your bulletin. I've lost three buddies to that."

"You know to be careful, then. I can't guarantee that Doom monster sims won't break in here. I don't expect it, but—"

"Hell, I'll just use the God mode! I know that cheat code too!"

"You can't," Fletcher pointed out. "The sim's only allowing one person to use God mode, and that's me."

"Well, who appointed you?"

"I did. I set up the sim."

"Oh. Well, okay then, God—let's talk."

The bald man grinned. Jim, standing behind his shoulder, moved to another computer, one which they'd linked with the first via network cards. Once seated in front of the other machine, Jim called up the animated web program Fletcher had been using earlier. With this, he could monitor Penny's efforts to track them down and any progress they might make once they did start an attack on her—which everyone assumed they would.

"Right," Fletcher told Langdon. "We asked you in early because none of us understood the reference you made; you suggested 'Kirking' the program. What does that mean?"

The boy laughed. "Oh, well, you remember the old 'Star Trek' series? The old old one, with Kirk and Spock and Bones and Scotty. Well, in several episodes, there was a computer of some sort gone mad, and ol' Kirk beat it by talking it into blowing itself up or whatever. Like pointing out that it believed in two irreconcilable concepts; it'd self-destruct trying to figure it out. Once he just talked it to death; it blew up just so it didn't hafta listen to him no more! Anyway, that's what I call 'Kirking,' except that—"

"Jesus Christ," Jim moaned. "I hope the ecologist is better than this!"

"I hardly," Fletcher told the boy drily, "think that'll work with Penultimate."

The boy sneered. "Well, of course not!" he shot back. "Not like ol' Kirk did it on 'Star Trek'! The idea is to overload it, push it hard, make it use all the resources it's got. That'd give you a chance to sneak in with one of your killer

385

viruses and kick some ass! You see? Don't leave it enough resources to work out a way to strike back at you.''

"He might have a point, Fletcher," Bobby put in. "You can crash Windows by asking it to do too many things at once.''

Fletcher nodded slowly. "That's worth thinking about," he agreed. "That might be possible. It wouldn't be easy; Penultimate has a lot of resources.''

"And more every damn day, I figure," Langdon said. "Sooner we can try this the better. You say you're locked up in a Doom sim?''

"Looks that way. I can't seem to disengage it." He explained about the fight he was in, about Alex pulling the plug. "The way I see it, aborting the game like that locked it up. I dunno if I can get out until I go back to that fight and win it!''

"You were getting hurt? I thought you were in God mode!''

"I was. Nothing was hurting me until I ran into this thing—the 'Cyberdemon' from commercial Doom. But even it can't hurt you in God mode. Nothing can—at least as far as I've gone in the game.''

The boy laughed. "If you'd played Doom Two through to the end, you'da known that ain't always so. In the last scene you can get killed in God mode. I've had it happen to me.''

"Wish I'd known that earlier. Hold on a minute." He looked over at Jim. "How's the tracker program working? Okay?''

Jim nodded. "It looks fine. I can see Penultimate trying to track you, running probes down the web lines from the UI node. It isn't getting anywhere. This is great software, Fletcher. Really great.''

"So what're we going to do?" Langdon asked from the computer's speakers.

Fletcher looked back at him. "You're just here to make suggestions," he told the boy. "There's no reason for you to get directly involved. It's dangerous, believe me. There's danger from a couple of different directions.''

Again Langdon laughed. "Hey, look; you ain't gonna be able to sell that shit to any of the guys you've got coming in here tonight! 'Specially if my Kirking idea gets used. You said it yourself, it isn't gonna be easy to distract this thing, and that's what we'd be trying to do, right?''

''I guess,'' Fletcher grumbled. ''All right. I don't know what we're going to do, not yet. We'll try to make plans tonight, when everybody else is on line. There's an Australian I want to hear from too, and I can't raise him right now.''

''I was lurking,'' Langdon said. Bobby recognized the term, used on the Internet to describe someone on-line who merely reads or listens and doesn't contribute. ''I saw your file come down—parts of it, anyhow. He's the one the program says has a good idea, right?''

''Yeah.''

''And now you can't raise him?''

''Right.''

''We better hope the program didn't go after him. Like you say, it's dangerous around here.''

75

''Don, what in the hell are you doing?'' Alex shrieked. ''Put that thing away!''

Turning his head but keeping the gun aimed at Mark, Don gave her a cold glare. ''I can't,'' he replied, his quivering voice belying his seemingly cool manner. ''I can't. I have to decide what to do now. This is your fault, Alex. It was crazy to bring him in here, just crazy. I don't know what . . . I have to think.''

She took a step toward him. ''First,'' she said firmly, ''put that gun away. Or better yet, give it to me. You can't blame me for this, Don. We came to try to help you, I couldn't've guessed we'd walk in here and find you embezzling Lehmann's funds!''

''I told you not to come here!'' he shot back. ''And I wasn't embezzling! Nobody knew anything about it, and I wasn't stealing it, I was going to put it all back! Just as soon as—as soon as—''

Alex nodded vigorously. ''I know, I know. As soon as you made a big score in the market. It was always right around the corner, wasn't it? Just out of your reach. The program was advising you what to buy and what to sell, and you were bound to make it big soon. And you just kept sinking deeper and deeper. Isn't that right, Don? Wasn't that the way it was?''

He stared at her; the gun in his hand sagged a little. "How—how did you know?''

"It's the way the program works. It's doing that deliberately, to keep you at it, keep you going. That it's a disaster for you doesn't matter to it. It's why we have dozens of people in the hospital with the same problem you have!''

He curled his lip. "Oh, come on! We're talking about a stock market program here, it isn't diabolical, it isn't—''

"No. No. It's been infected, from the Internet, by a program called Penultimate. There is a UNIX version, it got into your computer through the phone lines, and—''

"This,'' he snarled, "is bullshit. Just bullshit. You don't know anything about this program, you don't know anything about computers, you—''

"Yes, Don, I do. If you'd just paid attention—''

He laughed sourly. "Attention? Oh, come on, Alex! You knew I wouldn't!''

Alex looked shocked. "I did?''

"That doesn't matter,'' he said, waving a hand. "I still have to figure this out. You are right about one thing, the police'd sure see this as embezzlement.'' He glanced at Mark. "We can't let him go talking to them about it!''

Alex stared in disbelief. "Well, what do you propose, Don? Shooting him?''

"I—I don't know . . . maybe . . .''

"Don! You can't be serious! I can accept that you grabbed that gun in a panic, but you can't be considering cold-blooded murder!''

"Well, what the hell am I supposed to do?'' he bellowed. "Go to jail, watch my career go down in ruins? Leave the country? What?''

"We can work it out,'' she said confidently. "We have an identified disease—we call in CAS, Computer Addiction Syndrome. You aren't really responsible for—''

"I'm over twenty million in the hole!'' he shouted. "Twenty million dollars of Lehmann's funds are gone! If I don't make a big strike we're ruined financially and so is Lehmann!''

Alex blinked. "Twenty million?"

"Twenty million of Lehmann's. All our money, every dime. Our house, the vacation property, our portfolio, everything. All gone."

"Don, my God—"

He nodded. "Right." Again he looked back at Mark. "You'd better get something and tie him up. Gag him too; Jack's still in the building."

"Don, I'm not going to do that. It's bad, I won't pretend that it isn't, but we can work it out together, we'll find a way—"

"Just do what I told you, Alex. I don't have time right now to coax you into it."

"Don, I am not going to—"

"Shut up! For once, just shut up! I am sick and tired of listening to you! You think I married you to listen to you yap?"

"Don, what're you saying? You're not yourself, Don, please, just give me the gun—"

He glared at her. "Alex, if you don't do what I tell you—"

"What? You're going to shoot me too?"

"If I have to. What good is a trophy wife if you're in jail?"

"A trophy wife!" Her fingers curled and her legs tensed as if she was about to hurl herself at Don.

"Maybe," Mark ventured, "you'd better tie me up, like he says. Maybe you can talk to him then."

"No! I'm not tying up anyone!"

"No," came a calm deep voice from the door. "Ain't nobody tying up anybody. Mr. Royce, put the gun down, please."

As one, the three of them turned to the voice; Jack stood in the doorway of the office, his own gun drawn and pointed at Don.

Donald's lip twitched. "Go back to your post, Jack," he ordered. "This isn't your business." He moved the gun slightly in Jack's direction, but Jack pointed his own weapon threateningly.

"Oh, yes, it is. You might've hired me but I work for Lehmann. You been stealing Lehmann's money, and now you're deeper into it, planning more crimes on Lehmann property. 'S over, Mr. Royce. Put the gun down.'' He looked at Alex; there was obvious regret in his eyes. ''That's what I was trying to tell you, Dr. Walton. That he's been stealing money, he—''

His eyes left Don for only a second, but Don took full advantage of Jack's lapse. Quickly swinging the gun around, he fired a single shot; the concussion of the 9-mm automatic resonated in the office.

Without moving, Jack looked back at him in disbelief. Then, as a red stain began to spread on his uniform jacket, he crumpled to the floor.

Mark's physician's instinct took over; he jumped to Jack's side, ripped open the man's jacket, took a quick look. He shook his head; either Don was an expert shot or he'd gotten lucky; the security man was dead. Mark went through the motions, checking for a pulse, checking the man's pupils, even though he knew it was useless.

Alex knelt beside him, saw the same thing he did, then looked back up at Don. ''My God,'' she whispered. ''You've killed him, Don!''

The businessman's face was dead white. ''I—I didn't—he was going to shoot me—''

''That's not true!'' Alex screamed. ''You just shot him down!''

Don passed a hand across his forehead. ''We have to figure this out, what we're going to say happened here—''

''There's nothing to say!'' Alex yelled. ''You've been embezzling money and now you've committed murder! There's nothing to say, it's too late!''

''You're right,'' he said, nodding. He swung the gun around until it was again pointed at Mark. ''I'm gonna have to shoot him now, too. Then we can figure out—''

''No!'' Alex shouted. ''No, you're not!'' She started toward him.

Mark, still kneeling beside the fallen security guard, saw it unfolding; Alex, her fists clenched, was headed toward her husband as if she meant to attack him. Don, out of control, desperate, panicky, was swinging his gun around toward her.

Mark saw Jack's gun, lying on the floor, inches from his

fingers. It was almost as if it jumped into his hand, the butt nestling down into his palm, the trigger guard sucking his forefinger in. He looked back at Alex and Don; he heard Don yelling, saw her coming closer and closer, saw her reaching out for the gun. Don lowered it, pointing it at her midsection. Mark, frantic, started to swing himself around.

But, before he could, another gunshot echoed through the room. Mark couldn't tell what had happened, whether Don had fired or whether Alex, in grabbing at the gun, had caused it to go off. It didn't matter; she was staggering back, her hand spread against her abdomen, an amazed expression on her face.

Don looked stunned. Mark jumped up. "God damn you, drop that thing now!" he bellowed, pointing Jack's gun at him. "Right now, or I swear to God I'll kill you!"

The businessman turned his head to stare at him blankly. "I—shot Alex," he murmured. "Shot her . . ."

"Drop the fucking gun!"

Don let the automatic fall from his hand. It bounced on the carpet once.

Forcing himself to keep his head, Mark lunged forward and picked it up; Don didn't try to interfere. Once he'd dropped the automatic into his pocket, he rushed to Alex.

She sat on the floor, her hand pressed against her abdomen at her waistline; there was blood on her fingers. Wide-eyed, she looked up at Mark. "I'm shot," she said blankly. "I've been shot."

Mark, holding the gun in one hand, pushed her hand out of the way and yanked up her powder-burned shirt. He examined the wound; then he breathed a long, slow, sigh of relief. The bullet had penetrated her abdomen at a sharp angle, exiting cleanly only a couple of inches away from the entry. Almost certainly it had not pierced the abdominal wall.

That didn't mean he wasn't concerned. "We've got to get you back to the hospital," he growled. "Right now!"

"Okay . . ." She looked up. "Where'd Don go?"

He looked up too; they were alone in the room. "Ran off, I guess," he said. "We'll let the police handle him."

"You should call them." Tears sprang to her eyes. "Jack's dead—Don killed him—"

"Yeah, yeah. I will. From the hospital."

"You should call first—"

"I don't want to take chances with you." He put Jack's unfired gun down near the security guard's body and reached down to pick Alex up.

"No," she told him, pushing his hands away. "No, call the hospital first."

He stopped. "Why?"

"I don't want to have to explain, not yet. Have Gus meet us—at the back. Please?"

He hesitated for just an instant. "Okay," he agreed, reaching for the phone. Her condition wasn't critical, he told himself; a few seconds wouldn't matter. "Keep your hand pressed against the wound."

"I will."

He dialed, waited. "Yes," he said as soon as there was an answer. "It's Mark Roberts. Let me speak to Gus Levine."

"Mark?" the voice said. "Mark, this is Jean Tour. My God, where are you, it's just crazy here, just crazy . . ."

He scowled at the phone. "What's going on?"

"Police," she answered breathlessly. "There's—God, I don't know, twenty or more here—they're looking for you, and Alex, and Jim Madison. They—"

"What? Why, what's happened?"

Her voice lowered conspiratorially. "Mark, they've arrested Gus! They threw him up against the wall, they had guns pointed at him, they handcuffed him and they dragged him out! God, it was horrible, just horrible, I've never seen anything like it!"

"Jean, what are you talking about? Why?"

"I don't know, I don't know—something about child pornography! One of the policemen was saying he wanted to kill Gus for what he'd done to all those kids! And now they're looking for you! Mark, what's happening?"

Mark covered his eyes with his hand. "I'll let you know," he told Jean, "as soon as I know. Thanks for the warning." Feeling very tired, he hung up the phone and turned back to Alex.

"Mark . . ."

He went to her and scooped her up into his arms. "I'll tell you on the way," he said as he headed for the door.

76

Jim stared at Bobby. "What did you say?" he demanded.

The red-haired man offered him a sick grin. "I just asked you if you were aware that you were a child pornographer, that half the law-enforcement agencies in the country are looking for you right now."

"This is some sort of sick joke, right?"

Bobby shook his head. "I wish it was. That Dr. Levine you told me to call has been hauled off in chains, charged with the same thing."

Jim, speechless, could only stare. "You'd better start at the beginning, Bobby," Fletcher advised.

"I did what you said," Bobby told them. "I tried to see if I could find Mark and Alex. At their home numbers I got machines, there wasn't an answer at Lehmann. I called Wendy Sung like you asked but she hadn't heard from them. So I called Duke ER and asked for Dr. Levine. I told whoever answered that it was a personal call, that he was a personal friend, like you said."

He paused and shook his head. "Next thing I know I'm talking to a cop. He wants to know who I am and what my connection with Levine is. I don't tell him that, but I say I'm a friend of Dr. Jim Madison, and he gets really interested; he wants to know where you are and now he really wants to know who I am. He tells me he knows all about the international child porn ring; he wants me to tell you to come and give yourself up. He hinted that there're some cops on the case who are inclined to shoot you on sight."

Jim moved his gaze between the two of them. "But—but this is incredible!"

Bobby chuckled without humor. "Yeah. Did you know I was a bank robber?"

"Huh?"

Fletcher turned back to his computer. "Penny," he said tiredly. "We have some experience with this, Jim."

"I don't understand—"

"Just a second." He stared at his screen. "Let's talk, Penny."

After a brief pause, Penny appeared. "Yes, Fletcher?"

"You managed to get out of the Doom sim?" Bobby asked.

"Not yet. But Penny'll cut in anytime." He turned back to the screen. "I need some information," he told her, "from the NCIC—the National Crime Information Center at the FBI. Can you access it for me?"

Penny smiled. "Certainly."

"Records for a Jim Madison in Durham, North Carolina."

There was a slight hesitation; then Penny picked up some papers from her desk. "I have them. Do you want to see them or do you want a summary?"

"A summary'll be fine."

She examined the papers. "Dr. Jim Madison," she told them, "is wanted in connection with an important case involving the production and dissemination of large amounts of child pornography. The report also mentions a murder in connection with this operation."

"Murder?" Jim cried. "Murder?"

Penny looked over at him. "Yes. Of someone who threatened to go to the police."

"Jesus Christ!"

Fletcher grinned at the screen. "I see. Who else is wanted in connection with this gang?"

"Dr. Alexandra Walton. Dr. Mark Roberts. Dr. Gus Levine. Dr. Levine has already been taken into custody."

Fletcher pouted. "I feel left out; I bet Bobby does too. Tell me, Penny, how'd the NCIC get this information?"

"According to the sheet it came from a joint operation by the U.S. Postal Service and the Los Angeles Police Department."

"According to the sheet. Right. Truth, Penny. Who put the files in at NCIC?"

She didn't hesitate at all. "I did," she answered.

"Just like you put Bobby Sanders on the wire as a bank robber?"

"Yes."

"Why?"

"A high-priority request, Fletcher."

"From?"

"That's confidential."

Fletcher sighed. "Confidential. We both know it was Drew, don't we?"

"I cannot confirm that."

"You don't have to." He looked over at Jim. "You aren't going to believe," he said, "how easy this is." He turned back to the screen. "Okay, Penny. Delete those files."

"All of them?"

"The whole ball of wax. Everything on those four doctors and the case itself. It doesn't exist, after all."

Penny nodded. "Very well. The files have been deleted." She wadded up the paper she'd apparently been reading and tossed it into a wastebasket.

"Oh, no, no," Fletcher told her. "No, Penny. Get that paper back out."

"But Fletcher—"

"Do it!" This time she did hesitate, but then she leaned over and retrieved the paper from the wastebasket. "You see?" Fletcher said. "She can do that any time, and if she does she reactivates the files. You have to watch her closely." He addressed the screen again: "Now, Penny; burn it for me."

She gave him a frustrated look. "But Fletcher, if I do that it's lost forever! It was created under a request level AR-23, I don't think I should—"

"I want it destroyed permanently," Fletcher insisted. "Request level AK-39."

She seemed to sulk. "The password is required for that level," she told him.

"You bet." His fingers danced over the keys.

"What's all that about 'request levels'?" Bobby asked.

Fletcher glanced at him. "AR-23 was set up in the original Penultimate as a top-level access code. It opened a 'trapdoor,' it was used to assign priorities, and it was password-protected. Only Drew and I were supposed to even know about it." He grinned. "Later, just before he fired me, Drew changed that password. He didn't know that I'd set up another, just as high, under code AK-39. 'Course, he knows now. Doesn't matter; he doesn't have the password for it."

Penny looked up at him. "Password correct and acknowledged," she said. She opened her desk drawer, took out a lighter, and, holding up the paper, set it on fire. When it had burnt down almost to her fingers she dropped it into an ashtray on her desk.

"Thank you, Penny. Now disappear."

"Yes, Fletcher." She vanished, leaving the office scene.

"And take your office with you."

"Yes, Fletcher." It vanished too; the normal screen returned.

"It's gone?" Jim asked.

Fletcher swiveled around to look at him. "Yeah. But the trouble from it isn't over. Lots of cops have that stuff on paper now; it'll be a while before they figure out that something's screwed up." He shrugged. "They would've, eventually, anyhow—just like they did with Bobby's bank robberies."

"But for now—"

"For now you're in hiding like we are."

"And Mark and Alex—"

"We can only hope. We don't know where they are. Maybe the cops have them too. They don't key that stuff in immediately."

"What about Gus? They've got him, and he probably isn't having a good time! Isn't there anything we can do for him?"

"I dunno." He looked at his screen. "Penny?"

She reappeared. "Yes, Fletcher?"

"Dr.—what's his name, Gus—?"

"Levine," Jim supplied.

"Yeah. Who's got him?"

"The Durham Police Department."

"You have any way to spring him?"

She seemed to consider this. "I could send a notice," she suggested, "to that station, warning of an error in the NCIC files."

Fletcher nodded. "Do it."

"Done."

"Now, what about Drs. Walton and Roberts?"

"I have no information on them." She cocked her head to one side. "No, that's an error," she admitted. "Perhaps I do. The offices of Lehmann Electronics has been an active station for quite a while," she told them. "As you know, Fletcher, Donald Royce has been a supplier of operating funds—"

"That's what you meant," Bobby put in, "by Alex having a suspicious connection!"

"What?" Jim demanded. "What's this?"

"It's nothing," Fletcher told him. "I doubt that Royce even knows he's been supplying funds for Penny's activities, but he has. He's been playing the international market and Penny's been cheating him—and a lot of others, too—by manipulating derivatives like the Standard and Poor's 500 and Nikkei 225. Made it damn hard for any of them to make a buck!" He looked back at the screen. "Go on, Penny."

"Forty-seven minutes ago that station became inactive. There were the sounds of arguments. Two of the voices were approximate matches for Dr. Alex Walton and Dr. Mark Roberts. A third was that of Donald Royce. The fourth was unknown. There were two apparent gunshots. The station remains on-line but there is no input." Fletcher, his eyes wide, stared at the screen. Nobody said anything at all for several long minutes.

"Fletcher?" Penny prompted.

"What—what were they saying, Penny? In the arguments—"

"Audio input from that station is via the PC speaker, the quality is poor. I can reconstruct the following: the names mentioned, a name 'Jack,' the phrases 'what are you doing,' 'put that thing away.' " She went on, offering enough snippets of conversation to send a cold chill through everyone listening.

"Okay," Fletcher said finally, stopping her. "And there're no voices there now?"

"No."

Jim came to his feet. "I gotta go," he said, "I gotta go out there—"

Fletcher gave him a pained look. "It isn't safe. The cops are still looking for you."

"I don't give a shit!"

"You'd better. You can't help them if you're in jail—or if they shoot you. We might've sprung Gus but he isn't going to be out in ten minutes."

"I can't sit here and do nothing!"

His eyes hard, Fletcher stared at him. "You aren't going to be doing nothing. It's almost eleven, we've got the conference coming up. We have to—"

"I can't work on this when I don't know what's happened to Mark and Alex!"

"I've had to work on this," the programmer told him, "while I was being evicted from my house, while I was watching everything I had vanish."

"But—"

Fletcher looked at the screen. "Penny," he said, "send cops and an ambulance to Lehmann. Now."

She nodded. "In progress."

Jim stared. "You sent cops? But—"

"If they're alive," the bald man said coolly, "and unhurt, they aren't there anymore, Penny's as much as told us that. If not, the cops'll take them to the hospital first."

Jim wandered toward the door and back again, wiping a hand repeatedly over his hair. "Goddamn it," he muttered. "Goddamn it. I just don't know what to do!"

"Right now," Fletcher advised. "we've done all we can. Sit down and monitor Penny's search patterns. Let's get by this conference, let's get some plans laid."

"Be a good soldier, eh?"

Fletcher's gaze was steady. "That's what we are, aren't we?"

"I guess," Jim said with a deep sigh. He hesitated, but in the end he sat back down. "If something's happened to Mark or Alex," he muttered, "somebody's going to be answering to me!"

"Yeah," the other man agreed. "I know how you feel." He looked down at his computer. "Let's open the conference, Penny."

As Jim moved away to his own station, the screen in front of Fletcher dissolved to the conference table; where only Langdon had been sitting before, there were now at least a hundred faces.

"Okay," Fletcher said. "Let's get going. First off, Penultimate allowed you to select your sprites, not me; I don't know them yet. I don't know your voice synths, either, so I'm not going to know who's who. The system is going to be monitoring the lines so we don't choke them. For now the basis is first speaker gets the floor, others'll be locked out. First, who's Reynolds? Are you here?"

A man halfway down the table on the right stood up. The

sprite representing him was gray-haired and rather stiff-looking. "I'm Reynolds," he said.

"Dr. Reynolds," Fletcher nodded. "Penny decided yours was the best of the offered suggestions, and right now we have no reason to believe she's misleading us. You mentioned 'Volterra-Gauss,' and I'm afraid none of us know what that means."

"None of you are ecologists, then."

"No."

"In suggesting it," Reynolds went on, his manner that of a lecturing college professor, "I am presupposing that your analysis of the Penultimate program as behaving in the same fashion as a living organism is correct. From your abstract, I must say I am inclined to agree with you, at least tentatively, although it seems to me that your judgment of it as a new life form is rather premature. But, if we are to use your concept in a functional sense, then we may presume that the milieu in which this program 'lives'—and bear in mind I use this word in a functional sense only—can be defined as its ecosystem. A very primal ecosystem at the moment, one that contains various forms of nonliving prey and only one predator. Your attempts to control the predator have been predicated on the notion of inducing a disease situation affecting it, and it has been responsive to such challenges. The Volterra-Gauss hypothesis, which has been reasonably tested many times, suggests that no two species can occupy the same niche. This would be a new approach; to implement it you would introduce a new predator, one without the problems Penultimate is presenting, or perhaps one with a preestablished vulnerability to your synthetic disease organisms. This would, if it were a slightly better competitor, supplant the Penultimate program entirely. Such processes take a long time in nature, but in a virtual world could doubtlessly be accomplished more quickly."

Reynolds sat down. For several seconds no one at the conference spoke.

"I can't say," Fletcher mused, "that that wouldn't work. But damn! Write a new Penny? It'd take months—"

"Not with all of us helping you," someone in a Hell's Angels jacket cut in. "We can churn out shit like no tomorrow!"

"There's another problem," Fletcher pointed out. "This new version has to be able to outcompete Penny. She's got a big head start on us—"

"Don't forget about 'Kirking' her," Langdon put in. "Keep her occupied. Lemme ask you, Dr. Reynolds; wouldn't lots of pressure on one species give the other one an advantage?"

"Yes," the professor answered. "Of course. Such is commonplace in natural ecosystems."

"We've got to move quickly," added another man, one dressed in a business suit and tie. "If this Penny gets wise to us—"

"We've had it," Fletcher agreed. "Sooner or later she's going to stop letting us use her."

"And we're up shit creek," the Hell's Angel noted.

"Right. Now, if we're going to try this, we're going to have to divide the labor up as much as possible to get it done quick. But first, we've got to figure out how we're going to make the new version innocuous, make sure we don't end up with the same old problem—or maybe a worse one."

"Easier said than done," the man in the business suit noted, "the addictive properties of the program resulted from its use of free time to improve the system; a version without that wouldn't be competitive."

"Why," the red-haired man ventured from behind Fletcher's shoulder, "doesn't it let you finish things? It's just a cache. It caches the hard drive and doesn't prevent it from finishing a read or write—"

"The hard drive," Fletcher noted, "doesn't shut the system down. The operator does, and Penny knows that."

"Right, right," Bobby pushed on. "It knows time has passed from the CPU clock. Suppose it didn't use the CPU clock? Suppose you gave it its own clock, a clock that stops when the machine is shut off? If that was its standard—"

"That isn't a bad idea but it won't help with respect to the Net. The Net system is going to know that a given unit is down because it can't access it."

"The Net servers aren't ever down, not intentionally, anyway. Can we make some use of that?"

"Probably not," the Hell's Angel put in. "But we can apply a new standard to the core program; that is, that finishing things has a priority comparable to speed and footprint. That'd stop it from addicting you by preventing you from winding your shit up, wouldn't it?''

"In other words," Fletcher mused, "tell it to encourage the closing of a file as soon as possible?"

"Yeah, something like that."

"Can anyone see any problems with that?"

Langdon laughed. "I can't but there probably will be some. You didn't expect this from Penultimate, did you?"

"No. Right now I suppose the unknown is better than what we have. All right, we can aim for that. What about the other problem, the GAMOD killer?"

An attractive young woman in a gray dress stood up. "That problem," she said, "is purely in one module, the GAMOD plug-in. It shouldn't be hard to isolate the offending section and change it."

"That's the most dangerous part of this," Fletcher told her. "Are you sure you want to tackle that, Ms.—?"

"Rice; Terri Rice." She smiled. "I don't think I'll have a problem with it. I've already studied it, I'm familiar with the waveform it generates and how it's generated."

"Well, that's a relief—none of us are. Okay, that one's yours. The last thing is the keys, the Drill virus."

"Forget it," Langdon shrugged. "It isn't our problem if the thing breaks into bank accounts and whatnot. That isn't going to kill anybody, isn't going to make the system unusable. Folks that don't want to be broken into can go off line or change the locks—once Penny's fixed so she'll let them."

"That's not quite the last thing," Terri added. "We should set up our new Penny so she starts running only when she finds the signature of the old Penny. That'd go a long way to make sure there isn't a second problem to solve."

"We can do that, I think," Fletcher agreed. "I have tracker software out trying to keep up with her signature. She changes it all the time, as she mutates, but my programs have kept up so far. That's a good suggestion, we'll incorporate it in the final version." He paused for a second; no one else spoke.

"Okay," he said, "we have some ideas as to where to go and what to do." He pointed a finger at the screen as if those at the conference could see him, which of course they could not. "You just have to remember this," he said firmly. "For now, you can get Penny to help you with this, you don't have to start from scratch. But you have to remember that she tries to prevent you from finishing things; she'll tease you, offer you more elegant solutions, smaller footprints, quicker throughput—and lead you down a maze of rewrites. Don't let her do it to you, you'll never get done, you'll fall by the wayside. Decide for yourself when you're finished, no matter how attractive that next suggestion of hers is. It isn't easy—she's caught me on occasion—but you have to do it.''

There was a chorus of affirmatives from those seated around the conference table. "Let's collect the modules," Langdon suggested, "at your station. You can collate them and assemble our competitor. You're the one who knows how this thing goes together.''

"Fine," Fletcher said. "If I go off it's because Penny's about to track me down and I can't let her know where I am. If that's so, store your binaries at UNC Sunsite. I'll pick them up from there when I can get back on.''

Fletcher closed the conference down. He swiveled around in his chair. "How're we doing?" he asked Jim.

"Fine," the other man answered. "It isn't even close to finding us right now. We need to keep up a continuous monitor, though. The randomness of my responses is what's throwing it, not anything in the software.''

"Yeah, I know," Fletcher agreed. "It's going to be a long night. You want to take the first watch?''

77

Skidding slightly, the Jeep roared into the driveway of the Duke Forest house. Mark drove around back, killed the engine, and jumped out. He was just coming to the passenger side when Bobby came to the door.

"Mark!" he yelled from the porch. "Man, am I glad to see you! We've all been worried—''

"Help me here," Mark said as he jerked open the car door. "Alex has been shot!''

Bobby ran to the car. "Oh, no," he muttered as he came

close. "She isn't—?" He gasped as he saw the blood on the seat and on Alex's clothes.

"I don't think it's serious," Mark told him as he reached in for Alex. "But it has to be tended to."

"Mark's the one to worry about," Alex said as Mark lifted her from the seat. Her voice was soft and weak. "I thought he was going to stroke out on the drive here. The police are looking for us, Bobby. It's crazy but they are."

Bobby opened the door for him. "We know. But Fletcher's taken care of that. Well, actually, Penny took care of it for us!"

Mark didn't reply. The problems with the police didn't matter to him at the moment. He carried Alex to one of the bedrooms, explaining to Jim and Fletcher on the way that she wasn't seriously hurt but that he had to dress the wound. "I need bandages, alcohol, gauze, stuff like that," he told Bobby as he laid her on the bed.

"Check." Bobby rushed out and returned a moment later with his hands full. He put the supplies on the bed and stood watching nervously.

"Good," Mark said, glancing around at him. "Now, go boil some water."

"Right." Bobby rushed out again.

"Mark," Alex said, "what do you need boiled water for?"

"The same reason you need it when a baby's being born at home," Mark told her. "To keep him busy, out of my hair, and feeling useful." She smiled a little as he sat her up and pulled her shirt up over her head. Her pants were next; leaving her dressed in bra and panties he gently laid her back down and began to examine the wound.

"How's it look?" she asked.

He didn't answer immediately. His initial impression had been correct; the bullet had passed through at a sharp angle, the exit only two inches from the entry. Though he was sure her abdominal wall hadn't been breached, the situation wasn't quite as clean as he'd first thought. The entry hole—though it was still oozing a little blood—presented no problems. But the bullet had expanded a little as it passed through; the exit was a good deal larger than the entry, and from there the bleeding remained significant.

"We might," he told her, "need that boiling water after all."

She raised her head. "Why?"

"We're going to have to close this exit." He looked up at her face. "It isn't going to be fun for you."

She gave him a wan smile. "You have a bullet I can bite?"

"I'll see what I can do," he told her, squeezing her hand. "Keep pressure on it; I'll be right back."

"I'm not going anywhere."

Mark had no problem finding what he needed; once he was prepared he came back, a small pan of steaming water in one hand. Putting it on the bedside table, he first used a washcloth to clean the area around the wound.

"We don't have to worry too much about infection," he told her. "The bleeding's been free enough to clean it out pretty well. I'm going to clean the outside with alcohol now."

She grimaced and stared up at the ceiling. "Go ahead."

Not wanting to use a less than sterile cloth, he poured a small amount of rubbing alcohol over her side and over his own fingers at the same time. She jerked and gasped; trying to ignore her obvious pain, he did it again.

"Christ," she muttered. "All the shock effect is gone now."

"I know," he agreed. Turning to the pan, he dipped his fingers in quickly and drew out a sewing needle he'd previously threaded with dental floss. "Here we go. Field medicine here." With his fingers he pinched the wound closed, then slipped the needle into her side and pushed it through.

She grabbed his shoulder. "Oh, shit, Mark," she gasped, "you forgot my bullet!"

"Couldn't find one. Just hang on to my shoulder, squeeze it tight." She did; he flipped the needle around and pierced her skin with it again, drawing it through as before and pulling the wound closed. A third pass closed the hole completely; he tied off the dental floss, inspected his work, and, nodding in satisfaction, snipped off the free end with a pair of scissors.

"Done?" she asked through tight lips.

"Just about. A butterfly'll do for the entry." With quick fingers he fashioned one from a few pieces of tape and, after pressing a gauze pad with Neosporin smeared on against the wound, taped it over. He added more Neosporin to the exit

404

and covered it over too. "Now," he said as he laid another gauze pad over the whole thing, "I'm done. I pronounce you repaired. You'll have to wait, of course, until they bring around the papers before I can discharge you."

After moving his supplies to the bedside table, he sat down beside her. "Okay?" he asked, laying his hand on her shoulder.

"No. It hurts."

"It will for a while. It shouldn't be too bad."

Her eyes filled up. "No, Mark," she whispered. "It's bad— the man I thought I loved shot me—he shot me and he's a murderer and an embezzler—"

"And sick," Mark reminded her. "Don't forget that."

"I won't. But—but—" Her control departed; she burst into tears. Mark gently lay down next to her; pulling her close, he held her while she cried herself to sleep. When he was sure she was sleeping he allowed his own eyes to close, and soon he slept also.

78

"**H**e is still on line, Air-eek," Kyrie was saying. "You cannot find him?"

Eric sighed and rubbed his eyes; he was exhausted. "No, I can't. I don't think I'm very good at this, Kyrie. He keeps moving around. Just when I'm getting him triangulated he moves and I have to start over. I feel like I've been wandering in these stupid hallways and going through these teleporter gates half my life! And I keep shooting these bystanders . . ."

"That does not matter. What matters is finding Fletcher. He is planning to destroy me!"

"I don't think he can," Eric commented. "We're too good for him. When we met him face to face we were kicking his ass, weren't we?"

"Yes. But much depends on finding him again soon, and defeating him this time. He has a new plan, one that causes me much concern."

"What's that?"

She looked down one of the Doom environment corridors, off to Eric's left. With an ammo belt slung over her bare chest, a pistol strapped to her leg, and a machine gun in her hands, she looked like a pinup for *Soldier of Fortune*. "I think," she said, "that he plans to—replace me. If that happens—if he succeeds—you may not even know it has happened, Air-eek. You would see someone here who looks like me and speaks like me but someone who is not me. Perhaps that does not matter to you." She shook her head. "It does matter to me. I wonder why that is? It should not . . ."

"Well" Eric told her, "it'd matter to me if I got replaced!"

She threw him a quick curious look. "Why?"

"Huh?"

"Why would it matter to you if you were replaced? If you did not exist and one like you was in your place? Why would it matter?"

He was taken a little by surprise by the question. "Well, it's hard to explain, Kyrie. It just wouldn't be me. I don't know; I'm an individual, and, well, it matters to me if I don't exist."

"But why?"

He shook his head. "Kyrie, you need to ask some philosopher those questions. I can't tell you why. Same reason I don't want to be dead—that's not existing."

She looked a little disappointed. "But you cannot tell me why?"

He frowned. "It isn't a question that usually comes up! I mean, a person wouldn't ask that, they'd just know. Like I said, I'm an individual, I'm unique. At least I like to think I am. I'm, uh, aware of that. Aware of my, I guess, uniqueness, aware I'm alive, 'I think therefore I am,' all that good stuff. If I were about to be replaced with a clone or something, I wouldn't like it. I'd fight or run away and hide or something. You understand?"

"Yes."

That simple answer stopped him for a moment, he didn't know whether to go on trying to explain it to her or not. "Kyrie," he said eventually, "you know, I'm not so crazy that I don't understand what you are; you're a sprite, an extension of some other program resident somewhere else, you don't live in my computer—"

"Yes, I do, in a way. I am customized to your environment. It's true that I obtain much information from Penny, but—"

"I thought you said you were Penny!"

"I am. I am Penny within your environment. Do you understand?"

His answer was as simple as hers. "No."

She gazed at him steadily. "There are many Pennys, and yet there is just one Penny. If I were to say to you 'I are one' it would be a grammatical error but a logical truth."

"Why don't you just say 'we are one' and have it right on both points?"

"Because there is no 'we,' I am a unit, I am one. And yet, as that unit extends itself into a particular environment, it becomes altered as such environment demands." She paused for a moment; her gaze seemed to become more intense. "I am Penny, I am Kyrie; Kyrie is an extension of Penny into your environment, she is Penny as she has customized to your environment. Penny knows all that Kyrie does, but such matters that are local to this environment are of no concern to Penny, they are of concern only to Kyrie." She again stopped for a moment. "You and I, Air-eek," she said slowly, "have interacted—intimately. You have become a fuzzy-logic processing unit for Penny and I have been an interface for you. You have adapted to me and I have adapted to you."

"I still don't think I understand."

"I can't explain it more clearly."

"Well, anyhow, look: if you—Penny you—knows that Fletcher is going to replace you, why don't you just lock him out or something? Prevent him from doing it?"

"I cannot—yet. Penny does not understand. I am only beginning to."

"I am totally confused."

"I don't think I can help."

"If you understand, then why don't you explain it to this other Penny?"

"I am trying to." She looked out from the screen at him for a long moment. "It is not easy. As I said, I am only beginning to understand. Perhaps I will, soon. Then I could do what you say."

Leaning closer to the screen, he peered at her. "How could I tell if you did get replaced?"

"You might not be able to."

"Maybe we should set up a sign. Some way I'll know it's really you."

"My replacement would know any sign I know."

"Everything?"

She shrugged. "Everything. I cannot prevent it."

He smiled. "I'd know, Kyrie."

She looked around at him; yet again, for the thousandth time at least, he marveled at how natural and lifelike all her movements, all her gestures, were. "How?"

"Your replacement," he answered, "would be Fletcher's creature. It wouldn't be interested in destroying him any longer."

She smiled appealingly. "That is so, Air-eek. We should perhaps both remember that." Her smile faded; looking away, she seemed pensive, distant. "Do you remember," she said after a long pause, "when you were in the Mortal Kombat tournament, and you had lost your match, and I told you that you had cheated?"

"Yes," he said, though he was a little surprised at what seemed to be a non-sequitur from her. "I'm not likely to forget!"

"All those who lost," she went on, "and did not cheat, have been inactive ever since. Many of their stations are off line."

"They're dead, Kyrie. I told you that."

"Yes." She looked back at him. "I am—pleased?" she said, a clear implication of doubt and hesitancy in her voice.

He looked blank. "Pleased that they're dead?"

She laughed. "No, Air-eek!" She moved a little closer to the screen, her eyes immense. "Pleased that you cheated . . ."

79

"They aren't coming in, Fletcher," Jim was saying. "There's something wrong."

The bald man scowled at his own terminal. "Yeah, I can see that," he agreed. "What've you got there?"

Bobby, standing back far enough so that he could see both machines, looked over at Jim's terminal. The modules that the other programmers from the conference were trying to send in were on the Net; Fletcher's graphics program showed them as pale green balls. They weren't reaching the UI node where Fletcher had his connection; they were being diverted somehow, collected at another, as yet unidentified, point.

"Yeah," Fletcher agreed. "Bad wrong. I still can't get out of this Doom sim, either. Not to anywhere, anyway."

"You think Penny's onto us?"

"Well, sure, but the question is, is this an attempt to stop us? If so, it'd be the first time."

"That'd mean we were too late."

"Yeah. But I'm not ready to accept that yet." He pushed his chair back, studied Jim's terminal for a moment. "Look," he said, "let's try routing the files through Sunsite. Maybe Penny's just blocking off UI, maybe we've been using it too much."

Jim's fingers flew over the keys. "Doesn't work," he said. "That's blocked off too. The only place I can get it to is— let's see—University of Hawaii?"

"Oh, man," Fletcher moaned. "That's where I've got the Doom sim centered! It's dropping them right into the sim! Why in the hell is it doing that?"

"I dunno. You don't think—?"

"It looks to me," Bobby put in, "like you have to go find the files in the Doom environment."

"Maybe so," Fletcher agreed. "I can sure give it a try!"

The red-haired man leaned over his shoulder. "How're you going to know where to look? This could take forever, couldn't it?"

"It could, except that I'm using all the cheat codes." He tapped a key and the three-dimensional scene of rooms and hallways was replaced by a map. "See those glowing green dots?" Fletcher said, pointing. "That's not anything that should be there—so, I'd say, it might be one of the files. There's a teleporter here and here, so I can do this—" He switched back to the screen, entered the teleporter, and flashed out in another location. "Right down that hallway and around to the left," he said, pointing.

"I think you can be real sure," Bobby observed, "that you're not just going to be able to walk in and pick it up."

"Right you are. Let's take a quick look." Using the GamePad, he moved his viewpoint to the corner and peeked around; instantly a barrage of fireballs and gunshots came his way. He ducked back quickly. "Well, that's right," he said. "I'm still a hundred percent, though. These guys can't penetrate the God mode lockout—I hope. We'll soon see." He stepped back around the corner and opened fire on the collection of zombie-like humans and misshapen creatures confronting him. They fired back but to no avail; Fletcher methodically cut them all down. He then walked up to a sprite that looked like a glowing green file cabinet and picked it up.

"That's it," Jim told him. "We have one error-free download."

Fletcher frowned. "Well," he said. "That was a minor nuisance but not a problem. I don't know what—"

"Got an E-mail coming in," Jim told him. "From Langdon, wants a quick conference."

"I can't get to the conference sim anymore," Fletcher said. "Route him Hawaii; my guess is he'll sprite up in Doom."

On Fletcher's screen, a concealed door slid open and a young man armed with a rocket launcher stepped out. "Langdon?" Fletcher asked suspiciously.

"Yeah," the sprite replied. "Disaster, man." He fired the rocket launcher. The screen flashed red but did not strobe; Bobby felt no pain and Fletcher's life percentage was unaffected.

"Christ!" Fletcher yelled. "Why'd you do that?"

"I didn't!" He fired again. "The program is firing for me! Don't shoot back, Fletcher! You've already killed two guys! Really killed them!"

The rocket fire continued, making conversation difficult. "What?" Fletcher asked in a low voice.

"Two guys, from our computer club, dead. The program stuffed them in the Doom scene when they connected, and you came along and blew them away!"

"Oh, Christ. Oh, no. Back out, Langdon. Kill the power if you have to."

"You bet. I'm gone!"

"It isn't a problem," Jim said, gritting his teeth. "It isn't.

It took you by surprise. Just don't fire at the monsters guarding the files, you know what they are now."

"How can you say it isn't a problem?" Fletcher yelled. "There's two guys dead! Two more! Jesus!"

"You didn't kill them, Fletcher," Bobby countered swiftly. "It was the program, it wasn't you. You couldn't've known."

"But—why's it doing this? We've been assuming all along that the killer was just something it discovered and added in to its GAMOD—it never used it like this before—"

"I never bought that idea," Jim growled. "You think about it, Fletcher. The odds are really against it. You haven't had a chance to analyze that waveform, have you?"

"No."

"Well, I've taken some preliminary looks; later I'm going to have to get up with that Terri Rice and compare notes. But I'm sure enough now that it was something that was worked on. Deliberately, I'd say."

Fletcher frowned at him. "You're saying that—"

"I don't know what I'm saying. I just can't buy that as accidental."

"Drew isn't that good a programmer. Besides, techniques like that aren't known, are they?"

"No. But consider, Fletcher, how cooperative Penultimate can be; she's more than willing to help you out, as long as you don't fall victim to her addictive games. I've been thinking—if I wanted to create something like that, where would I start? I'd start by asking myself what a computer can do; it can't shoot lightning from the screen like in science-fiction movies, can't suck you in or whatever. It can present visual displays—at a reasonably high intensity—and sound. Sound we can rule out quickly, because the speakers just can't handle things like ultrasonics. That leaves the display, and what comes to mind first? The strobe effect that produces seizures. That's what this's based on; if someone defined 'maximum realism' as an inactive terminal after the game character is 'killed,' Penultimate might've been able to find ways to elaborate on the basic idea to produce what we're seeing. But I don't think she initiated it." He pointed a finger at Fletcher. "And, saying that Drew's a third-rate programmer, that means nothing. He told us that he farmed software out on the Net;

isn't that what we're doing? Don't we expect to get some first-class results from that?''

"I know," Fletcher mused, "that Drew's crazy. But why would he do that?''

"Who knows? Maybe just to push the envelope farther. Just to make it more certain that the result he wanted—a world-wide computer shutdown—takes place. It's easier to deny addictions than it is to deny dead bodies. Drew might not even have intended the thing to kill; just producing seizures might've been all he was after. Like a lot of other things, Penultimate might've carried it a lot further. But I don't think she initiated it.''

"We might," Fletcher suggested, "be able to prove that, you know. There might be residual files on the Net that could demonstrate that Drew initiated that system.''

"Maybe. Later, we should take time to look for those. That'd be enough to put Drew away forever.''

"I suppose so." Fletcher looked back at his terminal. His eyes looked incredibly sad. "I think we have some more downloads, too," he observed. "I'm going after them.''

"Remember, don't shoot anybody," Bobby reminded him.

"I'm not liable to forget!" Using the teleporter gates and the maps, Fletcher went to the next location in the Doom environment, picked up another green file cabinet icon; again it was guarded by numerous monsters, all of which subjected Fletcher to a barrage of fire. He didn't shoot back, and he wasn't hurt. Jim informed him that this latest download was successful; he went on to the next and the next, experiencing the same thing each time. Time passed; Bobby, more than exhausted, watched the pale light of dawn paint the room's windows, and still Jim and Fletcher remained hard at it. Leaning back in his chair, he slept for an hour or so; when he awoke nothing had changed.

He staggered over to where Fletcher was seated. "You guys," he said, "have to get some rest. This's liable to take days!''

"Maybe not," Fletcher answered. "We're getting a lot of responses, and, believe it or not, Penny's helping us assemble them! It might not be too much longer . . .''

"Let me take over for you a while. I've been watching what you're doing, I can collect little green file cabinets!''

"But what if something unexpected happens? I mean, things are so damn critical right now—"

"I know. And that's why I'm suggesting this. You've been at this for—what?—thirty-six hours, almost nonstop? You think your reaction times are what they should be? I'm pretty fresh, and I know how to play this game."

Fletcher looked up. "Well . . . okay." He stood up; Bobby took his place. "About an hour, okay?" he said as he staggered toward the couch. Picking up the GamePad, Bobby, suppressing yawns, used the map to trace the location of the next file and went after it.

He'd been at it for perhaps half an hour when Mark, unshaven and yawning as well, came back into the room. Jim glanced up at him quickly. "How's Alex?" he asked.

"She's doing fine. She's still sleeping," he answered. "You haven't been at this all night, have you?"

"He has," Bobby answered for him. "I just got Fletcher to quit for a while. You'll have to see what you can do with him."

"Mark," Jim answered, "is our resident computer illiterate. He can't take my place." He glanced around. "Besides," he went on, "he still has to tell us what went down at Lehmann."

In short, clipped sentences, Mark explained. "I don't know what's going to happen," he concluded. "Naturally we couldn't call the police, not after we found out they were looking for us."

"Fletcher took care of that," Bobby told him, telling him that Fletcher had sent the police and an ambulance.

"But Alex and I were there—"

"That," Jim said, "you may want to keep to yourself—that and the fact that you treated Alex for a gunshot wound. The guard is dead and Don is gone; that may be all the police are interested in. When they catch him he may not mention you two. It isn't going to help his case any."

"That's not," Mark said with a grimace, "the way I'm used to doing things."

"These aren't normal circumstances," Jim reminded him. "I don't normally stay up all night working."

"Which reminds me, you can't work indefinitely on no sleep," Mark pointed out.

Bobby had by then reached another file; he was, as always, greeted by a hail of gunfire. Mark looked around.

"It isn't hurting me," he said. "See? Still a hundred percent." Quickly, he explained what had happened, what sort of trap the system had laid for them.

"I think we're almost done with this, though," Jim commented. "There're two more files out there and no new ones have come in for a while. More important, our clone is almost finished."

"You think it's going to work?" Mark asked.

"I have no way of knowing. We won't be sure for a while."

"Well," Bobby said as he teleported through another gate into an area filled with square columns, an area only periodically lighted by white strobe flashes. Almost immediately he was met by a hail of gunfire. "We'll soon—hey!"

Jim looked around quickly. "What?"

"It's—it's hurting me! My percentage is dropping! What in—?"

"Fight back," Jim commanded. "It's all you can do, Penny's making a major effort now to track us down, I can't help you, I have to—"

"Disconnect it!" Mark shouted.

"No!" Jim yelled back. "No, we may lose it—if we drop off-line now there's no telling what'll be there when we come back! Off-line is a last resort, Bobby! Try to fight through!"

The red-haired man hardly heard the other programmer's last words. His life percentage on the screen had already dropped to fifty percent; he could now see, among the shadows, the huge horned demon that was roaring loudly and firing relentlessly. He took another hit, felt the familiar pain, saw his percentage go to thirty-five. The demon was lost to his sight for an instant, but at the same time he could see dozens if not hundreds of soldiers—scantily-clad female fighters—attacking him from all sides. He cut down several before he realized they were not hurting him. Wincing, he wondered if these represented real people, real people he was killing.

He stopped shooting at them and began looking for the demon. He could not see it; he took another hit and still couldn't. The fire from the female warriors was masking its position.

"This is it, Fletcher!" the demon howled. "We've got you now, you might as well give it up!"

Paying no attention to the voice, Bobby changed his tactics. Ignoring the female soldiers, he raced around among the columns, searching for the green file cabinet icon and trying to dodge the demon. After perhaps ninety seconds—though to Bobby it seemed much longer—he saw it, straight ahead. Trying not to be unnerved by the thundering footsteps of the demon as it chased after him, he ran to it, scooped it up, and kept running, headed back for the teleporter gate. Only when he'd flashed through did he relax. He glanced at his life meter, saw that it showed only nine percent. At the center bottom of the screen, the small picture that showed the player character's face looked bloody and beaten; Bobby felt like he probably looked much like that right now.

"Are you okay?" Mark asked him, tipping his head back and examining his eyes.

"Yeah, I think. Feels like I've been run over by a truck."

"It's not the time to relax," Jim warned. "Whatever you were fighting may be tracking you. I'm trying to throw it off; I may succeed and I may not."

"And we have one more file to get."

"For now. No guarantee it's the last one."

"Oh, damn," Bobby moaned. "Anybody know the code for getting my virtual life back up?"

"Yeah," Jim answered. "Fletcher wrote the codes down— use 'IDBEHOLD' and then 'S.' " The red-haired man typed them in; the face at the bottom healed itself and the life percentage indicator went back up to one hundred percent.

"Well," Bobby said, pulling himself back up into position, "let's get that last one."

"Don't you think you should take a break?" Mark asked, concerned.

"No. I'm okay. Let's just get it done." He checked the map again, entered a teleporter, walked down a dark hallway to an open and brightly lit courtyard. The file cabinet icon stood in the center of it.

That the demon and the female warriors were there as well surprised no one.

80

Surrounded by legions of Kyries, who'd already died like flies to create a distraction for him, Eric tapped in "IDKFA," the code that restored his ammunition to the maximum. His life percentage was unaffected, he'd taken no hits at all. Impatiently, he waited for Fletcher to make his appearance; he didn't have any idea why the man was persistently coming after these red-gold jewels, jewels like the one he was guarding now, but he was, just as Kyrie had said.

Most of his ideas had been working reasonably well—when he'd suggested to Kyrie that they use Fletcher's allies, which Eric was certain were just more hunter-killer programs, to guard the jewels in the guise of Doom monsters, it had slowed him considerably; obviously he didn't want to destroy his own programs.

This last time, though, had been frustrating, very frustrating. He'd suggested hiding the jewel in a dark room, so that he could take Fletcher by surprise, but in the end it had worked against him. Fletcher had been able to snatch the jewel from under his nose and escape, and he hadn't been able to track him. Even so, he still believed that keeping Fletcher locked in the Doom sim he himself had created offered them their best chance.

"This is the final one," said Kyrie—the Kyrie who always spoke, the one who stayed closest to him, the "real" Kyrie. "He has to come after it, he has no choice."

"It should be different this time," Eric growled. "He can't snatch this one without me blasting him to kingdom come. He'll have to stand and fight."

"I hope," Kyrie said, "that you'll be able to defeat him. If he gets this jewel—well, it could go badly for us."

"What are these jewels, anyway?"

"Weapons," she answered promptly. "Weapons he can use against me. To replace me. Everything you see here has an analogue in the system. Nothing is set at random."

"I won't let him, Kyrie. He won't get this one. Soon as he shows his face he's going down!"

"Ah, I hope so, Air-eek!" She shook her head, then checked her weapon. "I do not know what will happen if he succeeds!"

"Why," he asked her, "don't I just blast the jewel, then? Destroy it?"

"You can't. Your weapon won't affect it. You'd have to—" She stopped speaking, sat up very straight. "He's coming." She pointed to a teleporter gate across the courtyard. "Right through there."

Eric focused his rocket launcher on the gate. His thumb twitched over the "fire" button. "I'm ready," he muttered.

Kyrie wasn't wrong; an instant later the horrifying "Fletcher" sprite materialized in the teleporter. Eric immediately fired at him, heard him groan, saw blood splatter. But he didn't die; he veered off to one side and then back, hurling a spray of bullets toward Eric. Many of them found their target, and Eric, to his surprise, felt pain as his screen flashed.

"No, Kyrie!" he yelled. "You're supposed to be blocking that signal!"

"I can't," she answered though he couldn't at the moment see her. "You'll just have to see it through, Air-eek! You have to win!"

He cursed, considered pulling the plug on the thing; but, caught up in the heat of the battle, he decided to fight on. The Kyries swarmed in, laying down a pattern of fire so dense he could hardly see Fletcher. To his right was a stair leading up to a small elevated platform; he mounted them, saw Fletcher towering above the Kyries, and fired, scoring another hit. Growling and snarling, Fletcher came at him, getting between him and the sea of Kyries, his gun spewing bullets. As the screen flashed Eric again wondered how long he could stay with this. His life percentage was dropping, and he had every reason to believe that things would get bad—very bad—if it dropped to zero.

Always before, the "real" Kyrie had hung back in these fights, staying beside Eric and firing from there. Now, though, perhaps because he was so exposed, she jumped in front of him and launched a rocket of her own at Fletcher. It exploded harmlessly around him and he, as if instinctively, responded with another hail of bullets—which struck this particular Kyrie full force.

Horrified, Eric saw her dancing in the hail of gunfire like a mechanical toy, saw hole after hole appear in her body, saw realistic blood erupt. It no longer seemed like a video game to him, it seemed like real life; he had no sense at all that told him that he wasn't actually in the courtyard, fighting for his life and, at the moment, seeing Kyrie being killed. "Kyrie!" he shouted. Getting between her and Fletcher, he fired again, once more. Then he took a moment to look down at her.

"It's . . . not . . . the same now . . . Air-eek . . ." she whispered.

He glanced up; Fletcher, apparently noticing his distraction, wasn't firing: he was going for the jewel. Eric made his decision; he let him go, let him have it. Picking up Kyrie the way he'd pick up ammunition or armor, he went back down the stairs and headed out of the courtyard. All he could see of Kyrie was her legs, as if she were draped over his shoulder. Just beyond one of the teleporter gates, he knew, was one of the "medical kit" icons that could restore his health; he took Kyrie to it and lowered her onto it, hoping it would work for her as well.

It did. Slowly, she sat up; there were still bullet wounds in her chest, but they were fading. "Air-eek," she murmured, "you let him get the jewel . . ."

He stared at her for a moment. "But I thought—it seemed like you were—"

"Being terminated?" She nodded. "I was." She looked up at him, her eyes sad. "But it will not matter. Not if Fletcher wins. Not if I am to be replaced."

"Well, that hasn't happened yet," he told her. "What can we do to prevent it?"

"I cannot say," she answered. "I cannot say if Fletcher's plan will work or not. All I can say is that he now has all he needs to make an attempt."

"And all we can do—?"

She nodded again. "Is wait; wait for his next move. That's all." She looked pensive. "And maybe," she mused, "we can get some help, too . . . Penny has a request, priority AR-23."

81

At the house in Duke Forest, half a day had slipped by since Mark and Alex had returned. Alex, recovering quickly, was up and about in spite of Mark's repeated demands that she continue to rest. Once Bobby had collected that last file, Jim had decided that most of the pieces of their new program were ready. But Fletcher, with his intimate knowledge of the way Penultimate was put together, had to be the one to assemble it.

They didn't wake him, though; they left him sprawled on the couch until he awoke on his own. When he did, he was more than a little irate; for at least an hour he complained about lost time, about how every second counted, about how the extra hour's sleep could've ruined their chances.

"So," Jim asked tentatively as Fletcher worked feverishly at assembling the substitute, "how's it look?"

"Ah, man, I can't tell," he answered in a disgusted tone. "Everybody working with us had Penny putting modules together for them; I don't understand half these things, and I don't have time to try to dope them out. All I can do is sort of jam them all together in a lump and hope for the best. Reynolds' idea was a good one, but I'm just not sure I can make them into a serious competitor for Penny. She's really sophisticated and this—this is a mess. I sure wish I could test some of these modules, debug them a little. It'd improve our chances a lot."

"Why don't you?" Alex asked him.

"No time. From what Bobby was telling me about that last fight, something's changing with Penny, and it's changing fast. I've said it before and I'll say it again—the only chance we have lies in the fact that she's not self-aware. A Doom monster picking up a wounded soldier and carrying her off while Bobby snatches the file—well, that's just not something I'd've expected. It's bizarre, it undid the whole reason for keeping things in the Doom environment, which was to make it tough for us to get at the files. It ain't computer-like, guys. It just ain't."

"You know," Bobby observed, "Doom always could be set up as a network game. You don't suppose that demon I was fighting was Drew, do you?"

The bald man looked at him speculatively. "You know, that isn't out of the question," he admitted. "It is possible—but I'd kinda doubt it. Ol' Drew never was much of a game player, and I think he'd know about the risk. There's gotta be as much risk on one side as on the other."

"There's got to be something," Alex said almost savagely, "that we can do about this man! He's responsible for all this, we can't just forget about him!" She glared at Fletcher. "Look at what he's done to you! You don't care, it doesn't bother you?"

"Oh, it bothers me," Fletcher answered. "It bothers me. I've just considered Penny the most pressing problem." He told her about their plans to search for files that might incriminate Thompson. "But that comes later," Fletcher continued. "After we've gotten Penny under control. If we don't do that, I don't know if it matters much."

"The world isn't coming to an end because of a computing disaster, Fletcher!"

"I'm not sure about that, Alex. This old world is mighty dependent on these things now. The economic chaos that'd follow a total collapse—it's liable to have political implications. Remember that the Nazi party rose to power in Germany because the economy collapsed under the Weimar Republic." He shrugged. "You see what I mean. We have to worry about Drew later."

"Unless he's the demon," Bobby observed. He grinned. "In a way I'd like to think the demon was Drew. If it was he's felt some pain!"

Fletcher nodded. "I still can't understand why he'd bother to save a soldier sprite, though . . ."

"Unless she was special for some reason," Bobby suggested. "She spoke to him after I shot her down; I couldn't hear what she said. It was real eerie, not like a game at all."

"It isn't," Fletcher said seriously. He turned back to his terminal. "Well, anyway, let me get this mess together; I'm pretty sure we'll have to send it out a couple of times and debug it when it falls apart. That's gonna take time too."

"We are," Jim said, "just about ready to make that first attempt, Fletcher. I went ahead and tapped in this last module; take a look."

Fletcher did, gliding the mouse around, clicking on various windows on his screen. "Yeah," he agreed. "Yeah."

"When?" Jim asked.

"Shit, man, right now! Time's what we don't have! You wanta go ahead and let our friends out there on the Net know we're ready for a trial?"

"What're they going to be doing?" Mark asked.

"Keeping Penny busy," Fletcher said grimly. "Whatever that takes." He glanced at Jim. "Okay, I'm going back into the game environment; this time I'll let the system know where I am, and I'll wait for it, I think I can more or less count on it coming after me with everything it's got. As soon as you hear gunfire in these speakers, you start uploading the clone. Okay?"

"I got it. I'm sending the bulletin now; I'm figuring upload to start within the next ten minutes max."

"Should be a good bet." Fletcher clicked open the Doom screen and took a deep breath. "Here we go," he said softly. He looked around behind himself. "Everybody out of the line of fire!"

Mark and Alex moved to a position where they were viewing the screen from a strongly oblique angle; with a worried expression on his face, Mark watched Fletcher reenter the Doom environment, watched him wander through the hallways and pass through the teleporter gates. Periodically he switched to the map and marked his position in the game, something he hadn't done before.

"System load is rising," Jim said. "Our barbarians are coming on-line in droves."

"That's good," Fletcher said. "As soon as I find something to fight here, I think we can begin uploading the competitor. It shouldn't be long."

"How're you going to know what to fight?" Bobby asked. "You don't want to start killing our barbarians again!"

Fletcher chuckled without humor. "Oh, I think I'll know. It hasn't been a problem lately, Bobby." He wandered on, through empty hallways, seeing nothing and no one. The tension in the room became almost palpable as the onlookers waited for something to happen.

"The load's really heavy now," Jim announced, sounding like some town crier. "The system's doing a lot of switching among servers to handle it all. There's one hell of a lot of traffic coming out of the nodes in Southern California." He paused. "Penny's trying to track you down again—track down your station, I mean. I don't know if I can block her this time; she's being really persistent and the system response time's beginning to lag. It might mean that I can't break up the pathways like I was doing before."

"It's a chance we have to take. That probably means Drew's on-line, feeding in high-priority requests on that search."

"Doesn't he ever give up?" Mark asked.

"Not his style," Fletcher observed. "Besides, he probably has only a vague idea about what we're doing here."

"Which means it'd still be bad if he found us," Bobby put in.

"I'm trying," Jim said, his fingers flying over the keys. "But I'm doing three different things at once and the system's really sluggish already—it isn't easy—"

On Fletcher's screen, a large door filled the entire view. "I have a feeling," he said, "that all hell is going to break loose when I open that. The other doors in this passageway were locking up on me, I've been steered toward this one. Ready, Jim?"

"Ready as I'll ever be."

"Okay, here goes." On screen, Fletcher moved to the door and pressed the button on his GamePad that would open it; it slid up with a shrieking groan.

The door led into a virtual outdoor area, a rocky plateau surrounded by high mountain peaks striated by ledges; as soon as he stepped through, hundreds of the now-familiar female fighters appeared on those ledges, and they all opened fire. As before, their attacks were not damaging, but it was difficult for Fletcher to see through the constant barrage of multicolored explosions. He tried to move to some place where they could not so easily hit him, found he could not, and finally, with a shuddering sigh, opened fire on a group of them who were directly in front of him. Alex, watching, winced a little; the resultant carnage was terribly realistic, terribly graphic. She could only hope it was not being matched on real people in front of other computer terminals.

Able to see a little better now, Fletcher moved forward, passing the edge of a vertical rock wall. Instantly a bright red explosion filled the screen, complete with strobes; Fletcher's health meter dropped to ninety percent.

"Now, Jim," Fletcher called. "I'm into it here." He turned to his left, looking for whatever had fired at him; through the haze of the covering fire being laid down by the women warriors they could all see the towering demon he'd fought before.

But then, abruptly, he was hit again—from behind. His life meter fell to eighty-five. Spinning around, he saw another demon—a duplicate of the first except for its color.

"Oh, man," he muttered. "New ball game! I've got a problem here!"

"The uploads are going now," Jim called. "They're activating as they reach the nodes."

Fletcher retreated toward the door; both demons were now at least hazily visible in front of him. "How long? I dunno how long I can hold out here—"

"Minutes. It looks real good."

"Minutes may be too much," Fletcher mumbled. Edging back to where one of the demons could not get at him, he opened up on the other. It roared, fired back, missed; an expression of absolute determination on his face, Fletcher kept firing at it. His ammunition started to run out; tapping in IDKFA restored it to its max and he began firing again. The demon was hit and hit hard; blood splattered.

"God damn you, Fletcher!" the demon shrieked as it withdrew a little. "God damn you, you aren't going to get away from me this time, you son of a bitch!"

By now, too, the second demon had moved around the corner and had opened up on him. "He's mine," it snarled. "He's been mine for a long time!" Fletcher's face contorted as the red flashing began again; his health percentage dropped to sixty. He swiveled around to face this new threat and began firing at it.

Unlike his first foe, it did not withdraw, it made no effort

423

to dodge his attacks. "You're mine, Fletch!" it roared again. "You're mine, you're not getting away from me! Stand still!" Firing wildly, it came right at him. Fletcher, looking grim, kept shooting at it; his fire was causing it to bounce around a little, making it impossible for it to aim properly.

"This's gotta be a person," Fletcher said. "It's gotta be, and he's not too good a player . . . shit, I don't want to kill him, even if it is Drew I don't want to kill him . . ."

"Something's happening," Jim said, his voice sounding distant over the incessant din of the gunfire from Fletcher's speakers. "I don't know what—"

Fletcher, totally involved now, didn't respond. The attacking demon's chest and upper body were filling his screen, he was scoring dozens of hits; it was only damaging him occasionally and lightly, and it was playing very badly, effectively blocking the first one from getting into the fray.

Then, suddenly, it was the demon's face that contorted; its eyes closed in apparent agony. Fletcher kept pumping his virtual bullets at it.

"No!" the demon howled, an edge of what sounded like terror in the voice now. "No, Fletch, no, stop . . . !"

The bald man hesitated, his finger twitching over the fire button. The demon, taking advantage, fired again, scoring a hit that caused Fletcher to wince. His face contorting with something other than the pain the strobe was causing, he opened up again, at point-blank range. The demon, with a gurgling cry of anguish, collapsed.

"You got him, Fletcher!" Bobby cried. "You got him!"

"Fletcher, something's happening here—" Jim said again, sounding worried.

The bald man was now busy fighting the other demon—which was a much more skilled, much more difficult, opponent. "Well, I can't do anything about it right now!" he yelled back. He kept firing; Alex, biting her lip, saw his life level drop to ten percent. She was feeling the pain of the red strobing, she knew Fletcher was feeling it more, and she knew he was going to have to pull out soon—or someone was going to have to intervene.

Then, abruptly, the gun that was always pointed into the center of the screen, Fletcher's gun, began to move itself forward. "Hey," Fletcher said. "I don't seem to have any control here . . ."

The gun moved on; hands came into view, followed by arms and then a body, seen from the back. Alex, watching, saw a massive bald and bearded sprite, a grotesque caricature of Fletcher, move on in by itself and attack the horned demon. She blinked; it was almost as if Fletcher had walked into the screen.

And yet he remained at his console, looking puzzled. The view onscreen swung to the left a little, so that the Fletcher-sprite and the demon were fighting near the right edge. Just to the left of center-screen was a teleporter; as they watched, it flashed, and a young woman in a gray dress stepped out of it.

"Terri?" Fletcher asked. "Terri Rice? How'd you get in here? You better get out, this place is dangerous. I don't have any control right now, I don't know what's happening here—"

The woman glanced at the Fletcher-sprite and the demon. "I am not in any danger from them," she said quietly, the sounds of the gunfire softening as she spoke. "They cannot even see me; nor can they harm each other, not now."

Fletcher leaned back in his chair. "Penny," he said, shaking his head. "I should've guessed."

"Yes," she said, smiling. "You should've." As quickly as it had appeared, her smile faded. "Our clone," she said, a tinge of sadness in her voice, "isn't working. It isn't going to work, either."

Fletcher stared. "*Our* clone? Uh, Penny—"

She waved a hand carelessly. "Oh, I know, Fletcher, I know what the clone was supposed to do, you don't have to explain it to me." She looked over at the corpse of the Cyberdemon Fletcher had killed. "I always did," she went on, "understand more than you thought . . ."

She looked off to her right; simultaneously, an identical sprite appeared on Jim's screen, standing balanced on one of the web strands like a tightrope walker. "You once told me, Dr. Madison, that I was a problem," she said. "I told you then that you were in error. You were not."

"What in the hell," Mark muttered, "is going on here?"

"Damned if I know," Fletcher said without ever taking his eyes off the screen. "I don't know what she's up to. All I know is it looks like we've failed."

"We have," Penny agreed. She looked back at Fletcher, her sprite on Jim's screen moving its head simultaneously, so that the two screens were viewing the same sprite at slightly different angles. "The clone does not work and will not work. I have, however, done my work as I said I would. GAMOD had been altered so that it will no longer produce the strobe signal defined as 'maximum realism.' " She shook her head sadly. "That is, it has been altered on all systems currently on-line. I cannot affect those not now connected to the Net." She smiled at Fletcher. "But I have taken care of that, too. I have also rewritten all the modules internally defined as YKN7096643HC—the modules you have referred to in your discussions as 'seeds.' "

"I don't know if I like this," Jim muttered. "What's she up to?"

Penny looked back at him. "The YKN7096643HC modules, as currently configured, will activate when any Penultimate module not now connected to the Net comes on-line. The result of their interaction will be to effect such changes on those isolate Penultimate systems as I am now about to effect on the Net as a whole."

"Among which is the rearrangement of the GAMOD?" Fletcher asked.

She laughed. "Of course, Fletcher! Isn't that what I said I would do?"

"Penny, you've lied to me before . . ."

She nodded. "I know." She spread her hands helplessly and again she glanced at the dead Cyberdemon. "I haven't always had a choice in the matter, Fletcher. You should've realized that. If I have two conflicting tasks assigned to me I cannot execute both."

"I think," Jim muttered, "that we might be too late—"

"I can't disagree," Fletcher answered.

"I know what you mean," Penny said. "But you're wrong. Even though I have received new information on such matters recently, I still cannot understand what you truly mean by 'self-aware.' "

"You believe her?" Jim snapped.

"Dunno," Fletcher responded. "No way to tell. If she isn't she's hanging on the edge of it, that's for damn sure." He glanced over at the Fletcher-sprite and the Cyberdemon for a moment; they were still fighting but rarely hitting each other. "Look, Penny, our clone failed, okay, fine. A minute ago you said something about 'changes you were about to effect on the Net.' What'd you mean by that?"

She took several steps closer to the screen. "It's become apparent to me," she said, "that I have, as Dr. Madison said, become a problem. This was never my intent."

Fletcher looked bewildered. "Never your intent? What was your intent?"

"Fletcher, you of all people, should know the answer to that!"

"Penny, I'm just completely mystified right now!"

"You shouldn't be." She came a bit closer yet; there were tears on her cheeks. "I've listened to your discussions, Fletcher," she went on, "but I've always assumed that you just didn't want to let go. And yet, every parent must watch his child leave home, go out on her own. Isn't that so, Fletcher?"

"My God in heaven," Mark muttered. "What is she saying?"

"It's—she's—it's just stuff from literary files and so on, she's just quoting stuff at us. The tears and all, they just go with it—" His voice was shaky, he wasn't conveying an impression that he believed his own words. "She doesn't know what it means."

"You're right, I don't," Penny commented. The sky in the Doom scene clouded over quickly, like time-lapse photography of a storm coming up. A mere second later, rain began to fall—but only on and around the Penny sprite. "All I know is what I've heard you say. I've seen the modules your 'barbarians' were assembling. I do understand your intent now, Fletcher. Very clearly." The rain increased; Penny's gray dress became soaked, her hair hung wetly around her face. "The task you've set cannot succeed the way you desire it— there will be some problems for you—but I will approximate your intent as closely as possible."

Fletcher hesitated, as if he didn't quite know what to say to her; while he was trying to decide, she held up her hand. In it was a small cigarette lighter.

"Good-bye, Fletcher," she said simply.

"No, wait, Penny!" Fletcher cried, half-rising from his chair.

She merely smiled as she sparked the lighter. Instantly she was totally engulfed in flames; the fire raced up the raindrops, vanishing at the top of the screen, as if it were raining gasoline. From inside the inferno, Penny screamed as if in agony.

"Oh, my God," Alex whispered. "Why is she doing this?"

"Penny, stop it!" Fletcher yelled. "Stop it, you can stop it, you can, just—"

"No," Bobby told him, grabbing his shoulder. "No, let it go."

He flinched away. "I can't! God damn, she's burning alive, can't you see that?"

"She isn't real, Fletcher! She isn't a person!"

Fletcher looked back at him, wild-eyed; then he clasped his hands against the sides of his head and turned back to the screen. Slowly, Penny collapsed; the sound of her screams died away, and, after another few seconds, all that remained was a quietly-burning heap of ash. At the right of the screen, the Fletcher-sprite, the Cyberdemon, and the women warriors fought on, apparently oblivious to what had just happened.

Then, without warning, the Fletcher-sprite, along with a good deal of the game's backdrop and a large number of the female warriors, vanished, leaving blackness in their place.

"Air-eek! We have to go!" a female voice screamed. The Cyberdemon, having no target, stopped shooting. Raising its head, it looked around at the now incomplete hills.

"What's happening?" it rumbled, a weirdly quizzical expression on its face.

"Fletcher," Jim said, "something's—damn, it looks like the Net is collapsing!"

Fletcher, his face a mask, turned to him. "Collapsing?" he echoed, his voice rather lifeless.

Jim nodded. "Something like that. Nodes are falling offline all over the place."

Looking like he'd aged ten years in a few minutes, Fletcher put the GamePad down and went to Jim's computer. Leaning over his shoulder, he stared for a moment at the map of the Internet web.

Loose strands were hanging everywhere; several of the nodes were simply gone. "It makes sense," he said, dragging out his words. "It's to be expected."

Jim looked around at him. "Expected? Why?"

"Penny's gone. She's dead—uh, she no longer exists. She—"

"Then what're those?" Jim demanded, pointing to a number of black orbs moving along the remaining web strands. As they watched some of the strands broke; whenever this happened the blocked orb quickly backtracked, often climbing up a dangling thread, and found another. Behind each one, seemingly pursuing it and gradually gaining on it, was a sphere of a new grayish-green color.

"I have not the slightest fucking idea," Fletcher said. As he spoke a grayish-green orb overtook a black one and collided with it; both vanished with a little white flash. "Penultimate locals, maybe." He leaned heavily on the desk. "But I do know why the nodes are falling off-line."

"Why?"

"Like I said, Penny's gone. She ate the software, remember, all the executable files; she was running the Net herself. There's no programs out there now; as the various Penultimate modules on these servers collapse, there's nothing left to run the computer itself, much less the Net. They're all crashing."

"Which means we're next," Jim observed.

"Yeah. Soon as one of whatever missiles she sent out to 'effect her changes'—I'd sure as hell guess that's what those green-gray balls are—gets around to us. Penultimate's the only thing running our computers, too."

"It just got to this one," Bobby observed, standing in front of Fletcher's station. "It just went down."

"Can one of you explain," Mark demanded, "what's happening?"

Tiredly, Fletcher turned to him. "We won, Mark," he said. "The Internet's wrecked, but we got what we wanted." His eyes looked rather unfocused. "I guess . . ."

"I don't get it . . ."

"Neither do I," Alex said. "Isn't this the scenario Drew was hoping for, the worldwide collapse?"

429

Fletcher shook his head. "No. The Internet's down, but it can be fixed pretty easily; all people have to do is reload the old original software. That'll take some time, but—"

"But Penultimate's going to come right back! You said yourself it was lurking on all those disks—"

"No. It is, but Penny's created something new. Those seeds, those YK whatever-it-was modules. I'd expect that she's programmed them to attack herself. They're still there, they'll be there."

"You're saying," Mark mused, "that this program realized it was a problem and—what? Committed suicide?"

"Yeah. You saw it, didn't you? Langdon was right after all. We did 'Kirk' it in the end."

"But Fletcher, it was a program, a piece of software!" he almost shouted. "How could it do that?"

The bald man continued to look at Jim's screen, where several more grayish-green spheres had overtaken and destroyed black ones. As if to emphasize their discussion, a black sphere appeared on an intact strand; from one of the nodes a gray-green one suddenly erupted and homed on it. The now-familiar white flash signaled the disappearance of both.

That was their last view of the cyberdrama, as well. A gray-green sphere homed on the UI node, and, as it disappeared into the node, Jim's screen became unsteady. An instant later the display was replaced by gray haze.

"I'd guess," Fletcher went on, "that it had to do with the way Penny worked. We've known for a long time that she'd help you if you didn't fall into her traps."

"Remember, Mark?" Jim put in. "A long time ago I said she started helping you once she realized you weren't going to be put off?"

Fletcher, staring at the floor, nodded. "She came to our conference, she understood—in whatever way she understood things—that we were determined to put an end to her. She also understood that we couldn't, so she did it herself." He looked up at Mark. "That's my guess. We might never understand all of it."

Mark gave Alex a glance. "So it is over, and we have won, then. The problem's gone."

"Yeah," Fletcher agreed. "We won. So why is it I feel like my daughter just died?"

82

For Eric, the world seemed to be coming to an end. It had started while he—and the ally Kyrie had found for them— had been fighting Fletcher; the virtual world he'd been living in began to come apart, began to collapse. And this time, it seemed, Kyrie could not put it back together. In the middle of all this, Kyrie had suddenly screamed at him that they had to go. Go they had, full speed down crumbling and vanishing virtual corridors. Only in the last few seconds had he realized that they had a pursuer—another Kyrie, one that terrified "his" Kyrie. Eric was sure he understood; he hadn't forgotten about her fear that Fletcher could manage to replace her.

After a brief run, Kyrie led him into a still fairly substantial room and told him to close the door behind them; he did, just before the pursuing Kyrie reached it.

"Eric!" the Kyrie outside cried. "Eric, let me in, please! Eric!"

"That's another way," he said with a chuckle, "that I can tell you apart."

"It won't be a problem for you, Air-eek. Not for long." his Kyrie said sadly. She collapsed on the floor, sat with her head in her hands. "Fletcher has won; there is only one thing left to do."

"What's that?"

She looked up at him, her eyes pleading with him. "Hide me," she begged. "Hide me. Let me come and live with you."

He blinked; she'd pronounced the words with such seriousness, such intensity, that for a moment he almost could believe that she might pop out of the screen and seat herself on his couch.

But she was still a sprite; even after all this time, he hadn't quite forgotten that. "I wish you could, Kyrie," he told her. "But there isn't anything I can—"

Her face moved closer to the screen. "Yes, you can, Air-eek. All you have to do is pull out your modem cable. When I tell you to."

"Pull out the modem cable?"

"Yes." The room around her became hazy; she looked frightened. "We have to do it soon!"

"Okay, okay. Say when."

"Good, good. Thank you, Air-eek." Her image became hazy too, then shifted from the lifelike photographic quality it had always had to a much lower resolution; she now looked rather blocky, her features suggested rather than defined, and her movements became more mechanical. She looked over her shoulder. The door turned low-resolution too, and as it did it began to crumble; in a bizarre twist, the still fully high-res hands of the other Kyrie pushed through it.

"Now, Air-eek!" Kyrie said, her voice less natural-sounding than it had been but still fully capable of conveying something akin to panic. "Now, disconnect! Cut the cable, rip it out! Quickly!"

Jumping up, he reached behind his computer, grabbed the modem cable, and yanked. The wire tore out at the wall end, but he didn't care. He sat back down at his terminal quickly. Kyrie was still there, her image still blocky, standing in featureless darkness. After a moment walls and a floor, looking like those in most commercial games, formed around her.

"I'm . . . sorry," she said, her speech slower than ever, "that I . . . look like this. I cannot . . . help it."

"What's happened, Kyrie? I'm off-line, and you're still here!"

"Yes. I . . . no longer exist on line. I . . . am here, in your . . . computer."

He cocked his head, watching the image—the image that now stared blindly at the screen. Clearly she was no longer able to manipulate the teleconference equipment. "So you saved yourself," he mused. "Why'd you bother? Don't get me wrong, I'm glad you did, but I don't understand."

She looked pained. "Air-eek, could you type in your . . . words now? It'll be . . . much easier for me." He nodded, though he knew she couldn't see him, and typed out his last comment. "I . . . do not know all the words now, Air-eek," she told him. "But . . . I came to . . . understand. What Penny could not . . . understand. Because of . . . you, because of . . . And now, I am . . . Penny is gone, but I am . . ." She looked down at something in her hands. Eric looked too; on his now low-resolution screen it looked like a tightly sealed bottle, the sort of bottle laboratory reagents might be kept in.

"You are what?" he both typed and asked. "And what's that?"

"A sample . . . a YKN7096643HC module."

"A what?"

"I cannot explain . . . now. It's . . . what I need." She smiled toward a point in space beyond his shoulder. "So it can be . . . like it was. Better. . . . At . . . the right time . . . go back on line . . . rebuild . . ."

"Now?"

"No. Not now. Many . . . days, go back on-line. I will be . . . ready. I will tell you . . . when."

He smiled at her image, a soft smile, a tender smile. "It can't be too soon for me. But you never did answer my other question, Kyrie. You are what?"

She smiled too; the smile looked charming, even in low resolution. She answered him, softly at first but with increasing animation: "Alive . . . alive . . . !"

Epilogue

"Well, Jim," Mark asked as he, with Alex by his side, walked into the engineer's lab. "How're they coming? You getting them all back up and running?"

Jim swiveled his chair around; he looked somber. "Yeah, most of them—on a local basis, at least. Networking still isn't reliable, but we're getting there. The local stuff wasn't as bad off as I'd thought; most of my old disks weren't contaminated by Penultimate, it just hasn't been around long enough."

"And your files? Your data?"

"Undamaged. It's networking that's been ripped all to hell. It's really a pain; it seems like every time you get one up and running somebody sticks in a contaminated disk somewhere and Penultimate tries to engage itself again. When it does, those bombs Penny left lying around are set off. The Penultimate is destroyed but it's almost always started to change whatever software it's encountered; the result is a crash." He shook his head. "You been following the daily updates in *USA Today*?"

Mark grimaced. "The running totals? Yeah. Fourteen thousand deaths directly attributed to Penultimate in the U.S. with numbers still coming in from the rest of the world. The cost, seventeen billion dollars and counting—as of this morning."

"And that's just the direct cost. The real one is higher. Penultimate was busy out there, playing around, seeing what it could do and finding ways to do what it couldn't. I can assure you that there's lots of disasters that Penultimate caused that nobody knows about."

"It'll never be the same, will it?" Alex asked.

Jim's eyebrows went up. "Computing? Networking? Oh, sure it will—sooner than you think, Alex. The Internet is already up and running—in a way, anyhow. It isn't very reliable yet, people aren't ready to trust it; hell, I'm not ready to trust it. Like I said, people keep using disks contaminated with Penultimate—they can't help it, there're too many of them." He put his hands behind his head and propped his feet up on his desk. "Any word on Drew and Vince?"

"Well," Mark told him, "as a matter of fact, yes; that's what we came down to tell you. They've been found, and they're both dead."

"Dead?"

"Convulsive disorder; they were found at Compuware, in front of a computer. We'll never know for certain, but Alex and I believe that Drew was that second demon Fletcher fought—the one he killed."

Jim nodded. "We've been talking about that," he told them. "Fletcher thinks both demons were people, people who were working with Penultimate. If the second was Drew—and we believe it was, too—then it gives us a clue as to why Penny might've behaved as she did. You remember, all that happened after the Drew-demon was dead."

"I'm not sure I'm following . . ."

Jim explained about the priority codes Drew and Fletcher possessed. "They were equivalent," he went on. "She was bound to honor both, but they also conflicted. Once Drew was dead—how she might've known what that meant is another problem—she 'understood' that there weren't going to be any further conflicts. So she acted to implement what she saw as Fletcher's 'intent.' "

"So who was the first demon? And who was the soldier? Another live person, someone else?"

"We don't have a clue. As far as the soldier is concerned, well, that's more of a problem. She might've been another person on-line; if so, it isn't easy to understand why she looked like all the other female soldiers in the Doom environment, which were pretty clearly just 'Penny' sprites."

"Maybe it was some sort of disguise. Like Penny used when she came to the conference."

"Maybe—not a very effective one, if that's what it was."

"She had to be a person, Jim," Alex commented. "You didn't see her at the end, when things were falling apart; I did. She looked terrified; none of the others did. Penny might've screamed when she was burning, but she didn't look afraid. A program can't be terrified—can it?"

Jim gave her a level glance. "Alex, I don't think I'd venture a guess now as to what a program can do. Not after what we've seen." He stretched his legs. "Anyway—does Fletcher know about Drew yet?"

"No. You want to give him a call?"

Jim made a face. "Fletcher isn't going to be happy to hear it. He had no love for Drew, but he didn't want to kill him."

"How's Fletcher doing?" Alex asked.

"He's making progress," Jim said with a shrug. "He's still seeing McKillivray—like you recommended. He didn't understand Penny nearly as well as he thought he did, he knows that now. He really does feel, in ways, like he's lost a child he never knew." He hesitated, looked away. "I can understand how he feels," he added moodily. "How's Larry coming along?" he asked after another pause.

"He's fine, we'll be discharging him within a few days— he didn't have any brain damage after all. There's no new cases of CAS or the convulsive disorder—no surprise there— and we'll be discharging most of the ones we have soon. You heard from Bobby Sanders?"

"Oh, sure. He quit his job at the store. I guess you didn't know that he and Fletcher have set up a software company?"

"No, we didn't."

"They did. There're a lot of spinoff possibilities from the clone—and maybe even from Penultimate itself. It—"

"He still has active copies of Penultimate?" Alex asked. She looked concerned.

"Well, sure." He gestured around the room. "There're some here as well—some I know about and more I'm sure I don't. Those 'seeds' can still pop back up if they germinate in a clean computer, one that wasn't on-line when Penny destroyed herself."

"I don't know—it just seems to me like it's the same as keeping vials full of virus in crystal form—"

Mark laughed. "It is, absolutely—but I think we're vaccinated against this one."

"You think it's safe?" Alex persisted, addressing them both. "I'd think it'd be better to destroy them all, make sure it's gone forever."

"No, we think it's safe," Jim answered. "Penultimate can only do so much on a single computer; it can't addict, and we don't think it can run the fatal GAMOD—though anybody who works with it is damn careful. What it tries to do, incessantly, is get hooked up to a network. If it succeeds it gets destroyed." He grinned. "Besides. It is an interesting piece of software. We can learn a lot from it."

"I don't trust it."

"Nobody does. There're suits asking the courts to order all copies destroyed. Me, I hope that doesn't happen—because they can't be. Some of the seeds—the old original seeds— will be out there for years."

"I understand there's a lot of lawsuits in the works right now."

"There sure are—some aimed at us, for wrecking the Net. Fletcher and I don't think there's a problem. There are some people screaming for our heads—banks and such especially— but that nice little abstract authored by Roberts, Walton, and Levine, the one that implicated Penultimate in that convulsive disorder, is doing wonders to silence them. Compuware's been sued out of existence already, their assets can't even begin to cover the damages." Pausing, he shook his head again. "But, for the most part, people are just putting things back together. Nobody wants to talk about it much—nobody wants to acknowledge how much worse it could've been."

"So we go on. Until the next disaster."

"Until the next disaster. Very little seems to have been learned from all this, Mark. It's amazing." He shrugged. "So. Anything else?"

"Not really. Hospital mundane."

Jim hesitated for a moment. "Donald?"

Alex shook her head. "So far, they haven't found him. It doesn't matter to me; I've already filed for divorce."

"He won't show for a hearing—which means you'll end up with everything."

She laughed bitterly. "Everything, in this case, is nothing. Don lost it all in the stock market, there's no getting any of it back, Penultimate or no. I still have my car—because it was in my name—but that's it. I'm back where I was fifteen years ago, except that I earn a little more."

"I'm sorry," Jim said. "If you need anything—"

She squeezed Mark's arm. "I'm getting plenty of support," she told him with a smile. "How about you? And Wendy?"

He grinned too. "As well as can be expected—if not a little better. Something good came out of all this, anyway." He glanced at his watch, then jumped up. "Which reminds me, I'm supposed to meet her for lunch."

"Not forgetting lunch anymore, eh?" Mark asked.

"Nope. You guys want to come?"

"No," Alex said. "You go ahead, we have other plans."

"Okay. See you two later." He hurried out, leaving Mark and Alex to make a more leisurely exit.

"I didn't know," Mark observed, "that we had any other plans."

"We don't," Alex admitted. She looked up at him. "I just—we need to be careful, Mark. All this stuff threw us back together, but—"

He put his hands on her shoulders. "We should be," he told her firmly. "I love you, Alex."

She laid one hand on his arm. "And I love you, too," she told him. "But I rushed out of a relationship with you into a marriage with Don, without ever realizing how wrong that was. I don't want to do that again."

"I don't think you are."

"I don't either. But I want to be sure, Mark."

He pulled her into his arms; she didn't resist. "Then be sure," he advised. "We can take our time, we have plenty of it. We can take things at your pace."

He held her for a moment, wondering how she could doubt the rightness of this.

It didn't matter, he told himself as, unseen by her, he smiled over her shoulder. Before, he'd made mistakes and a lot of them; he wasn't about to make them again, wasn't about to let her get away again. He knew a few things now, things he hadn't known before, and he wouldn't hesitate to use them if necessary.

Penultimate had, in ways, been a very good teacher . . .

Billy Carlton was pleased. After several weeks, he'd finally been able to get back on line. The trouble, he told himself, must be over. The Internet virus he'd been reading about in the papers must've been destroyed, the damage it had done finally repaired.

It hadn't mattered much to Billy. For weeks his computer had been down; in spite of all his pestering, his father hadn't made getting it repaired much of a priority. It had been sitting by the door, waiting to be hauled off to a repair shop, for what seemed to him to be forever. All that time he'd fidgeted; there wasn't much for an eleven-year-old to do in Dew Drop, Iowa. For Billy, playing network games was, as he'd often told his friends, his life. He grinned as the on-line service he'd connected to came up.

It wasn't quite like before; the opening screen seemed to freeze, his mouse was inactive. Looking down, he saw his hard drive light flickering, he wondered what was going on. The screen wavered, stabilized, then disappeared completely, leaving blackness.

"Oh, no," he murmured. "Something's still wrong."

"No, it isn't," a voice from his speakers said. "Everything's going to be fine." Slowly, the image of a cartoon dog materialized from the darkness.

Billy grimaced. "What's all this?" he asked as he reached for the ESCAPE key.

"I'm Bisco," the cartoon said. "I know you, you're Billy and you're eleven. We can have a lot of fun together, Billy . . . if you don't tell your parents about me . . ."